THE WINNER AND THE PRIZE

by

Margaret Whitford

Published by Hardcopys DPS Inc.
Vancouver, British Columbia, Canada 2006

Copyright © 2004 by Margaret Whitford

This book is published by arrangement with the author by
Hardcopys Digital Publishing Solutions, Inc., of Vancouver, B.C.
Canada

Printed in Canada

Reach the publisher on the Web at www.hardcopys.com

ISBN: 978-0-9735820-1-7

To my family

Chapter 1

The First Dinner

"Tomorrow's the Big Day for Maureen Ash, winner of Cetapac Film's recent Movie Quiz Contest. Her prize is an intimate dinner for two at Trader Vic's at the Bayshore Inn with craggy, tough-guy movie star Harry Wentworth himself. Harry's currently filming his latest epic, "Hometown Hobo", in and around Vancouver. "Hobo" is slated for release in spring of 1969 Eat your hearts out, girls, Maureen gets to do this all by herself!"

"I need a dinner with Harry Wentworth at Trader Vic's like I need a hole in the head," the woman said firmly. "Give me the fifty dollar second prize instead."

She stood, feet apart, in front of Sam Price's desk in his p.r. office at the Cetapac Studios in West Vancouver, whence she had chased him from the reception desk. He stood at bay behind his desk, uncertain how, and unwilling to handle this prickly woman.

"But you won first prize in the How well do you know Harry Wentworth? Quiz," he said plaintively.

"No I didn't. Rob did. Rob filled in all the answers and

then signed my name at the bottom. Rob actually won the prize."

"But it can't be awarded to a man. It's women only – it said so on the form."

"I know," the woman said patiently. "I know, Mr. Price. That's why I'm suggesting you let me swap with the second-prize winner. She'll probably be thrilled to have dinner with Harry Wentworth - me, I'd rather have the money. Who's Harry Wentworth, anyway? I only see his movies by mistake, and I don't even like them - in fact I don't like him."

"He...", she stopped, puzzled by the glazed look in Sam Price's eyes, which were fixed on a space above and behind her head. She turned slowly, following his gaze, and found herself to be the object of a none too friendly visual examination by none other than Harry Wentworth himself.

Harry was an actor's actor. Fifty years old, six foot two and well built, with prematurely white hair and watchful blue eyes, his features too blunt and craggy to be called handsome, he was, nevertheless, a striking man. He extended a powerful, dominating charisma that inspired men to challenge him physically, and women to find him either repellant or fascinating: few people were indifferent to him.

For the twenty years since Dell's death Harry had looked upon women as nothing more than a commodity. One acted with them (as little as possible), one took them to parties, one went to bed with them and one said good-bye to them. One neither talked nor listened intelligently to them, nor did one treat them as equals. One kept them at a distance and changed them frequently - like cheap socks.

This was because for all of Harry's outward toughness, he was a vulnerable man who had been deeply hurt once and was reluctant to put himself at risk again by engaging in another personal relationship with a woman.

He was aware that this left a dimension missing in his life, but he was more willing to endure this lack than he was to risk another hurt.

So he grunted and growled his way past women and smoked cigars and shot pool and drank with 'the boys', and occasionally brawled when he had too much to drink. He wore three-piece suits as to the manner born, which, as the son of a prairie grain farmer, he was not, but it was a skill he had learned in acting school along with the grace to move his lean body smoothly, and the art of using his naturally deep-toned voice to its full advantage. He had likewise taught himself to raise either eyebrow independently and to arrange his mouth to express a wide range of emotions. He had a broad, professional, tooth-filled smile for the public, but in private, since Dell's death, he smiled little; when be did, fleetingly, people were astonished by the warmth and gentleness it gave to his face.

An observant person would also notice that Harry's hands (so often doubled into fists or gripping guns or knives or crowbars in his film roles) were elegant and well-shaped, and touched things with care and sensitivity. He knew that his hands did not match his macho movie image and frequently hid them in his pockets.

Harry was adept at self-deception too. Operating on the principle that what was not said could be assumed not to exist, he consistently refused to verbalize his feelings about life. Particularly life without Dell. So long as he never said 'I miss Dell' he could pretend he did not. This dark side of his soul he was afraid to explore.

Like many actors, he preferred to explore the darkness of the characters he portrayed and vicariously expressed the emotions he dare not admit to in real life.

A complex man with more warmth in him than most people believed, Harry was essentially lonely. He dressed well, he lived well, he was competent and professional at his job and respected by his peers, yet Harry lacked the one thing he seemed to have so much of—inner confidence.

What he needed, but was not yet ready to admit lest it seem disloyal to Dell's memory, was a second wife. Someone as young and lithe and striking as Dell had been, of course, and no one he had met so far had ever come up to these standards, so the question had never even arisen.

Now this man lounged against the doorjamb, the ubiquitous white raincoat that was his trademark in the Skinner and his Men TV series slung across one shoulder. He wore the usual immaculate three-piece suit, complete with silk handkerchief in the top pocket that was also a trademark. His rugged face was tanned from spring skiing at Whistler, and his hair, cropped short, really was as silver-white as it appeared on the screen. He had heard the woman's remarks as he came down the corridor towards the open office door, and made no attempt to hide his hostility.

The woman's back view had momentarily intrigued Harry, the feet-apart stance in the knee-high boots, the squared shoulders, the casual jacket and skirt, the untidy straggling blonde hair, but he was not prepared for the frankly middle-thirties face that she turned to him. She wore little makeup, just lipstick and eye shadow, certainly not enough to mask the fine lines of age and fatigue and strain. Their eyes met and for a jolting second a message flashed between them that neither had expected.

"Oh," said the woman, collecting herself, "Mr. Wentworth, how do you do?"

He straightened up, inclined his head briefly in reply and moved forward into the room. "I was just trying to tell Mr. Price -- "

"I heard," Harry said shortly, circling her, his eyes never leaving her. He leant against the desk, blotting out Sam Price. "Do go on, Miss Ash."

"Mrs."

"Ah." He put a wealth of expression into the word, glancing at her ringless hand and up at her face again. He took the raincoat from his shoulder and let it hang over the hands he clasped in front of him.

"Don't like my movies, eh?"

"No."

"Nor me?"

"Since you ask—no. What I know of you."

"Why not?" It was a bark, intended to intimidate.

"Your movies, or you?"

"Both."

"I don't think it's necessary—", she started.

"It's necessary to me," Harry cut in.

She sighed.

"You may not like it."

"I'm sure I won't," he said dryly. "Shoot."

"Your movies are brutal and violent. You play mean, hard, feelingless men who treat women like things—"

"Oh, God," he said flatly, turning away. "A women's libber, Sam."

"Is there something wrong with that?" she bristled.

"Yes, makes you rude and ungracious."

"I don't mean to be," Molly Ash said quickly. "I'm sorry, but you asked me, and I'd like to go on."

"I've heard enough. Give her the fifty, Sam."

"I'll take the fifty," she said agreeably, "but at least let me finish. After all, you asked." Before Harry could stop her she went on. "I find your movies unpleasant because your character is always so damned cool and detached, nothing moves him. He shoots people and punches people as though they don't matter." It sounded priggish and artificial even to her own years, but she ploughed on.

"There's never any warmth or depth . . . or emotion . . . or . . you . . . ummh . . . " her voice petered out, impaled as she was by Harry's flinty blue eyes, feeling like a butterfly pinned in a showcase. Oh damn, she thought, now I've gone too far; why did I have to open my big mouth?

"Anything else, Mrs. Ash?" the man asked politely—icily.

Molly swallowed, opened her mouth to say no, but he cut in quickly.

"Sam, I don't want to have dinner with this woman any more than she wants to have dinner with me. Right?" He turned to Molly.

"Right," she said faintly.

"So give her the money and get the other winner. Hopefully she's (a) a fan of mine, (b) young, (c) attractive, and (d) feminine—which is the way this cold fish likes them."

Only the feeling that the man was deliberately baiting her kept Molly from responding angrily. She clamped her mouth shut and breathed hard through her nose, making a play of opening her handbag and getting out her wallet to cover her discomfiture. Had she looked up she would have seen a glint of humanizing amusement in Harry's eyes.

"Sorry, Harry," said Sam, surfacing from behind the desk,

"...can't do that, I'm afraid. The contest is one hundred per cent legally binding—all prizes must be accepted as awarded— no substitutions or cash equivalents—it's all written in. Sorry." He looked from one to the other of them anxiously, wondering who was going to blow up first.

There was a moment of silence while they all thought.

"I could get sick," Molly suggested at last.

"No good." Sam shook his head. "Only postpone it. You see we've commitments to the restaurant and the media and the fan mags, not to mention the producers of Hometown Hobo. The whole thing's a publicity stunt to advertise the fact we're making the movie here in Vancouver. They expect an article and pics on the dinner—interviews afterwards—everything." He looked genuinely upset and Molly felt sorry for him, but not for Harry Wentworth.

She sighed and Harry grunted at the same time.

"Well," Molly said brightly, "at least we agree on something."

"OK," Harry said with resignation after a moment. "OK, We go ahead with it. But get wardrobe to fix her up with a decent dress and have John do something with her hair."

"No!" Molly said loudly, and when Harry turned to her, she jabbed him in the chest with her forefinger to emphasize her words.

"I wear my own dress and I do my own hair, and if they're not good enough for Harry Wentworth to be seen with—too bad! I'm me and that's the way I'm staying!"

"Told you she was a women's libber", said Harry wryly, looking over her head at Sam. "Probably why Mr. Ash divorced her."

It struck very close to the truth and Molly was annoyed to feel a betraying blush spread across her face. She started for the door.

"Until tomorrow night, Mrs. Ash," the actor said, his voice purring seductively, full of innuendo, his eyes amused.

"Yes," she said, squaring her shoulders and not looking back.

Harry raised his hand and leveled his forefinger at her back and said "Phhhut!" softly, jerking his hand up and back in imitation of a gun recoiling, intending this gesture for Sam's eyes alone.

But Molly saw it out of the corner of her eye and spun around, one hand up to her shoulder, he mouth open in a soundless scream. She staggered backwards dramatically, hit the wall and slithered down it; sat in an ungainly heap on the floor, shuddered, rolled her eyes up, kinked her head to one side, her tongue drooling from her mouth and froze in the stillness of death.

The two men stared at her in speechless astonishment.

"Ah," she said. "Yes...well."

Automatically Harry thrust out a hand to help her up and just as automatically she took it.

"Sorry," she said. "Automatic reflex action. I've been ambushed and shot by my kids so many times it's instinctive." Then seeming to react belatedly to his touch she snatched her hand from Harry's grasp. She smoothed her skirt and looked a little embarrassed and for the moment not sure what to do, thinking, oh hell, I've overdone it again.

"Well," she said again, disconcerted by the men's continued stunned silence.

"Well, good-bye." She gathered what dignity she could salvage around her and left the room.

"Hmmph," Harry grunted, which he was wont to do when reluctant to verbalize his thoughts. He looked at Sam.

"She's a klutz," he said disgustedly, only somehow it did not come out sounding disgusted, and Harry realized too late that he should have stuck with the grunt.

"Rob," Molly said with mock viciousness, flinging down her jacket and dragging off her boots," I will probably never forgive you for entering my name in that damn quiz."

"What's he like, Mum?"

"Harry Wentworth? Just like he is in his movies—old, hard, mean, cold..."

"Mum, no he's not!" Rob laughed. "He's very sexy. Most of the girls in my grade go for him."

"To me he's not...and I don't. End of subject. The dinner

will be a bore and a disaster—I couldn't get out of it. May you get pimples on your next date. Zap! You're cursed." She struck a pose, her pointed finger circling his face.

The twins giggled—but then they giggled at everything that was outside their private shared world. All they really wanted was a father—preferably someone they already knew and liked, but basically any male old enough and wise enough to manage their mother.

Harry dressed the next evening with his usual care—after all he was going to be on public display—but with little sense of anticipation—had the winner been a young woman, or even a teenager he would have looked forward to exercising his charm upon her, and at least having a little fun watching her bridle under his expert hands. But this woman—this Maureen Ash—and yet? There had been that moment when their eyes had met and he had surprised a naked jolt of attraction in her look which she had quickly stifled, which had intrigued him. Maybe she was not as impervious to his charms as she thought?

When he had reluctantly agreed to the wretched contest, Harry had never anticipated this kind of outcome. The winner he had naturally assumed would be a fan of his, a film and TV buff, and, of course, as specified on the entry form, a woman…a young woman like the girls who acted as his leads, and with a little bit of luck…attractive. Not that Harry found too many women really attractive, though he could pretend very nicely that he did (which was sometimes a bore).   But this Maureen Ash…

It was ridiculous: not only was she not a fan—her son had apparently completed the contest in her name—but she actively disliked his movies. And him. Also she was a solidly built mousy blonde in her late thirties—not at all the kind to turn a man on. She was rude, opinionated, defensive and aggressive all at the same time, and the evening promised to be a washout. Her instant refusal of a suitable gown from wardrobe and a hairdo from makeup, simply on the principle of 'being herself,' prepared him for drabness and tatter. What woman would not leap at the chance to borrow a film star's dress and be coiffured by a film studio hairdresser? A middle-aged, liberated divorcee, that's who, he thought grimly, and who needs an evening out with a middle-aged, liberated, divorcee?

Furthermore, he had anticipated the pleasure of knowing he was giving someone a thrill, but this Maureen Ash was about as thrilled at the prospect of dinner with him as the thought of a bout with an orangutan. He didn't know why that simile jumped into his head. Besides, what would they talk about if she were not interested in films, his films in particular? He had already planned on dazzling the winner of the contest with name-dropping shop talk of Hollywood and Roman and London Studios. But now what?

Would she dance—this Ash woman—or inanely jiggle in front of him? And if she could neither talk nor dance with him what did that leave? Eating and drinking. Probably wouldn't drink, he thought gloomily; probably teetotal on principle too. Ex-husband an alcoholic or something.

And then there had been the long-range thought that the dinner might lead to a more private and intimate encounter in his suite on the top floor of the Bayshore, culminating in a satisfying sexual experience (which he was having less and less frequently these days). But that, too, was obviously, definitely...OUT.

Yet whenever he thought of her jerking around and sliding down the wall in a parody of a movie death, Harry could not help smiling.

Molly dressed with equal care, but for different reasons. Stung by the actor's immediate assumption that she had no suitable clothes for a dinner at the Bayshore, and well aware that he was as disgruntled with the whole affair as she, she was determined to surprise him with her presentability. Not that she had any interest in impressing him, mind you. It was simply a matter of pride and proving worth. And then there was Rob: so pathetically pleased with himself for winning the contest in her name and getting her a rare night out on the town with a celebrity, no less; she could not disappoint him by going and looking like a slob on the promised TV interview, and in the film magazines which would be taking pictures— pix, they called them—of the whole evening. So for Rob's sake she dressed carefully in her only good evening dress, and did her hair in what was for her an unusually sophisticated style.

Molly also made mental promises to herself to keep her big mouth shut, but without too much confidence that she would be able to keep them when it came to the crunch. The man rubbed her the wrong way. Thought he was so damned handsome and macho with that white hair and sardonic eyebrows that women would fall swooning at his feet, or leap into his bed, did he? Well, she would show him there were other kinds of women in the world not so easily or superficially pleased.

And he probably couldn't dance, just stand on the floor and shuffle while he pawed — that's all that kind were capable of. Big, physical, insensitive animals.

At this point in her life Molly needed a macho show business, sex symbol like she needed a hole in the head — as she had said at their first, brief, uncordial meeting. It was annoying that his touch apparently weakened her knees.

No, Molly had no apprehensions about the evening — it was nothing she couldn't handle — she just wanted to get it over with and get back to normal living again.

She could easily have driven across town to the hotel in her compact station wagon, but Sam Price insisted on sending the Studio limousine, which caused quite a stir on the Vancouver-East Street where Molly lived. After pictures had been taken by a representative of the local community newspaper, she was waved off by Rob and the twins, the Puccinis, the Costas, the Iwasekis, the Yeungs and the Singhs.

Sam Price met her at the door of the Bayshore Inn and escorted her into the foyer where the TV lights snapped on and blinded her. But not before she had had a glimpse of Harry Wentworth waiting for her, resplendent in evening clothes more elegant and intimidating even than his three-piece suit. There were other hotel guests in the foyer, all looking studiously disinterested in the vulgar display of lights and cameras and celebrities. Most of them were also celebrities in their own right, after all.

Sam introduced Harry and Molly formally as though they had not met before, and they shook hands briefly and maintained the pretense. Harry was smiling with tooth-filled professional charm, the smile that Molly had seen him use on the screen as he seduced (that was her interpretation) girls young enough to be his daughters. It left her unmoved. She saw his eyes travel briefly up and down her.

"Do I pass" she asked sweetly.

"Admirably," he replied with ironic gallantry, partly for the benefit of the Press but partly because he was pleasantly surprised by Molly's outfit. The floor-length white sleeveless dress suited her, its gold belt complementing the gold chain at her throat, from which hung a single pendant pearl that in turn matched her pearl ear studs. The overall effect was one of cool grace. The upswept hair, too, gave her added height and slimmed her face, albeit it was obviously not a professional job... it suited her.

"Shall we go in?" he said, indicating the maitre d' hovering.

"Of course." Molly started forward alone, but Harry quickly reached her side and took her elbow in a firm warm grip. Unexpectedly disturbed by his touch she tried to shake his hand off, but his grip only tightened and he pulled her closer to his side.

"We'll do it my way, Mrs. Ash," he said grimly from between smiling teeth. "Smile—you're on TV."

Their shoulders and hips touching, they promenaded down the corridor, preceded by the TV cameras backing up in front of them. Thinking of the children watching, Molly made herself smile. She had an impish desire to loom into the camera, smile hugely and mouth "Hi, kids", but managed to curb it. Or so she thought, but something must have shown because Harry looked down at her from the corners of his eyes and growled,

"Don't!"

They were seated at a table for two, prominently placed at the center of the dining room where all could see them, and ordered cocktails.

"Like the dress," Harry said.

"Thank you. I considered wearing jeans and T-shirt."

"I've no doubt. What made you change your mind?"

"Rob. Rob insisted." (It was a lie: he had not said a word.)

Harry Wentworth cocked an inquiring eyebrow, recognizing the lie for what it was, knowing that she had enjoyed dressing up.

"Rob?"

"My son. The one who won the contest and put my name on the entry. He's sixteen. I also have twins of eight. Please don't ask me why there's such a gap between them."

"I wasn't going to."

"Why do we have to sit in the middle of the room?" Molly looked around uneasily.

"Because this is a Studio publicity gimmick and I'm part of the Studio and you're part of the gimmick."

"That's undignified for both of us. We're just things being used by the Studio. I'd rather have had the fifty dollars."

"So you said before." Harry sipped his drink, his mouth a thin line.

"I suppose you like it?"

He shrugged non-commitally.

"I like my job—acting. This goes with the job." He gave her a sour look.

"It can be fun, Mrs. Ash."

"I'm sorry," she said. "As you guessed yesterday, my husband and I divorced five years ago. I'm struggling to raise three kids on a small alimony and part-time job; I really haven't the time, or the money, for this sort of thing..." (she gestured at the well-dressed diners, the elegant room, the food, and drinks being consumed) "...but Rob wanted me to come. I'd rather..." She stopped, aware that she was sounding like a prig again.

"Have had the fifty dollars. I know." He was disgruntled and having trouble remembering to smile, and that was bad because flash bulbs kept popping in their direction from all over the room.

"Just what do you have against me?"

"Ah," Molly settled back in her chair, starting on her second gin fizz and beginning to relax.

"Three things, actually. Your clothes, your parts and your attitude to women." She ticked them off on her fingers.

"My clothes?"

"Those suits you always wear."

"So? Nothing wrong with a good suit." Harry said huffily.

"Well, no—in its place. But for jumping out of trains and airplanes? For brawling in bars and trekking through the forest and crashing cars? Looks impractical."

"I happen to be comfortable in a suit, whatever I'm called upon to do. I'm a suit man, whether you like it or not, Mrs. Ash—not that it matters to me. My parts?"

"As I said yesterday—the men you play are callous and brutal and insensitive. Chauvinists."

"Ah-ha!" He saw the feminist in her coming through.

"Treat my women like toys, do I? Mere sex-symbols to be exploited, is that it?"

"Yes. And they're all so young, too— your leading ladies and your dates."

"What's wrong with that?" Harry asked sharply.

"It's a little unlikely, isn't it, that beautiful twenty-year olds would fall for a man of your age, on screen or off?"

"What would you know about that?"

"Well...I...well..."

"For someone who's not a fan of mine you seem to be very well informed about my films. And me."

"Er...my son, Rob...he keeps me up to date." Molly was backing down now, on the defensive.

"I'll bet," Harry said grimly. "You're a liar, Mrs. Ash. Actually you're jealous as hell of those twenty-year olds."

There was a moment of shocked silence and Molly sat transfixed, her glass halfway to her mouth, the colour draining from her face. At that moment the TV lights blazed into life again and Harry leaned forward and covered her hand, where it lay on the table with his, and smiled a huge film star smile that was all on his mouth and none in his eyes, and said,

" Smile...react...say something, dammit, they're filming."

"That wasn't fair," she said, swallowing and smiling like him, with her lips only. She tried to pull her hand away from under his but he only held it the harder, noting as he did so with one part of his mind that it was trembling, and wondering why.

He leaned towards her intimately so that their heads were nearly touching, aware of the cameras all around the room pointed their way, trusting that the clasped hands were prominent in the view-finders, and said coldly, from between his ever-smiling teeth,

"You're nothing but a sex-starved divorcee pretending to be a feminist." It was as callous and brutal as she had said his parts were and he knew he had hurt her and had not really wanted to but was somehow helpless in the grip of his own screen image. He hoped fervently that she would neither start to cry nor leap up from the table, and to that end he kept her hand firmly 'prisoner' and deliberately engaged her eyes in a long hard look. "Keep talking," he said, less grimly, relaxing the insincere smile, "at least until the lights go out."

Molly had been stunned by a moment of unwelcome self-perception and had, in fact, envisaged herself jumping up and running from the room; but the man's steady gaze stayed her, and she was aware that in some way his hand on hers, and his eyes, were saying different things than his mouth was.

"It may be true," she acknowledged in a low voice, "but it was rotten of you to say it."

"Hmmph." He grunted. It might have been meant as an apology, Molly did not know the man well enough to guess. The lights dimmed and Harry released her hand and sat back.

Molly finished her second gin in one swallow. It was going to be a long night and she was not doing much to make it any more pleasant. She kicked herself for her dumb, defensive 'unwitty' conversation. Being divorced had not improved her social skills, she noted ruefully: their lack had been one of Tom's grounds for the action —not specified, of course, but she knew and felt bitter and degraded every time she thought about it.

Because as an actor he had learned to use body language, Harry was also skilled at reading it. He saw Molly's insecurity and unaccountably warmed to it. There was depth to this woman, and he felt an unusual curiosity about what he would find if he could peel away the layers of protection.

"Dance?" the man's voice intruded on her thoughts: he was looking at her, one eyebrow up and he spoke more gently than before.

"Yes," Molly said. "Yes, of course."

The both knew from the first three steps that they could dance together, and they exchanged a look of surprise. Harry dropped a wink, pulled Molly closer and said in her ear,

"Let's show 'em," and led her into a complex series of steps which she was able to follow effortlessly, for his hands told her clearly what to do, which way to turn, and their feet never stumbling, their legs stride for stride they moved in harmony. It was sheer joy for Molly—the more so for being so unexpected; she was metamorphosed from a thick-waisted, rather tired middle-aged mother into a lissome girl, carefree, joyous, ethereal, her lips parted in a smile of undisguised pleasure, her eyes shining, dreamy. So carried away was she, she never noticed the TV lights blaze on again, or the cameramen at the side of the floor, or that the floor cleared and the other dancers ringed it, giving them all the room they needed.

Harry saw these things, of course, but they did not interfere with his pleasure. Not since Dell had he danced so well with anyone—and Dell had been a professional dancer. He did not know why it pleased him so much to see Molly's face relaxed and happy, but it did. Perhaps because he regretted the 'ungallant' remark of a few minutes before and was glad to see her mood change; perhaps because when she smiled she became a different person.

They dipped and whirled and glided in unison—the band ad-libbing madly to heighten the performance—until the music worked to an obvious climax and Harry swung her in a heel-toe, heel-toe spin faster and faster; and with the concluding drum roll pushed her out to arm's length where she sank in a curtsy and he bowed over her hand—and applause rattled around the room.

Molly came out of the dream and stood up, confused by the lights and the clapping people, and Harry cupped her elbow quickly with his hand and led her back to their table, saying ironically in her ear,

"I think they liked us."

Their dinner was served then, and when Molly opened her mouth to speak, Harry held up his fork and said,

"Eat, woman," and she ate obediently, still dancing in her head.

The waiter poured wine and she drank: Harry refilled her glass and she drank again. Well, he thought, maybe with wine and dancing the evening won't be a dead loss. He topped up her glass again, noting that she ate and drank neatly and cleanly. He studied her face, trying to decide what it was about her that was different from the women he usually escorted.

"Make-up," he said suddenly, and Molly looked up inquiringly.

"Decent make-up would take ten years off you."

"Why would I want to take ten years off?"

"Don't all women?" Certainly those of Harry's acquaintance did.

"No," she said. "If I took off ten years I'd have to have been eleven when Rob was born. I don't mind looking thirty-seven."

Dell would have been forty-eight. (Why was Dell so near the surface all the time, even now, so many years later?) Harry regarded the phenomenon of a woman who did not mind looking her age.

"By the same token," she said, "why don't' you dye your hair? I keep expecting you to whip out a garbage bag and show me how strong it is."

Harry had been called the "Man from Glad" before, and it did not amuse him.

"My hair," he said clearly and flatly, the pleasure suddenly gone from the evening, "turned white the week after my wife was killed twenty years ago. Didn't know that, did you?"

"No. No, I didn't. I'm so sorry. Really, I am sorry."

The woman's voice was filled with concern and sympathy, as though the accident had happened yesterday, for she saw the pain in the man's face. For the first time Molly acknowledged that there was a real person living inside the glossy exterior of the successful movie star—a man who had experienced pain and trained himself to hide it. She reached across and laid her hand on his arm in a simple warm, friendly—maternal—gesture of comfort, and was momentarily ashamed of the smart-alecky things she had said earlier.

Harry looked at the hand in surprise—a capable, practical hand, the nails short and neat—and then glanced up at her face suspiciously, reluctant to believe in her sincerity and was astonished to see that her eyes were wet with tears. Tears. For him? Too much wine obviously.

Not just for him, as it happened. Molly went on:

"I know about death. I lost four babies in those seven years between Rob and the twins. Four. And I never got a line or a wrinkle or a grey hair. Not one. But not because I didn't care. Oh God, I cared for those little fetuses. You wouldn't understand. They were people to me, already. Men don't realize...Tom didn't..." She stopped, amazed at herself. She had not thought emotionally about those miscarriages for years, why now of all times, and here of all places?

Harry stood up and soberly they danced again, but the mood was gone. The physical harmony was there but the mutual pleasure was not. They sat down before the music finished.

"I'll tell you about the Hometown Hobo", Harry said, dutifully remembering his obligation to Cetapac Studios.

He was being too kind. Molly felt impelled to squash him.

"Please don't," she said thinly. "I'm not really interested in your movies. Remember? They're all the same anyway."

He glared, not caring now whether the other diners were watching or not.

"What gives with you, woman? Why are you so prickly?"

She shrugged, adding, "Something to do with being a single parent probably."

"I was a single parent too." (It was a long time ago.)

"Your wife died — that's different."

"Damn right it's different," Harry said with feeling.

Dessert was in front of them now and they ate in silence. There was nothing they had to say to each other. Nothing or everything. The evening was going downhill fast. Molly replenished her own glass. Who's interested in a thirty-seven year old divorcee with three kids and a history of miscarriages, anyway?

Harry retreated inside himself, deep in thought, and presently got out a cigar and lit it, forgetting that Molly was still eating. He glanced up and saw her staring and reached guiltily for an ashtray, but she gestured it's OK, don't bother. He pulled out cigarettes and offered her one, but she shook her head and reached for her wineglass instead and he emptied the bottle into it. He noticed two spots of colour high on her cheeks. She drank some coffee then downed half her liqueur in one gulp, ignoring Harry's look of disapproval. Stupid woman, he thought.

Sam Price came across the room and bent discreetly by Harry's ear.

"Is she all right?" he hissed in a penetrating whisper into a pool of silence as the band stopped playing.

"Yes," said Molly very precisely. "Why?"

"Well, Maureen..." Sam started nervously.

"That's Molly," she interrupted, holding up an imperious hand. "Nobody calls me Maureen. I'm Molly."

"Molly," said Harry thoughtfully.

"Yes?"

"Nothing. Trying it out. My name is Harry."

"I know." There was an expectant silence, but Molly did not reciprocate by using his name. She turned to Sam Price. "What did you want?" she asked abruptly.

"The TV people are set up in the lobby and they're ready for you to go out and do an interview to put on after the Late News. They'd like you to go out now."

"Let's go then," said Harry briskly, suddenly wanting to get the evening over with.

"OK." Molly tossed off the last of the liqueur and stood up.

She grabbed the back of her chair and froze, sending a look of naked panic and appeal across the table. Harry stood up at once, moving between her and Sam, incidentally shielding her from most of the rest of the room.

"Go ahead, Sam," he said easily. "We'll be with you in a minute. He put a hand on Molly's shoulder. "What's the matter, Molly?" though he knew.

"I had too much wine," she said flatly. "Oh, God, I'm sorry." She kept her eyes on Harry's shirt front, desperately trying to focus. "You'd...you'd better go on out alone and do your interview. If I let go of this chair I'll fall flat on my face."

"Hmm," Harry considered, holding her shoulder firmly, feeling her sway and knowing that the room was spinning around her; he was oddly touched by her honesty and her evident self-disgust, and her suggestion that he would do better not to be seen with her. "You'll make it", he said. "You're not that bad."

He pried one of Molly's hands off the chair-back and holding it firmly, tucked her arm inside his, pulling her close to his side. She groped blindly for her purse and he took it from the table and gave it to her.

"Now look up," he said. "Slowly. Don't look at your feet, look straight ahead. I'll do the navigating. And smile."

She beamed; Harry almost laughed.

"Not so much." She turned it down. "Good."

He led her from the dining room at a measured pace, smiling and inclining his head at the other guests who recognized him and greeted him by name, the 'gracious star' from his heels to his startling white head, deliberately eclipsing Molly.

In the lobby she stumbled as the lights blinded her and gripped his hand hard, for courage and for balance. He gave her both.

"I'll do the talking," he murmured as the elegant TV hostess Wendy Hills approached them with a microphone in her hand.

"I can talk," Molly retorted from between clenched smiling teeth. "I just can't stand."

"And here they come," Wendy enunciated with gay enthusiasm, "Harry Wentworth, star of the "Stringer and his Men" series we all watch each week—and many, many movies—and his once-in-a-lifetime date for tonight, Maureen Ash…"

"That's Molly," said Harry, smiling his craggy smile. "She prefers to be called Molly."

"Ah, Molly-well, yes. Tell us-Molly-have you had a good time tonight?"

Harry held his breath—at least figuratively speaking.

"The dinner was—fantastic," Molly said seriously.

"And I understand you were dancing up a storm in there."

"That's right," said Harry quickly. "Molly's a great dancer."

"Thank you," she said, almost inaudibly, catching the sincerity in his tone.

"And I suppose he told you all about Hometown Hobo— his new movie that's being shot in and around Vancouver right now, on the streets and the beaches."

"Oh, no," said Molly indifferently smiling.

"No?" Wendy was taken aback.

"We…found other things to talk about," Harry interposed hastily, his fingers tightening on Molly's wrist.

"Well, now, Molly—of course you won this dinner as a prize—the first prize, in fact, - in the "How Well Do You Know Harry Wentworth Contest", so you must be an expert. So tell us which is your favourite Wentworth movie."

"Ummh," she appeared to consider, staring hard at the camera, wishing it would stand still in front of her, and feeling Harry's foot crunch warningly down on her toes. "Actually I don't have a favourite." His foot came up again. She was about to add 'I hate them all', but thought better of it.

In despair of getting any interesting reaction from Molly, Wendy Hills turned to Harry.

"And Harry? How was it for you? It must have been fascinating for you to meet such an expert on your own career."

Harry suppressed the wrong king of smile and said, (gravely aware that Molly was suddenly all attention),

"It was an experience I don't expect to repeat."

At which Molly pealed with laughter, delighted genuine laughter that took them all by surprise. Wendy turned to her quickly to catch her in a moment of animation.

"Finally, Molly," she trilled, "do you have a message for all us Harry Wentworth fans, or a word or two for your three children, who I understand are watching this show?"

"If they are they shouldn't be –it's much too late." Molly looked straight into the camera again."

"Go to bed, you little pikers," she said sternly. " Go straight to bed. Do not pass go. Do not collect—."

"Thank you!" said Harry loudly, stepping between her and the camera. " Thank you, people, thanks a lot. Now Mrs. Ash has to get home to her family and since I'm due on the set at seven tomorrow I need to turn in. So please excuse us both."

The lights faded, leaving dazzling blobs in triplicate on Molly's gyrating eyeballs.

"Where's the door?" she murmured. "Can't see a thing."

Harry let go her wrist and locked his arm about her waist

instead so that he could support her better.

"Straight ahead," he said. "No steps." He swept her through the doors and out to the waiting limousine, his face craggy and impersonal again, and wordlessly handed her into the back seat.

Molly sighed and looked up at him.

"It was a bust, wasn't it?" she said wryly.

"Yes, " Harry replied levelly. "It was a bust and you are drunk."

"Who kept filling my glass?"

"I did. Go home and drink black coffee and go to bed." He thought she looked tired and vulnerable and unassertive, her makeup fading and her hair beginning to come down. Without thinking he reached in and pushed back a lock of hair that had straggled across her forehead—an oddly intimate gesture. To his own surprise as much as hers he leant in and kissed her lightly.

"Goodnight, Molly."

"Goo'night, Mr. Wentworth."

He closed the door and moved to the driver's window.

"Drive slowly," he said. "Don't cut any corners and help her up to the house if she needs it." He passed the driver a twenty-dollar bill.

The big car pulled out smoothly and for a few seconds Harry was treated to Molly's graciously nodding head and royally fluttering hand at the window, before she disappeared abruptly into the depths of the back seat. He returned to the lobby grinning.

"Gee, I'm sorry, Harry. Real sorry." Sam Price met him. "Dumb broad. I'll never put you through anything like that again. I promise."

"You couldn't," Harry said. "There can't be two like her in the world. There can't be."

"We saw you on TV!" the twins shouted.

"You did? Then why the hell aren't you in bed? I told you-"

"Did he kiss you, Mum?"

"Yes—as a matter of fact. But not the way you mean."

"Will you have a baby?"

"No."

"Mum," Rob looked at her quizzically. "I think you're a little tipsy."

"I certainly am, thanks to you for fixing me up with that fiend—that monster—that…"

"Didn't you like him, Mum? He had his arm around you."

"Like him? I—well, no—I mean—perhaps. We had a terrible evening. He was rude to me. I was rude to him. Oh, I don't know, I've got to think about it."

"They showed you dancing together."

"Yes," she said softly, remembering those moments on the dance floor. "We danced. Oh, how we danced."

Chapter 2

The Second Dinner

Seen boarding the skybus to Toronto today—tough guy actor Harry Wentworth. Wentworth, limping slightly and wearing dark glasses will be absent from the set of 'Hometown Hobo' for a week or ten days, a spokesman for Cetapac Studios said. No explanation was given.

"Sam!" Harry yelled. "Get me that Ash woman's phone number. Now!" He got it and dialed quickly.

"Hello. Molly Ash, please. What do you mean—who's this? Ken? Are you a twin? Get your mother to the phone. Yes, she can. Just do as I —."

"Get off the extension, Ken. This is Rob, can I help you?"

"Certainly can. This is Harry Wentworth, and I want to speak to your mother. I don't care if she's busy, just call her to the phone."

"O.K.," said Rob. "But she'll be mad."

Harry waited impatiently.

"Hallo?" said a cautious, sweet little girl voice.

"Hallo," said Harry shortly.

"Please help me, my mother's mean to me."

"My God."

"She beats me and she feeds us cat food and makes us wear old clothes." Heart rending fake sobs came down the line.

"She's stuffing my brother in the washing machine—OW!"

"Yes?" said Molly. "Sorry about that. What can I do for you, Mr. Wentworth?"

"I want you to come over and have dinner with me. Now."

"That's impossible. I've been working all day, I'm cooking supper for the kids and trying to do a wash."

"It's not impossible. Forget the wash: call in a neighbour."

"Who d'you think you are? I'm not about to drop everything and come running just because you call."

"Yes you are. Please."

The last word surprised Molly, and the (quietly desperate) tone it was spoken in.

"What's the matter?"

"I just want your company for dinner. Now."

"Now? It'll take time to get changed—."

"Come as you are, we're eating in my suite."

"As I am! You don't know how I am."

"I can guess. It doesn't matter. Just grab a coat and come. Please." Again that word. Molly wavered.

"I don't know…"

"Go on, Mum," said Rob over the extension. "I can baby-sit and Mrs. Trent will help put the wash through."

"You rotten fink, get off the line."

"You seem to have problems with your kids."

"Certainly not," she retorted. "They have problems with me. There's not enough of me to go round, that's all."

"Are you coming?"

"God help me, I don't know why—yes, I'm on my way."

"The door'll be on the latch."

Driving across town, Molly's mood veered from resentment at Harry's high-handed way of demanding her presence, annoyance at her own weakness at giving in, and curiosity about the strangely uncharacteristic tone of the two 'pleases'. By the time she arrived at the Bayshore, the resentment and annoyance had far outweighed the curiosity, and as the elevator took her to the top floor, so her mood became higher. She tore out of the elevator and bumped into Sam Price.

"Oh, Mrs. Ash, just a minute—"

"I haven't got a minute. I've got to get back to my kids."

"You don't understand. Harry…"

"Oh, I understand Harry all right."

"No, you don't, Mrs. Ash, wait—let me warn you…" his voice trailed away as Molly flung open the door and stalked in.

Harry Wentworth was standing in front of the window admiring the view across Coal Harbour.

"Shut the door," he said without turning around.

She kicked it shut behind her.

"I can't stay. I must have been mad to say I'd come. You have no right to expect people to run when you say run."

"Oh, be quiet!" he said shortly.

"Just tell me why I'm here, and do me the courtesy of looking at me when you speak."

He turned around quickly.

"Oh, Harry! Molly exclaimed. "Your poor face. What happened?" She started forward, full of concern, for the left side of the man's face was scraped raw, his eye was swollen shut and discolouring badly, and several stitches strained to hold together the edges of a cut over his eyebrow.

"Didn't Sam tell you? There was an accident on the set today." He had been warmed by the sudden change in her tone.

Molly was close now, examining the damage with a professional eye.

"It reminds me of when Rob went over the handlebars of his ten-speed. Are you hurt anywhere else?"

He held out his bandaged left hand.

"And my leg," he said. "Took a few stitches there, too." He watched Molly's face carefully for signs of pity or revulsion and found none.

"So," she said, standing back, "you're feeling sore and lonely and you want company for dinner, and that company has to be someone who won't swoon or cluck."

"You're very perceptive," he said, a little taken aback but not showing it. "That's it exactly. Will you stay?"

"Like this?" she said, spreading her coat open and revealing the fact that she was in scruffy blue jeans and a faded T-shirt with 'SUPERMOM' emblazoned across the front.

"In the penthouse suite in the Bayshore?"

"Why not?" Amusement glinted in his good eye. "I expected no less. Who cares, anyway?"

There was a knock.

"Room service, Mr. Wentworth. Your dinner for two."

"Just a moment. Give me your coat, Molly." He took it and headed for the bedroom door, limping stiffly.

Realizing that he didn't want to be seen, Molly waited until he was safely out and then said, "Come in, please."

The waiter fussed around setting up the table, the ice bucket, the candlesticks, and the heated chafing dishes. He looked to Molly for approval, not allowing so much as a flicker of surprise to cross his face at her informal garb. She stood amidst the splendour with as much aplomb as she could muster in the circumstances.

"Thank you," she said with dignity. "I'm sure Mr. Wentworth will be pleased. Will you uncork the wine?"

When he heard the door click shut, Harry creaked back into the room.

"Thanks," he said brusquely. "Sit down."

He picked up the wine bottle and started to pour, but the wine came out in spurts and splashes because his hand was shaking. He said 'Damn!' and put the bottle down. Molly looked at the good side of his face that he had made sure was presented to her, and saw that he was making a very conscious effort to relax and overcome the shaking.

"I guess I don't bounce as well at fifty as I did at twenty-five. I think you'd better pour the wine if it's to go in the glasses."

"Sure." She also served out the meal and without being asked to cut up Harry's Beef Wellington.

"This reminds me of when Rob broke his wrist."

"Woman," he said, "don't patronize me. I'm not your son and I have not gone over the handlebars of my bike or fallen out of a tree. I'm Harry Wentworth." It was not true—at that moment he felt more like little Henry Worthington after he had been thrown by his pony.

"I know," Molly said. "And you're incredible. I can just imagine you hurrying back from the hospital eager to change into a fresh suit and shirt and tie, and even polished shoes."

"Got something against my suits, haven't you?" he said catching the sarcasm in her tone.

"Well, it's not very natural, is it? Any normal man after being in an accident would want to relax in something casual — say, sweater and slacks and slippers. It's as though you have to wear a suit to be Harry Wentworth; if you took it off you'd fall apart like runny Jello."

"I don't appreciate the simile," he said shortly, realizing he did indeed feel a lot like runny Jello. She put her elbow on the table and her chin on her hand and studied him.

"I bet you have three-piece pajamas," she said.

"No," Harry said, "I sleep in a suit. My birthday suit."

Molly laughed, and bent forward to look at the battered side of his face.

"Your eye's running," she said, and reached and pulled the silk handkerchief from his breast pocket and tried to dab his cheek, but he caught her wrist, pushed her hand away and retrieved the handkerchief.

"Don't come the Supermom on me," he said sharply.

"Sorry, I'm sure." She bent her head and ate, rebuffed, realizing that she had taken a liberty and offended the man with her familiarity.

He picked up a strand of her hair.

"You didn't even comb it."

"You said come as you are."

"Why don't you do something with it? Get a good cut and perm." He tweaked the lock and let it drop.

"That takes time. And money. Of course, if I'd won the fifty dollars instead of the dinner with you, I'd have been able to."

"Is fifty dollars so much?"

"To me, yes. You don't live in the real world Har — Mr.Wentworth — ."

" — Harry will do — ."

" — To me fifty dollars is the difference between just getting by and enjoying a few small luxuries. However, my hair is unimportant, it's how I am inside that counts — it's being me, a person of worth — ."

"Spare me the feminist garbage," he interrupted rudely. He

pulled out his wallet and threw it on the table. "Take what you want and get yourself a hairdo."

"My God!" Molly jumped up, and threw down her napkin. "You bastard. Screw your dinner and screw your money and screw you." She strode to the door, face flaming.

"Wait." She stopped. "Don't go." She waited. "Please." She turned round slowly.

"I'm sorry." He had not intended to insult her. She sat down again, reached forward and pushed the wallet across the table with the tips of her fingers as though it was contaminated.

"I don't know what it is about you that makes me react like that. I don't usually use that kind of language."

He stroked her hair as though calming an excitable animal, smoothing it from the crown to the nape of her neck.

"You are the most unusual woman I have ever met."

"I'm only unusual to you because you don't get around to meeting ordinary housewives in your profession."

"You're no ordinary housewife." He gripped her hair at the back of her neck. "Will you go to bed with me?"

Only his grip kept her from learning up again.

"No!"

"Why not?"

"Why should I?" D'you think because I'm a divorcee I'm easy meat, or something panting for fulfillment? If it's sex you want, I'm sure the Bell Captain downstairs can fix you up, or any city taxi driver— there are plenty of girls in this town who do it for a living." Molly sat very still, looking down at her plate, anchored by his hand on her neck, strangely disappointed for a reason she could not analyze.

"Only asking," he said mildly. "Didn't think you would." Her disappointment receded. "Will you stay and keep me company, then? Hmm?" He coaxed, trying to smile, but the swollen side of his mouth would not respond and when he saw that Molly noticed, he was faintly embarrassed.

"The kids are expecting me home soon," she said resolutely.

"Call them. But stay a little while first. Remember...I'm sore and lonely..." His voice was vibrant, pleading, vintage Wounded Hero.

She leaned away from him, her face registering suspicion.

"Don't come the actor on me."

"I don't know what you mean," he spread his hands. "It's what I am. I can be no other."

"It's phony. I liked you better the other way."

"OK," he responded briskly. "Siddown, and if you don't want to talk, turn on the TV."

Molly tuned in to a symphony concert on Channel Nine and they sat in separate chairs in silence and let the music flow over them. Presently, Harry slipped lower in his chair, his chin dropped to his chest, his good eyelid dropped. The wine, the painkillers he had had, and the reaction were setting in and making him drowsy. Molly rose and went quietly to the phone, told the children she would be back soon, and then she tiptoed to the bedroom for her coat.

Harry was not asleep. He followed her movements with his ears and from under his eyelashes. In the bedroom she moved out of his direct line of vision but he could see her clearly in the big wall mirror. She took up her coat from the bed and put it on, then she noticed the pile of soiled clothing on the floor. She picked up the trousers first, found the bloodstained tear in the leg and spent a moment matching up the ragged edges to see if it was mendable, then she folded them neatly and put them on the bed and picked up the jacket. She held it out and carefully brushed it down with one hand, paused and examined the frayed and bloodied left sleeve, before folding it, too, laying it with the trousers. The vest was clean—she added it quickly to the pile and picked up the shirt, the collar and left front of which was heavily bloodstained. Quickly she moved out of range of the mirror and into the bathroom and Harry heard the rush of water filling the basin. What—? It dawned on him that she was putting the shirt in to soak, and he felt strangely touched by her simple 'housewifely' actions. He had planned to throw all the clothes away.

Molly came into the main room and Harry shut his eye quickly. He felt the air stir as she moved towards his chair, and divined that she had stopped and was standing looking down at him. For a long moment he breathed the slow regular breaths of a sleeping man and waited. When her lips gently brushed his forehead he grunted involuntarily, but managed to restrain the impulse to open his eye and reach out his hand.

"Don't go," he said.

"I have to." She spoke gently.

"You don't." He kept his eye shut.

"I do," she replied firmly. "My children are expecting me."

It was like a breath of fresh air to Harry to be contradicted and denied by this woman, and he was surprised by the unexpected pleasure it gave him. Harry Wentworth the Star was used to wielding his tough charm and exercising his powerful charisma to dominate those around him, particularly women. But here was someone unswayed, apparently by his toughness, his charm, his charisma or his status as the 'Wounded Hero', and giving no apology either. He had been right: this was a woman he had to get to know better.

Her coat swished and brushed him as she turned away and Harry risked another glance under his eyelashes. Molly walked to the door, paused, and looked back at him thoughtfully, and once more he was touched by the concern on her face. She frowned and looked more attentively, as though she had seen the glint of his slightly open eye. She raised her hand in a brief gesture of good-bye, uncertain whether he was watching or not, opened the door and noiselessly left.

Harry went straight to the phone and called Sam.

"I want you to get a gift voucher for a haircut and style and perm from the best place in Vancouver and have it sent Special Delivery to Mrs. Ash. No, don't make it worth any special amount. Pay the guy whatever his top price is and tell him not to tell her. And Sam, no signature on it, no message, no mention of me or Cetapac—understood?"

"Right, Harry, I got you."

"You're back early, Mum."

"He fell asleep in front of the TV, Rob."

"I heard on the News he was hurt filming down at Jericho Beach this afternoon."

"Yes. He was cut up and bruised."

"Did you kiss him better, Mum?" This from one of the twins.

She smiled. He had looked so tired and vulnerable and unassertive she had been unable to stop herself, and was still wondering why.

"As a matter of fact I did."

"Will you have a baby?"

"It wasn't that kind of a kiss, darling."

Harry dropped from sight for nearly two weeks while his cuts healed, and in that time went to Toronto and New York and taped some voice-overs for commercials and kept out of the public eye.

For the first week Molly jumped every time the telephone rang, and tried to convince herself it was not because she hoped it was Harry Wentworth calling.

Halfway through the second week she realized that he was not going to call, realized that to him she was nothing, he had used her briefly for amusement and forgotten her. She had one day of dark depression such as she had not experienced since she was fifteen and then in response to curious looks from her children had pulled herself out of it.

Another chauvinistic pig she did not need. Tom had been enough. She was lucky to have escaped from Harry Wentworth unscathed.

Then, belatedly, courtesy of a procrastinating Sam Price and an inefficient Post Office, she received the hairdresser's voucher. Her immediate reaction was anger: she crumpled it up and threw it in the fireplace. Fortunately the fire was not alight, so that later in the evening after second and third thoughts she was able to retrieve it—guiltily—and smooth it out and read it again.

No name of sender, no explanation, but of course it had to be Harry. She phoned the Bayshore, quickly, before she could change her mind or decide what to say, but was thwarted when told that Mr. Wentworth was out of town and had been for ten days.

She showed Rob the voucher.

"Use it, Mum," he said. Privately he thought her hair was a mess. "Who cares who sent it?"

"I do," Molly said seriously. "It's an insult, Rob, a criticism. It implies my hair's a mess."

"It is," the boy said before he could stop himself.

"Oh. Thank you. So you think I should use it?"

"Yes."

"I'll think it over."

She did—for two days—and the voucher burned a hole in her purse.

Could it have been intended merely as a kind gesture, an expression of concern rather than criticism? Maybe it was not from Harry Wentworth at all—but it had to be...didn't it? After much thought it occurred to Molly that having the voucher sent was Harry's way of relieving himself of any further obligation to her. Thus self-convinced that using it put her under no obligation to him, Molly presented the voucher to the salon and spent her entire half-day being re-coiffured.

Grudgingly, she had to admit that the style not only looked good on her, but it made her feel good too. But for what purpose? Logically she should have shared her feeling with the donor, but Harry Wentworth was not only out of town, but also out of her life, and inexplicably that left a lonely hole in Molly's pleasure. She kicked herself for that crass feeling, but the hole remained, and had to be hidden from the children.

Harry got back into Vancouver on the Friday and it was Sunday afternoon before he could take the time to drive out to the East End and find the house. It looked deserted, and repeated knocking and ringing at the front door elicited no response, until a neighbour stuck her head out of a window and called,

"Try the garage at the back, mister."

"Thanks."

Sounds of work came from the garage and when Harry ambled in, he was not surprised to find a lanky teenage boy bent double over a small bike. He looked up.

"Hi!" he said, recognizing Harry at once but determined not to be overawed by him.

"Hi. You must be Rob."

"Yeah, you're Harry Wentworth, aren't you?"

"Right."

"Mum's out."

"So I gathered. What are you doing?"

"Mending Ken's bike. He wiped out yesterday and bashed up the front wheel; I'm trying to straighten it."

"I used to be good at bikes. Let me look."

" Well," the boy looked doubtful, "it's kinda dirty—"

"That's OK," Harry stripped off his raincoat and noticed the boy eyeing him skeptically. "What's the matter? You got something against my suit too?"

Rob laughed. "No, that's just Mum. When Dad came out of University he started wearing suits, and she's had this thing against them ever since. I don't care what you wear as long as you have at least one good fight in each of your movies."

Harry grinned. "Give me the spoke key."

But Rob was still thinking, his face sombre.

"When dad graduated—and started wearing suits—it was like Mum wasn't' good enough for him any more."

Harry remembered his first encounter with Molly and how she had bristled at his suggestion of being dressed for their dinner date by the Cetapac wardrobe department. It fitted in.

"That's nonsense," he said. "You're mother is the equal of anyone anywhere anytime—in an evening dress, or a T-shirt with 'SUPERMOM' written on it."

Rob brightened.

"She likes that one. The twins gave it to her for her birthday; she says it boosts her morale." He was surprised to find himself talking to this famous man as easily as though he was Mr. Puccini from next door.

Harry grinned and nodded. "Well," he said briskly, "let's get on with the bike."

For a while the man and boy worked together setting the wheel in a clamp and replacing the broken spokes, and tightening and loosening them in turn until the wheel spun true.

"That's good," said Rob. "Thanks. I can put it back on the frame. You can wash up in the house if you want."

Harry wiped his hands on a rag.

"Do you like my mother?" the boy asked abruptly.

"I don't know, Rob. Sometimes I think I do, and sometimes I don't. Does she like me?"

"I don't think she knows either, Mr. Wentworth."

"Call me Harry. Where is she, anyway?" He tried to sound casual.

"Took the kids to Stanley Park for the afternoon."

"I guess there's no way I could find them there—it's a big park."

"Oh, I don't know, Harry. She said they'd be at Lumberman's Arch at four o'clock, in case—you know—anyone wanted to...meet her."

"Anyone?"

"Sure, anyone."

"Have I got time to get there?"

"Sure, lots."

"Rotten kid," Harry said happily, punching him lightly on the shoulder. "Why didn't you tell me before?"

The boy grinned.

"You didn't ask. By the way," he added, "she used it in the end."

"Used what?"

"The thing to get her hair done. It looks nice."

Harry parked his car and walked across the grass to the refreshment booth, searching for Molly and the twins, somewhat surprised by his own sudden anxiety that he may have missed them. They were sitting on the damp grass eating ice cream cones, and as he approached them Harry noted that the twins—unlike Rob—were replicas of their mother.

"Hi," he said, standing over them. "Rob was right. Your hair looks nice."

The done-over curly-haired Molly appeared to be struck dumb.

"Who's he?" asked Sue.

"Harry Wentworth," said Ken. "You know. He's on TV. Sometimes."

"Oh him. He took Mum out. I don't like those cop shows."

"You shouldn't be watching," said Harry sternly. "They're adult shows."

"What's that mean?"

"For grown-ups only." He held out his hand to Molly.

"Come on. I've got a car just over there, let's go for a ride."

"No," said Molly, staring up at him dazedly, still hardly able to believe that after two weeks, and just when she had accepted the fact that there had actually been no feeling between them, he had taken the trouble to seek her out. She found her voice.

" The children want to play in the park."

"I want to see his car," said Ken.

"And I want to ride in it," said Sue.

"You're outnumbered three to one," Harry said, pulling Molly to her feet, and she looked and noted automatically that his eyebrow had a new kink in it but otherwise there were no scars.

" And if we don't get a move on I'll be signing autographs here for the next half hour."

The children chattered excitedly and their chatter served to cover the unusual silence of the man and woman as they drove slowly round the park in Harry's magnificent Lincoln Continental. He turned it into the Third Beach car park and stopped.

" Go and play on the sand, kids," he said.

"Don't want to."

"Let's drive some more."

Harry swiveled round and fixed them with a fierce glare.

"The sand—now! Out!"

The doors opened simultaneously and the twins scampered down to the beach in mock terror.

"Now," he said. "Say something."

"I don't know what to say." It was true—for once she was speechless.

"Hallo Harry, how are you, would do for starters."

"Hallo Harry, how are you?"

"I think I'm fine. When you walked out on me two weeks ago, I couldn't decide whether to be angry or hurt."

"Maybe you should just have been grateful, and left it at that."'

"That's a dumb thing to say, Molly, and you know it." His arm was along the back of the seat and slipping gradually towards her shoulders.

"Oh," said Molly suddenly, "I can't see the kids anywhere." She got out of the car hastily, pretending not to see his arm, and walked to the little deck overlooking the beach. Harry followed and stopped close behind her.

"I can't see them anywhere," she said again, distractedly.

"Don't worry—they're there—probably watching us."

Harry put his hand lightly on her shoulders, and she started and moved a little forward. He increased the pressure, feeling the trembling in her body through her coat, and pulled her back against his chest. He knew what he wanted, turned her round quickly and kissed her. For a moment she held back stiffly, then relaxed and responded, kissing him freely. Her knees turned to water and she sagged against him, and only Harry's arms locked around her waist held her up.

"Oh, God," she gasped. "I'm one of them after all."

"Them?"

"Those stupid women who worship the ground you walk on."

Harry chuckled, laid his cheek against hers.

"I never doubted it from the first moment I met you."

"Now will she have a baby?" asked Sue, sprawled on the sand behind a log with her brother, peeking through a crack at the couple on the deck above them.

"No, silly," said Ken. "She has to go to bed with him for that."

Chapter 3

Harry's Place

"Canadian actor Harry Wentworth seems to have taken up residence again in his West Vancouver home in the British Properties. He has lived in it only intermittently since his wife's death twenty years ago."

"This is Sam Price from Cetapac Films," the man's voice on the phone said. "I'm calling for Harry Wentworth, Mrs. Ash."

"Oh, yes? Can't he do his own calling?"

"He's been working since 7 am, Mrs. Ash. He'd like to take you out to dinner tonight."

"Really?"

"He'll pick you up at seven-thirty, he said."

"Oh. Well. Let me think." There was nothing on Molly's calendar, and no earthly reason why she should not go. Rob could baby-sit quite easily, and surely she was entitled to a bit of fun once in while? If Rob grumbled she would point out that it was his fault anyway since he had been responsible for her first meeting with the actor. "Yes, she said, "that would be all right. Should I wear evening dress?"

"I don't know what Harry has in mind, Mrs. Ash. But he always appreciates a well-dressed woman."

I'll bet, she thought, especially when she gets well

undressed.

The black dress with the big pink floral design on it really did not suit her, Molly had to admit, as she looked at herself in the mirror that night, but at least it was different from the one she had worn before.

She opened the door when Harry rang and he stepped inside right away. The twins were hovering on the landing, peeking through the bannisters, and Rob was listening from behind the living-room door.

Harry looked her up and down.

"Don't like it," he said. "Whoever you borrowed it from is brunette and a size bigger than you. Probably looks good on her. Change."

Molly kept her hands at her sides with great difficulty—the urge to slap the man's face almost overcoming her. Through smiling, gritted teeth she said, "I'm ready." It was so true-Charmian was dark and a size bigger than her. "Shall we go?"

The silence between them lasted so long that Rob moved to look through the crack between the door and the jamb to see what was happening. His mother and the actor were glaring at each other, equally imperious and resolute, and notwithstanding the fact that he too thought the dress was unbecoming, Rob hoped his mother would win the silent battle.

"Change," Harry said again, making his voice deep, warm, vibrant and masterful.

In answer, Molly picked up her coat from the hall chair, swung it around her shoulders and said again,

"I'm ready. Let's go." Her body, her chin said clearly 'don't try to dominate me.' She walked stiffly through the door that he held open—equally stiffly—without a backward glance.

The twins dashed downstairs to join Rob in the hall.

"She never even said good-bye!"

"She was too upset," Rob said bitterly. "He was rude. He didn't like Mrs. Trent's dress."

"Neither did I," said Sue.

"It's too big," said Ken.

"But he said so, and a gentleman isn't supposed to say so. Poor Mum was terribly put out. You know how she hates being told what to do by a man. You remember how it was with Dad?"

"D'you think she'll make a baby with him tonight?"

"I'll kill him if he does," Rob said fiercely. He had a sudden thought. "I'm going to call Diane to come and sit with you; I have to go out, kids."

"He doesn't like Harry," said Ken as Rob went to phone.

"I do," said Sue.

"You're like a porcupine," said Harry, "ready to throw a tail full of quills in my face."

"You're insufferable. Conceited. Domineering. Chauvinistic."

"Because I asked you to change into a dress that suits you?"

"You didn't ask—you told."

"Don't get so defensive. I don't care if you wear the same dress every time I take you out, so long as it's one that suits you."

"I'm still me whatever I wear."

"So I noticed," Harry retorted. "You should work on that."

She swallowed an angry answer, and sat in silence on the drive through downtown Vancouver, along the Stanley Park causeway and across Lion's Gate Bridge.

"You're very quiet," Harry said at length, gently. "What are you thinking?"

"I'm trying hard to smooth my quills down."

"Hmm." Harry grunted, reached out and touched her hair, let his hand rest on her neck.

"Where are we going?" Molly asked.

"You'll see."

"Frank Baker's? The Salmon House?"

"My place."

"Oh. Are you planning to seduce me, because—?"

"No," he said shortly. "Not unless you want to be. I don't waste my time seducing women who don't want me to." He returned his hand to the steering wheel.

Oh, hell, Molly flagellated herself, stop saying the wrong thing, you idiot. She smoothed the hideous dress, not recognizing her own knees.

Harry glanced at her, aware that she was kicking herself and wondering why she was so nervous this time, wishing she were not. He preferred her stubborn and assertive: she was not sure why he liked her, or even if he did, or what he found attractive about her. The fact that she was real, he supposed, as opposed to artificial— that she was incapable of hiding her feelings and actually saw no necessity to do so. This was in marked contrast to the people he worked with who acted constantly, both behind and in front of the camera, who usually had an axe to grind or an ulterior motive to forward, or were simply afraid to be themselves. That was it, he realized, that was what he liked—Molly's determination to be herself no matter where the chips may fall—it was very refreshing. If she was sad or mad or glad you knew it, and that made her very vulnerable. Without thinking, he stretched his arm along the back of the seat behind her in a protective gesture. He had not felt protective of a woman for a long time (not since Dell's death) and he found it a pleasant sensation.

Molly was aware of the arm behind her and though it was physically impossible, since he did not touch her, she felt the warmth enclose her shoulders. He removed his arm to change gears as they turned up the mountain into British Properties, and then returned it, indicating that it was no accidental gesture, and Molly sensed his change of mood and relaxed herself, accordingly. Without a word being spoken the atmosphere in the car changed, and by the time Harry turned into a driveway high on the side of the mountain they were both feeling positive about each other.

They were met in the hall of the gracious but unpretentious house by a stocky woman in her mid-forties, with curly hair going grey at the edges. She was wearing an apron.

"Molly, this is Mavis Topham, my housekeeper. Mrs. Molly Ash."

The two women eye each other curiously.

"Don't judge her by the dress," Harry said. "It's borrowed."

"Hallo," Molly said, holding out her hand.

" How d'you do?" Mavis shook hands. "Didn't I see you on TV a couple of weeks ago, Mrs. Ash?"

"I was drunk, as you probably noticed." Molly took off her coat.

Mavis grinned, cocked her head to one side.

"I must confess, I wondered." She took the coat.

"Mr. Wentworth filled my glass too many times."

"Mrs. Ash emptied her glass too many times."

"It takes two to tango they say," Mavis hastily interpolated.

"That we did very well," said Harry.

"Give me a shout when you want dinner."

They mounted four steps into the main living area of the house, the dining room to the left, the fireplace and easy chairs down two steps again to the right. Huge windows covered the wall giving a fabulous view of English Bay, and across the water, West Point Grey; French doors opened onto a large sun deck. The dining table was laid for two.

"It's lovely." Molly said. "I didn't know you lived here. I thought you were in the Bayshore Inn."

" I often live with the crew when we're shooting—just came back here for special occasions."

"Is this a special occasion?"

"Of course."

"I'm flattered."

Harry mixed drinks and they took them out onto the sun deck, Molly going quickly ahead so that he had no chance to take her elbow and escort her. Once out she kept her distance from him, talked lightly of the view, drank in quick little sips. Harry noticed that her glass shook a little when she held it in one hand, and that she noticed too and quickly cupped the other hand around it.

When they sat down to dinner, Harry opened the wine and poured a glass for each of them. Seeing Molly's guarded look he said, "Don't worry, I won't keep filling it." She smiled thinly. "Dammit!" he said suddenly. "Why are you so nervous tonight? You weren't afraid of me before."

"I'm not afraid of you -I'm afraid of me, I think. From the moment I put on this damn dress and realized it was a mistake and yet didn't change it, I knew there was something wrong with me. I've never compromised on my own standards before-why now? I could have worn my own dress again. Why did I think I had to have a different dress? I've never done that before."

"I should have been more perceptive and bought you a

dress and had it sent around."

" I wouldn't have worn it."

"Why not?"

" I'm not a Barbie doll, to be dressed up and played with."

"No," he agreed. "You're not a 'Barbie doll and I'm no Ken. Nevertheless, you accepted the hairdo from me-why not the dress?"

She turned a look of wide-eyed innocence on him.

" You sent the certificate for the hairdo?"

"You know damn well I did."

" It wasn't signed. And anyway that was different-I needed a hairdo and if I'd won the fifty dollars I'd have got it for myself. I don't need a dress."

"Bullshit. Eat your dinner. Mavis went to a lot of trouble."

He watched her covertly and was pleased to notice her hands were not shaking anymore.

"What are you grinning at?" Molly asked suddenly.

"Was I? I'm enjoying sharing my dinner table with a woman again, I guess. Are you going to take exception to that?" Molly shook her head. "Of course not."

They ate then in a companionable silence, and Harry refilled his wineglass generously and Molly's conservatively, and she made no comment, merely eating and drinking what was set in front of her.

Mavis served the coffee on the low table in front of the fireplace, and Harry poured liquor and coffee on the occasional table by his side in such a way that Molly had no doubt that it was 'his' chair. He gestured to the chair on the other side.

"Sit," he said.

Molly considered the chair and how far it was from Harry's and she considered the comfortably long looking white shag rug at their feet, and crossing her ankles she sank gracefully down. Harry seemed to enjoy merely watching her, notwithstanding the dress, though the amount of wine he had consumed at dinner might have had something to do with that. After a while he spread his legs apart, nodded at the floor between them, and said,

"In here, woman."

Again Molly considered for a while, gathered into at to the

pale flames, before getting up on her knees and moving over. She settled herself against his chair and he closed his legs so that his thighs were warm on her shoulders and his calves pressed against her bent legs. He lit a small cigar and in a few moments started to stroke her hair gently, and like a cat she moved her head up into his touch.

A great feeling of peace and safety and protection enveloped Molly, such as she had not felt for years. Since the divorce-no, since long before-she had had to fend for herself it seemed, without support or protection from Tom: life had been a constant tension. She had always been fighting something, real or imagined.

Harry's hand rested on her head now, and its strength and warmth spread through her body. She sat very still, enjoying every second of the sensation, relaxed yet more totally aware than ever before. Let this last forever: let me remember it forever as an oasis in a desert of cacti.

Presently the hand on her head became noticeably heavier and the man's breathing became regular and deep. Harry was asleep. Inwardly Molly laughed at herself. Just your luck, she thought, a romantic moment and you're so stimulating and exciting he falls asleep. Inside she knew that was an unfair comment, unfair on both her and Harry.

Very gently she slid down and down until Harry's hand drooped onto his thigh, then on her backside she eased herself away from between his legs.

Almost prone on her back she turned her head and found Mavis standing in the dining room watching her movements in fascination. Molly put her finger to her lips and indicated that Harry was asleep. Together the two women went quietly to the kitchen.

"That was an excellent dinner, Mrs. Topham."

"Thank you."

The women regarded each other more frankly than they had at the front door, both obviously wondering what the other's relationship was to Harry Wentworth.

"Do you...live here...all the time?"

"Yes, Mrs. Ash." Mavis moved around the kitchen scraping plates and packing the dishwasher. "I keep it clean and aired when Mr. Wentworth is away on location and I do it for him when he's here." She caught Molly's eye. "I mean I cook and clean and change the linen and keep my mouth shut."

Molly flushed.

"Does he often bring guests for dinner then?"

"Not of your age, Mrs. Ash."

"And I'll bet he doesn't usually fall asleep in front of the fire afterwards either."

"No."

"That doesn't say much for my talents as a companion."

Mavis smiled.

"It means that he feels very relaxed with you, Mrs. Ash."

"A lot of good that does me. Do you think I should just call a cab and go home?"

"That's up to you."

"I would if I felt insulted, but I don't. I think I'd like to see the house."

"The master bedroom is two doors down the passage, on the left."

"I'm not interested in the bedroom, Mrs. Topham," Molly said shortly.

"Just testing," said Mavis. The women smiled at each other then. "There's a family room and two bedrooms and a bathroom downstairs, if you want to look."

"Thank you."

Molly explored the lower floor, which had French doors opening onto a patio and swimming pool. The bathroom was a mess, in the process of being painted, plastic covering the fixtures. Overalls, paint, brushes and roller waited on the floor. A crazy idea crept into Molly's head. Why not pass the time doing a bit of painting? It had always been one her favourite pastimes. She unzipped her dress and stepped out of it, leaving it lying on the floor, and pulled on the overalls, hiking up her long slip inside them. The legs and sleeves were much too long so she rolled them up in great bands at her ankles and wrists, them she stuffed her hair inside the painter's cap and went to work. Soon she was totally absorbed.

Half an hour later, Harry came quietly down the passage, saw the dress on the floor and picked it up with curiosity. He leant against the doorjamb, arms folded, the dress draped over one shoulder and watched, and an unexpected feeling of warm affection came over him-not love with its sexual equation-but an asexual fondness. The phrase 'Be ye kindly affectioned one to another' dropped into his mind. He could not remember when he had last looked at a woman with this emotion.

Sensing his presence Molly turned.

"Hi," he said. "What d'you think you're doing?"

"Would you believe painting the downstairs bathroom?"

"I invited you to dinner, not to paint house."

"You fell asleep."

"I know. I'm sorry."

"It's all right," she spread her arms, "I love painting. And I had a look around the house. It's a big house for one person."

"Not bad for a couple with three kids."

"Right. Oh, yes, right," Molly heard herself babbling. "The two younger ones could be down here on this floor and the eldest upstairs with the parents and the housekeeper."

The warmth in Harry's gaze surprised her.

"You look ridiculous," he said. "Put your dress back on." He held it out. There was sudden clatter on the patio and he turned quickly. "We've got a prowler." He was through the family room and out the French doors in a second: Molly followed him. She heard feet pounding around the pool, saw two figures collide and struggle and then Harry was coming back to the house pushing a young man in front of him, twisting one arm up behind his back.

"Yours, I think," he said crisply, thrusting Rob into the room ahead of him.

"Rob!"

"Mum!"

They stared at each other in shock and surprise, Rob rubbing his twisted arm.

Harry unbuttoned his jacket, put his fists on his hips.

"What the hell are you doing here?"

"Rob..."

"No!" Harry thrust out an arm and pushed Molly back. "You keep out of this. It's between him and me. Well?"

"It's...difficult...to explain," the boy said unevenly, obviously very shaken.

"OK, so it's difficult," said Harry. "So we'll go upstairs and have a beer and you'll tell me."

"He doesn't drink..."

"Shut up, Molly. Want a beer, Rob?"

The boy ran his tongue around his lips, looked at his mother and back to Harry.

"Yes," he said.

"OK, up the stairs, kid. You," he turned to Molly, "change back into your dress and clean the paint off your face."
"I haven't got..." she started, but Harry pulled the paintbrush out of her hand, swiped it across her cheek and handed it back before she could finish. "Don't forget to clean the brush. And take your time about it."

He turned at the bottom of the stairs and the sternness on his face softened and he dropped her a wink. Molly stood motionless for a few minutes trying to assimilate what had happened — it had all been so quick.

The man and the boy stood on either side of the fireplace, each with a bottle of beer in his hand.

"If you're not used to that stuff, Rob," Harry said not unkindly, "don't drink it too fast."

"No, sir," said Rob. "I won't." He was confused by Harry's apparent change from the belligerence with which he had pushed him into the house, but also grateful for it. He sipped the beer and tried to calm down. Since Harry did not seem to be about to say anything else, he spoke again, a little hesitantly. "Why is my mother wearing Painter's overalls?"

Harry cocked an eyebrow.

"Because she decided to paint the bathroom, why else? Isn't that what you would expect of your mother?"

"I never know what to expect."

"That's what I mean. How did you know we were here?"

"I took Mum's car and followed you most of the way."

"The twins? You left them alone?"

"My girl friend came over. I lost you half way up the Properties and I've been going up and down streets looking for your car for the last two hours."

"Very resourceful. Why? Don't you trust your mother?"

Harry's voice was getting harsh again, and Rob cringed inwardly, but managed to speak calmly.

"I didn't want her to get into any trouble."

"Trouble. What sort of trouble?"

"Well...you know."

"No, I don't know. Tell me. What sort of trouble?"

"Like..." Rob squirmed.

"Like what?" Harry thrust his face into Rob's. "What?"

"Like you fucking her!" the boy shouted.

"And what damn business is it of yours if your mother and I do...fuck...as you so crudely put it?"

"Well, she's our mother..."

"And that gives you a right to tell her how to live? Because she's your mother she's not allowed to have a normal relationship with a man, is that it? Because you don't approve?"

"The twins-not me so much—but the twins...."

"Ah," said Harry grisly. "Now I see, it's not so much you want to protect her, as you don't want to share her."

"She's all we've got, Mr. Wentworth."

"Name's Harry."

"Harry, then. Dad doesn't want us. Suppose she didn't want us either...where would we go?"

"The Molly I know," Harry said quietly, "would never abandon her kids."

"But when she's with you," Rob said earnestly, "she doesn't act like our mother anymore. She's different in a way."

"How?"

"Younger. Soft, somehow. It's hard to explain. She used to be so sure of herself."

Harry considered that, then he asked shrewdly, "What are you afraid of, Rob?"

"Of being left, I suppose," the boy said slowly. "I don't think I could hack having to look after the twins. Like I want to finish school and go to University."

Harry shook his head, drank from his beer bottle and gave the boy a long thoughtful look.

"You have some problems, don't you, Rob? What did you think when you looked in the window downstairs?"

"I saw Mum's dress over your shoulder-well, what d'you

think I thought, for heaven's sake?"

"That I'd torn it off her in a mad passion and raped her?"

"Something like that."

"What would you have done if you had broken in?"

"Hit you, I suppose. Yeah, it's silly, isn't it? I wouldn't have had a chance—but I'd have tried."

"Good." Harry put his hand on the thin shoulder. "I'm glad to hear that. It's nice to know Molly has a son who's prepared to defend her honour, however mistaken he is, or confused his motives are. I'm not mad at you. Do you understand that?"

Rob took a long swig of this beer.

"Not really," he said honestly. "But it's OK with me."

"You'll have to learn to let your mother be a person as well as a mother."

"And I'm a person as well as a son. I don't think she knows that." He looked at the beer bottle in his hand, a symbol of his personage.

Harry clinked bottles with him.

"After tonight she will."

"I don't think I understand women, Harry."

"Join the club."

Harry was satisfied the way the conversation had gone.

Having missed the teen years of his own son, he had lost the feeling of being a father, and he realized now what a loss it had been. He liked being a father-even to this scrawny youngster-and wondered if Richard had been like this at the same age. He wondered, in fact, for the first time in years what his son looked like now.

Had it not been for the wink, Molly would have been really disturbed as to what was going to happen between Harry and Rob upstairs. But the wink had given her confidence in Harry's ability to control his temper and be fair. She had been shocked-totally-to see Rob there, shocked and mystified. What on earth had the boy thought he was doing? The bit about the beer was disturbing too. Were the men going to gang up on her and override her rules? Did Rob really like beer? How could she not have known that? Had he been sending out signals that she had not seen, nor had purposely ignored? She began to think that life was slipping out of her control. She changed, washed, combed her hair and went cautiously upstairs, listening as she went to catch the tone of the masculine voices. There were no voices.

When Molly entered the living-room space it was to find Harry and her son standing in companionable silence in front of the fire warming their backsides and just finishing their beer. Was it her imagination or did Rob look more of a man and less of a boy than he had fifteen minutes ago?

"Well, what's his story?" She tried unsuccessfully to keep the edge out of her voice.

"Ask him, " said Harry.

"Rob?"

"I'm sorry, Mum. I borrowed the car and followed you here."

"You haven't a license."

"I have —learner's."

"Not good enough," Harry said, holding out his hand. "Cough up the keys." Without demur Rob gave them to him.

"And Ken and Sue?"

"Diane's with them."

"You're in real trouble, aren't you?" Harry said.

"Stole your mother's car, drove without a proper license, abandoned your brother and sister after being left in charge of them, broke into my yard and violated my privacy by spying in at the window. What are you looking so cocky about? We could throw the book at you."

"Yes, sir," said Rob strongly. "I've said I'm sorry-to both of you. But I'm not really."

"Neither am I." Harry said. "Now, get out of here and go home."

"Do not pass Go; do to collect two hundred dollars," Molly added softly.

"And kid..." —Rob paused by the front door—"you'd better take up weight lifting and put some meat on those bones." Rob nodded and closed the door carefully.

Molly spread her hands.

"What was he doing here?"

"He thought I might have plans to rape you and came to

protect you," Harry said smiling. "He's not a bad kid. Don't be hard on him. Let him grow up."

"Why does life have to be so damned complicated?"

"It doesn't" Harry turned on his warmest and most vibrant voice, put his hands on her shoulders, ran them down her arms to cup her elbows and drew her to him.

The telephone shrilled.

"Damn." Harry turned away, picked up the telephone and said curtly, "yes?"

"Is my mother there?" It was the voice of the Eternal Woman, sweet, arch, melting-and about eight years old.

"Yes, she is. How the hell did you get this number?"

"It's in the book," the voice was aggrieved. "I can read, you know."

"And what do you want?" As roughly as Harry spoke, he was aware that Sue, on the other end of the line, was not in the least intimidated by him, and he found that both pleasing and amusing-as well as annoying.

Molly, listening to Harry's end of the conversation only, and watching his face, was puzzled and curious.

"My brother, Rob, left ages ago and he's not back yet...."

"He's on his way. By bus."

"Oh. Did he crash the car?"

"No. I took the keys."

"Diane's asleep."

"Good for Diane."

"Ken's watching the Late News."

"Good for Ken."

"Rob said if you made a baby with Mum he'd kill you."

Harry snorted, a cross between a laugh and a shout of anger, and doubled up. Molly started forward, guessing by the names Diane and Ken who the caller was, but he pushed her back with his free arm.

"Are you ill?" the voice asked solicitously.

"No!" Harry roared. "I'm very, very angry and insulted."

"Don't shout at her," Molly pleaded. "You'll frighten her."

"Frighten her?" he put his hand over the mouthpiece. "Your daughter? Not a chance. She's too like you."

"Well, did you? Make a baby?"

"We did not," he said tersely. "Not that it's any of your damn business, you nosy little brat."

"Did not what?" Molly asked. "What's she saying?"

"You'll never guess." Harry changed his tone to a more conversational one. "Your mother's all right, Sue. We'll be coming back soon, and if you and your brother are not in bed and at least pretending to be fast asleep when we get there, I'll wallop you both. Is that clear?"

"Yes, Mr. Wentworth." The voice was sweetly submissive, apparently well content with his fierceness.

"You can call me Harry," he said gruffly. "Good night, Sue."

"Goodnight, Harry."

"What was all that about?"

"Oh," Harry put his arm around Molly's shoulder and led her back to the fireplace, "your daughter just wanted to know if I'd raped you yet. Not in so many words but that was the gist of it."

"Harry, I'm sorry."

"Don't be."

"My family-this stupid dress-me. It's been another bust, hasn't it?"

"No," he said quietly. He pushed up the shoulder strap that was falling down her arm. "It's been one of the most interesting evenings I've had in many years."

Taking her by surprise, he wrapped his arms around her and kissed her hand. "Now we're going home, you in your car and I in mine. Yes, I know you're quite capable of getting there by yourself, but you're not going to. Understand?"

"Yes, Mr. Wentworth," Molly said meekly, unconsciously parodying her daughter, and looking up at him under her lashes.

The next day a large dress box arrived at the house by Special Delivery. Resentment and pleasure pulling her apart, Molly ripped off the wrapping paper and opened the box. On top of the tissue was a card inscribed briefly: TO BARBIE - FROM KEN.

Her heart pounding, Molly folded back the layers of tissue paper, a delicious anticipation thrilling her reluctant soul, until the garment lay revealed. She laughed out loud. A new pair of blue denim bib overalls looked up at her, a one and a half inch paint brush tucked in one pocket.

Chapter 4

Molly's Place

"Yes, Virginia, the Lincoln Continental you saw outside the modest Vancouver East home of Molly Ash (recent winner of the Cetapac Film Quiz) was indeed that of popular actor Harry Wentworth."

Molly's feelings about Harry were disturbingly ambivalent. She had to laugh wryly at the eager way she had opened the dress box—after having objected so strongly to the idea of him buying her a dress she had no business being so excited as she pushed back the layers of tissue. The overalls had been a delightful surprise; and they took her off the hook of having to be indignant about him sending her a dress, and revealed that he had an impish sense of humour which she had not suspected.

How far was the relationship going to go? Just as far as the bedroom? Molly dreaded the disillusionment of being dumped after he had got her to bed. Maybe it would be better to finish it now so that could not happen. Yet she enjoyed his company and his physical presence, his touch and his kisses. Maybe it would be worth being dumped just for the pleasure of making love with such a man, for however short a time?

No.

That would make her a traitor to her principles, and also a lousy example for the children, for however discrete they might be she was sure the media would report on their friendship and speculate on its outcome. She would not be used as a sex object, a plaything, she decided virtuously—while at the same time another part of her mind told her that was not how Harry Wentworth viewed her.

But Harry Wentworth was an actor, a star, a personality— how could he be interested (really personally interested) in an unextraordinary, late-thirties divorcee with three children? Compared to the glamourous girls his name was usually associated with she was nothing.... Nothing in his world. Molly hastily qualified the thought: she did not think she was nothing, of course. She squared her shoulders mentally. I'm as good as any of those glamour girls—in my way—it's just that I don't have anything in common with him like they do: for heaven's sake, I don't even like his films! On the face of it a productive friendship between Harry Wentworth and Molly Ash was unlikely and illogical –and yet it seemed to be happening.

Still, by sending the overalls he had hit the ball into her court and Molly knew it was up to her to respond. Finally she wrote a note, after several attempts, in a lighthearted vein that she felt gave them both a fair chance of deciding whether to carry on the game or let it drop.

"Dear Ken," she wrote,

"Thank you for the gift, they will be so useful next time I paint a bathroom. I like painting bathrooms. I like eating dinner too. Will you eat dinner with me on Friday at 7:30? And if you want to , you can paint my bathroom.

Your friendly, eat-out dress-up doll,

Barbie."

She sent it by Special Delivery to Harry's suite at the Bayshore, pushing it quickly over the counter quickly before she could change her mind —which happened almost immediately the envelope was dropped into the bag, and then it was too late. Molly was annoyed to find herself anticipating the answer with trepidation—she would have preferred to feel indifference. When the telephone rang the next afternoon she found herself snatching it eagerly off the hook.

"Mrs. Ash? This is Sam Price from Cetapac Films. I have a message for you from Harry Wentworth…"

"No, you don't, Mr. Price," Molly said crisply, interrupting him. "I have a message for Mr. Wentworth. You tell him that if he wants to say anything to me I'd appreciate it if he'd take the time to do it in person. No offense meant to you, Mr. Price."

"Well, of course…I understand, but Harry is very busy filming."

"If he's too busy to call me himself, or drop me a line that's too bad. I'm not accepting messages from a third party. Tell him. Good-bye, Mr. Price," she said sweetly and hung up.

The next time the phone rang some hours late she picked it up with considerably less eagerness, having had ample time for second thoughts.

"The message was," Harry said without preamble, "Ken says yes." His tone was brusque. Molly took a deep breath.

"Oh, hallo Harry, how nice to hear from you," she said pleasantly.

"And in the future," Harry went on as if she had not spoken, "if you want to tear a strip off me I'd appreciate it if you'd do it in person and not through a third party." There was no mistaking his sarcasm. "Poor Sam is still pulling porcupine quills out of his face."

"Oh," said Molly, for once at a total loss for words, and wishing she did not feel so like an uncertain teenager. "You said, 'the message was' …does that mean", she let her voice drop to a throbbing melodramatic whisper, "does that mean (Dear God) that all is over between us?"

To her relief Harry chuckled.

"No, you fool, it means I'll be there at 7:30 on Friday— providing your protective kids don't booby-trap the driveway."

"The kids won't be here; it's their weekend to go with their father."

"Ah" he said with a rising inflection, and Molly had a quick mental picture of his eyebrow raising, "that means we'll have the house to ourselves, eh?"

"Of course they'll lock me into my chastity belt before they leave."

"Of course."

"And Harry—tell Sam I'm sorry about the quills. I suppose I shouldn't come on so strong but we single parents get very touchy about not being treated as equals sometimes."

"You're equal to me, Molly," he said warmly.

"Just one thing. Could you possible come in a more ordinary car?"

"Nothing wrong with a Lincoln Continental."

"Last time you came the neighbours thought I was going out with the Godfather."

"My car is as much a part of me as my suits and my raincoat. You'll just have to get used to it, Molly. I'll bring the wine."

Yes, she thought, hanging up, there's so much to get used to I don't know if I can cope with it all.

On Friday afternoon Rob went off to play basketball in a tournament up the Valley, and Tom collected the twins for their monthly weekend, and that left Molly free to clean and tidy the house and prepare the dinner for Harry and herself. She had felt absurdly excited all day and now a delicious purring feeling pervaded her body as she worked.

At six, she lit the fire and set the table; at seven she went to get dressed. All day long she had planned what she would wear but now that the moment had come to change, she found herself getting out a T-shirt and the new overalls. She looked at herself in the mirror—they fit so well, how did Harry guess her size so accurately? Not exactly dinner party accoutrements perhaps, but somehow she felt Harry would appreciate the joke if she wore them.

He arrived at 7:30, wearing a splendid grey suit that positively shimmered as he moved, a white shirt and grey and black patterned tie and breast pocket handkerchief. He stood in the tiny hall and overwhelmed it, holding out a bottle of wine.

"I see you dressed for dinner," he said gravely. He put his hands oh her shoulders and turned her around. "Nice fit."

"I'll be able to wear them at work."

"Painting?"

"No—my job. In a day-care centre for kids."

"You like that?."

"I'm good at it."

"That wasn't the question."

"It's satisfying to do something you're good at."

"But do you like it?"

"I don't even ask myself. It's not material. I have to have a job and that's a job I can do well."

"I love my job," Harry said. "Every minute of it. Acting, travelling, meeting people — even people who win me as a prize in some silly p.r. contest."

"Might have been better if I'd been twenty years younger and…"

"No," he interrupted. "That's not the point. The whole concept was a bloody insult to both of us. I was very angry with Sam for getting me into that."

"Still angry?"

"No." He looked around. "I like your house; it reminds me…" he was going to say 'of a place Dell and I lived in when we were first married and I was doing bit parts' but the words would not come; he could not speak of Dell or share memories. "…it reminds me of my parent's place in Winnipeg."

Molly was aware that he had shifted gears in mid-sentence. She had seen him open a door in his mind and close it quickly. She wondered.

"Where's the paint brush?" Harry asked suddenly, breaking the mood.

"In the hammer loop." She stuck out her hip.

"Uh-huh. Well, here's a little something to add to your wardrobe. You'll be the best-dressed painter in town." He pulled a jeweler's box out of his pocket and handed it to her.

Molly took the box slowly, held it in both hands without opening it, surprised, almost afraid to lift the lid. She led the way into the living-room room and with her back to Harry opened the box. Inside lay a triple strand gold chain necklace, simple, elegant, and very expensive, she knew. It was undoubtedly the most valuable piece of jewelry she had ever held or touched or owned.

"Harry," she breathed. "It's beautiful. I love it. Is it really for me?"

"It is," he said, relieved that she had not thrown it at his feet with an angry remark as he had quite anticipated she might, and pleased at her appreciative reaction. "Let me put it on you." He took the necklace from the box and standing behind Molly put it round her neck and fastened the clasp.

"Damn. I should have worn a dress."

"No." His hand lingered on her neck, caressing it.

"Look." She moved to the mirror over the fireplace and admired the gold strands as they lay in shining loops across her T-shirt. She made a face. "I'll go and change. But first I have to thank you properly, don't I?" She put her arms around his neck, crossing her wrists, and stood on tip-toe and kissed him on either cheek and then on the end of his nose. It was not what Harry had expected and he was charmed. "Thank you, Harry. I think you really are the Godfather."

He put his hands lightly on her hips, prolonging the moment. The doorbell shrilled.

"Now what?" Molly turned away in exasperation and went down the hall to the door and opened it. She stepped back in dismay.

"Hi, Mum, we're back!"

"Daddy has to go to Toronto."

The twins stood, looking up at her with a mixture of guilt and relief on their faces. Tom Ash came in after them.

"I'm sorry, Molly, but it's true. I got an urgent call and I have take the midnight flight."

Harry watched from the living-room with interest. Tom Ash was wearing an almost identical grey suit, but because he was shorter than Harry and beginning to go to fat, it did not look smart. The open jacket revealed a watch chain spread across a little round pot. His hair was styled and cunningly brushed forward, possibly to hide a receding hairline, and he wore a fashionable thick moustache. In a flash of perception Harry saw him as a sad figure of a man trying to be something that he was not.

Molly was protesting.

"But couldn't Wendy....?"

"Wendy's busy tonight. Sorry. Oh—I see you have company."

"Yes. Come on in. I suppose you might as well meet Harry. Kids, go and take off your things and get ready for bed."

"Hi," Harry said briefly. He had arranged himself carefully, leaning negligently against the mantlepiece, one foot crossed over the other, one elbow on the mantelpiece, his arm swinging elegantly, showing off the French cuff of his shirt and his tasteful silver cufflinks. His eyelids drooped, his expression was haughty; he looked every inch the decadent actor, he hoped, disliking Tom on sight. Idly he toyed with his breast-pocket handkerchief, pulling it up into an extravagant puff. Glancing down, he saw Sue clap her hand over her mouth and stifle a giggle: she was not deceived. His eyelid twitched in a quick wink.

"Tom, this is Harry Wentworth. Tom Ash, my late—er—ex-husband."

"That was a Freudian slip of the tongue, wasn't it?" Tom said sharply. "My God—are you the—?"

"Yes!" said Harry, making no move towards the other man, holding his territorial right in front of the hearth. As it was obvious that he was not going to move, Tom walked up to him and thrust out his hand and was taken aback by the hardness and strength of Harry's grip, as Harry had intended he should be.

"Ah!" Tom waggled his crushed hand. "Harry Wentworth, eh? Well. Glad to meet you. Always enjoy your films—lots of action—good fun."

"Really? Molly doesn't like them."

"Well," Tom gave a jolly laugh, " can't all have good taste, can we?"

Harry glanced at Molly and held out his hand to her, but she shook her head almost imperceptibly and stood apart, declining his offer of moral support. He noticed that she had stuffed the gold necklace down inside her T-shirt and at the same moment so did Ken.

"Hey, Mum," he said, "why did you push that..." at which point Sue, always the more perceptive, fell on him with a savage yell and they ended up on the floor in a rolling windmill of arms and legs.

Molly and Tom both stepped back out of the way, but Harry

moved in quickly, waded between the children and pulled them apart.

"That's enough of that, " he said sternly, holding them each in a vice-like grip an arm's length of each other. "Molly, deal with them."

"Come on, I'll get you a snack and you can go downstairs and watch TV for a while. OK? Excuse us, gentlemen." Shepherding the twins ahead of her, Molly went off towards the kitchen.

"A drink," said Tom immediately. "Can I get you a drink? I imagine it's in the usual place—if the dear girl remembered to buy any. Ah, yes," he opened the cupboard under the buffet, "here we are. Rye or Scotch?"

"Rye."

"She never was much of a housekeeper. No ice—of course," he opened the ice bucket and tipped it towards Harry.

"I'll take it straight."

"Look at the place," Tom gestured around the room, down to the dining area. "Candlesticks on the table and her knitting on the floor by that chair. Absolutely no idea, poor girl."

Harry, looking noncommittal, sipped his warm whiskey. He had already noticed both the candlesticks and the knitting, and the other evidence of a warm lived-in family room that had been superficially spruced-up for company.

"Confidentially," " Tom lowered his voice, "no dress sense either. Imagine inviting a man to dinner and wearing blue-jeans. No idea of what's right, don't you know. One of the reasons we separated. Man in my position—when I graduated—couldn't afford to be humiliated by my wife's naivete, if you understand me. Frankly, I can't see what a man like you sees in her—unless it's sex."

"A man like me", said Harry, "can get all the sex he wants without having dinner with a woman like Molly."

"Not that she's bad in bed," Tom said, tapping Harry's chest with his whiskey glass, and winking knowingly. "But not for a chap like you, I don't think. I mean to say, you're out of her class, aren't you?"

"And she's out of yours, " said Harry.

"Oh, yes, yes indeed," Tom agreed heartily, taking the

statement entirely opposite to the way Harry meant it. "What I mean," he went on seriously, "is, I hope you're not going to lead her up the garden path, so to speak. I may not be married to her anymore, but I do still feel responsible for her. I mean to say it's obvious you haven't much in common. How did you meet anyway?"

Harry had stepped back to the fireplace and he leaned again on the mantelpiece.

"We met over dinner at the Bayshore."

"Ah, yes, now I remember!" Tom snapped his fingers. "I read about it in the Sun. Won a contest, didn't she? Friend of mine saw her on TV that night—said she was sloshed. Didn't do my reputation much good I can tell you. No head for wine, you know. Have to watch her like a hawk—knocks it back like water. No idea."

Harry looked down at him from under drooping lids, somehow concealing his rage and scorn and suppressing an urge to pick up the pompous little man and throw him bodily through the picture window.

Fortunately at that moment of impasse, the twins marched sedately through from the kitchen and down the basement stairs, carrying mugs of milk, and Molly came into the living room.

"Oh," she said, seeing the glasses in the men's hands. "No ice. Damn," She turned.

"It doesn't matter, " said Tom. "I'll be leaving now." He tossed off the last of his drink. "Nice meeting you, Wentworth. Remember what I said, eh? About the garden path and all that. Sorry to have messed up your evening, but it's just one of those things, you know."

Molly held the door open for him, closed it behind him, leaned against it, her forehead on the wood, defeated, deflated, and disappointed. Harry, watching, felt for her but deliberately said nothing, hoping she would pull herself out of it. She came back to him her mouth a thin line.

"So," she said, "my house is a mess, I have no head for wine and no dress sense, but I'm good in bed."

"You heard all that?"

"I didn't have to—he's said it so many times. You may not

believe this, but he was not like that when we first married. He changed and I didn't."

"I'm glad you didn't." He reached forward and hooked the necklace out from under her T-shirt. "Why did you hide it? Ashamed of it?"

"No, of course not!" She covered the three strands with her hands protectively as though afraid he was going to strip them off her. "I just didn't want to lay myself open to any snide remarks. Oh, Harry, I'm so sorry this happened. It seems that something always goes wrong . . . do you want to give up and go home?"

"I came for dinner."

"Dinner! Oh God. I'd better go and see if that's all ruined too." She hurried off to the kitchen.

Harry sat down by the fire and lit a cigar, and presently Ken and Sue—who had been listening from halfway down the basement stairs and not watching TV at all—came in and stood on either side of him.

"Well," said Harry, "you really buggered things up for your mother and me."

"Wasn't our fault. We knew you were coming—we begged Dad to take us back to his place, but he wouldn't."

"Aunt Wendy doesn't like us," said Sue in amazement.

"Not since I left a snake in bed one weekend," said Ken.

"And I gave the dog a drink of water in her Royal Wooster teacup."

"Rotten kids. I wouldn't like you if you did that to me."

"Mum doesn't mind if I leave Sam in the bed to keep warm—she likes snakes,' said Ken.

"And Patticake always drinks out of a good cup like us because she's one of the family. Why are you smoking? Don't you know it's bad for you?"

"Yes, but I like it."

"I don't like people who smoke," Sue said virtuously.

"That's OK with me," said Harry, puffing.

"I don't mind," said Ken, indicating that we men must stick together.

"Will you kiss me?" Sue asked.

"No, you're too young."

"It's 'Show and Tell' in school tomorrow. I want something to Tell."

"In that case…" with a show of distaste, Harry kissed Sue's cheek, and she giggled and covered the place with her hand.

"Are you going to kiss Mum?"

"Later. If I get the chance."

Ken looked around and then whispered, "I think she might like it now."

Molly stood in the entrance to the room, oven mitts on her hands, a tragic look on her face.

"The souffle fell, the steaks are like leather, the gravy turned to brown paste, the vegetables boiled dry and the ice cream melted. As far as I can see the cheese and crackers are OK."

She threw her hands up, sending the oven mitts flying. "I give up. Life is hell." And she gave a short bitter laugh and turned back to the kitchen.

Harry and the twins trooped out after her to see what they could salvage of the meal and the evening. It was not much, for it was obvious that the sun had gone behind cloud for Molly. She sat quietly, caressing the gold chains and looking into the far distance: only the twin's chatter kept the evening from falling with a dull thud, like the souffle—and when they went to bed it did.

Harry prepared to leave.

"I want to see you tomorrow," he said.

"I don't know…."

"What will you be doing?"

"Walking around the Sea Wall with the kids."

"I'll meet you at Third Beach."

"If you like," she said listlessly. "Is it worth it? Won't you be recognized?"

"With a woman and two children? I'll blend into the background."

At least that drew a smile from her.

"I hardly think so."

He kissed her and her lips were unresponsive, her knees did not buckle.

"What happened?" he asked.

"Tom."

In silence Molly resolved not to go to Third Beach, to send the gold necklace back tomorrow, to write and tell Harry it was all no good. She could not tell him to his face.

Chapter Five

With This Ring

"Shooting of a scene for Hometown Hobo on location at Third Beach in Stanley Park was interrupted briefly today by two children, who slipped through the security guards' cordon to ask Harry Wentworth for his autograph. Though visibly annoyed, Wentworth obliged."

Harry had been in a rotten mood for a week since receiving Molly's letter, and the gold chain necklace, both of which he now carried in his pocket with him wherever he went for reasons known only to his subconscious. He snarled at all and sundry and only pulled himself out of the mood when actually filming a scene.

Hanging around on Third Beach, waiting for the sun to come out and the tide to come in far enough in coincidental proportions to shoot a scene that would probably be on screen for only fifteen or twenty seconds, was not helping his frame of mind. He was cold and bored, notwithstanding the raincoat he had pulled on over the jeans and jean jacket and roll-neck sweater that he wore for the part of the "Hometown Hobo."

He glanced at the patient crowds thronging the Stanley Park Sea Wall watching the filming, and he was mildly interested by a noisy diversion taking place at the edge of the sand where a security guard was struggling to hold some children back.

One of the Production Assistants picked up a bull-horn and shouted,

"Get those kids off the sand, please! Everybody off the sand, please – it has to be unmarked!"

At that moment the children, a boy and a girl, broke loose from the guard and started running towards the film crew.

"Harry! Harry!" they screamed, floundering in the soft sand.

"Get those two!" Bullhorn shouted.

"Wait a minute!" Harry was on his feet. "I know them. Let 'em come." He snatched the bullhorn. "Let 'em come, man," his voice boomed across the beach, and a ragged cheer went up from the spectators as he went down on one knee and caught Ken and Sue in his arms as they flung themselves at him. "What the hell –?"

"Harry, Harry, you've got to come!"

"Come where?"

"To the hospital."

"What hospital? Why?"

"It's Mum. She's hurt – you've got to come – it's all horrible – I hate spaghetti –" they were talking together, a jumble of words, panting and gasping at the same time.

"Spaghetti? Just a minute – whoa!" he shook them both. "Now, calm down and talk one at a time. Ken – What's the idea interrupting the filming like this?"

"It's the only way we could get to see you. They wouldn't let us talk to you when we telephoned –"

"Because we're kids," said Sue angrily.

"We saw in the paper about the movie being done on the beach today so we skipped school –"

"Mrs. Puccini won't let us out after school – it's like being in prison."

"You're not making sense. Who's Mrs. Puccini? No, forget that- let's get to the hospital."

"Lion's Gate," said Ken.

"Let's go now," said Sue.

"Why?" Harry asked, trying to keep his voice low and calm

(Was Molly dying? What, in God's name, had happened?) "Is your mother ill?"

"She's hurt," Ken gulped. "She's all black and blue and her arm's broken and she can't walk."

"My God. What happened?"

"The car," said Sue, "she was hit in the car –"

"All right," Harry stopped her. "All right, I'll come. Did she ask you to tell me?"

"Oh, no," said Ken. "She wouldn't do that."

"She'll probably kill us when she finds out, "Sue added, looking tragic. "But we thought you ought to know," she finished virtuously.

"You were right, both of you. When did this happen?"

"Three days ago."

Three days. That would explain why the phone had rung and rung unanswered when he had swallowed his anger and tried to get in touch with Molly.

"What took you so long to find me?"

"We told you. Mrs. Puccini wouldn't let us out."

"Has she got something to do with spaghetti?" Harry asked.

"They eat it all the time."

"I hate it."

"We're staying with them, you see," said Ken. "While Mum's in the hospital. But we hate it. We thought p'raps we could come and stay in your house –"

"What about your father?"

"Oh, we haven't told him."

"Wendy doesn't like us."

"Mum told us def'nitely not to tell him."

"So." Harry stood up. "And Rob?"

"He's all right. He's with the Davidsons."

"And you want me to move you out of the Puccini's and then visit your mother, is that it? In that order?"

"Yes please, Harry."

"I don't think your mother wants to see me." He turned away. "Take off," he said harshly.

"But I thought you were friends." Sue's small puzzled voice stopped him in his tracks and he looked back at them standing stricken, close together, apparently close to tears. "I thought you'd want to. I thought you'd want to help." Her lower lip trembled and pouted and her eyes blinked rapidly.

"Cut that out, Sue," Harry said sharply. "I can tell when you're pretending. All right. Since, as you say, we're friends, I'll go and see her, and I'll ask her about Mrs. Puccini."

"Oh, thank you, Harry! Thank you!" The twins launched themselves at him, reaching up to hug him as high as their arms would go. Grudgingly he bent again and put an arm around each of them.

"I'll go as soon as we finish here. If we ever finish." He glared at the Director, the sky and the sea.

"Please," Ken was patting his thigh. "Can you lend us some bus fare?"

"And a note," Sue hissed in her brother's ear.

"Oh yes, and we need a note for our teacher." Ken pulled a folded page from a school scribbler, and a pencil from his pocket and held them out.

"This was a well-planned operation, I can see," said Harry, starting to write.

"That's forgery."

"Our teacher won't believe it if you sign it."

"She'll believe this," Harry said grimly, folding the paper several times. "Don't you dare read it."

"I can't read writing," Ken said. Sue smiled a secret little smile and turned away.

The sun finally came out, but it took ten takes to get the film in the can to the Director's satisfaction, by which time Harry was tired, bruised and covered in sand from repeatedly jumping off a log, rolling, running, fighting off a fellow-actor and making his getaway. The patient crowd applauded enthusiastically when it was all over, pleased to see that 'tough-guy' Harry Wentworth really did do his own action shots, and really was a fit hard man. He acknowledged the applause with a brief wave and hurried to his car, knocking the sand off himself as he went.

He drove straight to the hospital, forgetting that he had not shaved for several days to promote a realistic growth of stubble, and for once oblivious of the fact that he had not changed. Checking quickly to make sure the jewel box was still in his raincoat pocket, he hurried up to the floor, where the Information Desk had informed him Molly was being treated.

Hastening along the corridor looking at the numbers on the doors of the wards he was halfway past Molly's room before he realized it; he stopped, glanced in, saw her, stepped back out of sight with a sharply indrawn breath. It was not so much the sight of Molly propped against the pillows, one side of her face mottled and swollen and her right arm in a heavy bandage on the covers, (the rest of her face pale and drawn), as the sudden searing memory it jolted free – a sickening memory of the moment when he had to identify Dell's body.

He drew a deep breath and was surprised to find himself shaking, shocked, the wound still raw after all these years – years of denial and concealment. There was no way he could go in and see Molly, he told himself; he was closer to breaking down than he had been in years. And at the same time there was no way he could not see her. He was an actor. The only way he could carry it off would be by acting, acting indifference, anger (his hand touched the jeweller's box), and he closed his eyes and concentrated, psyching himself into the part.

Molly's eyes flew open in surprise when Harry strode into the room and stood at the foot of the bed, wrathful and accusing.

"What the hell's the idea not letting me know you were here?" he barked.

"I'm none of your business. I didn't want anyone coming here. I look a mess," she retorted, turning her head away.

"I don't care what you look like – I want a few explanations. Like where you've been for the last week, why you stood me up, and why you wrote that bloody silly note."

"Because what I said is true. We've nothing in common; my life and yours have no meeting points. The relationship is futile."

"That's your opinion – not mine. You don't make unilateral decisions that are going to affect me, woman," Harry said harshly, levelling a finger at her. "Look at me. I've never been stood up by anyone, or dumped by a woman in my life, and you'd better have some better reasons than the crap you've given me so far." He stalked to the side of the bed, tossed the jeweller's box on the covers. "And neither has anyone ever had the gall to throw a gift back in my face."

Molly looked at him now, struck by the pain in his voice, vaguely aware that it went deeper than the mere words he was saying.

"When I give a gift it's given," he went on tightly. "You don't like it, you can pawn it; you can melt it down and fill your teeth with it; you can throw it in the garbage – but don't you dare give it back to me." Somewhere in the course of this tirade he had snatched her good hand up off the bed covers and was holding it hard, apparently unconscious of his action.

Molly glared up at him, nevertheless gripping his hand in response.

"If it's mine to do what I like with," she said, "then I can damn well send it back if I want. Now leave me alone, you bastard, and let me go back to living a life I can cope with." She wrenched her band from his grip and turned away again.

Harry opened the box and scooped out the necklace; taking Molly's hand he dropped it in her palm and forcibly closed her fingers over it. He leaned over the bed, put his hand under her bruised cheek and turned her face towards him.

"Now," he said furiously, "throw it in my face if you dare!"

Oh God, what's happening? This is all wrong. Her eyes meeting his, Molly suddenly realized that Harry was acting – that his mouth and his eyes were saying different things.

"You know I can't do that," she said quietly. "I love it. It took me all my will power to send it back. This time I'll keep it. Even if people do think it's payment for services rendered."

"What people?"

"People like Tom."

"Did he say –?"

"He didn't have to – I saw him look. It made me feel dirty."

"That's your problem," Harry retorted curtly, standing up.

"I know. I have a lot of problems, don't I?" Like pride and fear, she thought wryly. She swallowed, took a breath. "Well, where are my chocolates and flowers?" she asked lightly.

"You want chocolates and flowers from me?"

"No. Well ... a Bar 6 might be nice. And look at you – unshaven, dirty – where's your nice three-piece suit?"

"I came straight from doing location shots," he said huffily, not picking up the humour in her voice. "On Third Beach," he added pointedly.

"Well, would you tell whoever was there who told you I was here to butt out of my life?"

"Sure," he said coldly. "It was your own kids, Sue and Ken."

"Oh," Molly said, abashed. "Interfering little pikers."

"They didn't tell me what happened." It was a question as much as a statement.

"I was giving Rob a driving lesson – someone has to," she added quickly seeing he was about to say something. "It wasn't his fault. A fellow went through on the amber and broadsided us. I got it all down my right side. Rob's O.K. My arm's broken but they can't put a cast on it till the swelling goes down, then they'll let me out. The rest of me is just bruised."

"Just bruised," said Harry with sarcastic emphasis. He looked at the side of her face, black and blue and swollen, and imagined her shoulder, side, hip, thigh, leg the same way, and an instant desire to fold her in his arms and cradle and comfort her invaded his soul, and it was all he could do to remain standing there.

Molly saw the look in his eyes, the unguarded compassion, pity and tenderness.

Abruptly, Harry turned away, aware that he had lost control, lost his lines, forgotten his part – was unable to deal with his real self. He stalked to the door and out.

"Harry!" Molly's surprised cry followed him down the corridor, and he hurried to the stairwell and flung himself round and round down the eighteen flights of stairs, running from the past, running from a dead wife, running from pain and love and commitment. In the hospital lobby he stopped and for a long time stood in front of the Gift Shop staring, unseeing, into the window, feeling the sweat crawling under his arms, a big, grizzled man, his white hair cropped close to his head, his face closed and grim, remote. He was just one more tired worried relative. Finally he stripped off his raincoat, slung it over one shoulder and went into the little shop.

When Harry took the elevator upstairs again to the ninth floor he was Harry-Wentworth-real-person, ragged at the edges, hurting, uncertain – this he wanted Molly to see.

He stood quietly at the foot of the bed, taking in calmly the disfigurement of her face, as she lay with her eyes closed, unaware of his presence. He wanted to become accustomed enough to it so that the distress it gave would no longer show in his eyes or on his face. Molly had spread the three strands of gold chain at the base of her throat and there was wetness on both her cheeks. Responding to that sixth sense – a remnant of the awareness of the hunted animal – that she was being watched, she opened her eyes.

Harry moved forward. He plunked a single red rose in a bud vase on the bedside locker.

"That is my idea," he said. He dropped a Bar 6 on the bed near her hand. "And that was yours." Deliberately he put his raincoat on the end of the bed and stripped off his jean jacket. He leaned forward and carefully turned her head on the pillow and fastened the clasp of the necklace, letting his hand linger on her neck as he had when he had first put it on her. He pulled up a chair, took her hand in both of his, leaned his elbows on the bed and directed upon her a look of quizzical tenderness.

"I'm mad," he said. "We're both mad. I could kill the man who hit you." He reached one hand forward and with a gentle thumb wiped the moisture from her bruised cheek.

"I'm not crying," Molly said. "My eye's running."

"I know."

"But I will do soon if you don't stop being so terribly nice."

He smiled his famous tooth-filled screen smile – but nonetheless genuine for that – and kissed her cheek.

"You're scratchy, and you smell like a polecat," she said.

"Hmm-mm. Been working."

"I like it. It makes you a little less perfect and a little more human."

"I'm human."

"And so do the sweater and jeans. I like them too."

"So you like my sweat and my clothes – do you like me?"

"You know I do. Thank you for coming. What happened just now, when you left?"

"That's private." She saw him retreat.

"You can't share it?"

"No."

Molly considered. "O.K." she said. "O.K., I accept that."
Realizing that she had no alternative anyway.

"Now," Harry said briskly," I shall make arrangements for
the twins to go up to my house, and when they let you out of
here you can go there too, and Mavis can look after you."

"No, certainly not. The twins are looked after".

"They hate it at the Puccini's."

"I know, but spaghetti for a few days won't kill them.
They've got to learn to be adaptable."

"Mavis had nothing else to do –"

"That's not the point. I've made perfectly good
arrangements, I don't need you to waltz in and start taking
over and changing things."

"I wasn't –"

"Yes, you were. I may be battered and bloody but I am
unbowed."

"You're throwing those quills again."

"All right. But you haven't even stopped to think of practical
things like how do the kids get to school from West Van, and
Cubs and Brownies and swimming lessons? You don't know
where real life is at, Harry Wentworth. And what would your
neighbours think – that you'd moved in your latest lady-friend,
a new Barbie-doll to play with?"

"If my neighbours think like that they can stuff themselves."

"But what about me? I don't want people thinking about
me like that. And the kids, what would they think? Especially
Rob. Think again, Harry."

He smiled an amused smile, not angry this time.

"How about Mavis moving in to your house and looking
after the kids and you there?"

"Now you're making more sense. Would she?"

"Of course. She'll do what I tell her."

"Not like me." Molly started to laugh and stopped
suddenly, a spasm crossing her face. "Ouch! I shouldn't do
that. The doctor said I'm lucky my cheekbone and jaw weren't
smashed – then I would have been a mess. Harry," she had
seen the look of concern and pain he had been unable to
suppress –"Harry, it's O.K. I'm all right. I can handle it." But

she knew that the look stemmed from something deeper and more private than the bruises on her face.

"Don't run away from me again, Molly," he said seriously.

"I'll try, but I can't guarantee it. I scare easily. I pretend not to, but I do." They were words he would remember in later years.

Rob looked at the single rose and the Bar 6. "Harry gave you those?" he asked. "I call that pretty chintzy. The money he's making he could have given you a roomful of flowers and a huge box of chocolates." Still consumed with guilt and frightened and embarrassed by his mother's injuries he kept his eyes anywhere but on her face.

"Rob – one rose means more than a bunch, sometimes. And the Bar 6 was what I asked for. Sometimes it's more important to give someone something simple that they really want, than what you think they should get." And sometimes it's more important just to be there than to bring presents, she added inwardly.

Molly sat on the edge of the bed and swung her legs – one normal, the other swollen and bruised (and that one was uncomfortable and would have been better still but she was impatient to get dressed and go home). She needed help, the new cast on her arm feeling heavy and awkward.

The nurse came, bustling in and swung an Adidas bag up onto the bed.

"Your friend brought the clean clothes you asked for. He's waiting for you in the lobby."

She unzipped the bag and quickly laid out on the bed a bra, panties and camisole that Molly recognized, and a beautiful off-white silk shirt, navy blue slacks and a crushed velvet midnight-blue jacket that she did not. She clamped her mouth shut on her annoyance.

"What a lovely outfit, Mrs. Ash!" The nurse stroked the jacket. "You'll feel super in this. Oh – here's a note."

Molly unfolded it and recognized Sue's Grade three half-writing, half-printing.

"Dear Mum,

I showed Harry the close you like in the Catalog and Mrs. Poocheeni found the other stuff.

> Love,
>   Sue."

And at the bottom in a stronger masculine hand:

"Sue has good taste. Please wear these for her if not for me. Harry."

She held the note and had the strangest feeling that she was standing on the edge of a cliff about to step forward into space, and stranger yet, it was a delicious feeling.

The blouse had been carefully chosen for it's extra-wide sleeves that easily accommodated the cast on Molly's arm, and the nurse was most impressed that Molly's 'friend' had been thoughtful enough to remember this. She was even more impressed when she discovered that the right sleeve of the jacket had had an insert put in the inside seam from the elbow to the wrist to make it large enough for the cast too.

"Why, Mrs. Ash," the nurse enthused as she guided Molly's arm into the narrow sling she had fixed around her neck, "one would hardly guess you'd had an accident!"

"Really?" said Molly, glancing in the mirror at her rainbow coloured profile with a wry smile.

"Oh – well … I'll go and get a wheelchair to take you down in."

"I can walk."

"You're not allowed to, I'm afraid."

As she waited Molly walked back and forth around the bed trying out her stiff and aching leg, feeling disconcertingly wobbly. There was a knock and a young man carrying a small vanity case came in.

"Hallo, Molly," he said in a warm friendly voice. "I'm Percy Watt from make-up – call me Perc. Harry sent me to do your face." He opened the vanity case to reveal it as a travelling make-up kit.

"Well, hallo Perc. Harry does think of everything, doesn't

he?"

"Just sit down and shut your eyes," the young man said, fixing a cape around Molly's neck, "and when you open them again you'll be beautiful, dear."

"Now just a minute," Molly protested. "I feel like the young man who hurt his hand and asked the doctor, 'Doctor when it heals will I be able to play the violin?' and the doctor said, 'of course, my son', and the young man said, 'that's strange, I never could before.' I'm not beautiful on the side that isn't bashed up, so if you make me beautiful I won't be me. So how about just making me a decent me without any bruises?"

"If that's what you want, dear." Perc smiled again and Molly, wondering why she got no sexual vibes from the man realized it was a 'girls-together' smile and that Perc was homosexual. He lifted her hair away from her face and slipped on a bandeau to keep it in place. "Now," he said, and he stood back and studied her face so intently that Molly felt herself becoming embarrassed and self-conscious. "Don't be shy, dear," he said lightly, "it's only old Perc looking at you. You know, this is a real change of pace for me – usually I put on scars and bruises. Do you mind if I study it for a minute and make a few mental notes?"

Molly spread her hands. She felt safe and unthreatened. "Be my guest."

Perc worked gently with his fingers, with cotton batten, with brushes; his eyes – when Molly glanced up at him – impersonal, absorbed in the challenge of his task. She decided she liked him.

He powdered her, wiped off the excess and stood back to survey his handiwork.

"Can I see?"

"Not yet, dear. Not till I do your hair. Hospitals are hell on a girl's hair." He worked with brush and tail comb for a few minutes, and finally handed her a mirror.

Molly was impressed in spite of herself. Never having been a person to use much make-up she had tended to scorn people who did, thinking of them as a vain and artificial, and in a sense deceitful.

"That's very good, Perc. I'm still me – but better. You're an artist."

It was the right thing to say, and Perc smiled with pleasure as he packed up his little case of magic transformations.

The nurse wheeled Molly swiftly down the corridor.

"Wait. Don't we have to go to the cashier first to settle up?"

"Oh no, Mrs. Ash. Your friend has seen to all that."

"Oh," she said. Of course. He would have. I mustn't be angry; he's only being kind.

"He's so thoughtful, isn't he – your friend?" said the nurse chattily. "The clothes, the make-up and all." Molly realized with surprise that the girl actually did not know who Harry was.

"Yes," she said.

"And good-looking too – if only –"

"If only he'd shave more often," Molly finished for her.

"Well, yes. But perhaps his job –"

"That's it exactly," said Molly, grinning inwardly. "His job."

He was waiting in the lobby, relatively inconspicuous in his 'working' clothes – denims and crewneck sweater and heavy boots and two days' growth of stubble – and when he saw her he came forward with such a look of warm fondness that Molly felt herself blushing under the make-up, and the tart words that she had planned to say about the clothes and his paying the bill fled her mind. He took her left hand in his.

"Hi," he said, and in the silence that ensued neither of them noticed the nurse put the Adidas bag down and quietly backed away. "Can you walk?"

"Yes." He took her arm and helped her to stand.

"Prepare yourself. There are reporters and T.V. cameras outside."

"Oh," she said. "That's why the outfit and the facial I suppose. And I thought it was to make me feel good."

"It is."

"It's not. It's for your image. You don't want to be seen with a – a frump with a bashed up face and stringy hair."

Harry glared.

"Do you want to be seen like that on national T.V.?"

"I don't want to be seen on national T.V. any way. Isn't there a back door we can use?"

"Yup. There's a back door. But we're not using it."

"Why not?"

"Because I'm Harry Wentworth, and that's not the way I do things."

"Well, I'm Molly Ash and – "

"You're my girl," he put in quickly.

"Uh – " she said, momentarily speechless. "Uh – "

"Don't fight me, Molly. Let's go." He bent and picked up the bag.

"What do I say to them – the reporters?"

"As little as possible. Smile, if you can without it hurting, otherwise look brave and fragile."

"Ha! Me, fragile!" She snorted with laughter. "I'm no actress."

"I know. But you can try."

They went out and the T.V. lights blinded Molly and when Harry's arm went protectively around her she had no difficulty in leaning against him for support. She was vaguely aware of a hub-hub of voices around them and Harry saying something, then a microphone was thrust in front of her face and someone asked,

"Are you suing the driver, Mrs. Ash?"

"Er – "

"Her lawyer's looking after that."

"Is it true you're going up to Harry Wentworth's place in the British Properties to convalesce?"

"No," Molly said sharply, collecting herself all at once. "Certainly not, I'm going back to my home and my family in Vancouver East. Mr. Wentworth's housekeeper is going to come over and help me for a few days." They were moving down the steps now and towards the car park, the reporters in a phalanx around them.

"How would you describe your relationship with Harry Wentworth, Mrs. Ash"

"How? – Why – we're just good friends."

"Is it true that Cetapac Films –?"

"I'm sorry, fellows," Harry interrupted quickly, "I have to be back on the set in an hour, you'll really have to let us go."

The lights faded and the reporters moved away, packing

up their microphones and checking their tapes as they went.
Harry opened the car door for Molly and suddenly it was as
though an invisible barrier popped up in front of her, and she
stood rigidly in front of the opening unable to move. Unaware
that she was in a state of traumatic panic Harry gave her a
push and said briskly,

"Come on, get in, I'm in a hurry."

Somehow, as though she was pushing her way through a
lead curtain, Molly forced herself to climb into the car, her teeth
clenched hard to stop them chattering. When Harry slammed
the door she reared away from it, wanting to scream and fight
her way out again, but at the same time locked immobile in the
grip of a terror such as she had never experienced before. She
wanted to beg 'don't start the car, I'm scared stiff, let me get
used to it', but Harry was in a hurry, he'd said and she didn't
want to delay him. At the same time another part of her mind
was praying that he had not noticed anything was wrong. Oh
God, stop it. The sweat broke out on her temples and her palms
as Harry manoeuvred the car out of the car park and onto the
street. She squeezed her eyes shut and bent her head so as not
to see the other cars rushing towards them; she tried to blot
out the sounds of horns and engines and brakes. She found
herself waiting for the tearing, grinding scream of buckling
metal, waiting to feel the shock of impact, the blast of pain up
and down her side. It went on and on, happening even though
it never happened.

Harry took a sharp left turn and Molly slid along the seat
and bumped against his shoulder. Terrified lest she slide back
and into the door with her sore side, she reached and clutched
a handful of his jacket and anchored herself against him, her
head butting his shoulder. The immobile bulk of him was
comforting; she breathed a little easier. He kept both hands on
the steering wheel, his eyes straight ahead, aware now that
Molly was experiencing a panic reaction to being in a car again,
but not sure whether to comfort or ignore her.

They swept around another corner and stopped abruptly
at a light and Molly gasped.

"Sorry about that," Harry said matter-of-factly as they
waited for the light to change. "If you feel like throwing up let

me know."

Oh God, Molly thought, as they moved on, now he despises me. What's wrong? I've never been afraid in the car before. Will I never drive again? This is crazy. Stop it: pull yourself together. Sit up and look around. As luck would have it, at the existential moment when she opened her eyes, a car came careening up to a stop sign on their right and nearly overshot it. That was when Molly's bladder let go. Not much – thank God she had gone to the bathroom before leaving the hospital – but enough for the warm wetness to seep through her underwear into her new slacks. She endured the final fifteen minutes of the drive with her thighs pressed tightly together, praying that the wetness would not go through to the car seat.

"Here we are."

Stiffly she eased out of the car and almost collapsed on legs that buckled like over-cooked spaghetti, and grabbed the door for support.

"Give me a moment, Harry," she begged in a whisper, acutely aware of heads behind fluttering curtains up and down the street.

"Sorry," he said, "haven't got a minute," and he scooped her up with one arm under her knees and the other around her shoulders and carried her into the house where Mavis stood at the open door. He set her down in the hall.

"Why, Mrs. Ash, you look great!" said Mavis gaily. "And I love the outfit."

"I have to change," said Molly doggedly, and lurched down the hall towards her bedroom.

"Change?" Harry charged after her, pushed her up against the wall, a hand on either side of her head trapping her. "What the hell d'you mean 'change'? What's wrong with the clothes you're wearing? Because I gave them to you, you won't wear them, is that it? I'm getting a little –"

"No – no," she said, trying to push his hand away. "You don't understand. I just have to change. Don't ask me why."

"Why?"

"Please!"

Harshly: "Why?"

"Oh – because," she glared up at him, mortified and defiant, "damn, because I wet my pants!"

"Ah – Molly." His voice warmed and he put his arms around her and pulled her to him, enfolding her, and – her head against his chest – so could hear the laughter rumbling inside him.

"It's not funny," she protested, muffled against his sweater.

"I know," he said. He put a hand under her chin and raised her face. "I do know. Remind me to tell you about the time I was stuck on a rock-face on a Greek Island and the rope broke. It doesn't matter, my love. We'll go driving again and you'll get over it, I promise. Now change, rest, let Mavis look after things and I'll be back for supper about eight."

"You're not being very charming." They were at the dining-room table where Harry had sat down almost immediately after arriving immaculate, shaven, wearing a suit, and ravenous, and demanded Mavis serve them without further ado. He seemed to be preoccupied with some private pleasure that for the moment did not include Molly – hence her remark.

Harry ate busily.

"Damned if I'm going to waste my charm on someone who doesn't even like my movies. Besides," he glanced up with a twinkle in his eyes,. "You're already hooked. Eat up."

"Hooked, maybe," said Molly, "but not landed. I can't get this stuff on my fork with my left hand."

"Ah," said Harry. "Sorry." He took her fork, filled it with food and held it in front of her mouth. "Open wide." Molly blushed and turned her head away and tried to reach for the fork, but he followed her face around until she finally opened her mouth. "Don't be coy with me."

"I'm not coy, I'm embarrassed." She chewed and swallowed.

"Embarrassed! It's only un-charming old Harry Wentworth here." He piled her fork again, and this time handed it to her. "By the way…" he added conversationally, busy eating,…"there's something I've been meaning to ask you. Will you marry me?"

Molly chewed slower and slower and finally swallowed.

"Well?"

"I'm thinking, I'm thinking. I don't hear violins."

She looked around. "Shouldn't there be violins? And shouldn't you be down on one knee?" She spoke quickly and lightly, trying to cover her nervousness.

"No violins, no knees," he said brusquely. "You can look at these while you think." He pulled a ring box from his pocket and set it open on the table between them. The rings were simple – diamonds in a plain gold setting for the engagement ring and a matching wide gold wedding band. He had longed to buy a set worth several thousand dollars, but fearing its extravagance would overwhelm Molly, had opted for the more modest set in the end. He watched Molly anxiously. She held up the box and looked at the rings intently, and Harry could tell by the pleasure on her face that she liked them.

"They're lovely," she said quietly. She pulled the engagement ring from its slot and Harry took it and put it on her third finger, where it slipped around back to front. "It's too big."

"Grow fatter" He took her hand in both of his. "I love you," he said, and he forgot to pour Sincerity and Warmth and Vibrant Timbre into his voice, but it still came out sounding as though he really meant it.

"Now I hear violins."

"I'm serious, Molly."

"I know. And I love you, and you've known that from the first, haven't you?"

"Mm-mm."

"Since long before I knew it. I love you, against my better judgement, against my will, against all common sense."

"Marry me."

"I want to say 'yes' Harry, but I'm scared stiff."

"You think I'm not?"

"I'm scared of failing – again. I wasn't what Tom needed or expected, and when he wanted me to change, I was too pig-headed to try. I've been alone long enough to have gotten used to managing my own life; I don't know if I could go back to being a – a traditional wife, subjugating myself to my husband's life."

"First," said Harry, ticking off the points on his fingers, "I don't see you as a failure; second, yes you're pig-headed – I'll have to learn to cope with that; third, I've been alone for a long time too, so we'll be doing the adjusting together; and fourth, no, I won't expect you to subjugate yourself to me."

"But you're an actor, Harry, and a famous one at that – and I don't know beans about show business."

"You don't have to."

"And I'm so different from the kind of women you've been used to."

"I know. That's what I love about you. You're honest and frank and open and – without ulterior motives."

Molly gave him a sideways look and a small smile. "Don't underrate me," she said.

"Besides," he went on, "you already understand me better than most people who have known me for years."

"How do you figure that?"

"When I came to the hospital the first time and ranted and raved at you, you knew that wasn't what I was really saying, didn't you?"

"Yes." She nodded.

"And I knew when you swore back at me that wasn't what you were really saying, either. Surely, when two people can do that they must have something good going for them?"

Molly nodded again. "We have. But will it last, Harry? At first I thought it would just be until you got me to bed. I know my knees turn to jelly when you touch me but should I trust my knees?"

"Of course. They're telling you something."

"That I love you? I do, Harry. But I love a you that may not be there. I love the man I see behind the gruff tough outside, a man who's kind and gentle and generous –"

"Watch it!"

And a man who's been badly hurt once and is terribly vulnerable, she added to herself.

He picked up her hand again.

"Will you marry me, Molly?"

"Will you give me some time to think about it?"

"Not much."

"We know so little about each other."

"Enough."

"When I go swimming," Molly said thoughtfully, "I like to wade in from the shore and get used to the water gradually. I don't like to jump straight in out of my depth. Isn't that what I'd be doing if I married you right away?"

"It's the quickest way to learn to swim."

"Or drown."

"Only fools drown. Survivors learn to swim – you're a survivor, Molly."

"I'm also the mother of three children. How about them?"

"How about them? They're part of the deal. Unless you mean you're going to consult them first?"

"Consult? No. But they have to be told and given the chance to react. I mean, I'm not going to let them tell me what to do, but they're people, they have a right to an opinion. Rob's going to resent anyone I marry, he's used to being the man of the family and protecting me. But he's not going to be home very much longer, so I don't feel obligated to consider him too much."

"I like the kid. I think we can get along."

"The twins. I owe them love and attention and a home for at least ten years. Could you share me with them? Because you're going to have to."

Harry glanced instinctively at the stairs down to the rumpus room where Ken and Sue were watching T.V.

"How about you sharing them with me? I'm not used to kids, but I'm willing to try to be a father to them. Unless that's still Tom's territory."

"Tom spoils them – like most divorced fathers. I'm beginning to think they don't enjoy their weekends with him. Particularly since he married."

"That's sad."

"Yes." They lapsed into silence.

"We dance together so well," Harry said ruminatively.

"Life isn't all dancing."

"I mean there's a lot of harmony between us." He picked up the ring box. "Shall I have these made smaller?"

"Well, I don't intend to grow fatter fingers."

Mavis, who had been hovering at the kitchen door waiting for a break in the conversation, moved in now.

"Anyone want dessert?"

"Yes."

"No."

"Coming right up." She put a plate of fancy tarts on the table. "Shall I put the twins to bed, Mrs. Ash?"

"No. But call them, would you? I'll put them to bed." They had been so pathetically pleased to see her home, Molly knew they needed to be reassured that she really was there, and things really were back to normal. "I'll go and turn down their beds."

Harry was drinking coffee and eating a tart when Ken and Sue came through the room. They stopped by the table and watched him.

"They look good. Can we have one?" asked Ken.

"No," said Harry briefly, dismissing them. They stayed.

"Why are you having supper here?" Sue asked.

"Because I'm your mother's friend."

"Are you going to marry her?"

Harry was astounded at the boy's perspicuity.

"Perhaps. Do you think I should?"

"Will she have a baby then?" That was Sue. Ken kicked her shin.

"I told her not to ask that."

The idea had taken Harry off guard.

"I don't know," he said slowly. "Maybe I'm too old to be a father. Would you want her to have one?"

"Yes," said Ken.

"But they die," said Sue. "Before they're born." She looked wistful "But you can marry her if you like."

"Well, thank you."

"Will you be our father, then?" That was Ken, the practical one.

"Not if you don't want me to be."

"We've got a father."

"Then I'll just be Harry."

"Uncle Harry? One friend Mum had wanted us to call him uncle."

                    Margaret Whitford

"Definitely not uncle," said Harry, feeling a twinge of jealousy. "Just plain Harry."

This struck the twins as funny and they started to giggle. Ken controlled himself.

"Will you be nice to us?" he asked seriously.

"Or will you be a Wicked Step-Father?" added Sue, clearly capitalizing the words.

"Neither. I'll be Harry who won't let you eat tarts after supper and wallops you if you don't go to bed on time."

"Ken! Sue!" Molly's voice wafted down the stairs right on cue. The children scampered. Ken stopped at the foot of the stairs.

"You'd better ask Rob," he said.

"But don't mind what he says," said Sue with a sweetly comforting smile. "We like you."

Chapter Six

I Thee Wed

"Mrs. Molly Ash and Canadian actor Harry Wentworth – best known for his portrayal of Stringer in the series 'Stringer and His Men' – were married this morning in a quiet ceremony overlooking Third Beach."

Harry arrived at Third Beach early on the morning of the wedding – at least half an hour early. He wanted, he told himself, to meet the Minister first – Molly's Minister, He had given her the privilege of choosing both the location and the official for the ceremony, and had been prepared for anything from a J.P. at City Hall to a Minister in a Church; he had hinted strongly that he considered the living-room, the sun deck, or the lawn by the swimming pool at his West Van House all very desirable choices, but Molly had opted without hesitation for the small wooden deck on the bluff overlooking Third Beach. He understood the reason for her choice, it being the place where she had first surrendered and admitted that she loved him, but he felt hideously exposed to the public here, and since most of Harry's life was played to the public on both big and little screens and the occasional stage, he would have preferred his private life to be private.

At eight-thirty in the morning on a warm spring day he was aware of the incongruity of his smart grey suit, especially on looking down at the joggers on the Sea Wall below huffing and puffing by in shorts and sweatshirts.

Harry was also having serious second thoughts. Marriage? Again, after all these years of bachelorhood, was it really a good – sensible – idea? And to Molly, of all people? He looked around in vain for a Minister, but the only person in sight was a heavily pregnant young woman occupying the deck, leaning on the rail calling down to a small boy and girl playing in the sand. (She would have to be asked to leave soon.) Of all the women he could have had – rich, glamorous, talented (and young and beautiful) – Molly was the one he fell in love with. Molly the prickly divorcée, with no money and little sophistication, three children and no appreciation of his work on the screen, but an endearing honesty and straightforwardness that had conquered him from the first time they had met in Sam Price's office. Molly with her sudden spontaneous laughter, her warmth and compassion and love and wry acknowledgment of her own shortcomings, but marriage? An abiding friendship maybe – a companion, mistress (he had no doubt he could have persuaded Molly to abandon her principles and become his mistress, knowing the effect his physical presence had on her). And not only marriage but also the taking on of the parenthood of two eight-year-olds and a teenage boy. He was, he knew, illogical and mad even to be contemplating it, let alone embarking upon it. He paced thoughtfully, and then became aware that the pregnant woman had recognized him and was approaching with a friendly smile.

At this moment Harry had no desire at all to be a gracious star, and he turned away.

"Harry Wentworth?"

He had no option but to turn and face the woman, who was smiling and holding out her hand. Now some fans seem to get a great thrill out of shaking hands with a star, claiming to feel intimate vibrations or sense private emotions through the touch, and Harry specialized in bone-crushers with these people. However, this girl's handshake was firm and strong, and in deference to her condition he modified his grip.

"Hallo," she said. "My name is Sara Osgood. The Reverend Sara Osgood. Believe it or not, Mr. Wentworth, trapped inside this pregnant body there beats the heart of a duly licensed United Church Minister. "I'm here to marry you to Molly Ash"

"I should have known," said Harry.

"Meaning?"

"Trust her to find a Minister who is not only female but aggressively expectant."

Sara smiled cheerfully, not insulted.

"There have been times when I had a struggle to find the woman inside the Minister, Mr. Wentworth. I've known Molly for years – since High School, in fact. I hope you're going to make her happier than Tom did."

Deliberately Harry turned away and surveyed the beach.

"If those are your kids," he said coldly, "they're playing with a dead seagull."

"Probably giving it a Christian burial," Sara surmised equably. "I need some information from you to fill in these forms." She had produced a briefcase from her holdall, and from the briefcase pulled out a Marriage Register. "By the way, I have a gown and tabs in the car. I'll change before the wedding."

It was difficult not to like her, she was so incredibly comfortable with herself, and Harry found his initial reserve wearing off. They talked as she filled in the forms, and when he became aware that he was being skilfully interviewed as to his fitness as a husband, he held up a hand.

"Stop," he said. "Did Molly tell you to ask these things?"

"Of course not. I'm asking them for my information. I have to be satisfied as a Minister that this is a suitable union, based on acceptable premises, before I'll perform the ceremony."

"If I don't pass muster you won't marry us?"

"Exactly."

"Hmm." That took Harry by surprise. "And how about Molly?"

"I talked to her the other day. She's ready. Two weeks ago she wasn't, but now she is. What did you do to her?"

"Must have bowled her over with my charm", Harry said with some self-mockery, an ironic eyebrow cocking.

"Whatever it was," Sara said warmly, "it must have been good. I haven't seen her so happy in years. You do know, don't you, how terribly hurt she was by the failure of her first marriage? It's left scars."

"I know," Harry said shortly.

"And your first marriage, Mr. Wentworth, was it happy?" she asked gently.

"Of course. Until she died. It's over now."

"I don't think so."

There was a pause while Harry absorbed Sara's contradictory statement, wondering how a mere woman, a girl almost young enough to be his daughter, could be so knowledgeable about men, about relationships, about death, about him, and realizing it was the trained Minister he was speaking to now.

"You're right." He admitted tersely. "It's not over."

"Work on it, will you, please, for Molly's sake?"

That, he resented, but was forestalled from expressing his resentment by the familiar racket of Molly's un-tuned station wagon arriving in the parking lot. Harry started forward eagerly, then stopped in disappointment. Molly had got out of the car and was standing looking at him. She was wearing blue jeans and a T-shirt – her Super-Mom T-shirt, in fact – and the blue velvet jacket Harry had given her. His first thought was that she had changed her mind and no longer wanted to marry him, and he was shocked at the hollow depth of the hole of his disappointment, unaware of his already dependency on her. Quickly, but not quickly enough, he rearranged his face to indifference. But Molly had seen - had seen and been surprised. She had dressed deliberately to test him. Had he shown anger or scorn at her costume she was not sure what she would have done, but certainly not gone into the marriage with as much confidence. But she had seen, and correctly read his quite unexpected dismay, seen his fear that she had changed her mind, and thus her mind was confirmed in its purpose. This was the man she loved. She reached into the car for the shopping bag.

"I'll change," she called out. "Only be a minute."

Rob and the twins stood by the car undecided. Rob was

wearing a typical teenagers suit – did they specially make them for boys of his age short at the wrists and ankles, Harry wondered? The kid obviously needed some new clothes. He was carrying a portable tape recorder. Ken was precise and neat in jeans – pressed with a crease – and a jean jacket; Sue was in an untypical sprigged muslin dress, white knee socks, sandals, and a ribbon in her hair. She looked adorable. The more so because one sock was creeping down a smooth brown calf, and several strands of hair had escaped the ribbon and framed her face with charming disarray. Harry had an immediate impression that these were calculated effects that Sue had carefully created. He grinned; this one he would always understand.

The few friends they had invited were arriving now; the Reverend Sara's children – fresh from their sandy avian funeral – had come up from the beach and were standing with Ken and Sue eyeing Harry curiously, and obviously quizzing the twins about him; Rob was waiting for his mother by the entrance to the Lady's Change Room and fiddling with his tape deck. Sam Price was standing by Harry's Lincoln, pulling at his shirt cuffs, and when he caught Harry's eye he raised a circled thumb and forefinger, which Harry interpreted as meaning the Press were in attendance. Harry, glancing around and recognizing a few journalistic faces in the small crowd, had assumed – without consulting her – which Molly would realize that anything he did in a public place was going to be recorded and reported. That was part of the price of being a star. Surely she had already experienced the fishbowl existence enough times with him not to be fazed by it? Out of the corner of his eye he noted a T.V. crew, unable to bring their mobile van close enough, were scaling the wall of the Concession and setting up their camera on the roof.

The Reverend Sara emerged from her car in a blue clerical gown with white collar tabs, looking considerably less obviously pregnant, and simultaneously Molly came out of the Change Room in the long white dress she had worn for their first dinner together. Harry was a little disgusted with himself that he should feel relieved: he should have been prepared to marry her in her jeans if that was what she wanted. However, something about the way the dress hung gave him the distinct impression that she was still wearing the jeans underneath, and it pleased him to think that she had not completely compromised herself.

The Reverend Sara Osgood had a strange look on her face.

"I think we'd better get on with this," she said. Rob punched the button on his tape-recorder and music flooded the area, drowning out the traffic noises from the Park Driveway.

Twenty minutes later chaos reigned.

A second after declaring Harry and Molly man and wife, the Reverend Sara had given a strange little cry, clutched her abdomen, and her waters had broken in a flood onto the deck between her legs. The cameraman's assistant in his excitement had stepped forward off the roof of the Concession and crashed to the tarmac, cutting open his head and breaking an arm. Now a fire engine, a Rescue Squad van, a paramedic team and two ambulances had converged upon the car park, their sirens in various stages of alarm.

Harry leant against a tree and signed autographs and watched the activity in fascinated disbelief.

This was his wedding: The Minister was being loaded onto a stretcher, beaming seraphically and at the same time giving detailed instructions to someone about seeing that her children were taken home; the paramedics were staunching blood and setting up an IV for the TV man; a crowd had materialized in seconds; three cars had crashed in the car park in the confusion; a Mounted Policeman was trying to move people on; two police cars with sirens bleating were trying desperately to force a way through the traffic jam on the Driveway – and Harry's bride?

Molly had her white gown hiked up around her hips – revealing the fact that she was indeed wearing blue-jeans underneath – and she was squatting on the ground picking up broken headlight glass and dropping it into a plastic bag she had found in a garbage container, and directing two or three other people to help her. At the moment of crisis she had left Harry's side and efficiently organized coats and blankets for the two victims, commandeering towels from the Concession for the Reverend Sara to stuff up her skirt, and to make a rough pressure pad and bandage for the man's cut head. She alternated between the two of them until the Emergency Unit arrived, at which time she had faded into the background and started to pick up the broken glass.

Watching her Harry had to be wryly impressed. He could imagine other women being appalled, having hysterics, being creased with embarrassment, or even reacting with anger. Of course it was her fault (in a way) for choosing a public place for the wedding and a pregnant woman Minister ripe for parturition – but then, that was Molly.

Was his life henceforth going to be one crisis after another, he wondered? Tired of signing the pieces of paper thrust at him by awestruck fans (did they wonder why he wasn't helping?) he looked around for his new family.

The twins were down on the beach with the Reverend Sara's children – appeared unmoved by their mother's dramatic onset of labour – and all four were busy disinterring the dead seagull, amid a lot of flying sand. Rob had taken off his jacket and tie and retreated to the Sea Wall, where he sat listening to his tape recorder and gazing out to the sea busy disassociating himself from the melee by the Concession. Harry sympathized. He felt a strong need to disassociate himself.

He strode over to Molly, held out his hand.

"Get up," he said.

"Someone's going to come up from the beach and get a cut foot if I don't –"

"Let the others finish. Get up." He took her wrist and pulled her to her feet and the dress fell in graceful lines around her legs and she became a bride again. "We just got married," he said. "Remember? We didn't finish the ceremony." He put his arms around her and kissed her and the vigilant Press Corps popped their flash bulbs busily. The pose was a good one, his feet were firmly placed, and his hands spread elegantly, one on Molly's shoulder one on her waist, his head at a good angle so that their noses did not bump. He hoped they were getting his good side.

Molly, almost blinded by the flash bulbs, pulled her head back.

"Was that for my benefit or the media?" she asked between falsely smiling teeth.

"What do you think?" he replied enigmatically. "Come on," he hustled her towards his car, "our guests are waiting at the house."

"Wait! My bouquet – I dropped it –"

"It's gone," Harry said shortly, realizing that was what the twins had carried down to the beach; and with a flash of intuition he knew what they were doing with it.

He was right: the seagull's second funeral was almost complete and Molly's bridal bouquet was doing substitute duty as a graveyard decoration.

"The Lord giveth, the Lord taketh away," the Reverend Sara's son intoned.

"Let no man put asunder," Ken added, not to be outdone.

"Amen," said the girls in unison.

"I won't be long," Molly said, and disappeared into the bathroom, carefully closing the door behind her.

Harry stripped and climbed into the bed and sat up, propped against the padded headboard and waited for her, disappointed that she had chosen to change in the bathroom, and wondering if, after all, she was going to turn out to be a shy bride. True, there had been times when she had been embarrassed and self-conscious but somehow he had not expected that she would be on their wedding night. He hoped she wasn't changing into some frothy bridal negligee outfit that he would have to pretend he liked. The minutes ticked by and Harry's misgiving increased. Hell, he thought, I should have taken her to bed before this.

Molly came out of the bathroom and Harry's heart plummeted – she was still fully dressed in the suit she had travelled in. She came across the room to the side of the bed and bringing her hand from behind her back, she placed a small cassette tape-recorder in Harry's lap.

"This is my wedding present to you," she murmured, almost whispered, and walked back to the middle of the room, keeping her back to him.

Mystified, Harry looked at the recorder.

"Now," said Molly.

Comprehending, he punched the Play button and after a

brief pause music started – a saxophone, a clarinet, piano, percussion, a heavy, smoky, driving, nightclub beat, and looking up in surprise Harry saw Molly begin to move in time to it. Gently at first, her back still to him, her heels rising and falling, her shoulders moving alternately, her hips swaying. Slowly, almost dreamily, she undid her jacket and one sleeve at a time took it off, held it by the collar, turned suddenly – on the beat – and tossed it aside. Then she started to dance with her whole body, stepping, kicking, gliding, bumping, grinding, her hands tracing the lines of her bust, her hips and thighs, hiding her face, revealing it.

Oh yes! Said Harry silently. Oh yes!

She dropped her skirt and stepped out of it – 'a-one-a-two'- and kicked it away across the floor. Her face serene and remote, her eyes unfocussed, she undulated out of her blouse and threw that too aside, and she danced on, in her garter-belt and nylons, panties and bra; and looking at her face, Harry knew – as an actor – that she was inside herself and outside her real self and immersed in a Molly-fantasy that was a facet of herself that no one else had ever seen. And he was delighted. His smile was small on his mouth but big in his eyes.

The nylons were peeled off one at a time and left with the stepped-out-of shoes, she leant forward and the unclasped bra fell away from her breasts and with a wriggle of her shoulders dropped to the floor. The garter belt— (where had it come from,?— she always wore pantyhose.? That must have been why she was so long in the bathroom) slid out from inside her panties, was flaunted seductively before being thrown away. Now Molly turned her back and teasingly edged her panties down her buttocks an inch at a time, bumping and grinding as she went, glancing over her shoulder, peeping, mock-shy. Suddenly, they were down and with one toe she skied them across the room and turned, triumphant, naked, legs apart, arms up-stretched, head flung back – a long suppressed sex-dream fulfilled.

Harry punched the Stop button and for four silent beats Molly held the pose, then gradually she relaxed, like a melting wax figurine; her arms became loose, lowered, dropped, fell to her sides, her body settled into her pelvis, her legs became slack, knees slightly bent, her head dropped forward and she became once more Molly Ash Wentworth, housewife, mother of three, with stretch marks on her belly and breasts too small and hips too heavy, and she walked quietly over to the bed – offering herself, her whole self, saying I'm all I've got to give and I'm giving it all!.

Harry took her hand and kissed the back and then the palm, unable to speak his thanks, and with a growl of pleasure pulled her down on top of him.

If he had wondered what kind of a lover she would make he had no doubts now, after that performance. He knew he was going to enjoy her.

As for Molly, the fulfillment of actually living out her fantasy totally freed her. For years she had been constrained by Tom's concept of a 'perfect lady' and 'a good wife', someone who passively submitted to her husband's ministrations, had held herself back and filled that role for reasons of loyalty and obedience too deeply ingrained for her to fully understand. For years she had held in her natural instinct to take part in the love-play, initiate it, drive it on, withhold, tease, release, and now at last in Harry she had a man who had no preconceptions about what was right or wrong for a woman to do in bed. As long as it was creative and loving and mutually acceptable, it was good with him.

So their lovemaking was like a conversation – give and take, now you, now me, now we agree – ah-hahah! It was exciting, it was fun, it was emotionally marvellous and physically pleasure-able and, in the last analysis exhausting. Finally, they drifted off to sleep, Molly in the crook of Harry's arm, her head on his shoulder.

She woke some hours later with a crick in her neck and started cautiously to turn over. Harry grunted in his sleep, tightened his left arm around her and brought his right arm across her to meet it. She was now squashed against his chest, her face jammed up to his chin. She put her left hand on his chest and pushed gently, but nothing happened. Beginning to feel trapped, Molly pushed harder, but this only elicited another grunt from Harry, a shift down in the bed and a tightening of his arms.

Molly had slept alone long enough to not only become accustomed to it but to enjoy the freedom of having a whole bed to herself. Now she felt uncomfortable, hot and restricted. She pushed harder. Harry hugged harder, his arms around her ribs now so tight that she could hardly breathe. Molly fought down an irrational, claustrophobic panic. Harry grunted again, shifted again, turned, lay half on her, crushing her into complete immobility. Her mouth pressed hard against his neck, both arms pinned and her legs weighed down by Harry's Molly felt powerless to help herself, and lay tense and rigid as a stick in his embrace, until gradually common-sense overcame her fear.

This is my husband; he loves me; he's not going to hurt me, and it doesn't matter if I do wake him.

She had a further thought and her sense of humour overcame her latent hysteria and she found herself giggling into Harry's neck. He stirred.

"Joke?" he asked sleepily, his eyes silver glints in the light from the window. (Had he been awake all along?)

"Had a thought," Molly said with difficulty, forcing her head away from his neck. "Tomorrow's headlines: 'Show Biz Tragedy: rugged Harry Wentworth smothers new wife on Wedding Night. Didn't know my own strength, protests heartbroken Star'. "

Harry's arms relaxed then, and he moved until they were both comfortable, put his lips to her forehead and kissed it gently.

"I love you," he said in a strange different voice that Molly had never heard before, and guessed she was not likely to hear ever in daylight. "Don't ever leave me," and there was an urgency there that she did not fully understand, but she knew he was expressing a fear and a need, so she reached up and pulled his head down to hers and kissed his mouth.

"I won't," she murmured, an unexpectedly move. "I won't, Harry."

And, not knowing why, she thought, I'm really the strong one here, isn't that strange, and drifted off to sleep again.

She woke later and looked at the white head on the pillow beside hers, the features plain in the dawn light coming through the curtain. My God, she thought, who is this man in bed with me? I don't know anything about him; I don't even recognize his face. She raised herself on one elbow and stared down at him. His face isn't tough at all, she thought, it's gentle and sad and lived-in. Is it possible to love a person without even knowing him? Who were his parents, where did he grow up, did he finish High School – where has he been for the fifty years before I met him? Can we possibly have enough in common to even be in love, let alone married? Is this another one of my monumental boo-boos?

"Second thought?" asked Harry quietly, looking at her through half-opened eyes. She nearly said yes, but meeting his eyes and hearing his now-familiar voice, she found it was not true.

"No," she said. "Just finding it hard to believe I'm really married to you."

"You really are, " he said, and took her hand and guided it underneath the bedclothes and between his legs. Then he pulled her down in the bed again and for the first time in many years – since Dell died, in fact – he saw the future cast a solid shadow.

Chapter Seven

Adjustments

"Tough-guy actor Harry Wentworth shines in new role on stage at the Playhouse. Marriage seems to suit him."

Molly was in the pool at home one afternoon enjoying the feel of the water on her naked body as it swirled between her legs as she swam, her breasts supported, yet free – no cloth, no straps, no restrictions. She thought, it must be like this in the womb--

"Molly!" A roar came from the sun deck. "Get out of that pool!"

Startled and puzzled she looked up at Harry and the twins leaning over the rail. Her round white bosoms broke the water, the nipples standing up pink and hard.

She trod water. "What?" she asked mildly.

Harry had not realized until the family moved up to his British Properties home that Molly was a swimmer – not a dipper, but a serious distance swimmer. Before she married him she had been in the habit of going to the beach every day in the summer and the Britannia Pool some time every day during the winter. Now she swam in Harry's pool, and loved it.

She swam for pleasure, for contemplation, for exercise, for relaxation— to expiate her frustrations, and to wrestle with problems uninterrupted.

The element of water gave her sensual pleasure too; it supported her, but not wholly- she had to use it, to co-operate with it. It was a strong yet passive adversary against which she could test her anger or elation and neither win nor lose: like a punching bag she trained against it and developed mental and physical muscles, using it. It embraced and enveloped her when she dived- she floated and it caressed her gently: it tested and challenged her, length after length reeled off, subconsciously noted, past the point of first exhaustion and on into the euphoric period of seemingly unlimited strength and invincibility, and finally to satisfying tiredness when she trod water quietly, breathing deep, slow breaths, feeling her fingertips and toes tingling, and agreed with the water that it was time to get out. They always parted friends.

The neighbours thought she was a nut – especially when they saw that Harry kept the pool filled, heated and cleaned on into the fall and winter, and yet put no shelter over it so that often Molly had to patter out through the rain or snow for her daily swim. That was the way she wanted it; that was the way she really appreciated the water.

Sometimes Harry joined her, but for the most part he watched, taking pleasure from the grace and agility his new wife had in the water. But this time she had gone too far.

Molly heard him stamping through the house and presently he burst out onto the patio and came to the edge of the pool holding out the largest bath sheet they possessed.

"Get out," he said tightly. "Now." He was at his most authoritarian.

Molly considered simply swimming away and staying in the middle of the pool to tease him, but looking at his thunderous face she decided against it, and paddled quietly to the steps.

"What's the matter, Harry?"

"Out," he said tersely.

"O.K." Even before she was fully up the steps he had the towel around her, wrapping it tightly several times till she was covered from chin to ankles. He tucked the free end in at the neck.

"Don't ever swim in the nude again in this pool."

"And why not?" Molly was getting angry at his chauvinistic attitude. "It's my pool – it's private –"

"Because I say not – and it's not private. People can see. They try to see – because you're my wife. Next thing you know there'll be stories about wild parties here, naked debauchery, the lot."

"Oh, come on!" She wriggled, trying to free the end of the towel.

"Do as I say, Molly."

"I will not do as you say. I might do as you ask."

They locked eyes, both strong, both stubborn, both proud. For a long moment neither spoke.

"Very well," said Harry. "I am asking you not to swim in the nude again."

She nodded.

"I'll take it under consideration," she said formally, sweetly.

"I'll drain the pool until you give me your decision."

"Hey!" said Ken from the sun deck. "What's the matter? Mum often used to take us to Wreck Beach to swim with nothing on."

Harry glanced up. "That was before she married me."

"What's the difference?"

"A lot," he said quietly, looking not at Ken, but at Molly now. "A whole lot. Now go and get dressed."

"Oh, yes, sir. Yes, sir. Of course, sir." She turned and shuffled comically towards the house, almost totally restricted by the towel. The twins shrieked with laughter and disappeared from the rail, collapsed on the sundeck in glee.

"Wait!" Harry caught her by the shoulders and turned her. "Molly," he said earnestly, "I love your body. I want it to be mine alone. I don't want to share it with other people. Can you understand that?"

"I like it better than 'do as I say'."

He loosened the towel at the neck and as she pulled it free Molly had a sudden urge to drop it to the ground and dive into the pool again. She looked up at Harry: he had read her mind.

He stood with his hands out, ready to grab her. Their eyes met.

"No," he said. "Please?"

She laughed then, that sudden surprising laugh of hers, free and unselfconscious. He grinned, his wolfish sexy grin.

"Go on," he said. "Go, woman." He propelled her towards the house with his hand on her behind.

Rob came out of the twins' playroom.

"Thank you, Harry," he said. "I wish someone had said that to her years ago."

Harry raised a surprised eyebrow and the young man flushed. "It may have been alright for the twins at Wreck Beach," he said, "They were little. But it was damned embarrassing for me."

There were times when Harry and Rob were in complete agreement, and this was one of them.

Molly had to make another adjustment when Harry finished filming "Hometown Hobo" and went straight into rehearsals for a stage play at the Playhouse. For this part he grew his hair longer and developed a bushy grey moustache that completely changed his face. In time Molly would learn to accept both the physical changes and the personality changes he went through when creating a new part – the moody withdrawal – the trying on of a new persona which consistently slopped over into his private life and sometimes made his responses difficult to understand. But this first time was a little frightening; also she had trouble suppressing the naughty giggle that rose in her throat when she glanced at him and was taken by surprise by the walrus moustache.

The twins had no such problem; Harry was Harry to them, with or without facial hair, and they were never fooled by the superficial differences in the way he behaved.

Harry found that, like riding a bicycle, being married was something you never forgot and he quickly slipped back into the role of husband. The role of father was something else again…the twins took a bit of getting used to. He was relaxing in his chair one evening, moustache, hair and all, his long legs stretched out across the rug, studying the heavy typewritten script that tested on his knees, dressed in character for the role in a roll-neck sweater, jeans and sneakers, when he became aware of being watched. He looked up and found Ken and Sue on either side of his chair in pyjamas and exuding toothpaste with every breath.

"Well," he said gruffly, "What do you two want?"

"Will you read us a story?" Ken asked.

"No." Harry picked up his script again.

"Oh Harry!" Sue cried reproachfully, turning on a five hundred-watt gaze of wistful adoration.

Harry rigidly controlled the smile Sue's gaze triggered and said,

"Why me? Why not your mother or Rob?"

"Because you're a nactor."

"I'll bet you do it really well," Ken added.

"I am," Harry said sternly, "An actor."

"That's what I said," said Sue. "An actor."

Harry opened his mouth to correct her again, but suddenly got the feeling it was a lost cause and shut it. He glared at them fiercely.

"Did your mother put you up to this?"

"No," said Ken.

"She told us not to ask you," Sue added.

"She was right," Harry said briskly, closing his script. "What's the story?"

Ken handed him a lurid comic book filled with pictures of crudely drawn adults hitting each other and surrounded by words such as POW, BAM, BOP, and CRUNCH.

"I'm an actor, not a sound effects man," Harry said, handing it back. "That's garbage. Don't you have any better taste than that?"

"I thought you'd like it," said Ken stiffly. "It's like your movies."

"Touché," Harry said grimly.

"What does that mean?"

"It means out of the mouths of babes and sucklings. And I'm not telling you what that means either. Got another book?"

"Winnie the Pooh," Sue pulled it out from behind her back and laid it on his knee, a well-thumbed, well-loved copy, and Harry realized he had been conned.

"That's better." Before he had turned the pages to Chapter One he found he not only had a twin on either knee, but that they had burrowed up beneath his arms so that he encircled them both.

Sue laid her head on his chest with a contented sigh.

"This sweater's nicer than those nasty old suits."

"Another suit-hater! What's wrong with suits?"

"You can't cuddle in suits."

"I'm not a cuddly person."

"Yes you are," said Sue. "Really. You just pretend not to be."

Harry pulled back his head and looked from one to the other of them.

"You're too smart by half," he said sourly.

"Read," said Ken.

He read; slowly at first, the story and characters completely strange to him, then as he warmed to the task, he gave Pooh and Piglet and Tigger and Eeyore and the others different voices so that they came alive off the pages. The twins, their eyes fixed on his face, neither moved nor spoke. They stayed that way for several minutes after the chapter was finished, Harry as thoughtful as they were feeling their weight on his thighs, their shoulders under his arms.

Harry had never before been comfortable with children; (had not even cuddled his own son); had always felt their world and his were too far apart to meet; had felt that he lacked the special manner to relate to them.

"Hmmph," he said. "That's it. Off to bed. Scoot." He pushed them roughly off his knees.

Ken picked up the book.

"Thank you, Harry," he said gravely.

Sue said nothing but turned on him a look of such loving longing that he knew at once she wanted to be hugged and kissed, but for once was not sure enough of herself to make the first move – and neither was he. He allowed his face to soften.

"Goodnight, Sue," he said gently, and reached out and ruffled her hair. She turned away with a small sigh.

Later Molly came in and sat on the rug at his feet.

"Thank you, Harry, for reading to them. You didn't have

to."

"I know. What's with those kids, any way? I snap and snarl and it never seems to fizz on them."

"They like you."

"Why, for God's sake?"

"Because you treat them like real people. Not like adults, but like people. A lot of grown-ups talk down to children, you know, put on special faces, special voices – more so to twins, for some reason. They like you not giving them the special treatment. It makes them feel equal."

"What bothers me is they can read me like no one else can. How do they do that?"

"They're twins," said Molly, as though that explained everything.

So Molly and Harry adjusted, the twins settled down unaware of even making an adjustment and Rob remained – painfully – on the outside looking in. Sometimes he felt a bitter bewilderment to think that he had set this whole thing in motion. Now he had a stepfather he was not sure he liked, a new home, a new school and a subtly different mother. And he was demoted from man of the house to just a son – that probably rankled more than anything else. It would be some years before these resentments came to a head, but come to a violent head they inevitably would.

In the meantime the first Wentworth/Ash Christmas loomed in the near future, and Molly was pondering on a familiar physical phenomenon and wondering whether it was welcome or not.

Chapter Eight

Christmas in Hawaii

"Spotted yesterday at Vancouver International Airport – rugged veteran Canadian actor Harry Wentworth, being seen off on the Hawaiian Special by his wife of six months Molly (nee Ash). Stepchildren, Rob (17) and eight-year-old twins, Ken and Sue were not present."

Harry had breezed in, a self-satisfied look on his face, and dropped a fat envelope on the coffee table in front of Molly. "Surprise," he said. "We're going to Hawaii for Christmas – all five of us – there are the tickets, and I've rented a big condo."

"What!"

"I've been going to Hawaii for Christmas for years – didn't I tell you? It's the only place. You'll love it."

"We can't go," she said flatly.

There was an ominous silence.

"Explain that," Harry said tightly.

"Well – we never go away for Christmas. It's a family time. There's the tree to decorate and the twins are in the Nativity Play at the church and Rob has a basketball tournament between Christmas and New Year. And there's my Day Care Centre Party."

"Nothing important then?"

"Not to you, maybe – but to us, yes."

"And going to Hawaii is important to me. Done it for years. Nobody in their right minds would stay in the rain and fog in West Van when they could be on the beach at Maui."

He looked pointedly at the streaming December windows.

"I'm sorry, Harry." Molly could see how disappointed he was by her reaction, and one part of her bled for him, while the other part rebelled at his autocracy, which had been a problem for her from the beginning of their relationship. "We'll have to have a family conference. The children have a right to be part of the decision. If it's all right with them, I'll go, of course. Someone else can run the Party at the Centre."

"That's big of you," he said sarcastically.

Later they assembled around the table, the children curious, Molly tense, Harry showing no emotion, fairly convinced he held a winning hand. He opened the discussion on a positive note.

"Anyone want to go to Hawaii?"

"Yes!" they chorused. "When? When?"

"For Christmas, of course."

"Christmas," they looked at each other in consternation. "Mum?"

Molly said,

"Harry's been going to Hawaii for Christmas for years. He's booked a condominium and he wants us all to go for the holidays."

"But – the tournament," said Rob doubtfully. "I couldn't miss the tournament, could I?"

"Why not?" Harry asked.

"Well…." he said, "well – I'm part of the team, aren't I?"

"So. Aren't there other guys – subs?"

"Yes, but –"

"But what?"

Rob bit his lips and looked away, embarrassed.

"He's the Star," Sue hissed. "He gets all the baskets. They need him."

"Hmmph." Star was a word Harry could identify with.

"He's got a 'sponsibility to the team," said Ken earnestly,

obviously quoting. "Haven't you, Rob?"

Rob nodded.

"Yes. Sorry, Harry. Can't we go in the summer?"

"Too hot. This is the time to go."

"But it's Christmas," said Sue.

"So? What's special? It's just a holiday, an excuse to eat and drink and give presents. We can do that in Hawaii."

"It won't be the same," said Sue doubtfully. "There's our friends and parties and the Ice Capades and – oh, the 'Tivity Play at church. Ken and I are in that on Christmas Eve."

"Somebody can take your parts I'm sure," Harry said smoothly.

"Mary and Joseph?" said Molly. "At such short notice?"

Harry looked at his stepchildren sourly – playing leads already, eh?

"And just how did they get to choose you two for those parts?"

"Because I'm pretty," said Sue immodestly. "Holy Mary Mother of God has to be pretty." She posed serenely.

"Really?" said Harry.

"Besides, I was the only one who wasn't afraid to hold the baby – we have a real baby. Reverend Osgood's baby is Jesus."

"Harry doesn't believe in Jesus," said Ken. "Do you?"

"Why d'you say that?" Harry temporized hastily, taken aback.

"Oh – people like you never do."

Stunned by the perception of the child, Harry could only grunt.

"They chose me," Ken went on, "because I'm the tallest."

"So you wouldn't really mind giving up the parts?"

The twins looked at each other and shrugged.

"I suppose," said Ken.

"But what about Rob?" said Sue.

"Perhaps he could stay here with a friend –"

"No!" This time Sue and Molly spoke in unison.

"The family are not splitting up at Christmas," Molly added firmly.

"Supposing," Harry said, giving them all a level look, one after the other, "I told you I'm going to Hawaii anyway?"

"I'd say 'feel free to go, of course'. We'll miss you but –" Molly groped for words, a terrible ache in her heart.

"We, all four of us, have commitments we can't just throw aside, can't you see that? If you'd only told us earlier – you can't just expect us to drop everything and disrupt our lives to follow your whim –" It was the wrong word, and her voice trailed away. She was afraid he had been desperately hurt. She was also afraid that for some reason Christmas meant absolutely nothing to him, and that that was incomprehensible to the children. Had he never had a family Christmas? He never talked about his first marriage and she had never asked. After the years of loneliness following her divorce Molly had been looking forward to having a man by her side again on Christmas morning. Should she be a 'good wife' and say "we're going, children, because your stepfather wants it?" Did he really expect her to do this? That's not fair. We're people too, we have hopes, expectations, traditions, and promises to keep. A chill thought struck her – will this drive a wedge between us? Can our delicately balanced marriage survive a major conflict at this time?

Harry stood up, his face set in stone.

"That's it, then," he said, running a hand over his short grey hair. "I'll cancel the condo and four of the tickets and book into a hotel by myself. You don't know what you're missing"

There was a stunned silence. Nobody objected. No voice clamoured to him to change his mind. No one changed theirs. He was stuck with his decision. Molly wanted to say "don't be pig-headed and stubborn: don't cut off your nose to spite your face: don't go just because you can't bear to be overruled by the majority. Don't break my heart." But she remained silent, and in the silence an intuitive thought came to her – he's running away from something, he's run away for years and he can't stop running. And then her being was suffused with sadness for him. One look at his face told her he did not want sympathy.

Quietly the children left the table.

The days went by and nothing more was said. If the children were aware of a tension between Harry and Molly they did not make it obvious. Molly spent the days with her fingers mentally crossed, hoping that as the time got nearer Harry would quietly and graciously back down from his stand. That would have been atypical, of course, since Harry did not make a habit of backing down, and was seldom quiet and gracious about a thing like that. Unwilling to precipitate an argument, she made no mention of his rapidly approaching departure.

On December 18th Molly bought the Christmas tree and set it up in the living room, boxes of lights and decorations on the floor in front of it, waiting for the children to return from school. By the time Harry came back from a taping session at the CBC studio they were all hard at work.

Harry stepped around and over the mess on the floor, mixed himself a drink and sat down by the fire and regarded the activity with a plainly jaundiced eye. They had all been so absorbed no one – not even Sue – had taken the time for anything more than a cursory word of welcome home. He felt excluded – he excluded himself. He didn't like it. Christmas was a time of pain (remembered) and he didn't like that either. He hung on to the thought of the beach and the surf and the sun.

"Harry…" Sue was standing in front of him holding out a box of tree ornaments, "…Harry, don't you want to put one on?"

"No." He sipped his drink and looked at her steadily.

"Are you like Scrooge?" she asked.

"Yes," he said. "Bah. Humbug."

For once Sue was not sure whether to take him seriously or laugh. She took his hand and tugged. "Come on, Harry. Everybody has to put at least one on."

Reluctantly he allowed himself to be led to the tree.

"There," Sue pointed, "put one there, that branch wants a decoration."

"Needs," said Harry, "not wants. A tree can't want."

"Wants," said Sue firmly. "Poor little branch, can't you see how left out he feels? You think trees don't have feelings?" Her voice rose in passionate inquiry.

Feeling like a tree himself, Harry was silent. He hung the ornament carelessly and went back to his chair. Behind him Sue exchanged a look of puzzlement and pity with her mother, and without comment Molly reached up and set the shiny bell straight.

Two days later...
"Are you really going?"
"Of course. Will you come and see me off?"
"All of us?"
"No. Just you."
"You know I will."

It was not an easy good-bye: both felt guilty but neither was prepared to verbalize it. Molly wanted to beg him to stay but her pride locked her tongue: Harry wanted her to make him change her mind, but stubbornly waited for her to make the first move. They could not look each other in the eye in case their thoughts were too easily read. They kissed lightly, briefly, and a newsman's flash bulb popped, intruding on their privacy.

"Have a lovely time." Molly said brightly, trying to sound natural.

"You too."

"'Phone me?" A chink in her armour showed – her voice was suddenly anxious, a little sad, despairing.

"Of course. Every day." He opened a tiny chink in his own armour, his response warm and gentle. He touched her hair, turned and walked quickly through the boarding gate. Molly left the concourse without a backward glance, forcing herself to walk swiftly and steadily, her head up, face neutral for the benefit of the reporter who was still hovering.

"Well, I think it stinks!" said Rob hotly, from where he knelt on the floor examining the parcels under the tree. "Not one present here from Harry for any of us – not even you, Mum. I don't mind for myself" (it was a lie, he did) "but at least he could have got the twins something."

Silently Molly agreed, but loyally she defended her absent husband.

"He doesn't believe in Christmas, Rob, so why should he do any of the traditional things?"

Harry telephoned, sounding cheerful, describing the sea and the sun and the happy crowds. Fortunately Molly was too busy with preparations and cooking and parties with old pre-marriage friends (who tactfully pretended not to be curious about Harry's absence) to spend much time brooding and feeling lonely. The next time he called was Christmas Eve day and he asked Molly to put Sue on the line and Ken on the extension.

"All ready for the play tonight?"

"Yes," they chorused.

"Well, listen kids, in the profession we don't wish each other good luck on a first night we say 'break a leg', so that's what I'm saying to you two – break a leg." When they stopped giggling he added, "and keep your eyes open for Santa Claus tomorrow." To Molly, when she came back on the line, he said the same thing. He did not wish any of them a Merry Christmas. The line was clear and he sounded very cheerful. Molly hated him.

Christmas morning dawned in typical British Columbia fashion for West Vancouver, with windows streaming rain, the steep hills of the British Properties turned to shallow torrents, rockeries washing away into gardens and drains stopping up and making lakes at every intersection.

Molly felt like the weather but forced herself to be cheerful and excited for the children's benefit, as they gathered around the tree to open their presents. Suddenly their chatter was interrupted by the most extraordinary noise from outside. Garbled and distorted by the wind and rain, the strange cacophony grew louder and louder and gradually became recognizable as a recorded version of Rudolph the Red-nosed Reindeer played over a loudspeaker, complete with sound effects of clopping hooves and swishing sleigh runners. The twins sat on their heels, their eyes wide, staring at each other.

"It can't be," said Ken.

"It must be," said Sue.

The noise reached a crescendo outside the front door and stopped abruptly. The children were on their feet. There was a jangling of sleigh-bells and a pounding on the door.

"Merry Christmas! Merry Christmas in there!" boomed a jolly voice.

"It is!" the twins shrieked, and rushed to the door.

Santa Claus stood there, beaming, fat, jolly, a bulging sack over one shoulder, sleigh-bells in hand.

"Merry Christmas Santa!" They pulled him, laughing, into the room. "We knew you'd come! Harry said you'd come!"

Then Molly, standing transfixed herself, understood. Of course, Harry had hired a professional Santa – or maybe even an out of work actor friend – to do this for the twins, and she moved forward with a broad smile, warmed at last by the knowledge that Harry had not let them down. She watched with pleasure and admiration as the old man chatted with the children as they settled him in a chair by the tree and offered him cookies and milk.

He was a big man, but obviously padded to make him bigger, probably in his sixties: he had a neat white beard and moustache and grey eyebrows, and silver hair curled beneath his Santa hat. He wore old-fashioned eyeglasses, black leather boots and white cotton gloves. He was a storybook Santa Claus, and behaved like one too. He pulled gift-wrapped parcels out of his sack, one after the other, and gave them to the twins and they tore off the paper and discovered Atari games, puzzles, books, candy, jeans and sweaters.

Rob, who had not moved from his chair, regarded the scene with angry adolescent cynicism. Nothing for me, of course, he thought. I don't count. I'm too old to believe in Santa – or Harry.

"And now," said the old man importantly, "I do believe my elves are ready for you to go out to the garage."

"The garage -? Why? What's there?"

"Why don't you go and see."

They dashed out through the kitchen door and within seconds their voices came back to the room, high and delighted.

"BIKES!" They shouted. "Mum – Rob – come and see – bikes!"

They all stood in the doorway then, Molly, Rob and Santa and admired the identical purple five speed bikes that Sue and Ken were pushing around. Sue flicked out the kickstand and left the bike and came and held out her arms to Santa until he lifted her up.

"Thank you, Santa," she said. "Thank you – really, really thank you – it's just what I wanted." She put her arms around his neck and planted a big wet kiss on his cheek. The old man hugged her then, his head bent, and in the moment of stillness Molly sensed a deep emotion. Poor man, she thought, how lonely he must be, always hugging other people's kids.

"Boots and raincoats on," said Molly, "and only in the driveway."

When the twins were dressed and outside she went back to the living-room where the old man was sitting in his chair again, scrabbling in his almost empty sack, while Rob looked out of the window at the rain. That was when she realized just how left out Rob was feeling.

"Santa," she said quietly.

"I know, I know," he said, catching her look. "Don't worry, my dear, I have something for him. Ah, here it is." He pulled out an envelope. He cleared his throat. "This is for Rob Ash," he said loudly.

Rob turned from the window and idled across the room.

"Uh-huh," he said, seeing the envelope and thinking, ten bucks and a card, I suppose.

"Merry Christmas, son," said Santa. "Use it wisely."

"Yeah," said Rob. "Well, thanks." He started to stuff it in his pocket.

"No, no," Santa protested, "you must open it now, son."

"O.K...." Carelessly he ripped open the envelope and something fell to the floor with a jingle. Rob reached down and suddenly his whole attitude changed.

"Wow!" he said. "Mum – it's car keys! Harry's given me a car!" He looked at Santa for confirmation and the old man smiled broadly and nodded, his hands clasped across his padded stomach.

"Try the driveway, son," he said quietly.

Rob left at a run.

"Datsun pick-up. Not new. A boy doesn't need a new car at his age, eh?"

"No. How sensible. I guess this was all Harry's idea? He sent you?"

"That's right, my dear. Oh, there's something for you too." He reached in the sack and handed out the last parcel.

Molly turned it over in her hands.

"Maybe I should wait until Harry comes home, then we can open ours to each other together."

"No, no, no, my dear. He wants you to have it Christmas morning. You open it now. Please."

She sat on the floor at the old man's feet and opened the package carefully, untying and rolling up the ribbon and folding the paper. Inside the box was a gorgeous expensive, sexy black nightgown. She knew without a shadow of a doubt that Harry had chosen it for her, had held it up, looked at it, imagined her in it; he had touched it and selected it because it said something to him about her, and that brought him so close it was almost as though he was in the room, and for a moment Molly felt so desolate it was almost unbearable. To cover her emotion she searched for the card that she knew lay somewhere in the folds of nylon. It was characteristically terse and to the point.

TO MOLLY FROM HARRY. I LOVE YOU.

Almost overcome, Molly buried her face in the nightgown.

"Now, now," said Santa from behind her, and he patted her shoulder kindly. "No tears on Christmas, my dear."

"No. No, of course not." With an effort Molly controlled herself, set the nightgown in its box under the tree and stood up shakily, wishing she was alone. "I'm sorry, Santa…" she said quietly, keeping her back to the man "…it's just that I realized I made a mistake and I can't do anything about it for another five days, and that made me a little sad."

"Well, cheer up, my dear and give old Santa a kiss."

"Oh," she said. "Of course. I'm sorry." She turned and leant and kissed the old man's cheek, but before she could straighten up, his white-gloved hand snaked out and gripped her wrist with surprising strength.

"Surely you can do better than that," he said sharply, and jerked her arm so that she fell into his lap.

"No – please –" Molly threshed her legs and tried to get up, but the man's arms were wrapped around her and he crushed her against his padded chest. She had a vision of the whiskered face bearing down on hers, the disgusting red lips already parted. "Oh God! No!" She pushed against him with all her strength, thinking 'this is ridiculous – it's a trap – he's sent the children out – he know I'm alone – oh hell, oh damn, raped by a bogus Santa Claus under my own bloody tree!' Before she could scream, the mouth crushed down on hers, rough, repulsive, demanding...passionate...tender...and unmistakably Harry's. Her eyes, squeezed shut in revulsion, flew open and mouth to mouth, nose to nose, eyeball to eyeball they regarded each other.

"Mmmph!" she exclaimed, trying to pull apart, but Harry's hand was on the back of her head holding her to him, and he was laughing through the kiss, willing her to relax and enjoy it too. She gave in and when they were both breathless, he let her go and she sat back on his lap and looked at him.

"I'm mortified!" she said. "My own husband! I never had inkling —! Harry, how could I not have known you?"

He raised a false grey eyebrow.

"I'm a good actor I guess."

"That's not your nose!" she said accusingly.

"No," he agreed. "It's putty. Percy from Make-up at the studio did me. He's in the van outside. I'm hoping you'll invite him in for Christmas dinner."

"Of course," Molly said distractedly. "You must think I'm such a fool –"

"No."

"When did you get back?"

"Never went. After you left the Airport I got a cab and checked in at the Bayshore and did some thinking."

"The Bayshore! But the 'phone calls from Hawaii!"

"I got the girl on the switchboard to pretend the call was coming from Hawaii."

"I could hit you!"

"No, you couldn't."

"You've been there for five days, and I've been going through hell here for five days —!" Suddenly she saw the funny side of it. "Harry, you're impossible! –" She started to laugh.

"No – you're impossible."

"Is our marriage always going to be this – this –?"

"Creative? I hope so. Now, go and call Percy in, I'm roasting in this outfit."

She turned at the door.

"I meant it – what I said about realizing I'd made a mistake."

"I know," he said quietly, nothing more.

When the children came running in, breathless and wet, and found a strange young man standing in front of the Christmas tree they reacted with their usual directness.

"Who are you?"

Percy gave them a sad, beautiful – and to Molly — an unmistakably gay – smile.

"You might say I'm your Christmas fairy," he murmured, and winked at Molly and Harry.

"Fairies do magic," said Sue.

"What's your magic?" asked Ken.

"I turn people into other people," Percy said without hesitation. "Watch."

He walked over to Santa Claus, and standing between him and the twins, he pulled off the red and white trimmed cap; with a quick movement he peeled off the tuffs of grey eyebrows; taking hold of an end of the moustache with each hand he lifted it off and to the middle, and placed the two halves on the side table with the eyebrows. Then he pulled the whiskers loose under each ear and peeled them down to the chin; the putty nose came away with a gentle turn of the hand; finally, he lifted the wig from the front, and removing it with a flourish stepped aside.

"Voila!"

"Harry!" they squealed in delight, but they hung back from him while he was yet only half-transformed, Harry's face and Santa's body. Harry, sensitive to their uncertainty, quickly stood and stripped off the jacket, pants and boots of Santa, and became himself, immaculate in his best grey three-piece suit.

"Hi," he said laconically, thus completing the transformation from jolly, chatty Santa to the gruff taciturn man they knew.

"I knew it was you," Sue cried, hugging him as high up as she could reach, undeterred by the fact that now Harry was Harry, he made no responsive hugging or touching gestures as he had when he had been Santa. Molly noticed this and smiled to herself, a small smile of compassion for his locked-in-reserve as himself, and began to understand a little more why an actor is an actor.

"You didn't," he said flatly.

"Yes, I did – you smelt like you!"

He shook his fist at her in mock anger and as they all laughed the doorbell rang.

"Oh gosh!" Molly clapped a hand to her mouth. "I forgot to tell you – since you were going to be away I invited some friends to share our Christmas dinner."

"Friends?"

"Two single mothers from the Day Care Centre," she said over her shoulder, on the way to the door," and their four kids. They have no families to go to. You will be nice to them?" Her face was momentarily anxious.

Harry showed his teeth in a wolfish sexy grin.

"I'm always nice," he said, and the girls and their children came into a house gusting with laughter. For a moment Harry had been annoyed that their privacy was going to be intruded upon, and then he had remembered Percy and realized that Molly would not have been the Molly he had married without doing this, any more than he as Harry would not have been himself, if he had failed to invite Percy in.

Aware that his unexpected presence near the door might overpower and inhibit the young mother with shyness, Harry moved over to the fireplace and leant against the mantelpiece, negligently, studying the crackling log below him. In truth he was a little overwhelmed himself, by so many more women and children than he had been used to. It was here that Rob joined him, having come in through the kitchen door to avoid the mob of children and boots and raincoats in the hall, where Percy was happily helping out. He proffered his hand.

"Thanks, Harry."

Harry grunted, and took the boy's hand.

"For the truck – it's great – and for coming back and making Mum happy."

"Hmm-mm." Harry glanced at the rain bouncing an inch and a half off the sun deck and instantly dismissed Maui and the surf and the sun and the sand as being a very minor sacrifice. They would be there for along time, this day would only happen once.

Much, much later, when everyone was full of turkey and mince-pie and oranges and nuts and wine, and the children were all playing with new games and toys near the tree, Molly sat on the sofa before the fire suffused in a rosy glow. Harry was close beside her, his arm along the back of the sofa above her shoulders, talking to Percy, while Rob helped the young women scrape the plates and pack the dishwasher in the kitchen.

Molly did not know what Harry and Percy were talking about, she was sleepy and warm with food and wine, and it did not really seem to matter – they talked across her without excluding her. Presently she hiccupped lightly and realizing that – oh damn – she was a little drunk, she looked guiltily up at Harry and found in his answering look a message of such tenderness that her very being turned into liquid love. His arm slipped down around her shoulders and pulled her closer, and though his mouth went on talking to Percy, his body spoke to her most clearly. She beamed.

"Isn't this better than Hawaii!" she murmured.

"Next year," said Harry.

Chapter Nine

A Drinking Problem

"Rumour has it that actor Harry Wentworth's bride of six months, Molly, has a drinking problem. It certainly was not evident at the big party they threw recently in their, charming West Van home."

It was unfortunate that there was a lull in the conversation just as Harry reached across the dinner table and put his palm over his wife's glass and said,

"No more wine, Molly." His voice, deep and authoritarian dropped into the silence, and what was intended only for Molly's ears was heard by everyone at the table.

There was an awkward pause while they waited to see how Molly would react, while pretending not to.

Molly was shocked. She sat very still, her mouth clamped shut, her jaw jutting defiantly, refusing to show the instant humiliation that she felt. The worst of it was she knew Harry was not trying to humiliate her, only to protect her – from herself, as he would say. She met his eye across the table, and because they were guests and in a public place she forced her lips into a stiff smile. She wanted to say "Mind your own business, I know how many I've had, I'm not drunk yet." Instead she glanced back at the waiter, who was hovering, and

said, calmly and clearly for the benefit of the listening ears,
    "I think I'd like some coffee, please."

She immediately despised herself for being an abject, humble, cringing, obedient wife and had difficulty quashing an urge to grab the wine bottle from the centre of the table and refill her glass. Harry's foot came down heavily on hers under the table – at least she assumed it was Harry's – and she had no way of knowing whether he had read her mind and was saying 'don't do it', or was indicating his approval of her switch to coffee.

At least some of the women at the table found her behaviour admirable, but for Molly, no matter how hard she tried as she sipped her coffee while everyone else drank cocktails and liquors, the party was spoilt.

How can I be myself and have fun knowing that Big Brother is watching me, she wondered, and said so to Harry in the car going home.

"You know you get drunk on a few glasses of wine."

"Not drunk – dizzy."

"To anyone watching, you're falling-down drunk. I don't want a drunken wife."

"You could have been more subtle," she said bitterly.

He grunted, apparently unaware of how deeply he had offended her, and changed the subject.

"I start on the new Stringer series for CBC-TV next week. I think we'd better throw a party right away."

Molly was appalled.

"At the house?"

"Where else?"

"I mean – Harry, I can't cope with a party of that size."

"Won't have to. We'll get it catered. They do everything- drinks, food, and décor. All you have to do is be a gracious hostess. I'll see if Lance and Jack can come up and do some jazz for us."

Now Molly stood in the middle of the room and marvelled. The caterers had indeed done the décor, moving furniture around, bringing flowers and potted plants and even draperies, and altering the lighting. And the people – so many people – gave the space a whole new look. People, mostly standing, gesturing, posturing, posing, talking, laughing, noticing, being noticed, and scratching influential backs. People in everything from bare-shouldered cocktail dresses to Indian cotton floor-length granny-dresses and headbands; from five hundred dollar suits (like Harry's) with colourful matching ties and handy-puffs in the breast pocket (Harry's were black to complement his silver-grey suit), to frayed jeans and leather vests. Men with everything from flowing below-the-shoulder hair and beards to short back and sides and Errol Flynn moustaches; women with Eton crops (lesbians?), to girls with pigtails, and everything the hairdresser could create in between, including Wednesday Barnes' crown of gorgeous copper madness.

And yet by catching snatches of conversation, Molly knew that many of the 'Beautiful People' were worried about growing children, aging parents, the school system, the price of vegetables and local politics, like any other group in any other part of the City meeting for a hair-down session, as well as last performances, next performances, production costs, better parts, set design, the eternal search for backers and better scripts. She was learning that actors, artists, writers, producers, though creative and emotional and larger than life and sometimes sexually ambivalent, were still basically people like her, people she could relate to.

Even Wednesday Barnes. Wednesday had come with her agent and was quite obviously on show and up for sale, all five foot nine of her in a splendidly revealing, ostensibly simple, little grey silk jersey number slit three-quarters of the way up both thighs, and tight enough to show off admirably her magnificent forty-inch braless bosom. Instinctively, Molly glanced down at her own thirty-five inch neatly tethered breasts riding circumspectly inside her white silk blouse. No comparison. Yet Harry seemed to enjoy them. She could not dislike Wednesday for she thought she saw inside her a slightly bewildered girl trying to cope with living with a gorgeous face and body – and all the sex related stresses that brought upon her – and not quite managing. Even the ridiculous name – Wednesday, for the day her agent had first seen her – obviously more glamorous than Joan, yet still too unfamiliar to sit on her comfortably. Much of what she said and did was still Joan, and for that Molly liked her.

Molly surveyed the room, her eyes skipping from group to group until she found Harry, and experienced again that feeling of unreality – thin-isn't-really-happening-to-me, it's-all-a-dream – I'm married to that man, she thought, I fold his underwear, I watch him shave, he makes love to me. I adore him, I'm like a teenager in puppy love – and yet I don't even know him. And I doubt if he knows me; and yet we're making a life together,… how did I get to be so lucky?

Harry had a thing about husbands and wives staying together at parties – when they arrived he stayed with Molly only for as long as it took to introduce her to someone and get her talking and then he was off, doing his rounds. Not that he was a great talker; as Molly said, he liked to grunt at a lot at different people. And though they were apart they were always aware of each other in a comfortable telepathic way. Every now and then he or she would scan the room and find the other and their eyes would meet briefly saying, O.K.? Sometimes she would signal 'Help' if she was stuck with someone drunk or dull, and be confident that in a few minutes Harry would wander over and take her elbow and move her on, and because he was Harry the drunk or the dullard, would raise no objections. Sometimes – not often, but sometimes – Harry would be trapped, usually by a woman, and he would send out the 'Help' signal and Molly would rescue him.

It's funny, she thought, I know these women find him charming and sexy and yet I can watch them throwing themselves at him and I don't feel a thing – I'm so sure of him, so sure I don't have to compete. It's a beautiful feeling – they're glamorous and dazzling and stacked and I know Harry doesn't feel a thing for them. How can I be so sure? I'm middle-aged and fighting to keep my figure and certainly not beautiful, and yet I'm the one he chose…if choice came into it.

She knew the people looked at her curiously and wondered the same thing – what's she got? She stands apart and watches a lot of the time, she never hangs onto his arm and stakes her claim on him, and yet she's got him. Cool and sure and…. mature was the word they were looking for but seldom found.

Should I be jealous? Molly reached for a glass of wine from

a tray as a waitress passed, but somehow the girl turned deftly and Molly's hand grabbed air. What the hell, I don't need a drink.

Harry had surprisingly similar thoughts, looking across the room at Molly where she stood, alone, serene, her hands lightly clasped in front of her. She had nothing to prove and nothing to hide. She dressed in clothes that suited her, not the latest fad, and looked calm and confident and all together, as though she knew who she was and where she was going. He knew that this was not always so but marvelled that she could look as though it was. He loved her and felt infinitely lucky that she was his wife. Of all the women in the room – glamorous, talented, beautiful, exciting, exotic, intriguing – he was glad he was married to her. He knew well that other men found his choice of a wife strange, and wondered what he saw in her, and he was glad that their life together was so private that they could keep their relationship clean of pettiness and jealousy and envy and pride.

He saw that Molly was enjoying her role as hostess, despite her initial dismay at the idea of the party, and reflected what an odd mixture she was, sometimes so gauche and awkward and immature, and at others so much in command of herself. Human nature, he mused, is an amazingly complex creation. Now if she can just stay off the wine tonight we'll get through without anyone getting to see the klutzy side of her.

He knew that at parties she liked to catch his eye sometimes, and enjoyed exchanging wordless private messages, which doubtless bolstered her ego by giving her the feeling of having a special relationship with him. He was, after all, an international star whether she consciously acknowledged it or not. But tonight when he saw her head turning, looking for him, he deliberately dropped his eyes, shifted his stance, looked away at an oblique angle, and becoming aware of a vibrant presence close by, glanced up and found himself in direct non-verbal communication with the ubiquitous new starlet Wednesday Barnes. Despite the copper barbed-wire hair, the by-the-grace-of-God bosoms and the overtly sexy dress, he too saw through to the healthy, friendly, warm, ambitious small-town girl working hard to learn to be a star, to develop the talent that would exploit the charisma – and he warmed to her. And he had absolutely no premonition that his response to her bold unspoken message – 'I need you to help me be a star' (he read that quite clearly) – would have profound and lasting results on his life with Molly.

Molly watched Wednesday stride gracefully across the room, and following her directional path realized that she was stalking Harry, who had stepped down into the fireplace area and was momentarily alone. He stood resting one negligent elbow on the mantelpiece, a favourite pose, and turned his head, but before his eye could meet Molly's it met Wednesday's. She stopped in front of him – five feet nine inches on two and a half inch heels put her on an almost eyeball to eyeball level with him. She spoke and gestured with her arm and as she did so one perfect round ripe pink-nippled breast popped out of her dress. Molly drew a quick breath and put her hand over her mouth.

Harry answered Wednesday and without taking his eyes from her face reached out and unhurriedly tucked her bosom back inside its grey silk jersey nest. To Wednesday's credit she did not look down either, and Molly saw her mouth form the words,

"Thank you."

Molly found the little scene delightful. Dear Harry, how like him; people think he's rough and crude, like I did at first, but really he's the most gentle man. And not a warning bell sounded in her head. Later she would remember that. Now she turned to reach once more for a drink and once more the loaded tray was virtually whisked from under her hand. A little annoyed, she followed the young waiter and would have stopped him but was waylaid by a guest raving about the lovely party and how great it was that Harry was entertaining at last, after all it had been years, hadn't it?

When Molly tried for a third time to get a drink, only to have the waitress's back turned on her, a horrible suspicion began to form in her mind. The party turned to ashes in her mouth. She made for the kitchen.

"Ah, Madam," Albert Scott, the caterer's man, met her in the door, blocking her way. "I hope everything is satisfactory?"

"No," she said, "it's not. Let me in, please. Your boys and girls are too quick on their feet; I haven't been able to get a drink off a tray for the last half hour."

"Well, Madam," he followed her in, trying to get between her and the table where the wine was being poured. "I trust the guests are being attended to?"

"Is there a conspiracy to keep me from the wine?"

"Why, Madam –"

"Just a straight answer, Mr. Scott. Waitress –" the girl at the table turned – "give me – why Nancy Lee!"

"Hallo, Mrs. Wentworth," the young Chinese woman said quietly.

"Mrs. Wentworth! When did I stop being Molly?"

"Listen, I was Molly at the Day Care Centre when you started bringing the kids and I'm still Molly, no matter whose wife I am. How are the kids?"

"Oh, they're fine. Steve's baby-sitting Carol tonight. I figured at eleven he's old enough. They're good kids."

"I know they are. Now tell me about not serving me any wine."

"Oh. Well, Mr. Scott said Mr. Wentworth told him not to let you get a glass of anything to drink for as long as possible. I figured it was a joke, Molly."

"Yes," said Molly tightly, grasping the proffered straw that helped her to keep her dignity, "yes, I guess Harry was playing a joke on me. Thanks for telling me, Nancy."

Nancy picked up the tray-full of glasses and with barely a hesitation held it out towards Molly.

Molly shook her head.

"No. You've got your orders. I wouldn't want to spoil Harry's joke. Take it out – circulate. Thank you, Mr. Scott." She swept out of the kitchen as regally as she could, feeling shards of humiliation splinter off her in all directions.

Damn the man. How could he?

Back in the main room Molly was out of the party now, isolated. Everyone else was warm and friendly with drink – nobody stood alone – and for the first time at a party Molly actually felt lonely looking at the other people so busily communicating with each other. Furthermore, she felt suddenly unnecessary, at her own party in her own home. And particularly unnecessary to her own husband, still standing by the fireplace deep in conversation with the gorgeous Wednesday Barnes, too absorbed even to raise his head and search for her. How could she have thought those dumb, sentimental, lovesick things about him just a few minutes ago? Dictatorial, domineering, superior, behind the back, egomaniacal prig. Don't serve my wife with drinks, indeed!

Her anger rising, she willed him to look up, to meet her eye, see her fury; and the longer Harry did not do that the more her anger grew. She had a quick vision of herself striding across the room, slapping his face and telling him what she thought of his paternalistic 'joke' – and knowing that she would never do such a thing, but getting a measure of relief just imagining it.

It was as though she was invisible- people were not ignoring her; they were just not seeing her. She had to get away, leave the room. Quietly she went downstairs, through the family room and out onto the patio which was in darkness. Harry had deliberately left the pool and patio lights off to discourage his guests from wandering away from the main rooms. He didn't want, he had said, the kind of Hollywood idiocy where people were pushed into the pool fully dressed.

For a moment Molly had an impulse to give a great whoop and jump into the pool with as big a splash as she could make. This fantasy, too, she curbed. Instead, she kicked off her shoes, slipped out of her blouse and skirt and left them in a heap on the ground, and carefully lowered herself into the water in her bra and panties.

Ah! The relief of it! Water never failed to have a soothing effect on her, and as she swam her anger and frustration began to evaporate.

"Harry," Sam Price momentarily diverted his attention away from Wednesday. "Harry, I was out on the deck getting a breath of fresh air and I think you have a problem. Excuse us, Wednesday, darling?" The two men turned away from the girl. "There seems to be a nude woman swimming up and down your pool."

"Oh God." Harry's face turned to stone, knowing at once

who it was. "Thanks, Sam, I'll see to it." He left without so much as a backward glance at Wednesday, who made a moue of disappointment and raised beautifully shaped eyebrows at Sam. Sam shrugged.

Harry stood in the shadows cast by the deck, Molly's blouse and skirt over his arm, holding out a towel.

"Out," he said in low steely tones.

"Why?" Molly trod water, looking up at him.

"There is a party going on in there. Your guests are waiting for you," he said very distinctly, with a show of patience and self-control.

"I don't think so. I'm not part of that party. My husband gave orders that I wasn't to be served any drinks."

"Get out, please. We'll talk in the house."

"You bet we will." She paddled to the side and held out her hand for a pull up, but instead of taking it, Harry backed away a step and Molly realized with a twinge of amusement that he was afraid she would pull him into the water. She smiled in the dark; it was nice to know that he couldn't completely read her mind, that she was still a bit of a mystery to him. She climbed out and took the towel and noticed his eyes on her bra and panties.

"You thought I was skinny-dipping? I'm not that much of a fool."

He pushed her into the downstairs bathroom and shut the door and leaned against it.

"Dry," he said. "Dress."

She peeled off the wet underwear and posed provocatively in front of him. He grit his teeth and looked away, but not before noticing the fuller lines of her figure.

"You humiliated me," she said, towelling herself.

"Nonsense. I merely told the caterers not to serve you wine. You know you –"

"The caterers are not robots. They are people. They have families and friends, I know one of the waitresses; she's a nice woman and she was as embarrassed as I was when I went into the kitchen to ask why I wasn't being served."

"You should have stayed out of the kitchen."

"My kitchen?"

"Molly, I was only trying to save you from making a fool of yourself. You know how wine affects you," he added reasonably.

"Yes, I do, and I'd appreciate it if you'd give me credit for knowing it, and allow me to set my own limits." She pulled on her blouse and skirt over her naked body.

"But you don't."

"Then accept it – that's me. Look, I've driven home from enough parties to know you're no angel. How come it's all right for you to get sloshed but not me?"

"You're a woman."

"Oh – you noticed? Whoopee."

"Women don't get drunk gracefully."

"I've got news for you – neither do men. Harry, I wouldn't have minded drinking Perrier all night if only you'd discussed this with me first and let me be part of the decision. Male chauvinism is 'out' this year – didn't you know?"

She preceded him up the stairs and Harry noted her buttocks moving under the stuff of her skirt, and putting a possessive hand on them he murmured in her ear,

"You've got a nice ass, lady." He steered her towards the bedroom. "Get it covered."

Molly pulled panties on under her skirt.

"And a bra," he said.

"Why? Half the women in the room are braless –"

"They've got better boobs than you."

She swallowed, shocked at the bald cruelty of the words, and having a quick replay of Harry tucking Wednesday Barnes' magnificent breast back inside her dress. Harry realized at once he had been too brutal, and was sorry, but not sorry enough to say so. Instead he raised his arms to protect his face in mock fear that she was going to hit him.

"You should know," she said pointedly. "I saw you tucking Wednesday in."

"Yeah?" he said, shaken to know that he had been observed but not showing it, "but I married you, didn't I?"

"Yes, I wonder why."

"Don't ask."

"I'm asking."

"You're a small-boobed wino with a nice ass." He grinned his wolfish sexy grin and undressed her with his eyes, and Molly felt herself begin to melt. "Not now," he growled. "Later." Sometimes it was handy to be an actor.

Outside there was a cry, a thud, a crash and a diminishing crescendo of tinkling, breaking glass, then a frightened, pained exclamation:

"Oh. Oh! Oh, no!"

Nancy Lee sat on the floor surrounded by a rumpled scatter rug, an upside down tray and a pile of broken wine glasses, and she held up a hand dripping blood from a gash across the palm.

"Handkerchief, quick!" said Molly, taking in the situation at a glance. Harry slapped his clean, still folded handkerchief into her hand and watched as she scrunched across to the waitress, saying, "It's all right, everyone, I'll take care of her. Here, Nancy," she put the handkerchief firmly over the cut, "Hold that on tight and let's get into the kitchen. It's O.K. You'll be all right."

Harry moved forward to shoo the people away from the glass on the floor and the nasty little pool of blood, and assure them that the party was far from over.

Molly was in full command in the kitchen.

"Put your hand over the sink, Nancy, that's right. Mr. Scott, get someone out there to clean up the mess, starting with the blood. Someone bring a car round to the door, Mrs. Lee's going to have to go to the hospital for a few stitches. Now, Nancy, I'm going to run the cold tap over your hand for a minute to wash away any little bits of glass – don't worry about the blood, you've got lots of it and it'll help carry away any splinters too." The girl swayed. "Get a chair for Nancy, please. In that drawer, the third on the left, you'll find tea towels – give me two or three. Thank you. Shouldn't someone be out there serving drinks? Oh, Mr. Scott, Nancy's shivering. Will you get her coat?"

As she was speaking Molly was examining the cut, then making a pad of the handkerchief, bending Nancy's fingers down over it, making another pad with a tea towel and binding a second tea towel around the whole fist.

Harry, standing in the doorway, had time to reflect on the

many facets of his wife's personality: a moment ago she had been a piqued child, and now she was a mature responsible woman taking charge, exuding confidence and comfort, and turning what could have been moments of chaotic panic into an ordered exercise of emergency procedures.

"I'm s-sorry, I'm sorry, I'm so sorry, Molly" the waitress was murmuring, tears standing in her eyes.

"It's all right, Nancy, it's all right. It wasn't your fault, it was the damn scatter rug." Molly pulled the coat around her, tucking it and fussing with it and touching the girl's shoulders and neck and arms as she did so. "Hold your hand up – like so. Good girl. Is the car coming?"

She glanced back at Harry, a hard look that he did not understand, and he shrugged noncommittally, indicating that he did not know what all the fuss was about a caterer's waitress. Then Molly gave the girl a glass of water and came and stood in front of him and said in a low voice, barely moving her lips:

"Don't just stand there – do something for her, Harry." He grunted in surprise. "She's a person, Harry, a fan of yours. Her name's Nancy Lee and she's a single parent supporting two kids. The older one's baby-sitting while she's working here, so they won't have to go on welfare."

Harry moved forward at once, improvising his lines.

"Mrs. Lee," he said, "Nancy, my dear," and he poured Warmth and Sympathy and deep-toned Concern into his voice, and he put his hand on her shoulder. "I'm so sorry this happened."

"Oh, Mr. Wentworth, that's kind of you," the young woman looked up at him shyly. (Why am I surprised she's Chinese, Harry wondered?) "I hope I haven't interrupted your party. You didn't need to come…."

"No problem," said Harry. "Is there anything I can do for you?"

"Well – my boy – Steve – my son, he's a real fan of yours – he, sort of, asked me, knowing I was working here, if I could possibly get your autograph?"

Harry had already pulled out his wallet and extracted a one hundred dollar bill, now he folded it and put in into Nancy's hand.

"Perhaps this'll help more," he said.

While Nancy was struggling not to cry and thank Harry all at once, he was surprised to feel a paper thrust into his hand, and looking down found it was a glossy photograph of himself. In fact he recognized it as the one that usually sat on Molly's dressing table; he could see the crimp marks where the frame had pinched it at the edges. Molly had obviously just spent the last few minutes taking it out. Silently she proffered a felt pen.

He grunted, meaning, my God, you think of everything, don't you? And wrote in a bold hand across the bottom of the picture 'To Steven Lee, Best Wishes – Harry Wentworth'. And while Nancy was gasping with speechless gratitude he helped her up and with a strong arm around her shoulders walked her out to the waiting car.

As he went back into the house he realized that Molly had faded totally out of the scene since he had taken over, allowing him to have the limelight, and be the one that Nancy Lee would remember most clearly. Another facet of Molly's character, he thought-she's sometimes too damned self-effacing. He found her in the kitchen swilling out a blood-soaked cloth in the sink.

"Leave that," he said curtly, and took her hand wet as it was and led her out of the door and back to the party. He paused to pluck a full glass of wine from a tray.

"You look peaked," he said, giving it to Molly.

"I feel peaked," she responded, drinking so deeply that Harry could barely restrain himself from saying 'not so fast'. She quirked an eyebrow at him. "My reward?"

He shook his head. "Your due."

They remained together for the rest of the evening, arm in arm, the perfect affectionate couple, except that as Molly drank – and Harry never demurred when she reached for a fresh glass – his grip became a little tighter and a little more supporting. Then Molly finally put down a glass and said thoughtfully and carefully, "That was one past my limit." He shifted his arm to circle her waist, and even then few people were aware that if he had not done so, his quiet, graceful wife would have toppled in a dizzy heap onto the floor.

The last guest left; Jack and Lance the musicians left; the caterers left, and still Harry and Molly were glued together, side by side. They stood alone at last in front of the fireplace.

"Nice party," said Harry.

"Thank you, love. Wait a minute. Bathroom." He let her go gradually and she sank down onto the shag rug with a contented sigh. When Harry came back from the bathroom he found she had pulled a cushion from the sofa under her head and was fast asleep. He bent to pick her up, then thought better of it and went and found a spare blanket and tucked it carefully around her. He smiled fondly, in a way that he only did when there was no one there to see him, then shook his head and went to the bedroom.

He pulled of his jacket and tie and shoes, and then deciding the bed looked lonely and empty, dragged the comforter off it and went back into the living room and pulled the sofa close to where Molly lay and settled himself upon it. One hand reached down and touched the blanket that covered Molly.

He awoke gradually to brilliant, unfamiliar light seeping through his eyelids, and took a moment to orient himself. His head ached dully and his mouth was thick – not too bad, he thought, for a good party. He opened his eyes cautiously and groped for Molly with his left hand and found only space.

"She isn't there."

Ken and Sue were looking at him with interest but no apparent surprise. It was Ken who had spoken.

"Are you drunk?" asked Sue curiously.

"No. Hung-over, maybe."

"It must have been SOME PARTY," she said. "Cars were coming and going ALL NIGHT." They had spent the night at neighbour's house so as – ironically – not to be disturbed.

"I got Bruno Gerussi's autograph," said Ken. "He was nice."

"What's this black gravely stuff on the crackers?" Sue had a plate of left over canapés from the refrigerator. "It's de-lish-us," she said.

"It's horrible," said Ken.

"It's caviar," said Harry

"Can I have it in my school sandwiches?"

"Over my dead body. "Where's your mother?"

"In the bathroom throwing up," said Ken matter-of-factly, stuffing smoked oysters in his mouth.

Throwing up? Molly had never been sick on wine before. Harry frowned, puzzled. Maybe she'd got a chill in the pool?

Rob came in then and looked at Harry (who was dressed in dishevelled evening clothes wrapped in a comforter on the sofa) with unconcealed hostility and disapproval.

"Mother's ill," he said bleakly, and there was no mistaking the accusation in his voice. "She slept on the floor."

"I slept on the rug," Molly corrected him, coming briskly in, dressed in her bathrobe, her face shining and scrubbed and glowing with health. "I've always wanted to sleep on that rug since the first time I came here."

Rob and Harry stared at her in surprise, having expected her to look pale and sickly.

The twins, however, exchanged a worldly look and left the room giggling.

Chapter Ten

Molly Takes Off

'Seen at the Airport yesterday, Canadian star Harry Wentworth seeing off his distraught wife Molly, called away suddenly by a family emergency in Calgary. Wentworth's appearance at the Celebrity Bash later in the evening was cut short when he hurried home to await word from his wife.'

Harry was nearly ready. Resplendent in tux, ruffled shirt, black bow tie and cummerbund he peered in the mirror and smoothed his short-cut nearly white hair – and fumed. Molly sat on the bed, still in her day clothes.

"I'm not going," she said. "I mean it."

"You can't not go – we're committed."

"You're committed – I'm not. They don't want me there."

"I want you there."

"Harry, you're a grown man. You can survive without a woman. You did for twenty years after Dell died."

"Now I've got you, and I want you there, by my side. Is that too much to ask?"

"I need a life of my own – you knew that when you married me. Frankly, I'm tired of parties and actors and temperamental directors. I'm tired of plastic people wearing plastic clothes saying nothing to each other while they eat plastic food and drink too much."

"Thanks a lot – I'm one of those plastic people."

"Oh, Harry, you're not – you're you. I know you. I married the man inside the plastic suit because I loved him."

"Good," he said decisively, "then if you love me you'll hurry up and get dressed."

She stood up. "Don't lay that 'if you love me' stuff on me. I really can't go."

He went to the closet and pulled out a dress, a soft jersey dress in muted gold tones.

"Wear that. You look great in it."

"No."

"Part of being my wife is going to these things whether you like them or not, Molly."

"I'm not just your wife – I'm me, Molly, and Molly thinks the Celebrity Bash is a crummy way to raise money for crippled kids. And I'd probably say so if I came – which I'm not going to."

Harry's big blunt features registered towering rage – a lot more than he felt, but then he was an actor and used to expressing himself freely, and knew that Molly was equally well aware of that.

"Stop being so damn liberated!" he thundered. "And do as you're told. Get dressed."

"Go to hell!" she responded, and turned to leave the room.

"Just a minute." Harry strode across the room and grabbed her arm just as she reached for the door. "Don't you walk out on me, woman." He jerked her back more violently than he had intended and she swung away from him, stumbled, and fell down on all fours. Immediately sorry, Harry reached down to help her up, but Molly sprang away, her arm upraised, palm open.

"Leave me alone," she snapped.

"Don't threaten me!" He caught her wrist and twisted her arm up behind her back. "Don't you ever slap me – or even pretend to." She struggled, pushing him away with her free hand and they wrestled until he caught that wrist too and pulled it up behind her with the other. Now he held her tightly against his chest, a prisoner.

Molly had never in her life been physically abused by a man, never before been made aware of her physical inferiority and it shocked her. Not only the sensation of helplessness but the fact that it was Harry who was taking advantage of her.

"I knew it," she said bitterly, "You're just a damned animal, just like the men you play on the screen. Louts. Brutes. Chauvinist pigs!" She wrenched and wriggled in his grasp, panting.

"Shut up," he said.

"Let me go, or I'll scream for Rob."

"Don't you dare."

She opened her mouth but before any sound could come out Harry had transferred his grip on her wrists to one hand and clapped the other one over it, pushing her head back uncomfortably.

A mewling pitiful sound came out from under his hand and looking down at Molly's face Harry was appalled to see what he took to be fear in her eyes. He let go immediately and stood back a step, his hands spread.

"My God," he said. "What are we doing?" He tried to put his arms around her gently, but she broke away from him.

"I don't know about you," she said breathlessly, wiping her mouth and rubbing her wrists, "but I know what I'm doing." She crossed the room quickly, found a suitcase in the back of the closet, flung it on the bed and opened it.

"Oh, no, you're not."

"Oh, yes, I am." She scooped up an armful of underwear from a drawer, grabbed several blouses from the closet, threw them all in the suitcase.

Having followed her back and forth across the room, being careful not to touch her, Harry now sat on the bed.

"You've been watching too many soap operas."

"I never watch soap operas, Harry. This is real life."

"Where are you going?"

"That's my business."

"Wherever it is you're not going to need four nighties," he pointed out reasonably. Angrily she snatched up two and threw them on the bed. "And the children?" he asked.

"Mavis is a good housekeeper. They like her."

"Ah, Molly," he turned on his vocal after-burners and his voice vibrated with Warmth and Sincerity and Love. "Molly, you can't do this to us –"

"Harry," she said shortly, "You're acting again, I can always tell."

He opened his mouth and almost said 'I wish I could', but there was a knock on the door at that moment.

"Your cab's here, Mr. Wentworth," Mavis called through the door.

For a few seconds they both stood like statues, then Molly grabbed her handbag, a coat and the suitcase and called out;

"Thank you, Mavis, I'm on my way," and headed for the door.

Harry remained in the middle of the room, uncharacteristically stunned into inaction. In truth he was not much like the people he portrayed on the screen, being a basically kind man who over-defended his vulnerable places. By the time he reached the hall, the door had shut and the cab was gone. Mavis was waiting for him, holding out the car keys that he always left on the hall table.

"The airport. She told the cabbie the airport."

"Thanks, Mavis."

There was no way of telling whether he was ahead of or behind Molly's cab on the way across town, so when Harry arrived at the airport he parked in the ten minute zone and dashed into the building, going straight to the long line of ticket wickets. He was a conspicuous figure in his fine evening clothes, and heads turned and a buzz of conversation followed him as he was recognized.

He found her just as she was buying a ticket. Pushing to the head of the line he reached for her small suitcase saying,

"Come over here."

Molly grabbed for the handle of the case and for a moment they wrestled grimly over it.

"I'll carry it for you," he grated between clenched teeth, pushing her out of the lineup with his body.

She glanced at her ticket and started towards one of the Departure gates. Harry kept pace beside her, his head bent, muttering in her ear,

"Don't do this, Molly, please. You're making a fool of me."

"No." She looked at him for the first time, stopping by the gate she wanted. "You're making a fool of yourself, Harry. Let me go. I need to go." Then almost inaudibly she added, "I'm sorry."

His face was like stone, immobile, every expression severely curbed. Molly saw him physically restraining himself from taking hold of her; she saw the despair and bewilderment that nobody else could see; she saw him force himself to put down her case quietly and accept her right to her decision. And she was so moved by what she saw the tears welled up in her eyes and ran in streams down her cheeks. She made no sound, just cried uncontrollably as they held each other's gaze.

Harry had never seen her cry like this and he was touched by the honesty of the tears. He knew that at that moment she was so vulnerable he had only to say one tender word and she would be in his arms and his again. Deliberately he said nothing.

Molly became aware that the tears were dripping off her chin and made a helpless attempt to wipe them away with her fingers. Harry searched in his pockets for a handkerchief and found none, having come out before he was fully ready, so he pulled the big square of coloured silk from his breast pocket and pushed it into her hands.

"Madame," said the attendant, spotting the label on her case, "Your flight is being called. You'll have to hurry."

"Yes," she said, "yes." She wiped her eyes, her cheeks, and her chin, balled the wet handkerchief in one hand, picked up her case and went through the gate.

Harry watched until she was out of sight, waiting to see if she would turn for one last look at him, betting with himself that she would not, hoping she would have the strength not to, obscurely pleased when she did not. He felt emotionally drained and wondered what the people around had made of their little scene. For their benefit he looked up with a tired, grim smile, cocked an expressive eyebrow, caught a few sympathetic eyes, nodded his thanks, and gracefully exited through the nearest door.

He went to the Celebrity Bash and spent a miserable evening baring his teeth in a false hearty grin and explaining why he was alone. Molly, he told them, was called away suddenly, he had to drop her off at the airport on the way, hopefully she'd only be away for a few days. It was impossible to miss the knowing looks that were exchanged behind his back. Inwardly, he ground his teeth at Molly for putting him in this position, his anger growing as the evening – and the innuendoes – progressed.

He left early, explaining he was expecting a call from Molly. He was not. He knew she would not call. And yet –

At home he threw down his coat in the hall.

"Mavis!" he bellowed. She poked her head out of the kitchen. "Any calls?"

She shook her head regretfully. "Sorry, Mr. Wentworth."

He strode down the corridor to Rob's room, knocked, and when Rob answered, went in.

"Your mother's gone," he said abruptly. "I suppose you know?"

Rob looked up from his homework.

"Yeah."

"You know where she's gone?"

The boy considered Harry for a moment and then nodded his head. "Yeah, I think so."

"Are you going to tell me?" He stood over the boy, dominating him, unbuttoned his jacket, put his fists on his hips.

"No," said Rob, staring up at him, meeting his eyes unflinchingly. "Not yet."

"Sorry." Harry put his hand on the thin shoulder. "Didn't mean to come on so strong." He turned away. "I'm confused, Rob, I don't know what to do. Got any advice? You probably know her better than I do."

"Leave her be, Harry. She'll come back, or call, or something. She always has."

"You mean she's done this before – just up and left you kids?"

"Um-hmm." Rob smiled fondly. "Mum's a bit whacky, you know."

Harry nodded.

"That's one of the reasons I married her, I guess." He caught the boy's eye and they exchanged a masculine smile that bridged the years between them. "So, I'd better go and think this out." He gestured to the books on the desk. "Need any help?"

"Calculus?" Rob cocked a sceptical eyebrow.

"Uh – no," said Harry.

"It'll be all right," Rob said as Harry paused at the door. "She loves you – I know she does."

"Does she? I wonder."

Harry went downstairs then, rubbing his hands over his hair, his eyes unfocussed, deep in thought. He went through the family room and out onto the patio and raising his eyes to the stars for inspiration he walked straight into the swimming pool.

Coming up, spluttering, his first thought was a fervent hope that no one had heard or seen him. Cursing himself for being all kinds of a fool with one half of his mind, and laughing wryly with the other, he paddled as silently as he could to the ladder and climbed out and sat on the edge.

"It's fun, isn't it?" said a small voice behind him.

"Mum used to let us have a last swim with all our clothes on when we went to Qualicum for the summer holiday," said another, earnestly.

The twins. The last people in the house Harry wanted to see. He put his hands over his face and rubbed the water out of his eyes before turning round. They stood behind him in their pyjamas, the window of their downstairs bedroom open sending a shaft of light across the patio. They were not laughing.

"The only thing is," Ken went on. "You get cold quickly after."

"You'd better come into our bathroom and dry," said Sue practically, "before you catch cold."

Harry stood up and the water streamed out of his sleeves and down his pant legs. He spread his arms wide.

"That's O.K., kids, have a laugh, I don't mind. It isn't every day you see an adult fall in a swimming pool in his best suit." They looked up at him solemnly.

"Shh," said Ken warningly, "the others might hear."

"Come on," Sue took his hand and pulled him towards the

door. To Harry's intense surprise Ken took his other hand. Molly's children, he thought, were as unpredictable as she was. They led him to the downstairs bathroom, followed him in and stood by the door waiting expectantly.

"Well," said Ken. "Undress."

"Oh. Yes. Of course." Harry started to strip.

"I expect you're missing Mum," said Sue sympathetically. "Put your things in the bath."

"Of course I am. Know where she is?"

"Probably with Gran – oh!" Sue clapped her hand over her mouth guiltily.

"What's that?" said Harry, pretending he hadn't heard.

"You've still got your pants on," Ken pointed out. "And your shoes."

"Ah – yes." Harry kicked off his shoes and with a quick glance at Sue dropped his trousers and stepped out of them. "Sue, so you think you could sneak upstairs and get my robe and bring it down for me?"

"Course." She was gone.

Quickly Harry stripped off his jockey shorts and before he could grab a towel Ken said matter-of-factly,

"Your pee-thing's all shrivelled."

"Yes – well – that happens when it gets cold. And by the way the proper name for it is penis." He wrapped the towel around his waist.

"Oh," said Ken. "Nobody told me."

Breathlessly, Sue arrived at the door and held out Harry's robe.

"Thanks, Sue."

"Harry just told me my pee-thing's called a penis."

"Is that what mine's called too, Harry?"

"No," Harry swallowed. "I think yours is called a vulva."

"Oh, I like that," Sue squealed. "That sounds all soft and furry!"

Harry snorted, trying to disguise a shout of laughter.

"You kids are as crazy as your mother! Now, don't you dare use those words in company – they're private words for private parts of your body – O.K.?"

"O.K., Harry."

"Now, off to bed, you two. And not a word about me falling in the pool, eh?"

"Cross my heart and hope to die," said Ken.

"Our lips are sealed." Said Sue, but she glanced at the wet clothes in the bath.

"I'll think of something to explain those," Harry said quickly. They paused at the bathroom door.

"It'll be all right, you know," said Ken.

"Mum always comes back," said Sue.

Harry sighed. I hope so, at least I think I hope so, he said to himself. He felt a little as though he was drowning in an unfamiliar element.

"After all, she wouldn't leave us with you for the rest of our lives, would she?" Sue gave him an angelic smile, obviously under the impression that she had said something comforting.

Days went by: there was no letter, no message, and no call.

Rob and the twins went to school and ate and slept and seemed unperturbed, while Harry stewed and fumed, and snapped on the set and snarled at home. Finally he calmed down. That was the night the 'phone rang. He and Rob were in the living room together – Rob reached the 'phone first.

"Oh, hi Mum! Sure. Fine. Yes, he is. O.K. Hang on a minute." He put the receiver down on the table and looked across at Harry. "I'm going to my room to take Mum's call on the extension, if you don't mind. When I shout will you hang up here, please?"

"She doesn't want to talk to me?"

The boy had the grace to look embarrassed.

"No. I'm sorry, Harry."

"O.K.," he said, raising both hands palms out in a gesture of surrender. "O.K. I'll do that."

Rob left the room without a backward glance, implying complete trust in Harry's word, which at least was gratifying. Harry raised the receiver thoughtfully, his hand over the mouthpiece; he could hear Molly breathing. He moved his hand and breathed audibly in reply.

"Got it!" Rob yelled.

Quickly, guiltily Harry hung up. A moment later he heard

the twins pounding along the corridor to Rob's room. He waited bleakly, feeling angry and left out. Ten minutes later Rob returned.

"Well, is she coming back?"

"Yes."

"When?"

"I'm not supposed to say."

"So, are you going to?"

"Yes, I am. I thought about it and I don't think she's being fair."

"Well, thank you, Rob."

"Just because she's my mother doesn't mean I think she's always right, you know. She'll be on flight 901 from Calgary at five past five tomorrow afternoon. She's expecting me to meet her."

"Will you?"

"I've got a basketball game," Rob said. They looked at each other for a long moment then Harry nodded, crossed the room and put his hands on the boy's shoulders.

"Thanks, Rob," he said.

Molly put down the telephone.

"I'm going home, Ma."

"Well, good. Did he ask you to?"

"I didn't even speak to him. While Rob was out of the room he breathed over the phone."

"Really? How did you know it was him?"

"I knew. I breathed back."

"How romantic," said Mrs. Bragg dryly. "If you ask me you're damn lucky to have a man who's content with a wife who only breathes to him."

"I know. I know I am, Ma. And I don't want to spoil this one. Harry's such a nice man, and I really love him, but I want to be what he wants without abnegating what I really am – and I don't know how to do it."

"If you want, you'll find a way, though it may mean a compromise. Are you ready for that?" Mrs. Bragg put a hand on her daughter's shoulder and squeezed it. "One of these days I'll have to come and meet him. Now, what's your problem?"

"What d'you mean?"

"You didn't come here just because you had a row. I know that. There's something else on your mind, and if you're leaving soon you'd better get it out now."

Molly swallowed.

"Ma, I'm pregnant."

"Hmm. What does Harry think about that?"

"I haven't told him. That's my problem – I don't know how to."

Mrs. Bragg sat down beside her daughter and took her hand. "How do you feel about it, Molly?"

"That's another problem – I don't know either. I'm thirty-seven, Ma, and Harry's fifty, maybe we're too old to start a family. And Rob and the twins... they might not like it...."

"Are you afraid to tell him?"

Afraid of Harry? Molly's hand closed around his silk handkerchief in her skirt pocket and was comforted.

"No," she said softly, realizing. "No."

At five past five the next afternoon, Harry Wentworth was leaning casually against a pillar at the airport facing the Arrivals Gate, his raincoat collar turned up, and his hat brim turned well down over his face, his eyes hidden behind dark glasses. He stood out like a sore thumb.

Molly came through the gate, her handbag over her shoulder, her suitcase in her hand. She put the case down and stood and methodically scanned the crowd in front of her, looking for Rob. Her eyes slid over Harry, stopped, tracked back and rested on him with grave surprise, then moved on. Harry made a small gesture behind his back and suddenly lights blazed in Molly's face and a T.V. crew moved in on her. Blinded, she tried to back away but found herself surrounded by journalists with tape recorders and notebooks at the ready. Three or four microphones sprouted in front of her face like lollipops.

"How are you feeling, Mrs. Wentworth? Does Harry know you're coming back today? Why did you leave town so suddenly? Molly, are you and Harry splitting up?" The questions were fired from all sides.

"Would you like to make a statement?"

"Is it true you're contemplating divorce?"

"What?" she said. "No – I've got nothing – please – let me through." She tried unsuccessfully to push the journalists aside.

"Are you expecting Harry to meet you?"

"What d'you think of the movie he's shooting?"

"D'you think he'll be nominated for an Oscar?"

"Mrs. Wentworth, is it true you're a woman's libber?"

"Yes, it sure is, and I'd like to be liberated –"

"Darling!" Harry pushed hastily through the crowd at that juncture, sensing immediate disaster if he did not rescue her. Notwithstanding that it was he who had tipped off the press about her arrival, this was a bit much. "Sorry I'm late!" He cried heartily, swamping her in a bear hug. In her ear he murmured urgently, "Play up to me, Molly, please!" He pulled her head back and kissed her lightly on the mouth while the cameras whirred. "And how's Mother?"

Molly looked up at him and smiled brilliantly.

"She's fine, Harry," she trilled. "Just longing to meet you, of course."

He locked one arm around her, picked up her suitcase and turned his charm on the media people.

"Give us a break fellows – girls – let me get my wife home to the kids. She's had a busy time."

"One last question, Harry –"

"No. Another time. Sorry." He hustled her along through the crowd of reporters and the spectators who had been attracted by the lights like moths. Hands reached out to touch him. (I touched Harry Wentworth!) Then they were out in the open and heading down to the car park.

"Thanks," he said curtly, letting her go.

"Why you?" Molly asked breathlessly. "Where's Rob?"

"Basketball."

"The fink. He told you I was coming?"

"Didn't you mean him to?"

"Well... I, ... Well..." Molly looked at the granite profile beside her, leaned forward, trying to peer up into his face. "Do I know you?"

He glanced sideways at her.

"After six months? Not likely. But keep trying."

They stopped beside Molly's station wagon.

"Where's the gorgeous car?"

"Rob's got it. Thought I'd come incognito."

"Ah, yes, the disguise – dark glasses and a turned up coat collar. I couldn't miss you." She smiled, a real smile this time, but Harry turned away deliberately and opened the car door.

They sat in tense silence while Harry manoeuvred out of the car park and onto the road heading north into Vancouver.

"Harry. I'm sorry."

"That's nice," he said tightly.

"At the same time I'm glad I went."

"Really. Well, I'm glad you're back, I suppose. But I'm so damn mad you ever left that's all I can feel."

"Don't I have a right to be me?"

"Not if it's at my expense, no. I was humiliated, Molly. I couldn't tell anyone where you'd gone or when you'd be back. The kids knew but they wouldn't tell me. I didn't know… anything…what was going to happen…. My work suffered. I felt used and belittled. Dammit!" he shouted, "that's the truth! All you think about is you. And if you were still alone that'd be OK, but when you married your first husband and had the kids you should have accepted the responsibilities you created for being part of other people's lives and happiness; and when you married me you should have accepted the fact that I'm famous and have a public to serve. I'm Harry Wentworth, not Joe Blow, and you've got to be Harry Wentworth's wife first –"

"No!" she objected. "No, I was me long before I was anyone's wife. And you're the man I married and what your name was or your profession had nothing to do with it. I didn't marry you because you were a famous actor. I didn't marry you for your name, but for you. And I hoped you'd marry me for me as I am, not what you could change me to. I can't help it if I don't care for your friends and their parties. I don't see why I should pretend."

"You should try because I am Harry Wentworth, that's why. Whether you like it or not Harry Wentworth needs his wife at his side, preferably smiling and sober, or he gets a lot of rotten things written about him in the gossip columns and smut sheets, and that affects his career. It's your responsibility to subjugate your needs to my needs once in a while. That's what marriage is all about."

"And what about vice versa? My needs?" she said heatedly. "My needs for privacy and peace and quiet. Don't I have rights too? Don't you have a responsibility to me, to support me in public?"

"Who are you? You're nobody."

She gasped. "Nobody?" she exclaimed. "I'm me, I'm Molly. I don't have to be famous to be important. Molly Bragg – Molly Ash – Molly Wentworth – whatever. I'm very important to me!"

"That's a bloody selfish attitude."

"You think yours isn't?"

He kept his head straight, presenting her with a rigid profile. Molly stared at him, at the blunt features set in stone, the lines hard and uncompromising. She realised that if anyone were going to give, it would have to be her – this time anyway.

"I don't know you," she said quietly. "I don't know Harry Wentworth the movie star, but I do know Harry my husband who fell into the swimming pool because he was thinking about me."

"Oh," he said. "The little toads told you? They promised they wouldn't. Your family don't have any scruples about breaking promises, to they?"

"They use their discretion. They didn't tell me because they thought it was funny, but because they were worried about you. You should be glad they told me, that's why I came home." She looked at her hands in her lap and bit her lips to suppress the smile that was being born there. "Especially because Ken told me your – your – pee-thing was all shrivelled up." She tried unsuccessfully to stifle a giggle.

Harry glanced at her then, and his face softened momentarily.

"Didn't he use the right word? I told him the right word."

"Oh, yes. And so did Sue. Thanks for giving them the anatomy lesson." The tension in the car had eased somewhat and Molly felt a little more relaxed. She noticed they had turned off the Stanley Park Causeway. "Where are we going?"

"To Third Beach. Where all this started."

"You mean," she said hesitantly, dismayed, misreading his tone, "you mean, now it's finishing?"

He heard the note of desolation in her voice and without looking reached across and put his hand on her thigh and squeezed it, an intimate, possessive gesture.

"No, Molly, you idiot, no," he said.

They parked and Molly walked over to the deck overlooking the beach where they had been married on that bright spring morning not so many months ago. Coming up behind her Harry put his hands on her waist and pulled her back against his chest, and he could feel her trembling as he had that day they had discovered they were in love. Suddenly he wrapped his arms around her, holding her tightly, pinning her arms.

"Don't struggle, please," he said. She stood quietly. "I may get rough sometimes, Molly, that's the kind of guy I am, but I'll never hurt you. Do you know that?"

"Yes. I know that."

"And don't ever, ever, be afraid of me."

"I'm not," she said. "I won't be."

He turned her round and kissed her hard and as they had before her knees turned to water and she sagged against him.

"Whoa!" he said. "Not now, Molly." She laid her head on his shoulder, smiling.

"Excuse me," a young voice said. "Excuse me." Someone was tugging Harry's sleeve. "Aren't you Harry Wentworth?"

They broke apart and looked at the two small boys in front of them.

"Can I have your autograph, please?"

"Of course." Harry took the book and started to write.

The other boy looked up at Molly, undecided, a piece of paper in his hand.

"Excuse me, but who are you?"

"I'm Molly, Mr. Wentworth's wife."

"Are you someone important?"

"Yes," said Harry. "She's very important. You'd better get her autograph too."

Molly looked at him. He was serious. Smiling, she took the paper and signed it. They exchanged paper and book, then watched the boys go down the steps to the beach comparing notes.

Harry said: "Let's go home. My pee-thing isn't shrivelled any more."

Molly pealed with laughter, full of joy and freedom and love, and the startled gulls took off from the logs below and wheeled away across the sea, and she knew that as soon as they were home, she would tell him her news. She could not guess how he would react – she still did not know him well enough for that – but now at least she was confident that whatever happened they would be able to work it out. Hopefully, it was not a false confidence.

Chapter Eleven

Richard Arrives

"New lawyer in town Richard Worthington bears strong family resemblance to what famous actor? Only one guess – it's too easy."

Harry unbuttoned his wife's blouse and opened it; he unclipped her front-fastening bra, pushed it aside, and cupped her breasts in his hands. He bent his head and kissed them lovingly. He raised his head and looked at her.

"They're getting bigger," he said.

He ran his hands down her waist to her hips.

"You're putting on weight," he said.

Molly sat very still and said nothing, holding his gaze.

"You're having my baby?" There was a note of incredulity in his tone. "Molly. Is it true?"

She nodded. "Yes."

He sat on the bed beside her and took her hands in his.

"Is that why you ran away – you were afraid to tell me?"

"No, not exactly. More like – I needed time to think about it myself."

"And what do you think?"

"That at thirty-eight and fifty-one we'll be a bit old to be new parents."

"You want an abortion?" She caught the dismay in his voice.

"No. Never. I had four miscarriages, between Rob and the twins remember? I wouldn't want to lose one on purpose. Unless.... You felt...."

"I feel very satisfied," said Harry with a grin. He pushed her back on the bed. "Now, let's do what we were going to do."

Later he stood at the window admiring the view of English Bay, the cargo ships at anchor waiting to enter the harbour, the towers of the University buildings in the distance rising ethereally through the haze.

"Do you realize, Molly, it's nearly thirty years since I was a father?"

"My God," she said dryly, "I was eight. Tell me about your son. You never have."

"He's about twenty-nine, a lawyer, and an insufferable stuffed shirt."

"Harry!"

"He is. I hope you never meet him. He'll bore you stiff and he wouldn't approve of you at all. He never approved of me. He thought acting was a very unrespectable way of life. He was ashamed to have to admit what his father did for a living."

"Don't sound so bitter, Harry."

"Why shouldn't I? The little brat never refused a thing my money could buy – though he made it clear he despised the way I earned it. He didn't invite me to his Graduation when he got his law degree – Dell's mother told me about it (he lived with them after Dell died). When I went he pretended not to see me, so I walked out. I haven't seen him since."

"What's he like?"

"To look at? Like me. There the resemblance ends – the rest of him is from Dell's side."

"You never told me about Dell, either," Molly said sadly.

"No." He continued to gaze out of the window. "She's got nothing to do with us. I loved her for fifteen years- she died. That's a part of my life you can't share."

"I could – if you'd let me. I could tell you about Tom and our ten years…"

"I don't want to hear –"

"I know. Sometimes I feel I need to share it, though, so that you can understand why I am as I am."

"Rob's told me enough."

"Has he?" She looked surprised.

He came back to the bed and leant over her, his hands on either side of her head.

"I love you as you are," he said. "Regardless of what made you that way. I'm glad you're carrying my baby, not because it proves my manhood, but because it's going to be a unique child." He kissed the tip of her nose.

"Mum's just told me something," said Sue, bursting with eight-year-old importance. "She's going to have a baby!"

"Well, of course," said Ken, looking bored and superior. "I told you she would when they slept together – and they've been sleeping together for months."

"Don't be crude!" said Rob sharply.

"What's the matter, Rob? Don't you want Mum and Harry to have a baby?"

"No," he said, "not particularly. They're too old."

The twins looked puzzled; at eight all grown-ups are too old. They could not know that at nearly seventeen Rob was contemplating it as the supreme embarrassment to be the only guy in class to have a heavily pregnant mother present at Graduation exercises.

"Besides," he went on jealously, "why does she need more family than us?"

"That's all right for you," said Ken.

"You've got us to boss around," said Sue. "We'd like a baby brother or sister. Or twins like us."

Two, maybe three weeks and the baby would arrive. Molly was big, and she was tired; tired of resting and being careful and not eating this or drinking that, and walking slowly and avoiding stairs and not having sex. And incredibly grateful that she had not aborted because that made everything else worthwhile.

She went out onto the sundeck to relax on the chaise-lounge in the warm sun, the skirt of her maternity dress hiked up to her thighs.

She heard Mavis come to the French doors.

"Molly?" There was a puzzled, hesitant note to her voice.
"I'm awake."

"There's someone to see you. I told him you were resting, but he said it was important."

"Who is he?"

Mavis held out a business card.

"Richard Worthington, Barrister-at-Law."

"Never heard of him. Tell him to come back when Harry's home."

"I think you should see him, Molly." Again there was that strange note in Mavis' voice.

"You've whetted my curiosity. Send him through."

"Your skirt…"

"Oh," Molly pulled it down, sat up neatly, expectantly.

The man who came through the door in a light blue three-piece suit, blue and white pinstripe shirt and navy tie, carrying a black briefcase was Harry twenty years ago. Tall, well built, Harry's long face, big hands, short hair – blonde not grey – his face tight and private and legal, but for all his self-control registering a little shock.

Molly thought 'but he's my age' and had a moment of terror, it was so uncanny to see her husband in the flesh as a young man.

"How do you do, Mrs. Wentworth," he said formally, but not holding out his hand. "I'm…"

"It's obvious who you are. But why Worthington?"

Hostility flowed between them.

"It's my legal name. My father – your husband – changed it for 'professional reasons' I believe they call it. Too many letters for the marquees."

"To what do we owe this sudden visit, at long last?"

"At long last? How could I have come before? I didn't know where my father lived, I only found out recently that he had remarried, and I had no idea you were…er…" he gestured vaguely.

"Pregnant," said Molly, "is the word you're looking for. Heavily pregnant, in fact."

"It makes my visit more pertinent."

"You obviously don't read the show-biz columns – our

marriage and my condition have been well reported."

"No doubt. As you say, I don't read those columns."

"And you don't read your letters either."

"What letters?"

"The ones Harry wrote to you when you were a boy. The ones you never answered."

"I never received any letters."

"He wrote them."

"No doubt he told you that."

"He did – and I believed him, and still do." They were at an impasse. In the pause Molly rearranged her mental attitude and attempted to rearrange her physical one too by hauling herself laboriously up out of the chaise-lounge; an act with which Richard Worthington made no effort to help her. She bunched her skirt at the front trying to make the very large pregnancy a little less obvious.

"I'm sorry," she said. "Let's start over. My name is Maureen, but everybody calls me Molly. How do you do, Richard?" She reached out her hand and she was so close to him the man had little alternative but to take it and shake it, but as briefly as decency would allow. "Now, would you like to sit down? There's a chair –"

"No, thank you."

"In that case you won't mind if I stand too? I feel at a psychological disadvantage in that low chair. I think Mavis told you Harry is out? They're shooting interiors at the Studio today and he won't be in until about six. So, is there something you wanted to see me about?"

"Yes. I don't particularly want to see him at all."

"Why not?" Molly was chilled by his tone.

"We have nothing in common."

"Oh, yes, you do. You look exactly like him; you wear the same sort of suits; you stand like him–"

"Oh, externally, perhaps," the man said shortly. "Philosophically, no."

"How can you tell, you haven't met him for years?"

"I've seen his movies. One or two were enough."

"His movies!" Molly exclaimed. "They're not Harry. I can't stand them either. I only see them by mistake."

The young lawyer looked surprised and puzzled.

"Well then, how –?"

"Did I meet him? My son – I have a son of seventeen and twins of nine – entered me in a competition for which dinner with Harry, your father, was the prize. I was very annoyed, I would much rather have had the cheque for fifty dollars that was the second prize, but they wouldn't switch. You're looking confused – never mind, it's too complicated to explain. Suffice it to say that I was never an adoring fan of Harry Wentworth. Did you think I was?"

"It was reasonable to assume…"

"I suppose so." Molly had been moving restlessly around the sundeck as she spoke – since that was more comfortable than standing still. Now she stopped in front of him. "I'm not what you expected, am I?"

"Frankly, no."

"You expected a young bosomy ambitious sex-pot of a starlet, eager to get her hands on all Harry's lovely money, and ready to use him to further her career."

"Something like that," Richard Worthington admitted guardedly. "I have seen pictures of him with girls like that."

"I thought you didn't read the show-biz columns?"

"Well, one sees them in dentist's waiting rooms. I came to ask if Harry Wentworth has made a new will."

"You mean your father. Are you so bitter you can't even call him your father? If he's Harry Wentworth to you, what does that make me? Just Mrs. Wentworth the second? Well, maybe, but who do you think this is in here?" She placed her hands on her abdomen. "This, Richard Worthington, Barrister-at-Law, is your brother or sister, whether you like it or not."

"And that," the man said coldly, "adds a new dimension to my question."

"About the Will? You'd better ask Harry, it's none of my business."

"It's very much your business, especially if you have children from a previous alliance."

"Marriage!" she said sharply. "You make it sound as though I shacked up with someone for a few years. I'm ordinary pregnant, middle-aged Molly, as respectable as they come. I didn't even go to bed with your – Harry – until our wedding night. But if you're worried about getting your rightful share of the loot from your father's despised career, I'm sure you won't be disappointed. He's been more than generous to you already."

"Ha!"

"You mean you don't know –"

"I know," the man said angrily, "that my father dumped me two days after my mother died; that he went off to make a film and left me with my mother's parents and never attempted to see me again. That from the time I was ten my grandparents fed me and clothed me and housed me and loved me and put me through school and University –"

"With what? Whose money do you think kept you in bicycles and sweaters and sent you to Upper Canada College and Sir George William's? Granny and Grandpa's pensions? No, sir that was Harry Wentworth's money did that for you – your father, Richard Worthington – I've seen all the receipts. I've –" Molly clutched her abdomen with one hand and reached for support with the other; she had gone quite white.

"Are you all right?"

"No, I'm not all right, I want to sit down. Where's the bloody chair?"

"Here." Suddenly Richard's hand was under her elbow, supporting her in the same way as Harry so frequently did, and he had lowered her into the chaise-lounge. Her skirt pulled taut over the bulge and the baby's kicks were visibly moving the material.

"Look," said Molly fondly, "look at her kick." She grabbed the man's wrist and pulled his hand down on her abdomen and held it there against his pull. "Say Hi to your brother or sister, Richard." She let go of his wrist and in spite of himself, the man let his hand rest there and feel the baby moving. "It makes it more real, doesn't it?" Molly said quietly.

Embarrassed but reluctantly affected, the man stood up and moved away.

"Yes," he said, quietly also. "Mrs. Wentworth, I must apologize for upsetting you. I didn't know about... your condition."

"I don't expect you to call me Mother, but, please, not 'Mrs.

Wentworth'. Try and get your tongue around Molly. Please. After all, I'm not that much older than you – and I am married to your father."

"Yes," he said, and he ran his hand over his short hair in a very Harry-like gesture, and breathed deeply in and out in what amounted to a sigh. "I think... there are things... we have to talk about. Molly."

"I think so too. Drag over that deck chair and let's do it."

Richard sat down, clasped his hands between his spread knees and looked at the floor, thinking, for some moments. Slowly Molly relaxed as she waited, and the baby's violent movements subsided.

"I realize you came here expecting to dislike me," she said. "For whatever reasons – loyalty to your mother, disappointment in your father – and I know that deep down I have always disliked what little I knew of you because of how much you have hurt Harry – deliberately or unwittingly – over the years. Let's go back to square one and meet each other as complete strangers, tell each other what we know about a mutual friend called Harry."

"I'm afraid I can't be that dispassionate. When my mother died –"

"Harry was heartbroken. I know because he won't talk to me about her. He once said 'I loved her for fifteen years: she died. I can't share that part of my life with you'. But he has talked about you. How you never answered his letters –"

"There were no letters."

"Perhaps your grandparent didn't give them to you. You never thanked him for his gifts..."

"No gifts that I knew about."

"When he called to see you, you had always 'just gone out' or 'gone to bed' or 'had a cold'. When he made an appointment to fetch you for an outing, the house was locked and empty when he got there, and later your grandparents would say 'oh, sorry, we forgot'."

"I can't believe this."

"I'm just telling you what he told me. He was never good enough for your mother's parents: being an actor wasn't dignified or respectable: they were against the marriage from the start..."

"Yes," the man said, "that I have heard them say. 'Your mother could have done so much better than that man, he wasn't good enough for her'. I was devastated when she died. Why did – he – leave me? Did he tell you that?"

"He was offered a film part; he thought that if he didn't work he'd go insane with grief, so he took it."

"He told you that?"

"No. I'm guessing from what I know of him now. He doesn't show his emotions easily in real life, only on the screen can he let off steam in those wild and violent scenes in a way he won't do as himself. I'm saying that he made the movie to work through his grief."

"My grandparents thought he made the movie because he didn't really care. They told me that."

Molly looked at him with compassion.

"And what ten year-old boy would doubt Gran and Gran'pa?"

"Exactly. I grew up believing that he abandoned me. I'm not convinced yet that he didn't. But, you've given me food for thought."

"There's one other thing that he told me. He heard about your graduation from University in a round about way and went, because you were still his son and he wanted to be proud of you – and you cut him dead."

Richard nodded.

"I remember. I was so shocked and embarrassed to see him, I turned away. When I looked back he'd gone. I thought at the time that was typical of him – I was so unimportant, he couldn't be bothered to stay. You're trying to tell me I was wrong."

"Very wrong. He was very hurt. Now, he pretends he doesn't care whether he ever sees you again; he calls you an 'insufferable stuffed shirt' – Richard moved angrily – yes, and when you first came in I found myself agreeing with him," Molly said quickly. "Now I'm beginning to see signs of humanity. I'm sorry if I'm too blunt for you, it always was a failing of mine."

"You," said Richard, "and this – baby – you're carrying make quite a difference to my thinking. I need time to assimilate all this."

"Take all the time you need. You can move into the spare room."

"I'm booked in at the Hyatt."

"Then get on the 'phone and un-book yourself. Good grief, where else would you stay but here? – It's your home."

"And what will… your husband… say when he comes home and finds me installed?"

Molly grinned suddenly.

"Oh, he'll shout and stamp his feet a bit to, cover up his real feelings, but that's just the actor in him, you can ignore it. He'll come around. Let's go into the kitchen and get Mavis to make us some coffee."

Richard was drinking his coffee in the living room, contemplating the view, and Molly was in the kitchen with Mavis when Harry's car swept into the drive. Molly went quickly – as quickly as she could – down the four steps to the front door and met Harry as he came in.

"Darling!" She greeted him and he kissed her first and then put his hands on the swelling of the pregnancy and said softly,

"Hi, Caroline,"

"There's someone to see us," Molly said very quietly and turned her head. Harry followed her gaze.

"My God!" he said. "What the hell are you doing here?" He mounted the stairs and stood nose to nose with his son. "If you've been bothering my wife –!"

"I've no more bothered her than you've bothered with me over the past fifteen years –!"

"Wait a minute," Molly slipped between the two men, put a hand on each chest and pushed them apart. "Even boxers are civilized enough to shake hands before they come out fighting-
-"

"Molly, you keep out of this."

"I'm damned if I will. You're my husband and he's your son and I'm smack in the middle. For heaven's sake look at each other and say Hallo or something."

Harry turned away abruptly and went to the liquor cabinet.

"What d'you drink?" he asked curtly.

"Scotch."

He poured two large drinks and came back across the room.

"So," he said, looking the younger man up and down. "Little Richard has come home. What d'you want?"

"I want to know where I stand now you're married again. I didn't come for money. I didn't even want to meet you."

"I'll bet you didn't. Daddy never was good enough for you, was he? Just wanted to see what kind of a cheap trollop I'd married, I suppose. Well, there she is. What d'you think of her? eh?"

"That's a rotten thing to say in front of your wife."

"She knows I love her," said Harry harshly. "Don't you judge me. You don't know me."

"And whose fault is that?"

"Not mine, by God!" Harry shouted. "Those damn' grandparents of yours maybe –"

"Hold it," Molly interrupted strongly. "Let's not rush this. Richard's staying with us for a few days."

"The hell he is."

"I invited him. He's my stepson –"

"Not in my house. Go find a hotel."

"It's my house too, damn you."

"I'll go, of course," said Richard hastily,

"No! Harry, for God's sake, this is your son. Please! You held him when he was a baby, took him walks, taught him to ride a bike – he's not a stranger, not an enemy!" The men glared at each other, tight-lipped. "Richard, this is your father, he rocked you in his arms once, helped you take your first steps, and took you to school. Have you no... can't you... you're behaving like two stupid... " She ran out of words.

A wetness came between her legs and Molly turned and walked carefully out of the room, her thighs tight together. In the bedroom she pulled down her panties and looked at the show of blood on them. That's why, she thought, that's why the baby's so low, why I feel so odd. She washed herself, put on clean underwear, pulled on her jacket and picked up the small ready-packed suitcase, and returned to the living room. The men were talking, but not quite so loudly or aggressively as before. Molly did not hear the words for she was already partly removed from their world, beginning to experience the deep inner involvement of the woman in labour. She stopped in front of Harry and said in a calm voice,

"Harry, take me to the hospital, please."

He stared at her. "You mean –?"

"I mean I'm having the baby. "And no," she added quickly, "it's nothing to do with him being here. It started before he arrived."

Harry put down his glass, his face apparently impassive but his eyes tender and concerned: he put his arm around her waist, picked up the case and walked her out of the front door without a word or a backward look.

Richard stood in the middle of the room, nonplussed, not knowing whether to go or stay, feeling isolated and unreal, and emotionally drained. Two children came in, identical but of different sexes, and all three stared at each other.

"I'm Ken and she's Sue. Who are you?"

"You look like Harry," said the girl.

"I'm... related to him."

"Oh, then you must be our stepbrother."

"Yes," he said reluctantly. "I suppose so."

"Where's our mother?" the boy asked.

"She went to the hospital."

"To have the baby?"

"I think so."

"Oh, wow! Let's go tell Rob." They started out of the room, stopped in the doorway. "If you're staying in the spare room," Ken said, "don't open the bottom drawer of the dresser. Sam's in there."

"He's hinerbating," said Sue.

Richard smiled for the first time since entering the house, changed his mind about going to the Hyatt and decided to share the guest room with "hinerbating" Sam.

Chapter Twelve

Caroline

"Sombre-faced actor Harry Wentworth seen entering St. Paul's Hospital this morning carrying a huge bunch of flowers. His wife Molly was admitted to the Maternity Wing last night."

Dr. Pennington gestured to the nurse 'no more', pulled down his surgical mask and turned to Molly on the delivery table.

"I'm sorry," he said. "I'm so sorry, Mrs. Wentworth."

"She's dead?" He nodded. "Why?" she asked flatly.

"She died in the birth canal – asphyxiated – the cord was around her neck and constricted–"

"Let me see her." He heard the steel in her voice and where he would have demurred with another woman with Molly he acquiesced, and brought the small discolouring bundle to the side of the table.

Molly raised herself on one elbow and looked sadly, tearless, down at the little purple face.

"Like Harry," she said. She touched the cheek with one finger, a mother's caress. "Good-bye, Caroline." She lay back, tired, so terribly tired. Quickly the nurse took the dead infant. "Where's Harry?"

"In the waiting room. Do you want me to tell him, or do you –"

"Yes. Please. Now." The doctor nodded, stripped off his gloves, glad of an excuse to leave the scene of his failure (as he saw it), pulled off his apron and went out in his greens.

"Wentworth," he said, his face showing his news before his tongue did. "I'm sorry, but your daughter was stillborn. We did all we could to revive her –"

"Stillborn, what d'you mean stillborn?" Harry's voice was rough and angry.

Pennington swallowed.

"It was a long hard labour. She died in the birth canal."

"There was nothing you could do?"

He hesitated a fraction of a second. "No." There had been, of course. It was his fault, he knew it. He was afraid of Harry's anger.

"Let me see her." The same words Molly had used.

"Very well."

Dr. Pennington brought the bundle to the door of the delivery room, pulled back the blanket. Harry took the baby, cradling it against him with one big hand, touching the little blue face with the other. His own face was granite. "Caroline," he said.

"Why did she die?" he barked.

"We don't know for sure."

"Find out," he thrust the baby back at the doctor.

"An autopsy? Very well. Your wife is fine; she said –"

"Fuck my wife!" Harry said harshly and turned on his heel and strode away down the corridor.

Dr. Pennington showered and changed. It had been a long second stage of labour, twelve hours, on and off; he was tired, there were patients waiting in his office and he was conscious of having failed Molly Wentworth. Depressed and guilty he went in to see her in her private room.

Molly was clean and tidy, in a fresh bed and a fresh gown, her hair combed, her eyes dry; her womb empty of the baby that until a few hours ago had lived and moved and grown in there. She was alone.

The doctor – unprofessionally – sat on the edge of the bed,

his back to his patient, his head bent.

"I'm so sorry, Mrs. Wentworth," he began.

Oh God, Molly thought, he wants me to comfort him. She put her hand on the doctor's arm.

"It's all right, Dr. Pennington. I know you did all you could."

"No! I didn't. I should have foreseen the difficulty, I should have insisted on an Caesarean Section."

"I said no to that," she reminded him gently. "I'll take that responsibility. It was just my body that was inadequate – again." She could not keep the note of bitterness out of her voice.

"The twins came so easily."

"The twins were different," she reminded him. "The whole pregnancy was different, remember? But I'm nine years older. I was too old. The equipment was too worn out, I shouldn't have let it happen."

"Mrs. Wentworth," the doctor took a deep breath, turned to face her, "there's more than just the dead baby. I have to tell you, you should never get pregnant again, there's damage –"

She held up one hand.

"It doesn't matter. I have my family – my husband."

Their eyes met. Do you? She forced a cheerful smile. "He'll go to the nearest bar for a drink, then he'll be up to see me," she said with a confidence she did not really feel. Poor Harry, he would be angry and sad and bewildered and resentful and trying to cope in the only way he knew how, trying to be strong and masculine. But why couldn't he come to her when she needed him so badly? Why? Didn't he know how badly she would be feeling, for him as well as for herself? Didn't he know she needed his strength, his reassurance, and his shoulder to weep on?

The doctor was still wrapped in his own problem, reaching at straws.

"He asked for an autopsy. There may have been a defect we didn't know about –"

Again Molly touched his arm.

"Do it," she said. "If it'll help." It won't help me. Dead is dead. My baby, my Caroline, Harry's child is dead. She lay quietly, reassuring the doctor, smiling a little, tiredly patting his sleeve.

"You're a wonderful woman, Mrs. Wentworth. I appreciate your courage and your understanding." He stood up. "Now you need some rest."

She smiled with her teeth, her soul writhing in a paroxysm of grief on the graves of her four aborted foetuses and Caroline.

"Thank you, doctor," she said. "For all you tried to do."

He left the room with his head up, refreshed, grateful. In the corridor he recognized Rob, waiting, not yet having heard, and told him the bad news.

"How's – my mother?" Rob asked, not caring much about the baby.

"Being very brave, Rob. It's a rough one – she'll need some help."

"Can I –?"

"No, I think not, not until tomorrow. What she really needs now is her husband."

"Isn't he there?"

"No. He was very upset. He went – out."

"Out?"

"Of the hospital. For a drink, I believe."

"Harry left Mum," Rob asked incredulously. "At a time like this he left her to go for a drink?"

The doctor nodded.

"Perhaps you could go and find him, son, and bring him back. He's the one who can help her now."

Rob was dumbfounded; he left the hospital confused and uncertain what to do. A drink meant a bar. He would have to look in the bars nearby – but he was too young to go into bars. He stood on the sidewalk outside St. Paul's hospital and looked up and down Burrard. The Century-Plaza was to his left, the Burrard directly across the road. He tried the Century-Plaza first, walking into the bar as nonchalantly as he could, going from one end to the other, looking quickly around him as he went. No luck. Across the road the same thing. Now where? The only other hotels with bars he could think of were all further down Burrard and down Georgia. Grimly he set off on foot. At the Hotel Vancouver he was escorted out of the upstairs bar but in the dimness of the pub atmosphere of the Red Barrel downstairs he slipped in unnoticed as a minor. When a waiter looked at him questioningly he decided to ask.

"Harry Wentworth?" the man said over the blare of the entertainer's organ plus the skirl of tape-recorded bagpipes, "sure I know him. Yeah, he was here a while ago, had a couple of drinks and left. On a bender by the look of it."

"I have to find him. Where d'you think –"

"Try the Hyatt or the Henry V in the Georgia, or down the other way to the Ritz. You'd better be quick though, he was drinking fast."

Feeling sicker and angrier by the minute Rob ploughed on from bar to bar. After drawing a blank at the Ritz he suddenly remembered that the Bayshore was Harry's home away from home. That meant more footslogging down Georgia, and time was slipping by and Harry was probably getting drunker by the minute, and Rob had no idea how to handle a drunken man.

The hunch paid off. Sitting alone in a dark corner of Annabelle's Rob found Harry, two beers and two shot glasses lined up in front of him. He sat facing the wall, hunched over, his hands on the table near the glasses.

Swallowing his apprehension Rob wound his way between the tables.

"Harry?" he said, his voice coming out in the treble range. He tried again. "Er – Harry – hallo?"

"What the hell you doing here? You're too young to be here. You know that?"

"Yes, sir, I know that."

"Then get out before they throw you out."

"I was sent – to ask you to come to the hospital –"

"Sent?" Harry said sharply, glancing up at him. "Who the hell sent you?"

Rob gulped, intimidated by the man's belligerence.

"The doctor. He said my mother needed you."

"He did, did he? Well, I need a drink more than I need her. You know that? Your mother – my effing wife – had a dead baby – my baby. Bloody baby's dead. Sit down kid, before someone sees you're only a kid. You don't care about the damn' baby, do you? I do. Never had a daughter before – damn bloody incompetent effing doctor let her die." He was still gripping Rob's wrist that he had grabbed to pull him down into a chair.

"Please, Mr. Wentworth – Harry – Mum needs you –"

"Mum needs me. The hell with Mum. She's no Mum. No Mum to any kid of mine. My Baby's dead, Rob, and you don't care a shit. She doesn't care –"

"She does, I'm sure she does!"

"Nobody cares but me. I care. I'm the only one that cares. My little girl is dead. Dead, dead, dead, dead… Why should a dog, a horse, a rat, have life and her not any? King Lear, my friend. Probably didn't know that, did you? I played Lear once." He drank a long draught of beer, tossed back the whiskey chaser. "He had a daughter – three daughters. Lucky bastard." His voice was rising.

"Please, Harry," said Rob again, sickened, disgusted, afraid, not knowing what to do. "Let me get a cab –"

"Got a cab – waiting."

"Then let's go back to the hospital."

"I hate hospitals!" he said it loudly, causing heads to turn. "Go away, kid. I'm busy getting drunk."

Rob's composure left him, the anger boiled over.

"How can you sit there getting drunk when my mother's alone in the hospital wanting you? You mean rotten selfish bastard, I hate you! It's her baby that's dead, too, and she went through hell having it, not you, and she's lying there alone and sad while you swill beer. I think that's disgusting! If you were any kind of a man you'd be in there with her, holding her hand, being nice to her. But you're not. You're not a real man at all, not like in the movies, you're nothing but – a – gutless – actor!" He spat out the last word as though it were a deadly insult.

Two waiters converged on the table and took Rob's arms.

"Come along, sonny, you've got no business in here, anyway. Leave the gentleman alone."

"Wait!" said Harry raising an imperious hand and rising somewhat unsteadily, giving Rob a look of surprised respect. "The nasty boy is right. We will leave together." He put his hand on Rob's shoulder for support and they wove through the tables to the exit, followed by many curious stares.

Rob found the right taxi and bodily pushed his stepfather into it, where he crunched down in a corner and covered his face with one hand. Rob wondered if his mother would really want to see her husband like this. Maliciously he thought, why not, it's about time she knew what he really was.

He pulled Harry into the hospital – after finding his wallet and paying the taxi-driver (the first time he had ever been into anyone else's wallet; it felt like trespassing in a very private place, but it had to be done) and stuffing it back into his jacket pocket. Then he took him up to the right floor in the elevator.

"Down there," he said. "Second door on the left."

He gave Harry a push and turned and left quickly.

Richard had spent almost twenty-four hours in his father's house and oddly, considering the emotions with which he had first entered it, he was beginning to feel as though he belonged there. He had spent much of the time getting to know his stepbrothers and sister, and Mavis Topham, and vicariously, through them, his father. Harry himself had been absent since he had taken Molly to the hospital, but his personality dominated the household, and it was not the personality Richard had expected.

When the doctor telephoned the news of the baby's death, and the fact that Harry had left the hospital immediately with Rob in pursuit, Richard had been as concerned as Mavis, and after a while had gone to the hospital himself to see if there was anything he could do. There was not. He was not even allowed in to see Molly – who at this point was apparently alone, which seemed a bad thing in the circumstances – since he was not a close relative. But he waited anyway; in case there might be some way he could help.

He had discovered that he liked his father's second wife; and his original opinion of his father was returning more strongly as the moments ticked by. He was facing the elevator when Rob manoeuvred Harry out of it.

Richard watched his father progress down the hospital corridor with something approaching disbelief. Harry's tie was hanging loose, pulled down and away from his collar, the top button of which was undone; his vest and jacket were unbuttoned too and his raincoat was pulled on carelessly over both, crooked, the collar turned in half-way around, and a spill stain prominent on the front; his hair was too short to be untidy but his unshaven chin showed a grizzle of grey that aged him ten years; there were bags under his red-rimmed eyes and all his blunt features sagged. He walked unsteadily, almost shambled, his hands a little out from his body ready to ward off the unfriendly walls. He was drunk.

He passed Richard without seeing him and lurched into Molly's room. Sick inside, and knowing that he should leave, yet Richard felt impelled by a sort of morbid curiosity to see what happened. He moved to the doorway and watched, fascinated and repelled by his father's complete change of image.

"Oh, God, Molly, you look awful," Harry said in a rough uneven voice.

Molly looked up and smiled wearily at the irony of the remark. Wordlessly she opened her arms. Harry fell across the bed, buried his head between her breasts and started to cry with difficult masculine sobs. She put one arm around his shaking shoulders, stroked his hair soothingly, looking down at him with a tender understanding that touched the watching Richard.

Once again Molly had to be the strong one, once again she had to comfort and sustain, once again she sublimated her own grief and despair to the effort of calming and re-stringing someone on the verge of coming apart. As she patted and rubbed, and crooned her words of comfort inside her head, she silently screamed; Oh God, when will it be my turn? When can I cry? When will someone give me strength?

Harry gripped her shoulders, raised his head and looked at her with unseeing tear-filled eyes.

"Dell!" he cried. "Don't leave me, Dell. Oh God don't die!"

Richard drew in a quick breath of horror, realizing that Harry was reliving his own mother's death, releasing anguish and sorrow that had never been expressed before – emotions that Richard had assumed his father had never felt. He experienced a rush of sympathy for Molly and the pain Harry's words must have given her, and admiration when Molly responded by stroking Harry's forehead and saying gently,

"It's all right, Harry, I'm not going to die. I won't leave you. I promise." Richard thought that her heart must be breaking and stepped into the room, intent on stopping his father from hurting her any further. Yet he could not be angry with him. He put a firm hand on his shoulder.

"Dad," he said. "Dad, let me take you home."

Molly's eyes flew up to his in surprise and Richard realized he was astonished as she was to hear himself use the affectionate term for his father.

"You're tired," he said, pulling Harry upright. "You need a meal and a sleep. And Molly needs to rest."

"Richie?"

"Yes, it's me, Dad, little Richie. Can you walk?"

"Oh God," Harry said with some self-disgust. "Probably not."

"Here." Richard pulled his father's arm across his shoulder. "Lean on me."

They turned towards the door and Molly whispered,

"Richard, be kind to him." Richard glanced back and nodded reassuringly.

There were things Molly had to get straight in her mind before she went to sleep. Did she resent, accept or appreciate the fact that Harry had been the weak one in need of support and comfort? Supposing he had been strong and self-sufficient-would she the have felt unneeded either by little dead purple Caroline or by Harry? Had his need given her a motivation that the death of the baby might have erased?

Everyone needs to be needed and wanted, Molly thought, and when he lurched in all unshaven and broken up at least I knew that I still had a job to do in the world. Poor Harry... dear Harry. Not Harry Wentworth the tough, craggy movie star, but the Harry that she knew, that she had recognized behind the actor's face soon after she had met him.

Calling her Dell – Molly pushed the thought away.

And nice Dr. Pennington, he needed to be helped over his sense of guilt and loss, and I was able to do that. Thinking of others kept me from wallowing in my own grief. Oh, how I longed to cry and beat the pillow –

And Harry – he called me Dell. Should I hate him for that? Should I want to kill him? Should I feel demeaned and insulted? He loved her too.

More than me?

Does it matter?

It was my arms that held him, my words that pulled him together.

But her name he called on – Oh God, help me! I love him but I am so hurt! Why?

Why should I be hurt? Perhaps I'm the only person he's ever expressed his terrible grief about losing Dell to? She must have been nice – maybe I should be flattered to be called by her name? No.

NO.

I am me and I need to be needed as me, not as a substitute her. Help me, God.

What will I say when he comes in tomorrow? Who will I see in his eyes? Will he remember? Will he try to apologize? How will I reply?

Why is life so complicated? Oh God, why did poor little Caroline have to die? Why do you give me so much to handle?

I wish I could cry now and wallow in my grief, but the feeling is all gone... I'm too tired... I just have to sleep....

She woke slowly feeling rested, and adjusted her mind to her surroundings by registering noises and smells. An after-pain started to cramp her womb and as it gripped her, deep and grinding, so the black hole of the loss of yet another baby opened before her. In her head she moaned; in her head she indulged in a primeval wail of grief. She opened her eyes and saw a man's knee close by, a hand resting on it. Harry. She reached out and gripped the hand and knew at once it was not Harry. The fingers gripped hers back. She raised her eyes up the waist, the chest, to the face.

"Richard?" she said quietly, curiously.

"Hallo, Molly." He released her hand. Offered to pull his away but she tightened her grip.

"Where is he?"

"At home in bed, asleep. I came back because I didn't think you should be alone when you woke up."

She noticed his stubble of beard.

"You mean you've been here all night?"

"Yes."

"There was a nurse... "

"I sent her home. I thought you might need someone 'family'."

Molly pulled herself up in the bed, looking at him, at his tired face, the younger version of Harry.

"Am I 'family' to you, Richard, already? Really?"

He reached for and took her other hand.

"Yes, Molly. You are. Your baby was my sister."

"Then help me. Oh God, Richard, please help me!" She wrenched her hands away from his and covered her face as a deep dry sob choked her. He stood by the high bed and gathered her against his chest, his arms right around her body, held her tightly. Secure, hidden, muffled, protected, Molly cried deep abandoned sobs- a private grief such as can only be shared with a stranger.

Richard made no attempt to comfort her with words; he merely stood and held her. He was one who did not need her courage or her strength or her pretense; his only need was to be useful to her. Presently Molly's crying eased and she wrapped her arms around his body and held onto him as a drowning person clings for dear life to a spar of driftwood. Only when her grip relaxed did Richard allow his arms to slacken. Gently, she disengaged herself and laid back against the pillows. Looking at her, Richard felt a deep compassion – comparable to, and as strangely warming as that he had felt for his father the night before. It was a new experience for him.

Later, Rob came to the room hesitantly. The pain of the baby's death was nothing to him, but his mother's pain promised to be hard to bear. He was embarrassed, he was afraid, he was shy, he was sure he was going to do or say the wrong thing. He was not sure he would know what to do or say if she cried a lot. He felt guilty about not being sorry about the baby dying. He still resented bitterly Harry's getting drunk, and making it necessary for him to drag him out of the pub. A man – a grown man – a big strong tough man like that should not have to be told what to do by a boy. He was not good enough for his mother. Surely, she could never love him after this?

"Come in, Rob."

"Hi, Mum. I'm – "

"It's all right, you don't have to say anything if you don't want – I understand. Thank you so much for coming."

"Are you all right, Mum? Really?"

"Yes," No, I'm not, damn it. I want Harry, not you. "Where's Harry?"

"Getting shaved, I think." Rob had seen Richard half carry him into the house, had heard him putting him to bed. It was infamous that his mother should have to remain married to a common drunk – a man who didn't even have the decency to go to his wife when their baby died – a shame – a – a – whited sepulchre! He was unaware that much of his thought showed on his face.

"Don't blame him too much, Rob," Molly said gently. "His first wife died; he knows what death is all about."

"But he was drinking –"

"I know."

"I had to – I had to – nobody else would – go in the bar and get him to come."

"That was you? Oh Rob, thank you so much for doing that!"

"I can't respect him anymore."

"For being human? That's not very fair, Rob. Please don't be a moralistic prig." He moved angrily. "And don't be a judgmental teenager either."

"How can you love him after that?"

How indeed? And you don't know the half of it, boy.

Molly swallowed and forced herself to sound calm.

"What's between Harry and me is private, Rob. You have to accept that. I can't share it with you. I love him. Please don't stop liking him because he didn't behave like a superman."

Rob bent his head. Moved his hands awkwardly.

"I'm sorry – it – the – baby – died. But I'm glad you're OK, Mum." A sudden totally unexpected wave of emotion engulfed him and he choked. Molly reached for his hand and held it tightly, while the boy turned his head away and wiped his eyes with the back of his free hand. "I'll be going now," he said gruffly. "The twins and Mavis are waiting outside." He squeezed her hand briefly and strode out without looking at his mother again.

Not yet, Molly cried silently, don't come in yet. Give me a moment please, God. But God didn't. There seemed to be no end to what he expected of her. And she wanted and at the same time dreaded Harry's coming.

Harry woke furry-mouthed and hung-over and with a deep inward pain, the kind you carry around like a hump upon your back. He had behaved badly, he had hurt people, he had revealed a side of himself that disgusted him. He was not the man he wanted people to know him as.

He shaved gingerly, wincing at the sound of the electric razor on his beard. As he dressed in clean shirt, tie and suit, so piece by piece, he assembled himself. When he was fully together he lifted his shoulders, grunted and went out to the kitchen.

There was a note beside the coffee maker. Everyone had gone to the hospital to see Molly; she had had a good night; she was doing fine. Richard was in the guest room, asleep. Please don't disturb him.

He opened the guest room door quietly anyway, and went in and looked down at his sleeping son – this man he had just met – noting he was still dressed and guessing why – and he saw not the likeness to himself, but to Dell. He saw Dell plainly, and somehow that was a good thing.

He drove to the hospital not knowing what he would – could – say to Molly, trusting that as soon as he saw her words would come. He knew what he had said the night before; it did not bear thinking on. In the lobby, because reporters were there and it seemed a good thing to do, he bought a mass of flowers, but when he got to Molly's room he looked at the flowers and realized they were nothing, merely a traditional gesture, meaningless, so he threw them on the chair and sat down on the bed. He cupped Molly's face in his big hands, his eyes holding hers.

"You are my wife," he said. "Your name is Molly. I love you." He kissed her gently, tenderly.

Molly knew at once that it was all he was ever going to say – no remorse, no apology, no explanation – and she struggled to accept that as she looked at the actor's face set in lines of suffering and sincerity, and heard the actor's voice, trained and properly modulated. He could not help his face and his voice, she knew, when he was in control. Last night had been real,

real grief, real fear, real need. Inside Harry Wentworth's famous actor's skin there was still a real person visible to her, and perhaps her alone, and because of that Molly put her arms around his neck, leant her forehead against his and said, tearlessly,

"And I love you. I'm sorry, Harry, My inadequate body –"

"Shhh." He put three fingers across her lips. "Don't ever apologize to me."

There were no more words, but the time would come in the not-too-distant future when he would be called upon to act out his apology.

Chapter Thirteen

The Mother-In-Law

"Canadian actor Harry Wentworth started work yesterday on a new feature movie at Cetapac's West Vancouver Studios. We understand wife Molly's mother, Margaret Bragg, prominent Calgary realtor is in town helping her bereaved daughter."

Mavis had been watching for the car and when Harry drove in she was waiting for him in the hall.

"She's here," she said.

"Hmm," Harry grunted. "Where?"

"In the bedroom with Molly."

He grunted again and went and got himself a drink from the buffet and took it out onto the sun deck. He was tired, as he had been every evening since going back to work following the baby's death. He worked a twelve-hour day at the minimum, counting make-up time, shooting interiors at the Cetapac West Van Studio, driving himself hard on purpose to blot out the reality of death. It was his way of coping, but it did not help Molly much. She spent the long days alone, swimming for hours at a time, and was usually in bed by the time he got back.

Now his mother-in-law had arrived for a long-promised (threatened?) visit, and he was in no mood to meet her.

He went back in for a refill and while he was making the drink became aware of the twins watching him with something less than approval. He glared at them and bared his teeth and snarled menacingly, daring them to make a comment, and was disturbed to see them both flinch. Damn, he'd overdone it. He went moodily back to the deck and sat down on the chaise-lounge. The children followed him out.

The flinch bothered him; they had never been afraid of him before, and he knew it was his fault, he had been remote and unapproachable for weeks since.... He had never expected to want children to like him; he no longer knew how to bridge the gap between them and him. It occurred to him, watching them watch him, warily, - and for the first time to his shame – that they might have been as hurt by the baby's death as he and Molly. Unaccountably he wished they would come to either side of his chair so that he could put an arm around each, but he could not make the first move by opening his arms so that they would come. He cleared his throat and looked away, as though dismissing them, and sipped his drink.

"Gran's here," Sue said.

"Uh-huh."

"She brought me a minicomputer," said Ken.

"Nice."

"She brought me a little sewing machine, but it doesn't work because she forgot the batteries." He heard the wistful disappointment in the girl's voice. Sometimes, he thought, adults are fools. He became aware that they were there for a purpose.

"What are you trying to tell me, kids?"

"It's about Gran," said Ken. "She's not like a real Gran."

"A real Gran?"

"He means," said Sue, "Like on T.V., with grey hair and old-fashioned dresses and aprons with toffees in the pockets."

"Granny Ash is like that."

"But not Gran Bragg."

"Is that bad?" Harry asked.

"No!" they chorused. "She's fun," said Sue. "She's diff'rent," said Ken.

"Well, thank you, my children," said a voice from the door, and Harry looked up quickly, "I'm relieved to hear that."

She was definitely not a TV grandmother; shorter than Molly with trimmer figure, her bright blonde hair was swept up on top of her head in a style that gave her height and elegance. In fact, elegance was the word that best described her whole bearing. She wore a coral coloured linen suit with a peach silk blouse underneath, and a delicate gold bracelet showing at one cuff. Her slim legs were enhanced by sheer nylons and high-heeled sandals. Harry knew that she had to be several years older than he but her features were so good and her make-up so skilful that she looked at least five years younger.

Harry stood up, holding the woman's gaze, which was unexpectedly hostile. Or was she just nervous? Or attracted to him? Few women were indifferent to Harry; many were apparently repelled by his dominant masculinity, and some attracted, and they were all a little afraid of him. Except Molly. And Wednesday. That thought dropped into his head unbidden, and he pushed it away without further examination. This woman was afraid of him, unlike her daughter whom she resembled only faintly. He was not prepared to like her.

"Harry Wentworth," she said, stepping out onto the deck and holding out her hand. "How exciting to meet you," she added coolly.

"Mother!" said Harry with heavy irony.

"No," she said, giving his hand a brief businesslike shake, "I think not. My name is Margaret Bragg. I would prefer you to call me Margaret."

"Very well. Margaret. Can I get you a drink?"

"Thank you. Whiskey and water, please."

When he came back with the drink Margaret Bragg had a cigarette in her hand unlit. The twins had gone. He put the drink on the railing and got out his lighter. She leaned towards him and cupped the flame with two slim brown hands. Her fingers touched his and she started as though she had been burned. Harry smiled grimly – he had felt the sexual charge too. He got out a cigar, bit it between his teeth and lit it. He loomed over the woman, purposely dominating her.

"You must wonder why I never came before."

"No," he said.

"I've been busy. I sell real estate in Calgary, you know."

"I know."

"I suppose it sounds like a lame excuse?"

"Too busy – for over a year? Yes. If you cared –"

"You don't have a high opinion of me?"

"My first mother-in-law was a bitch."

"I'm sorry. I hope I don't fall into the same category. I don't find being a mother-in-law any easier than being a grandmother. I mean, I'm not sure that I can play the part. I never had a role model. My mother-in-law, Mother Bragg, lives in the north and wears ski-pants and drives a snowmobile and shoots bears."

Harry laughed suddenly.

"Molly never had a chance, did she?"

"A chance?"

"To be ordinary. With a mother and grandmother who are also one-of-a-kinds."

"Do you love her, Harry?"

"Yes, Margaret," he said with barely concealed anger at being asked. "I love her. Very much."

"I'm glad. She needs to be loved. I find it hard sometimes to comprehend that Harry Wentworth – the Harry Wentworth – actually fell in love with and married my daughter."

"What's so hard? Don't you think she's lovable?"

"Because," she said, looking him in the eyes. "I was a fan of yours when she was just a child. I've seen every movie you ever made, every TV series you ever did. When my husband died and your wife died, marrying you was my fantasy." She turned away. "I'm sorry. I didn't mean to tell you that."

"Why not?" said Harry lightly. "I'm flattered."

"That's why I didn't come before." Her voice got thick suddenly and she put down her drink and her cigarette and covered her face with both hands. "I didn't want to spoil it for Molly. God help me, I was jealous as hell." She drew a deep shuddering breath, her poise quite gone. "I didn't mean to do this either."

Harry leaned on the railing beside her, his shoulder

touching hers, understanding now the fear masked as hostility, and decided she was not so different from Molly at all, and liked her. He waited patiently, sipping his drink and saying nothing.

Presently she found a handkerchief in her jacket pocket and wiped her eyes delicately.

"Goodness," she said briskly, "how terribly juvenile of me, no wonder the twins think I'm a weird grandmother."

He ignored that.

"Why did you come now?" he asked.

"Because of the baby. Molly's letters have been so depressed. I had to come and see how she really was. It didn't sound as though you were helping much." It was a pointed accusation.

"I'm filming," Harry said shortly. "We have a schedule and a budget to keep to, Molly knows that." He looked away, closing the conversation.

Molly's mother was not deterred; in command of herself now she remained cool. She smoked thoughtfully, and looking at her out of the corner of his eye, Harry realized how long it was since he had enjoyed a companionable smoke side by side with a woman – Molly being a nonsmoker. Unexpectedly he heard himself saying,

"She was my baby too."

"I know. At first when Molly told me she was pregnant I was very angry with you – in fact I still am."

"Why?"

"Didn't you know her history of miscarriages?"

"Yes."

"At her age – your age- I thought you were both too old to start a family again. How could you have let it happen?"

"How? Are you so old, Margaret Bragg, you've forgotten how: It happened. Neither of us meant it to."

"Maybe you didn't realize how deeply Molly was hurt when she lost those babies all in a row."

"I realized. She told me. D'you think we married without knowing anything about each other?"

"Yes." Her short answer took him by surprise. He watched an eagle slowly circling the treetops below them, drew on his cigar and considered.

"We knew – know – enough. Not everything. But enough."

"I know more about you than Molly does, Harry. I know the parts you played, the films you made; I watched you grow on the screen."

"You like my films?"

"Yes."

"That's more than Molly does – you know that?"

"I know it. It proves I have better taste, doesn't it?"

"No. She's right. Most of my films are crap. Entertaining – but crap."

"You shouldn't say that. You're an admired and respected actor. You've done so much for the Canadian film industry, Harry –"

"Hah!" he grunted. "Your bias is showing, Margaret."

"Well," she felt herself, a woman of nearly sixty, blushing, and was both embarrassed and pleased at the same time to know that beneath her polished exterior her sexual fires still burned warmly. Harry grinned a wolfish grin, sensing her discomposure, but had the grace to make no comment.

"She doesn't know about your wife, either, does she? I remember the accident. I remember how the whole country suffered with you through that. She doesn't"

"She doesn't need to," Harry retorted. "My relationship with Dell has nothing to do with my marriage to Molly."

"I think it does. And your son – you had a son –"

"Molly knows about him."

"Where is he?"

"Here. Grown up and practising law somewhere in the city, I think."

"You don't know?" Margaret was incredulous.

"No, I don't know, because he only came a few weeks ago and I've been busy. My relationship with my son is none of your damn business, Margaret. You're beginning to sound like a prying mother-in-law."

"I'm sorry, that was the last thing I meant to do. I just want to be sure my daughter has the right man this time around. How much do you know about Tom, her first husband?"

"As much as she knows about Dell. That's as much as I need to know. It's not my business."

"Then you must know that poor Molly –"

"Don't say 'poor Molly' in that condescending tone," Harry interrupted roughly. "She may be a child to you, but she's a woman to me, and not 'poor' in any sense."

"Touché. Let me rephrase that. Molly seems to have a propensity for things to go wrong in her life. My husband used to say that when she was born she had a label around her neck that said 'Warning; this model will attempt to self-destruct at regular intervals." Harry chuckled. "I see you recognize the pattern. When she was a baby she tried to squeeze out of her crib and got her head stuck between the bars and we had to saw her out. Then she swan-dived out of her high chair and took six stitches in her chin. When she was six she managed to get the car in gear and drove it through the back of the garage – two black eyes. And school – Harry, I could write a book about the calls I got from her teachers, I had to go on my knees and practically sob to get them to let her stay in class. When she got the Scholarship Award from the Lt. Governor and gave him a five-minute speech on the inadequacies of the Provincial education system, I could have sunk through the floor – she was lucky he didn't snatch the cheque back. She almost missed her graduation from U.B.C. because she was thrown in jail for being in a parade protesting nuclear warfare and obstructing the police; she only got out by convincing the judge that she had meant to be in a parade supporting Native Indian Rights and had got into the wrong group by mistake – you're looking surprised?"

"I am. I didn't know Molly had a degree."

"Oh, yes, Molly was a bright girl, Honours English. Then she threw it all up to marry Tom Ash and he almost broke her as a person. Quite apart from the babies – one after the other, four miscarriages. I can't forgive Tom for putting her through that. I think it was only the twins surviving that kept her from losing her feeling of self worth. So now do you see why I am anxious to see if you're going to be a good husband to her? She needs a lot of loving, Harry."

"And I'm getting it, Mother, whatever you think."

They both turned quickly, guiltily, wondering how much she had heard, to face Molly in the doorway. She was, for the first time in weeks, dressed for dinner. She gave Harry a reassuring look.

"You're up!" Margaret said with a false gaiety to cover her dismay at being caught acting like a protective mother checking-up on her son-in-law.

"And dressed, too," Molly said crisply. "Aren't I a good girl?"

"Is this in my honour?" Margaret asked.

"You bet. Also self defence. I happen to know you've had a crush on Harry for years."

There was a moment's astonished silence, and then Harry laughed – the first time he had laughed since the baby died. He took an elbow of each of the too women and led them indoors.

Crouched under the window of the den that opened onto the sun deck and having heard everything, the twins looked at each other, speechless. It was a lot to take in, particularly their own apparent importance to their mother.

"Gran?" said Sue, dealing with simpler concept. "Gran had a crush on Harry?"

"Must have been a joke," said Ken. "She's much too old."

But I've got a crush on him, Sue thought, and I'm not too young.

Chapter Fourteen

Molly takes a Swim

*"Nice to see Molly Wentworth, wife of actor Harry Wentworth –
out of circulation since the stillborn death of their baby – down at
Third Beach the other day swimming with her famous husband."*

Dr. Pennington tapped his teeth thoughtfully with the end
of his pencil, wondering what to do. He called in his nurse.

"Mrs. Reed, can you get hold of Harry Wentworth?"

"I doubt it, Doctor, I believe he's filming right now. I could
'phone his home and leave a message with his housekeeper".

"Not good enough. I think – you saw Mrs. Wentworth? – I
think it's imperative I speak to him now."

"I'll do my best, doctor."

"Get a message through to him to call me immediately, and
when the call comes through, pull me from wherever I am,
whatever I'm doing."

Mrs. Reed called Mavis and Mavis called Richard and
Richard called the studio. Pulling all the authority he could
muster both as a lawyer and as Harry's son, Richard insisted
that Harry be fetched to take his call.

Thus Harry was an angry man when he got through to Dr.
Pennington.

"What the hell's the idea, Pennington?"

"I'm worried about your wife, Wentworth."

"Worried! You pull me off the set to tell me you're worried! She was fine when I left her this morning."

"Yes, she's just been in for a check-up, and you're right, she's fine. Physically. It's her mental state I'm worried about."

"Mental state?" Harry said sharply.

"There's a syndrome we call post-partum blues that many new mothers experience some weeks after they've given birth. Even when they have fine healthy babies women can be subject to this deep depression. Now, in your wife's case she not only lost her baby, but it was the fifth baby she has lost. The others aborted in much earlier stages of pregnancy, this one was actually full-term, and then –"

"Yeah. I know," Harry cut in brusquely, "it was my baby too, remember? Get to the point."

"Have you noticed that she's been quiet, withdrawn, lately?"

"Noticed? No, not particularly. I'm a pretty busy man, Doctor Pennington, this new picture –"

"You must have seen something."

"Look, Doc., I wasn't very impressed by the way you handled my wife's delivery – as you know – and I was pretty cut up when my daughter died. I was offered a part soon after and I took it because to me work is an anodyne to pain. When I'm working I don't notice anything around me. That may be wrong –"

"I understand, believe me," the doctor cut in, "and that's just the point. She's had nothing to do for these past weeks except sit around and realize what a failure she is."

"She's no failure."

"I know that, and so do you. But to her she is a failure – a failure as a woman, as a wife and as a mother. She said so."

"And?"

"Wentworth, I'm afraid she's suicidal," the doctor said heavily.

"Suici— Where is she now?"

"On her way to take the twins swimming, she said."

"My God," said Harry flatly. "You think she's suicidal and you let her leave your office to go swimming." He hung up far,

far too angry to shout. He left the studio at a run without even leaving a message.

"Where is she?" he yelled, bursting into the hall.

"Molly?" said Mavis, coming out of the kitchen, taken aback by Harry's sudden appearance and in such an evident state of shock. "Why she – she took the twins down to the beach a few minutes ago –"

"The beach – which beach?"

"Why, Third Beach, I guess, that's where they always go, isn't it? What's the matter? For God's sake, Harry, what's the matter? The doctor –"

"The doctor called," Harry said, hurrying into the bedroom and beginning to change, "to tell me that Molly is suffering from post-partum blues – you know what that is? Yes, I thought you would – and that she is suicidal. Suicidal, Mavis – and she's gone to the beach. To swim."

"Oh, my God!" Mavis covered her mouth with her hand. "She wouldn't – but it's true she's been awfully depressed – oh, Harry!"

"Yeah," he said grimly. "Oh, Harry." He pulled on slacks over his swim trunks, grabbed a jacket and came out of the room. "Call Richard – tell him. I'm going straight there."

The traffic crawled all the way to and over the Lion's Gate Bridge –— it crawled. And that gave him time to think and remember signs and hints of Molly's depression that he had conveniently ignored, and the statement Margaret Bragg had made when she had come to visit about Molly losing her feeling of self-worth, and he kicked himself. I should have seen, I should have seen –

It was a glorious sunny day and not unexpectedly the Third Beach car park was full, so Harry double-parked and to hell with it. He ran down the steps and across the Sea Wall and onto the sand, looking this way and that for Molly and the twins. The children were standing at the water's edge, their buckets and spades in their hands, looking out to sea. They showed no surprise when Harry stopped beside them in a flurry of sand.

"Where is she?" he asked urgently.

"Out there," Ken pointed.

"She said she was going for a swim," said Sue. "A long

swim."

"She said there was money in her purse if we wanted anything," said Ken.

"She kissed us," said Sue. "She never kisses us on the beach."

Harry's hands were shaking as he stripped off his slacks and jacket. The swimmer's head they had pointed to was a long way out. A very long way. He was not even sure if he could swim that far.

"Well," he said with assumed cheeriness, "I guess I'll just go in and join her."

"D'you think she's all right?"

"Your Mum's a good swimmer, you know that. It's just that... so soon after having the baby she may not be as strong as she thinks. You stay here, kids." He started into the water.

When Molly waded in and started swimming she had no clear idea of why she was there or what she was doing. The water was a familiar element in which she could be alone; she could think – or not think. Today she did not mean to think – thinking was painful, thoughts were bitter – she just wanted to swim and swim for ever, to swim away from the shore, from life, from responsibilities, from failures; to stroke and kick and stroke and kick and breathe and pause endlessly until there were no more strokes or kicks or breaths left. To be so tired, so alone, so comfortable that not stroking or kicking or breathing would be easy – even desirable. Despite herself she began to think.

Rob doesn't need me. (Sometimes I think he's embarrassed by me, would rather not have me as a mother.) The twins are old enough to get along without me, they'll adjust whatever happens, they always have, they're good kids that way. (Molly took no credit for their self-reliance.) Harry – Harry was long enough without me, I can't mean much to him, anyway, he still thinks of Dell (pain, pain) and his work – is acting work? – is more important than his home life, always has been; besides, he really likes younger women, glamorous elegant women, healthy women. I don't know why he fell for me; it's a mystery, a surprise, a glorious serendipity, not logical or reasonable. Who wants a barren woman? A forklift that won't lift, a typewriter without a ribbon… they kill chickens that don't lay eggs… they junk cars that don't run. A small wave slapped her in the face and broke her fanciful line of thought, and she glanced back at the shore.

I'm doing well… it's quite a long way away and I don't feel a bit tired – I can go on for ever, out into English Bay until it's too far to turn back, then I can float for a bit and then let myself sink – slowly – and spiral down into the calm green depths. Oh, beautiful Mother Sea, back into your womb – into the cradle of the deep, endlessly rocking – oh, wine-dark sea – the multitudinous seas incarnadine – the sea, the sea, the sea… She stroked in rhythm to her thoughts.

I hate my useless body. I hate my useless life. Is hate too strong a word? I despise? I dislike? I don't care for – I don't care about?

Harry.

She pushed his name away. Tom will say he expected no less, it's typical of her, Molly never could – what? Cope, manage, be successful? When he found out what I was like he didn't love me anymore. I am not lovable.

Harry.

Harry can't love me – not really. Maybe he was sorry for me. Harry. I don't know how I got so lucky for a while. But my luck never lasts. It's over now. It's a lovely day. I might just as well swim and swim and swim forever.

The twins.

They've got the money in my purse, they know where to get the bus.

When Harry entered the water he went straight into a fast and powerful crawl and for five minutes never even lifted his head. When at last he did, and paused long enough to locate Molly's head low in the water still far ahead of him, then he realized he would have to pace himself, he was not as young or as fit as he used to be. Short bursts of high energy he could manage, a long sustained effort was another thing. He slowed his stroke, lifted his head more often, slowed his breathing.

Dammit, Molly, don't do this to me.

I lost Dell. Not you too. Please, not you too.

He cursed her roundly in his head, loving her with every curse word, cursed her for finding him, attracting him, fascinating him, loving him. Cursed her for not believing in herself. Cursed her for being so hurt, so vulnerable. Never even thought of cursing her for losing their baby. He cursed her for not sharing her feelings with him, cursed her for hiding her depression, cursed her for being all kinds of a selfish-bitch fool.

And gradually he gained on her, for she was swimming slowly now, a leisurely breaststroke, head and shoulders high in the water. He wanted to shout to her, but decided he was too far away, it might frighten her, might precipitate a burst of stronger swimming away from him. Would she really swim away if she knew he was behind? Surely, not? But – in her state of mind – maybe. He had better not risk it.

He lost sense of time; they seemed to have been swimming forever, she ahead, he behind trying to catch up, the distance between never changing. But it was, inexorably he was getting nearer. He was also getting more tired. The thought dropped into his mind: if we don't turn soon we'll never make it back. Not making it back was unthinkable. So now was the time to make the effort to catch up with her – now or never, he thought grimly, forcing his arms and legs into a faster stroke. Coming up directly behind her seemed to be a poor idea so Harry swung wide to the right and made a half circle so that he came gradually up on her right shoulder and slightly ahead of her.

"Brad," the lifeguard on the beach stood on the sand at the base of the high chair and spoke to his partner up on the seat, "can you see two swimmers way out there? A little to your left?"

Brad had the binoculars to his eyes.

"Yeah. I've been watching them. He's about caught up on her now."

"That's Harry Wentworth the movie star."

"No kidding?"

"I recognized him when he came down the beach. I guess the woman's his wife, and see those two kids at the water's edge? They haven't moved since the woman went in – I think they're hers. I've seen them down here before. Usually they play."

"She's swimming awful slow. Wait – yes, they've both stopped now, they're treading water. What d'you want to do, Jim?"

"I think I'll take the boat out. Got your walkie-talkie?"

"Yeah."

"Keep an eye on them. If they look to be in any kind of trouble call me up. If I'm halfway there I've twice the chance of getting to them in time. I've never lost anyone off a beach of mine yet, and I sure as hell don't want to start with a movie star and his wife!"

"They look to be all right – they're floating now."

"Maybe – now – but they're a hell of a long way out for two older people." (Molly and Harry would have winced at that.)

Harry came up on Molly as he had planned, to her right and a little ahead of her.

"Hi," he said gruffly.

She looked at him without surprise, her face remote, unusually calm, living inside herself, almost trance-like.

"Oh," she said. "Hallo."

He slipped into a sidestroke, keeping station a little ahead of her still, so that they could look at each other without turning their heads.

"How far are you going?"

All the way, her mind said. "I don't know," her mouth said.

"Mind if I join you?"

She swam on, not answering, her mind dragged back to the real world unwilling to respond, and Harry dropped back until they were shoulder to shoulder. He had a mad vision of himself knocking her out and life-saving her back to the beach, but even as he had it, he knew it would never work – if they did not both drown, at the least she would never forgive him.

"Beautiful day for a swim," he said after a while.

She glanced at him then, and the nagging awareness of his presence, of something being wrong with him being there gradually obtruded into her reluctant mind. She swam; after a while she asked,

"Why are you here?" the words coming slowly, in rhythm with her strokes, knowing he should have been at the studio working, not knowing why he was not.

"Nobody should swim alone."

"I like it."

"I don't," he said, and she knew he was saying something else but was too tired to examine the thought and respond, so she swam on.

Harry said matter-of-factly,

"We're a long way out. If we go much further I doubt if I'll make it back."

Molly glanced towards the beach and assessed the distance as still within her range.

"You'd better turn then," she said. But he swam on, going ahead of her by half a length. She put on a spurt and drew level again. "Harry," she said, "turn back."

"I'm O.K."

"For how long?"

"For as long as it takes."

"But you said... you may not make it back if we go on."

"Don't want to go back alone, Molly. I'll go on, if that's what you want.

And suddenly she knew what he was saying and the dead little nub of her comatose heart warmed and turned over and swelled and painful life came back to it.

"Dammit, Harry!" she said, "it's not. Stop. Wait a minute." She trod water and he stopped swimming and turned and faced her, treading water too, his face already showing fatigue. She wanted to say 'If you're ready to go on with me and drown, then I guess I'm ready to go back with you and live,' however painfully, but what she actually said was,

"You look tired, we'd better float a while," not realizing that her concern for Harry signalled a turning point in her life, a turning away from the inward thoughts consumed with self and out towards the needs of others, and her responsibility to supply those needs.

Obediently Harry flipped onto his back and floated, and as they spread-eagled there on top of the water like a giant two-headed eight-legged starfish Molly's fingers found his and interlaced with them lightly, and she said,

"Hold on, or we might drift apart," not aware until she had said it, of the symbolism of her words.

"Let's go," she said after a while, and they swam in silence, shoulder to shoulder, at the pace she set, and for fifteen minutes the shore got no closer, to Harry's eyes. "I think we're fighting an ebb tide," she said, "we'll lose ground if we rest. Are you O.K.?"

Harry's arms and legs were beginning to feel heavy, his breathing was not as good as it should have been, and the cold was creeping into him.

"I'm O.K.," he said, calling on his actor's skill to make his voice light and confident.

You're not, you liar, Molly thought, recognizing the voice, but she did not challenge him. Instead she dropped a little behind, the better to keep an eye on him. She was tired herself – more tired than she had ever been, swimming – probably because of her recent pregnancy – but not too tired. My resent pregnancy, she thought. My recent – useless – unproductive pregnancy (thinking helped the swimming). So I lost the baby (things were coming into perspective) but I have others, and I have him (she looked ahead to Harry labouring in the water, his head and shoulders low). He lost a baby too and he doesn't want to die. It's different for a man – is it? – he doesn't carry it. It's still his seed, his child; he saw her, he wanted her. And now he might drown (his stroke was getting uneven and splashy) and I might live – what irony if that happened. It won't happen. It's unreal. What the hell are we doing out here?

Molly reached and touched his shoulder and together without words, they turned on their backs and floated, their fingers laced as before.

They swam again, and now the shore was closer, the water calmer, even warmer – but not close enough for Harry. He had never been so tired in all his life. Fear was not a part of his nature, but anger, anger at the inadequacy of his body, anger at it's failure to respond to the demands he gave it, anger kept him going; anger made him slap at a wave that broke in his face.

"Harry," he heard Molly's tired voice behind him. "Don't

fight the sea – use it – go with it."

He grunted, nodded without turning his head. The sea was her element, he trusted her judgment, she led him from the rear. He was conscious of her presence there behind him, supporting him in more ways than one. That gave him confidence; but not the strength he needed. He turned on his back again.

"Got to rest. You don't need to. You go on."

Molly trod water near his head.

"No." That was all she said.

They swam on again, at Harry's pace, and now she kept station abreast of him, her eyes anxious, on him alone, not seeing the beach or the lifeguard's boat coming up to their right.

"You people need any help?" Jim's voice took them by surprise, the dark hull of the boat coming suddenly within arm's reach and instinctively Harry's arm went up and he grasped the gunwhale, and hung there panting, his pride saying 'No' his common sense saying 'Yes."

Molly went on swimming and Jim stroked gently on the oars to keep pace.

"Ma'am?" he said,.

"She's all right," Harry rasped. "I'm the one that needs the help." He had made his decision. "I'm coming aboard." He gathered his strength and managed to pull himself inboard over the stern, flopping into the boat awkwardly. Once in, though, his strength left him and he lay in the bottom for a few moments exhausted, and quite careless of what the lifeguard thought.

"Mr. Wentworth? Shall I bring her in?" Jim nodded his head towards Molly.

Harry sat up on the stern thwart, wrapping himself in the thick towel the lifeguard handed him, and looked across the water at his wife. She was swimming quite strongly now, apparently spurred by the sight of the beach and the knowledge that Harry was safe.

"No," he said, struggling to stop his teeth from chattering as reaction set in, and rubbing himself hard with the towel to stop the shivering. "No, leave her. She'll make it." Somehow, he added to himself. She has to do it on her own or there's no point to this whole fiasco.

Molly was having the same thought. If I can't make it all the way back on my own then I won't have truly made a decision. I could drown right here if I wanted to, but the damn lifeguard would probably save me. If he takes me in I'll feel I've cheated myself. I took myself out; I must bring myself back – all the way – my way. But oh God, I'm tired... She glanced at the boat and saw Harry watching her and broke her stroke to flutter a hand to him. He raised his fingers to his forehead and gave her an answering salute.

"I think," said Jim, noticing Molly's stroke slowing again, "I'll keep pace out here awhile, until she's a bit closer to the beach. Is that OK?"

"Yeah," said Harry, not taking his eyes off Molly's head. "That's OK, kid. I need the time to warm up, anyway. But let her take herself in. She has to prove something, you see – that she can do it, on her own. I wasn't out to prove anything. I just went for the swim and over-extended myself. Got it?"

The young man nodded, vaguely aware that he was being instructed in what to say to the press, and that what he was being told to say was only half the truth. He watched the actor curiously.

People on the beach had noticed them now; word had spread that it was Harry Wentworth out there swimming with his wife. Someone had recognized Molly, someone had recognized him, and someone had heard the lifeguards talking. Seeing the boat go out had alerted them, and seeing Harry climb aboard had intrigued them. They stood up now and wandered down the sand to the water and paddled casually, watching; some had binoculars to their eyes. They lined the beach.

Harry saw, and swore inwardly.

"Look," he said briskly," she's OK now. Let's get in quickly. Go as far to the right as you can."

"But your wife –"

"Is coming in to the left. I know. Do it."

"OK," Jim bent to the oars, having satisfied himself that the woman was in fact all right. Somehow one did what Harry Wentworth said, he thought: he has as much authority in person as on the screen.

A curious thing happened as they approached the shore --

the spectators, like filings attracted to a magnet drifted, slowly at first and then with increased urgency, over to the right hand end of the beach where the boat was obviously going to land and Harry Wentworth shrank under the towel. His face, which had regained its colour, drained again, exhaustion etched his eyes and mouth, his head lowered and his hands, under control a few minutes before, shook. Jim was aware that for some reason that was beyond him, his famous passenger was psyching himself back into the role of someone who had nearly drowned. Not for sympathy surely? Not Harry Wentworth – his image of a strong tough man's man could only suffer from this show of weakness – so, why? He glanced across the beach to where the woman, Mrs. Wentworth, was just slowly dogpaddling in, and noticed that apart from the two children who were wading out to meet her, the sand was empty. He looked at Harry with a new respect. For some reason (again unknown to him) he was deliberately diverting attention away from his wife, even at the risk of destroying his own image.

The young man warmed to Harry, and as the boat grounded on the sand, he leaned forward and said solicitously,

"Come along, Mr. Wentworth, let's get you ashore." And as he bent over and helped Harry stand, their eyes met briefly in understanding and Harry nodded minimally, and grunted his thanks – and made a friend for life.

Not trusting her legs to bear her weight, Molly swam slowly in until the water got too shallow, then she pulled herself along with her hands on the sand, pretending she was playing, pretending she was enjoying the water so much she did not want to get out. The twins waded on either side of her, their buckets and spades trailing in the water, looking at her with huge anxious eyes. She turned on her back in the wavelets at the water's edge and raised herself on her elbows.

"Where's everybody?" she asked, brightly – she thought – but actually the words dragged out of her in exhausted gasps.

"Watching Harry," said Sue, sitting down beside her.

"They think he nearly drowned," said Ken. "I heard them talking. Did he?"

"No, of course not. He just got tired."

"Are you all right, Mum? You went out so far, we thought –

"

"I'm fine, Sue," she said firmly. "Just fine."

"Why are you such a funny colour?" asked Ken.

"Colour? Oh – I guess I'm a bit tired too."

"It's almost green in places," said Sue, looking with clinical interest into her mother's face.

"On this side," said Ken, "it's kind of yellowy-blue."

Molly sat up and put an arm around each of them, enjoying the feel of their small, warm, living bodies.

"You rotten kids," she said, and they heard the recently unfamiliar warmth in her voice again and giggled.

"Have you stopped being sad, Mum?"

"I've swum it all away," she said, realizing for the first time how her depression had affected everyone around her.

"Oh, good," said Ken. "Can we have our ice creams now?"

"Of course, and get coffees for Harry and me."

She watched them scamper up the sand, and then looked across the beach to where the people were gathered in a crowd around Harry as he stepped out of the boat, the lifeguard's arm supporting him. He wasn't that tired, she thought. Why is he pretending? And then she saw the empty sand around her and it dawned on her that he was deliberately giving her privacy to recover in, drawing attention away from her landfall to his, and her heart cracked with gratitude and love.

After a few minutes, seeing that the drama was over and Harry Wentworth was all right, the crowd began to drift apart and spread across the beach again in two's and three's, and into the water to swim. And Harry came across the beach too, shedding his apparent exhaustion with each step.

He squatted on his haunches in the shallows facing Molly and they exchanged a long deep look.

He wanted to do three things, he wanted to take her by the shoulders and shake her until her teeth rattled and tell her never to do such an idiot thing again; he wanted to take her in his arms and hold her tightly and protect her with his strength; and he wanted to kiss her and make love to her and thank her for coming back. But, because they were under the scrutiny of the curious who always watch celebrities he did neither of those things; instead he stripped the towel from his shoulder and dropped it over her head and rubbed her dripping hair with seeming roughness, pushing her head this way and that. Molly braced herself with her hands behind her on the sand and felt the angry love in his touch.

Harry took the towel from her head and roughly dried her face, bringing the blood back to her cheeks, and when she opened her mouth to say Harry, I know what you did there – or whatever else she was going to say – he put three fingers over her lips and shook his head.

Some things between us will never be said, Molly thought, but we know they are there- they bind us, without words.

"How are your legs?"

"Like spaghetti."

"O.K. I'm going to pull you up and we'll put our arms around each other, and we'll walk slowly up the beach, like any loving couple. And nobody will know how tired we are."

And nobody will guess, Molly thought, how nearly she came to committing suicide and he to nearly drowning with her rather than live alone.

Harry took her hands and hauled her up in one swift movement, and then locked his arm around her waist, taking all her weight. Molly reached around his waist then – not a thing she had ever done before – loving the feel of her skin across his back, and they walked, strolled up the beach, and somehow while supporting her Harry managed to bend to one side and give the impression she was supporting him.

Then they lay face down on the blanket on the sand and Harry kept his arm across her shoulders, not wanting to stop touching her.

"Where are the kids?" he mumbled into the blanket.

"I sent them up to the Concession for ice creams."

He looked up then and spotted the twins hurrying down the steps, each with an ice cream in one hand and a coffee cup in the other, and behind them a city park policeman, and they were chatting to him and quite evidently leading him down the beach to the blanket.

"Shit," he said, with sudden realization. "I double parked."

And Molly laughed. Another day and he might have been annoyed. But not today. Today her laugh was music.

Chapter Fifteen

The Kidnapping

"Recent unexpected weekend visitors at a well known up-the-Valley lakeshore resort hostelry – craggy actor and his wife Molly. Dressed casually they were evidently hoping not to be noticed. Shooting on "Tiger's Eye" is apparently held up temporarily by disputes on the set."

It was difficult for Molly to work down at the Day Care Centre these days. Most of the women knew she was Harry Wentworth's wife and all they wanted to do was gossip about him and any other stars they thought she must have met through him. They found it hard to believe that her disinterest in 'show-biz' was genuine.

"What's this Wednesday Barnes like?" Nancy Lee asked one day when she came in to pick up her little girl.

"Wednesday? She's a pretty girl with a helluva big bust and a fantastic hairdresser," Molly quipped lightly.

"No – but I mean what's she like?"

"Like? A bit out of her depth, I think. I've only met her at a couple of parties, Nancy."

"They say –"

"Who says?"

"The movie magazines – they say this movie she's making with Harry will make her a big star."

"Oh," said Molly, non-committal. "I hadn't heard. I don't read those magazines, I'm afraid, but I suppose it could be true."

"It must be exciting," Nancy signed, "meeting stars and going to parties and watching the filming and going to the Studio, and all that."

Molly smiled. "I probably sound unbearably dull, but actually the few stars I've met have been just people, and I don't watch the filming, Harry doesn't like it, and I've never been to the studio yet."

"What!? But Cetapac's right there in West Van!"

"I know, but – how can I explain it? Look, if Harry happened to own a ball-bearing factory, I wouldn't go down and watch the ball bearings being made, because ball bearings don't interest me. Well, I've never been stage-struck, so watching Harry act really wouldn't be very exciting for me. The way I look at it, I married Harry not his job – and that's what acting is to him, a job."

"But Molly," said Nancy with the earnestness of a single parent who has been on Personal Growth Courses, "how can you appreciate your husband as a man unless you understand what he's doing for eight or ten hours every day when he's at work?"

It was a point, Molly conceded, that she had not hitherto considered. Perhaps she had been lacking?

She quizzed a tired-eyed Harry that evening.

"Can people visit the studio?"

"Mm-mmm. Wish they wouldn't though."

"Why?"

"Get in the way. Poke around. Ask silly questions. Besides, it takes away our mystery."

"The girls at the Day Care Centre can't understand why I've never been"

Harry glanced at her.

"You wouldn't be interested," he said shortly, and went back to his script, closing the subject.

But maybe I should be interested, Molly counselled herself;

maybe you'd like me to be, but don't want to force the issue.

The next day she telephoned Sam Price and made an appointment to be shown around the studio. No problem – being Harry Wentworth's wife opened doors closed to other people. Sam, always a little wary of her, showed her, in a whirlwind tour, cutting and editing rooms; sound stages, deserted and cavernous; property, costume and make-up departments, and, as a triumphant climax, the video-taping of a game show – which Molly found incredibly juvenile and boring.

"I thought Harry was shooting "Tiger's Eye" here," she said, as they left the hysterical competitors and sycophantic host to their game.

"He is, Molly. But that's a closed set. See that door?" They were walking back across the car park towards the main entrance and Office building. "The one that says 'Positively No Admittance'? That's "Tiger's Eye" in there. Val – the director, Val Pedersen – can't stand visitors on the set and neither can Harry – I thought you knew that. Especially when they're working with someone as inexperienced as 'Dear Joan'."

"Dear – You mean Wednesday Barnes?"

"Yes." Sam looked discomfited. "Wednesday – that was a slip of the tongue. You didn't hear it, did you?"

"No," said Molly gravely. "I didn't hear it, Sam. But couldn't I go in? I don't count as a visitor, do I?"

"Anybody is a visitor. Cast and crew only. And that means cast of the individual scene that's being shot. Everyone else waits in their dressing rooms. It's a very tricky movie – emotional, you know. Very sensitive material."

Molly raised sceptical eyebrows – it did not sound like the sort of film she associated with Harry. She thanked Sam for the tour, sat in her car till he had gone back to his office, and watched the 'Positively No Admittance' door. Her curiosity was undeniably piqued. Surely actors liked having an audience – wasn't that what acting was all about? So why all the secrecy? A man went to the door, pushed down the handle and walked in – so it was not locked, and there was no guard on the inside. Evidently the closeness of the set worked on the honour system.

Molly considered carefully. I can walk in as though I belong

there, watch, and then slip out. If anyone stops me I'll say I'm
Harry's wife – and anyway, the most they can do is ask me to
leave. And I am Harry's wife, she rationalized, and that should
give me some standing; maybe they'll even let me stay. That
is, if I want to.

Despite her rationalization, her knees were knocking by
the time she reached the door, but she knew that if anyone was
watching she must show no hesitation or indecision or
furtiveness, so she grasped the handle firmly, pushed it down
and walked in quickly and quietly, closing the door very gently
behind her.

It was dark by the door of the barn-like building, all the
lights being concentrated on a set some fifty feet away. Molly
stood very still trying to look like a shadow until she was sure
no-one had noticed her entry, then she slipped off her shoes
and tip-toed around the wall until she had a better view of
what was going on.

The set was evidently meant to be a cheap bed-sitting room
in the East End or on the waterfront; it was sleazy and tatty
and jumbled. Harry was sitting on the edge of the grubby bed;
he was wearing a soiled check shirt with a tear in one sleeve
and a button missing, stained and frayed jeans and beat-up
work boots. So much for the Harry Wentworth three-piece-
suit image, Molly thought. Most startling, however, when he
turned towards the dark place where she stood (and even
though she knew there was no possible way he could see her
through the glare of the powerful lights nonetheless she felt
naked and guilty under his gaze) was the huge livid bruise on
his forehead. It took her a moment to realize it was only make-
up.

Standing in the middle of the set looking somewhat
bewildered and uncertain was Wednesday ('Dear Joan') Barnes,
dressed as a stripper or a show-girl in a skimpy shiny dress
that showed off her twin attributes to their best advantage.

Molly couldn't hear from where she stood but it was
obvious that they were rehearsing a scene without the cameras
running. Harry lay back on the bed looking exhausted and
desperate; Wednesday came in through the door gaily, saw him
and stopped in mid-stride, surprised, frightened, even repelled.

She turned to leave and Harry leapt up and dragged her down onto the bed, speaking as he did so. Wednesday's legs flopped around like bent sticks and the director stopped the scene. Then her legs were all right but Harry apparently got his words wrong. Then it was something else; a light was changed, a microphone moved, a camera brought forward.

Molly stepped from foot to foot feeling the cold of the concrete floor through her nylons. Goodness, what a boring process. She was about to creep away and go back to the door, when the scene progressed a step further. The Harry character pinned the showgirl down and kissed her roughly and she put her hands on his chest and pushed him away. They did it several times and when they sat up Wednesday was laughing and Harry was grinning in that special wolfish way of his – and that part definitely was not in the script. Molly's mouth went dry and she swallowed quickly. Oh God, they're only acting – aren't they? It looked so real – so... pleasurable.

Evidently Wednesday could not get her lines right. They went over and over them until finally she got up with her hands to her face and walked off the set. Harry followed her, put an arm around her shoulder, talked. Molly could not see his face, but his whole body was expressing concern, friendship, sympathy, encouragement – Molly was consumed with a sudden traumatic wave of jealousy that tore her insides apart, and she turned quickly to leave, knowing she had seen too much, knowing this was something she could never be a part of in Harry's life and regretting it bitterly, and she tripped on a cable and sent a light teetering and something metallic clattering noisily to the floor.

The reaction on the set was immediate – a curse and a blaze of lights. Molly froze.

"What the hell are you doing here? Can't you read? Get off the set!" A man, the director, was waving his arms at her, advancing towards her. "Who are you, anyway? A journalist?"

"No – no – I'm... I'm..." Molly, to her dismay, found herself stammering like a teenager.

"It's my wife," said Harry harshly, striding across the floor, boots ringing on the concrete. "Sorry, Val. I'll get rid of her." His face was blazing with anger. He gripped her arm tightly with an iron hand, a stranger with a big fake bruise on his forehead, fury in his eyes, and a mouth Molly could not help thinking that had just been kissing another woman – a girl – over and over again.

"Harry," she said. "I'm sorry, I just –"

"Shut up." He propelled her briskly towards the door. "Don't say anything."

"But, Harry, my –"

He pushed her out of the door, turned her, thrust her face at the sign.

"That means you, you silly bitch. Go home, where you belong."

"But Harry, my –" He was inside, had slammed the door in her face. "My – shoes," she finished lamely to the still vibrating door.

Oh damn. Blown it again. She walked across the car park in her stockinged feet, convinced that everyone must be staring at her, and not caring anyway, furious with Harry for acting in an entirely justifiable way. She seethed all the way home, trembling inside like a naughty child caught in a misdemeanour and dreading the inevitable punishment. She felt physically sick, nauseated. He had called her a silly bitch – it was abusive, crude, horrible – disappointing… the strange word came to her mind and she began to wonder if she had fallen in love with a man who existed only in her mind, not in reality.

Harry came home three hours early and unceremoniously threw Molly's shoes down at her feet.

"Yours," he said tersely.

"I tried to –"

"In future don't barge in where you're not invited."

"I just wanted to see you working –"

"Thanks to you, I'm not working. My director blew his top and my leading lady came apart and had hysterics. We're off for two days. Satisfied?"

"Harry. I'm sorry. I know now I was wrong, but try to see – I just wanted to show an interest in your work."

"I don't need you to show an interest in my work, you fool. You've never done it before – why now?"

"I just thought –"

"You don't think, Molly. That's your problem. You do first and think later. Acting is my work and I enjoy it; that's all you need to know."

"Oh, I could see you enjoying it." Molly listened with horror to her own sarcastic voice thinking, that's not me; I didn't mean to say that.

"My God! Because we were doing a love scene?" He threw up his hands, strode across the room. "You don't know a damn thing about actors or the dynamics of the relationships between actors, and you –"

"Well, maybe I should be on the set more often and then I could learn." She heard her own voice rising.

"God forbid. Bloody hell, woman, if I was a doctor would you expect to wander into the operating room to watch me take out appendixes? No, by God, you wouldn't. And by the same token I don't ever want to see you on a set of mine again. Is that clear? Now where are you going?" For she had picked up her handbag and headed towards the door.

"Down to the beach to think this out – maybe somewhere else later. Just leave me alone." He followed her.

"You always walk out of arguments, don't you?" he said grimly, holding the door. The last thing he wanted at this moment was for her to go on another unscheduled trip. "Maybe one day you'll have the guts to stay and fight it out."

"Oh no," said Molly, turning in the driveway, "we silly bitches are only good at barging in where we're not invited." She slammed the car door and started the engine. Childish, she thought, damn.

To his own surprise Harry found himself smiling. Silly bitch had probably been too strong, he reflected, and after all he and Wednesday had been making a meal of the love-scene. He turned back from the door to find Rob and the twins watching him closely from the dining area. He looked at them, shrugged his shoulders, and nodded towards the door.

"You heard that?"

"Yes," said Rob. "I think you were right, Harry."

"Now I s'pose she'll go to Gran for a few days to 'get over it'," said Ken unsympathetically.

"Oh no, and the school play's next week!" said Sue

tragically.

"What play?" Harry asked, easily sidetracked by anything connected to his profession.

"I told you before – the Wizard of Oz, and I'm a Munchkin. Now there'll be no-one to come and see me."

"I'll come," said Rob loyally

"I meant parents," said Sue. "Not brothers. Other people have parents." She turned huge meaningful eyes on Harry.

"Hmmph," he grunted, thinking it sounded like a Chinese torture. "I'll come if you want me to." He spoke sourly but Sue was not in the least deceived. Of Molly's three children, Sue was the one who understood Harry the easiest, and he her; there was a rapport between them which surprised and sometimes delighted him.

"Oh, would you, Harry, would you? Thank you! You can sit in the very back row and wear a disguise, if you like, and only my very best friends will ask for your autograph."

"In the meantime, what do I do about your mother?"

"Leave her alone," said Rob. "That's what she said she wants."

"There's a difference, Rob, between what a woman says she wants, and what she really wants."

"Well, I think you should bring her home by force," said Ken firmly. "She's your wife. She's not supposed to go away. Drag her off the beach, kicking and screaming, tie her up and throw her in the back of the car."

"What garbage have you been reading, kid?" Rob asked.

"Oh," said Sue, her chin in her hands, her eyes shining, "how romantic! Fancy – kidnapped by Harry Wentworth!" She signed in ecstasy.

Harry looked at her.

"Not a bad idea," he said thoughtfully. He had an unexpected two day's holiday – why not?

Harry was hiding behind a tree overlooking Third Beach, and so intent was he on what he was doing he did not even feel silly doing it. He was watching his wife.

A mounted park policeman spotted him and for a moment identified him as a suspicious character, and urged his horse a little nearer. Then he recognized Harry and following Harry's gaze saw and recognized Molly, and he rode on. Those film people. He'd seen them on this beach several times before. Quite mad. Like children. Probably playing some elaborate game of hide and seek. Once they'd run into the water fully clothed and stood there kissing each other. Lucky they didn't catch their death. For a brief disloyal second his own marriage seemed incredibly dull. Mary-Lou would never do a stupid thing like that. He looked back. Harry had moved around the tree, keeping it between him and Molly as she walked across the beach, so that if she glanced up he would still be hidden.

The constable rode on.

Molly ploughed back and forth across the sand, shoulders hunched against the wind (good thing I brought her parka, Harry thought), hands plunged in her jeans pockets, trying to come to terms with what had happened and trying to decide what to do about it, and where to go, if she went anywhere, for a few days.

Harry, you fool, he castigated himself, what in hell are you doing skulking behind a tree watching a dumb broad get her shoes full of sand?

I love her.

Why?

I don't know.

You're Harry Wentworth, for God's sakes, you don't have to do this.

I do. She's my wife.

Then let her act like a wife.

She did and I cussed her out.

Dammit, she deserved it. She broke into a closed set, infuriated your director, upset your leading lady and embarrassed you by behaving like a ninny.

Which she isn't. Now she's deciding whether to take off again.

So what? Let her go.

No, I can't. I hurt her. I love her but I hurt her.

You always hurt the one you –

Shut up. I don't know why I love Molly, only that I do and I don't want her to take off. I'm used to her.

That's the cheapest weakest dumbest reason I ever heard;

you can do better than that.

She excites me; she stimulates me; she gives me a warm feeling.

Now you're talking.

She gives me a reason for living – I didn't realize how shallow and bleak my life was until she came into it.

Better, better.

I need her to feel whole, is that what you want me to say?

That's heavy, man.

I'm not ready to say that yet. Maybe one day. Not yet. It's just that I love her.

Just?

Molly sat down on a log at the left hand end of the beach and her shoulders, hunched before, sagged now and her head drooped and she looked infinitely small and sad and undecided.

Now, said Harry to himself, now's the time to get her. He closed his eyes and breathed deeply and psyched himself into the part he had to play, because for it to work she had to be convinced and to be convinced she had to believe him and to be believable he had to believe the lie himself, at least with one part of his mind. It was an actor's trick.

He took several quick short breaths, came out from behind the tree, and yelled, making his voice hoarse and rough:

"Molly!"

He bounded down the bank and across the Sea Wall and leapt onto the sand.

"Molly!"

She had raised her head at the first shout, then turned it, now she stood up as he ploughed across the sand to her.

"Thank God I found you," and his gasps were genuine enough.

"Harry – what is it? Harry?"

"Quick," he gulped a breath, "back to the car – quickly –"

He put his arm around her and almost carried her up the steps and to the car. He opened the door and pulled out her parka from the seat.

"Kidnapping," he said tersely. "Put this on." He stripped off her light jacket and draped the parka around her shoulders and before she could get her arms in the armholes, he joined the zipper and slid it up to her neck.

"Kidnapping – oh, God – who? The twins?"

"No," he said, pulling the belt tight around her waist, his voice suddenly calm and businesslike. "You." He spun her around before she could even register surprise and pushed her into the front of the car, but she stumbled and fell in and landed face down on the seat, kicking wildly and mumbling into the seat cover. Smothering a grin Harry reached in and pulled her upright and fastened the seat belt across her chest.

"What d'you mean, kidnapping? You can't kidnap your wife."

"Oh no? Watch me. This all right?" He pulled the seat belt.

"I can't move if that's what you mean."

He shut the door and climbed in the driver's side.

"Where are we going?"

"My cabin the woods, where I will rape you, as you deserve."

"You don't have a cabin!"

"You'll see."

"You can't rape your own wife."

"Oh?" He looked sideways at her, an evil leer with one cynical eyebrow raised, and in spite of herself, Molly felt a chill – no, a thrill – in the pit of her stomach.

"You're mad. What about my car?"

"Rob came, down with me; he's taken it home."

"The kids know you've kidnapped me?"

"Know!" he snorted. "They suggested it!"

"Oh." That took the wind of indignation out of her sails. "And where is this cabin?"

"Secret."

"Some secret," she said scornfully, looking out of the window.

"Ah. Nearly forgot." Harry pulled in to the curb and leaning over unzipped the pocket of Molly's parka and pulled out her ski-toque.

"Now what?"

He put the toque on her head, pulled it right down to her

chin and then rolled it back up in a thick band over her eyes.

"See anything?" he asked sharply.

"Wouldn't tell you if I could, would I?" she retorted. "This is totally irresponsible," she protested as they drove on.

"Umm-hmm."

"Don't 'umm-hmm' me. Tell me where we're going and how long for and why."

He grunted again.

"Harry! We can't just up and leave the kids."

"Really! You mean it's O.K. if you up and leave by yourself but not if we do it together?" he asked coldly.

"It's not the same thing."

"Damn right. Now you shut up –"

"Harry, you can't –"

"Shut up, I said!" he roared, in apparent anger. "Now – you just sit quietly and think. Think about what happened today, and what's happening now, and don't say another word until we reach where we're going –"

"But Harry –"

" — Or so help me, I'll gag you too!"

Molly clamped her mouth shut. He wouldn't – of course he wouldn't – and yet he might, the mood he was in – or was he acting? – She wasn't going to risk finding out. She was uncomfortable enough as it was. She wriggled experimentally and found herself to be truly trapped inside the parka, her arms immobilized by the belt and by the seat belt that tied her in from shoulder to hip. For a moment beads of panic sweat prickled under her arms and on her face and her breathing got shallow and quick. She felt anger, fear, resentment building up within her and in a moment would have screamed and threshed and bucked against the restraining belts. But at that existential moment – as though he knew exactly what was happening to her internally, Harry's hand came down on her thigh, firm and warm and friendly.

"All right, love?" he asked, gently in his own voice.

The tension ran out of Molly then and she settled back in the seat and relaxed, knowing that for all the bizarreness of the situation she was loved and cherished. The endearment touched and calmed her, but not as much as the feel of his hand.

That told her that if she was truly frightened she had only to say 'I'm afraid, stop this, unstrap me, take me home' and he would. And knowing that, of course she did not have to.

Here I am, she thought, trussed up like a chicken, blindfolded, and being driven heaven-knows-where and I should be feeling sick and angry and terrified, and suddenly all I feel is secure. Very secure. And excited. This could only happen with Harry.

The warm hand stayed on her thigh as though Harry, too, needed the physical contact. She realized she had not answered him.

"I'm O.K.," she said quietly. Then she started to do as he had suggested – think, think about all that had happened that day.

Harry glanced across and saw by the relaxed line of her jaw that she had calmed down; he also noticed she was getting red in the face and leaned over and opened the air vent so that it blew cool air directly in on her. She grunted and wriggled and pushed her leg towards him impatiently until he put his hand down on her thigh again. Later she dozed.

The car slowed, turned in and stopped.

"Wake up," Harry said, "we're here," and he reached over and plucked the toque off Molly's head.

"Oh. Harrison Hot Springs. How nice. Where's your cabin in the woods?"

Harry jerked a laconic thumb over his shoulder and Molly glanced back at the imposing hotel behind them.

"Some cabin," she said.

"Yeah. I do things big." Harry got out, came around and opened her door, unclipped the seat belt and taking her by the shoulders pulled her out onto the tarmac. He undid the belt and the zipper of the parka and stripped it off her. She flapped her arms like a chicken, bent at the elbows.

"Oof!" he said. "You smell like a polecat, my love."

"What d'you expect, trapped inside that? Furthermore," she added with dignity, "I think I wet my pants."

"Hmmph," Harry grunted, struggling to suppress a grin which Molly struggled to suppress a responding smile too.

"I can't go in there," she said. "I've got nothing to wear."

"Mavis packed you a case."

"You think of everything."

"No – Sue does. Want to change somewhere before we go in?"

"She shot him a look.

"No way. If they don't accept me sweaty from a long hot journey then we'll find somewhere else. Right?"

Now Harry grinned. "Right." He reached into the car and handed Molly her light jacket and put on a navy pea jacket with brass buttons, and pulled a black toque on over his white hair.

"What's that?"

"Disguise."

Molly threw back her head and pealed with laughter.

"You don't honestly think no one will recognize you?"

"Well –" he said huffily, "why not?"

"Oh, Harry," she shook her head fondly. "You're so naive sometimes. Don't you know that you have a presence, a charisma that crackles around you whatever you're wearing? You're unmistakable – always."

He looked at her curiously. She had never said anything like that before; she had always treated him as though he was…ordinary? He thought it was perhaps the nicest thing she had said to him in a long time, but he made no comment.

"Well, for the next two days I'm Henry Worthington and you're my wife Maureen and I just won a Harry Wentworth look-alike contest – How's that?"

"Perfect."

"And because I am in disguise and using my real name everyone will realize we're trying to have a private holiday and they will pretend not to recognize me."

"Dreamer."

But Harry was right to a degree, and though they were recognized they were not stared at or pestered or intruded upon. Molly swam away many length's worth of tension in the outdoor pool while Harry had a sauna and a massage; they dined at a discreet corner table, danced a few times unobtrusively and went to bed early, where they made love leisurely, thoroughly and with great mutual satisfaction.

But at no time did they mention the incident that had brought them eighty miles up the Fraser Valley to the Harrison Hot Springs Hotel. Harry would not, and Molly could not. She had no confidence that he had any understanding of how she felt. It was something that would have to be dealt with internally, tucked away and forgotten, she determined before drifting off to sleep. So much for conscious rational thought.

Harry, on the other hand, went to sleep thinking 'Only with Molly. Only with Molly could I have done this mad thing and have it work; now she's happy again, and that's all that counts'. He knew he had been wrong when he awoke some time later to find the bed shaking with fine tremor transmitted through the mattress, and to hear muffled sounds of distress from the other side of the bed.

Molly had woken bathed in sweat and shaking. She had been reliving the incident at the studio in a dream; reliving the stab of jealousy, reliving the feeling of helplessness and reliving Harry's rejection of her. To make things worse she found she was, willy-nilly, starting to snivel. Fearful, for some reason, of waking Harry she wriggled as far away from him as possible and jammed the pillow up against her mouth. Oh damn, damn, damn, why do I have to react like this? If he wakes he won't understand, and how can I explain?

Harry moved cautiously, aware of the emptiness of the mattress beside him. He opened his eyes and turned his head and looked at the curled-up lump his wife made on the very edge of her side of the bed, and he knew he was not supposed to have woken. With a simulated sleepy grunt he moved across the bed, one hand flung out touched Molly's shoulder, pulled it down to turn her, the other dug under her neck and with a convulsive movement he rolled her over onto his chest and wrapped his arms around her in a strong protective hug. He pretended not to hear the stifled sob and not to feel the trembling of her body or the wetness of her tears on his chest. He steeled himself not to say 'Ah, Molly' and kiss her cheeks and stroke her hair – he recognized that she was trying to cope with her emotions without bothering him and wanted to give her the dignity of feeling that she had. Only if he appeared to be moving in his sleep could he do that. He was relieved when he felt the tension melt out of her and the trembling ease; her breathing became normal and finally she reached a cautious arm around his body and anchored herself to him. He smiled to himself, remembering their wedding night when he had hugged her so hard she had fought to free herself and lie alone, as she was used to doing. Things had changed. Now she not only lay in his grasp trustingly, taking comfort, but she held him too; and he realized his grip had changed subtlety from possessiveness to protectiveness. He wondered if she sensed this; it was not a thought he could verbalize.

Molly, awake, enjoying his solid proximity, knew that they would not speak in the morning of this nocturnal communication. She was not sure if he was awake, though she thought she saw the moonlight glint on his slightly opened eyes once, but that scarcely mattered. What mattered was that, waking or asleep Harry had demonstrated his intention to protect and comfort her, and that was all that she needed to know. She slept again, peacefully.

Harry too went back to sleep, thinking loving thoughts of Molly, and woke early – with an erection – thinking of Wednesday.

Everything in the garden was not as lovely or as simple as he pretended.

Is it ever?

Chapter Sixteen

Showdown – the End of the Honeymoon

"Mrs. Molly Wentworth was involved in a minor auto accident recently. She was not at fault and sustained no injuries. Well-known actor husband Harry and son Rob were not so lucky later the same day – both received facial injuries requiring treatment at Lion's Gate Hospital."

It had been a stupid unnecessary accident, as most are – quite the other driver's fault, and the damage had been relatively slight, slight enough that neither car needed a tow-truck, and they were able to pull over to the side of the road under their own power before getting out to exchange names and addresses. At first Molly felt quite calm – though the similarity to her previous accident (when she had been hurt) was striking. Then when she got out of the car and found that her legs were reacting though her mind was not, she became unnerved.

The man blustered and shouted – as shaken up as she – and tried to pin the blame on Molly, and as she listened she felt herself go numb and helpless. All she could think of was 'Harry

– Harry will help me' – so she interrupted the man and said,

"Excuse me, I'm going to make a 'phone call before I discuss this any further," and walked off towards a telephone booth.

Harry was at the Cetapac Studios and it was absolutely taboo to call him there, but surely it would take him only a few minutes to drive down to Park Royal and sort this whole thing out for her and then go back? Surely he would do that for her?

"Harry," she said, when at long last he came on the line after she had insisted to three different people that this was an emergency that warranted his immediate attention.

"Yeah?" he said warily.

"Harry," Molly said again, and swallowed, her mouth dry. "Harry, I've had a bump-up in the car."

"Uh-huh." He sounded non-committal and detached.

"A fender-bender."

"Well? Anybody hurt?"

"N-no."

"So what are you calling about? Does the car run?"

"Yes – oh, yes, it's O.K. – just… bent a little."

"So?" he sounded cold and uninterested, and it made it harder for her to go on.

"The other driver is… he's not being very… well, what I mean is – since you're so close – you know.." her voice trailed away.

"What – exactly – are you saying Molly?" he asked with studied patience.

"Oh, Harry," she blurted, suddenly warmed by his voice and feeling the tension drain out of her as she spoke. "Harry – help me – please, help me!" It was a cri-de-couer, leaving her wide open and vulnerable admitting her weakness; she had thrown herself, unprotected, on his mercy with total trust in his response. His answer, when it came, was like a bucket of ice water thrown over her.

"No," he said curtly.

"Wh-what?"

"I said no, I'm not coming down. You're a grown woman, not a fool"

"But, Harry –"

"You know what to do – do it. Then go home. I'll see you

at dinner." Then he hung up. He hung up on her! Molly stared at the dead telephone in her hand in disbelief. He hung up on me. Not a kind word, not a word of reassurance. Refused to help me. When she had been totally honest and exposed herself in her weakness he had, in effect, turned on his heel and walked away. Bastard! Bloody rotten bastard! No, it was more as though he had slapped her face –

Her confused thoughts were interrupted by the man rapping on the glass of the telephone booth. Shelving her painful disillusionment in her husband's quality of understanding and love, Molly went out on rubbery knees and proceeded, coldly and dazedly, to do business with him.

She filed an accident report at the Police Station; she made an appointment to see her Insurance man; then she went home.

"I don't want dinner," she said, and went to her room where, of course, Harry followed her.

"Are you all right?" There was not much warmth in his tone.

·"No," she said, equally coldly, "I'm not. Not because of the crash. Because of you."

"What did I do?"

"It's what you didn't do. I asked you for help – and you hung up on me."

"For God's sake, Molly, you surely don't expect me to come running down to fight your little battles."

"I thought," she said distinctly, "in my innocence, that because you love me – as you say – you'd want to help me."

" I did."

"You did not."

"Yes, I did. You got out of that phone booth and fixed things up by yourself, didn't you? Which you thought you couldn't do?"

"I was upset and shaken, and I relied on you for support and comfort and you gave me none. If I can't rely on my own husband whom can I rely on?"

"Yourself. You managed all right before you married me – and through a much worse accident. I didn't marry a weepy, clinging vine and I don't want one now, so don't change. I married a gutsy woman who could stand on her own feet and

manage her own affairs without any help from anyone –
certainly not me. I'm not Joe Blow, Molly, I'm Harry Wentworth,
and I'm damned if I'm going to make a fool of myself for the
gossip columnists by running down to hold your hand every
time you get into a spot. When I'm working I'm working and
short of death or mortal injury you leave me alone down there.
Is that understood? You live your life, woman, and I'll live
mine!"

"Don't shout at my mother," Rob stood in the doorway, pale
and angry.

"Shut up, kid!" said Harry shortly.

"I'm not a kid," said Rob. "And I think you should show
more respect to my mother."

"Oh, you do, do you? Well, that's my wife, kid and I'll do
what I bloody well like to her."

"Harry, Please!" Molly tried to come between them, but
Harry pushed her away.

"You don't have to defend him, Mummy, he's a big boy
now," he said sarcastically. "Aren't you, Rob?" He put a hand
on Rob's chest and pushed him away. "Go to your room, kid,
I'll talk to you later. You," he turned around and levelled a
finger at Molly, "You I'll talk to now."

"Mum, shall I – ?"

"Go to your room!" Harry bellowed ferociously.

"Go," said Molly urgently. "I'm all right, Rob. Go, please."

Clenching his fists in angry frustration Rob retreated down
the corridor, ashamed at his own inadequacy; slammed his door
hard.

"Now," said Harry, beginning to pace, "it's about time we
laid down some ground rules around here. Should have done
it two years ago."

"About what?"

"About that – young man – for one thing. He's resented me
and tried to interfere between us from the very beginning."

"He's only trying to protect me –"

"You don't need him to protect you from me, and I sure as
hell don't need a wife who needs protecting – from me or
anything else. And don't you protect him either," he added
quickly, seeing her draw a breath. "Rule number one, keep

out of my professional life; rule number two, don't try to understand me when I'm filming; and rule number three, don't butt in when I'm dealing with Rob." He started towards Rob's room, turned and added, "and when I've done that, I'll be packing."

It was a shocking exit line and left Molly stunned, her eyes wide and her mouth open, groping for an answer.

Rob heard Harry coming, opened his door and stood back against his desk, arms folded across his chest. Harry closed the door behind him.

"We'd better talk," he said grimly.

"I don't like the way you treat my mother."

"My wife," Harry enunciated distinctly. "Your mother happens to be my wife."

"That doesn't make you my father."

"Never said it did."

"Then don't try to come the heavy Dad on me."

"I'm not. I'm just telling you to keep the hell out of arguments between my wife and me."

"She was my mother first," Rob was beginning to sound a little shrill.

"She had no choice about that, did she?" Harry retorted with heavy sarcasm.

"You're doing what my father did to her."

"I am not!" Harry said angrily.

"You bully her. She's changed since she married you."

"If she has it's for the better."

"That's your opinion."

"Damn right it is. And I'm tired of your opinion, kid –"

"I'm not a kid," Rob cut in. "I'm in first year University, remember?"

"All right – young man. If you're not a kid what the hell are you doing living in my house, eating my food? When I was your age –"

"Oh, spare me 'when I was your age' ," said Rob rudely. "I'm living here with my mother like any normal son. The fact that she was dumb enough to marry you and move into your house is my bad luck. I'm stuck with it – I don't have to like it."

"Then you can pack your bags and get the hell out – the

sooner the better," said Harry loudly, getting angrier by the minute.

"Oh sure, you're tired of playing Daddy now. For a while there it was fun pretending I was the son you walked out on, wasn't it?"

That hit so close to the mark Harry's fists actually came up. "Watch it!" he growled.

"But now that I'm getting a bit difficult you want me out, eh?" Rob's arms were still folded and he affected a look of supercilious superiority. See, I'm in control and you're not, his stance said.

"You've always been difficult," Harry granted.

"And why not? You disrupted my life; you took my father's place, you took my place in the family; you stole my mother."

"Jealous little prig."

"You did. She doesn't have any time for me or the twins any more. It's all Harry, Harry, Harry –"

"That's not true. And anyway, you don't own her, Rob, any more than I do."

"You try to. You boss her around. You were shouting at her –"

"And for a damn good reason. She's my wife and if we have a row that's our business. Keep your sticky little nose out of it."

"I can't!" Rob cried, suddenly passionate. "I love her. I wish I'd never put her name in that damn contest."

"Well, I don't," said Harry firmly, deliberately trying to slow the momentum of the exchange, which was threatening to sweep Rob away, he could see.

"Some prize you turned out to be!" Rob cried.

"She seems to think so – she loves me."

"Oh yeah? I can't think why. You're nothing but a phoney, a lousy actor; you're no tough guy when the chips are down. You couldn't even act like a man when the baby died. I had to drag you out of the bar. I –"

"Shut up!" He had caught Harry on a raw nerve again.

"She doesn't even like your movies!"

"She married me, didn't she?" Harry found himself shouting back.

"Doesn't mean she loves you."

"Then why the hell marry me?"

"For your money, of course," Rob said with contempt. "For someone to educate her children and provide a home, what else?"

"That's a bloody lie!"

"O.K.," said Rob, in control now and gloatingly aware that he had got under Harry's skin, "now you're going to beat me up, I suppose. Next, it'll be mother, and then the twins – oh, but not Sue, you dote on Sue, don't you?"

Harry was aware that Rob was taunting him for a reason, a purpose, a psychological need of his own, but had no time to stop and analyze it. Rob delivered his 'coup de grace';

"Then you can dump Mum and go off with the redhead with the big boobs."

That was when Harry went to hit him, but Rob was ready with his fists up and deflected the blow and threw a quick left hook. His fist caught Harry square above the right eye, splitting the old scar tissue on his eyebrow into a two-inch gash, which immediately poured blood. Incensed, Harry lashed out with a quick left and right – the left Rob parried with his forearm, the right crunched hideously against flesh and bone, and Rob reeled back with a cry, both hands up to his face.

Molly, who had been standing transfixed in the corridor, sickened by the loud angry voices though unable to distinguish the words, heard the unmistakable grunts and thuds of the blows of a fight, now flung open the door and stood there in a frozen horror.

Oh God, stop this, make it not be happening to me.

Harry, to her left, had his handkerchief up to his eye and blood was already down his cheek and dripping off his chin, while Rob was collapsed against his desk, to her right, white as a sheet, both hands over his nose, free-running blood quickly staining his shirt.

"Mum!" It was the muffled cry of a hurt child.

"Molly!" The 'cri-de-couer' of a wounded man.

Sick, hurt, disgusted, torn with pity and love for both of them, she controlled herself rigidly. If I go to Rob, Harry will be hurt; if I go to Harry, Rob will never, never forgive me –

what can I do? Her eyes flicked from one to the other and Harry, sensitive to body language, immediately perceived her dilemma and dropped the hand he had raised in appeal towards her.

"My God!" she exclaimed, with heavy contempt (which she did not feel but which successfully masked her real emotions), "is this the most adult way you two can find to settle an argument?"

If he had not been so busy trying to stop his brow bleeding, Harry might have applauded – it was, he thought, a magnificent performance.

Molly wheeled and stalking to the bathroom next door, found two towels, came back, threw one to each of the men.

"Clean yourselves up," she said shortly, and strode away down the hall, anger and indignation and dismissal in the swing of her shoulders and set of her head.

Realizing that she really was not going to help, Harry turned his attention to Rob, who was bunching the towel up under his nose trying to stop the flow of blood, and gasping with pain at the same time. Pressing his own towel over his eye, Harry crossed the room.

"Let me see," he said, pushing the boy's hands aside.

"Is id brogud?" Rob asked miserably.

Seeing it was not only concaved, but sideways on Rob's face, Harry said, "Yeah – and how. And I need sewing up. We'd better get down to Emergency and get some repairs. Come on, son, get a jacket. We'll take the Lincoln. "Neither he nor Rob noticed at the time his use of the word 'son'.

In the hall Rob croaked from behind his gory towel.

"Where's Bub?"

"Out," said Mavis crisply, leaning on the kitchen doorjamb looking at both of them with the particular disdain that women have for men who fight each other. "She took the Lincoln and went out with the twins. Her car's in for a tune-up; mine's been borrowed by a friend."

"That leaves your Datsun," said Harry. Wordlessly Rob dug in his jeans pocket and handed Harry the keys, he being in the better condition to drive. Did no one care that he and Harry were hurt and bleeding? He wondered. Strangely, he no longer felt any animosity for the big man beside him, and instinctively knew that Harry felt none for him. It was as though the blows they had traded had evened the score, and given them the chance to start again on a different footing. In fact, Rob felt bonded by a masculine kinship, a sort of Us against Them feeling.

Crouched in the tiny cab of the Datsun pick-up, Harry thought wryly that if she had planned it, Molly could hardly have found a better way to cut him down to size than to force him to drive to the hospital in this vehicle. Having started the engine, he realized he had a problem, he did not have enough hands – he needed to steer, use the stick shift and hold the towel to his face at the same time.

"Rob," he said, "think you can change gear while I steer?"

"Sure."

It took about three blocks before they managed to co-ordinate their movements so the gears did not grind and the engine race, but after that it was smooth going, and by the time they reached the Lion's Gate Hospital, they were both taking an ironic pride in their skill as a team. Harry parked and switched off.

"Before we go in," he said, "let's settle on a story."

"A story?"

"Or do you want to say, 'Harry Wentworth slugged me?'" Rob considered in silence. "Frankly," Harry went on, "I don't want to have to admit my stepson hit me."

"Ad accidett," said Rob thickly.

"Uh-huh. I slammed on the brakes and caught my head on the rear-view mirror and you hit the windshield – how's that?"

"OK".

"OK".

Rob was taken in for treatment fairly quickly since he was bleeding so profusely, but Harry had to sit and wait for a while until his own Doctor, Hansen, came and stitched him up. Consequently, they came out of their treatment rooms almost simultaneously, Harry with a dressing taped across his brow and his eye swelling and blackening beneath it. He had been cut for stitches on that brow so many times now that it hardly bothered him to be conspicuously bandaged and bruised. Not so Rob, who sported a plaster cast over his nose taped into position by lengths of adhesive making a huge X across his face, and in addition his nostrils were packed and taped; he looked uncomfortable and embarrassed, and glanced quickly around the waiting room. He thought he had been hoping his mother would be there, but in fact he found he was relieved that she was not.

"She didn't come," said Harry, correctly interpreting Rob's look. "Let's get home." He put his arm companionably around the boy's shoulders, and made a point of looking at him without surprise or shock or pity, and made no comment on the bandages. Rob, however, looked at Harry in consternation, awed by the damage his own fist had perpetrated, and said,

"Oh shit, Harry, are you all right?" (The expletive surprising Harry.)

"Not the first time I've had a black eye."

They reached the truck.

"I'll drive," said Rob. "I can see better than you."

Arriving home they sat in the cab for a moment in silence.

"I think your mother is going to be very angry with me," Harry said.

"I think your wife is going to be very angry with me," said Rob, and Harry regarded the young man beside him with a new respect and slowly smiled, and Rob, as well as he could within the framework of plaster and tape on his face, smiled back.

"Aren't we supposed to shake hands and apologize now?" he said.

"Something like that," Harry agreed, and offered his hand. They shook warmly, but neither verbalized an apology.

They knew by the fact that the garage was empty that Molly was still out. Inwardly Harry was angry with her, convinced that she had cravenly run away from a bad scene that should have been faced. He was only half right; he was forgetting the cause of the original argument.

It was not, Molly thought, sitting in the cinema with the twins watching, but not seeing, a movie that she would later have absolutely no recollection of, that she was afraid of blood. Blood was the least of it, the blood she could have coped with quite easily, had often done so through the years when the children had had accidents (even before she was divorced in fact, because Tom had always been useless in emergencies) – no, not the blood, but the violence, the raw angriness of the scene had disturbed her. It was the trauma of not knowing who to go to first, of feeling so insecure about making a wrong decision that might affect her whole life. Also a basic rejection of the happening, a disbelief, a desperate desire to roll back the clock and change things, make them not happen, not force her to examine where she stood when it came to a conflict between her son and her new husband. She wanted not to have to look at that. She was not ready for it. On top of the fender-bender accident and Harry's refusal to help her, it was too much. She had already been wondering if Harry really loved her – if she could love a man who rejected her in the moment of need. Could their marriage survive not only her fundamental lack of understanding about his job but also this hostility towards her son? Who did she love best? If it came to the crunch and they stood there and said you must choose one or the other or us, who would she choose? Harry, she answered herself without hesitation – Harry, hands down – but after this afternoon does he want me? And Rob's too young to be alone, especially alone against a man as strong and dominant as Harry; he tries, bless him, but he's always overwhelmed by Harry's personality – he needs me as a buffer, a mediator. Oh God, right now I need a buffer and a mediator between Harry and me. I can't do it all. I wonder how they are, with their hurting faces. Poor Rob, his nose was probably broken; poor Harry, the same old cut reopened. He'll have to postpone shooting while it heals – that won't make him any easier to live with. It's time to go back, they both need me – I need to see them.

"Is it over yet?" she hissed to the twins beside her.

"Over?" they said in surprise, "it's halfway through again."

At the house Mavis waylaid Molly in the garage while the twins ran on in.

"Be prepared, Molly, they look awful – both of them."

"Oh dear. Are they speaking to each other?"

"Speaking? You'd better believe it – they're bosom pals. They've been drinking together for an hour."

That was the last thing Molly had expected.

Ken and Sue had gone straight in and found Harry and Rob lounging in chairs on either side of the fireplace, and their reactions had been immediate, typical and predictable. They had both stopped dead and stared in awe at the wounded combatants, then Ken had moved towards Rob, saying with undisguised admiration,

"Wow! You look terrible, does it hurt? Did Harry really do that to you, is it broken?"

"Thank you, little brother," said Rob with tipsy graciousness, "the answers are yes, yes and yes."

"I bet Mum screams when she sees you."

Sue meanwhile fixed huge eyes, limpid with sympathy upon Harry.

"Your poor face!" she said with sweet sorrow, and strangely Harry remembered that was just what Molly had said the first time she had seen him with his face battered from an accident on the set. "I hate Rob. How could he do that to you?"

"It's nothing," said Harry truthfully. "I'm all right, Sue. Rob's much worse than me – I broke his nose."

"Good." She came and stood beside him and studied his face seriously. "Do you have many stitches?"

Harry shrugged.

"About five."

"I had three in my chin once. I think Mum's mad at you. But don't worry," she put a hand on his arm, "I still love you."

"Thank you," said Harry gravely, stifling an urge to laugh, and also stifling an urge to cover her hand with his own and squeeze it.

Molly came through from the kitchen, stamping heavily on purpose to forewarn them of her entrance.

"Well!" she said, standing feet apart, hands on hips, and glaring at her son and husband in turn. She was jolted by the garish white X on Rob's face and the size of the dressing over Harry's eye, and the swelling and blackening of the eye itself but somehow managed not to show this on her face. Still torn between the desire to castigate them both roundly and to burst into tears, she instead suddenly found herself laughing, maybe from sheer nervous reaction.

"Oh God," she said, "What a pair of clowns!"

Harry, who had stood up as soon as she came in, was nonplussed. Laughter was the last thing he had expected. But then, when had Molly ever done the expected? He was vastly relieved.

"Ken, Sue— Mavis has your snack ready in the kitchen – go and eat, and then go to bed. "I'll gather the... men", she hesitated sarcastically before the word, "don't need anything more."

"Mum –"

"Not now, Rob."

The twins left, obediently but reluctantly. Rob stood up.

"I think," he said carefully, "I'll go to my room and lie down."

"Do that," Molly responded crisply, making no move to help him as he wove uncertainly past her. In fact, her physical body was rooted and immovable, while her psyche had conveniently split itself in half and the two halves had rushed out of her to simultaneously embrace and comfort the two men she loved. This was the only way she could cope with the ambivalence of her emotions.

Harry saw the anguish in her eyes and thought he understood what she was going through. He was no longer angry with her for having, as he had originally thought, run away from a bad scene. He was beginning to realize that her instinctive retreat had in fact been a move of great innate wisdom. He wanted very much to comfort her, having forgotten for the moment the original altercation that had led to the fight, but found it as impossible to move as she did. Wordless, they looked at each other across the room. Satisfied now that she was not totally disgusted with him for hitting her son, he moved his head towards the hall.

"Go to him", he said quietly.

Thus released from the obligation of making an invidious choice, Molly crossed the floor to Harry, stopped in front of him, kissed him lightly on either cheek –because it is difficult to remain genuinely angry with someone who is hurt – and went to Rob's room.

Rob was lying propped up on his bed, a textbook in his lap.

A mixture of reaction and alcohol rendered him quite incapable of reading, but he felt obliged to look as normal as possible. He knew his mother would come and he had important news to give her.

Molly looked at the slightly glazed eyes and the slightly silly grin with which he greeted her (which no fellow with a recently pulverized and re-set nose should have) and said,

"You're drunk," which was not at all what she had intended to say.

"So what? Would you rather I was crying into my pillow?"

"No. Of course not. Oh Rob, darling, it looks so uncomfortable – are you all right? Is there anything –?"

"I'm all right, Mum. Really. And Harry's an O.K. guy. But listen, Mum, listen please. We decided it would be better if I moved out –"

"No – you don't have to!"

"Yes, I do. I want to. I've got a friend begging me to share a place on West Fourth. I'd have gone at the beginning of term, but I just didn't dare suggest it. I thought you'd be mad, or something."

"You wanted to leave? You're not just making this up?"

"Nope."

"And it's not because – because of that awful fight?"

"Hell, Mum, that was no fight. Two punches! Gee! We were both lucky."

"Lucky! A broken nose and a busted eyebrow?"

"So?" said Rob airily. "Maybe it'll give my face a little character. I'll be a one-day sensation up at U.B.C. – might even get a new girlfriend."

"You're not mad at Harry for doing that to you?"

"Hell, no. Besides, not many guys can say that Harry Wentworth broke their nose."

"You're not going to tell people?" Molly said faintly.

"Why not? Nothing wrong with a bit of a punch-up. Clear's the air."

"Wait a minute," Molly sat down on the edge of the bed. "Let me get this straight. You're telling me that you don't resent Harry's hitting you?, you don't think he's some kind of creep, that you're not leaving just to get away from him?"

"Right. Right, and right again."

"Three hours ago you were shouting at each other."

"That was three hours ago."

"Then you smashed each other's faces, had to go to hospital for repairs, and now all is forgotten and forgiven and you're bosom friends? Is that what you're telling me?"

"Yup."

"Pardon me for being a stupid middle-aged woman, but that doesn't make sense."

"It would if you were a man.

"Spare me the chauvinism. Just explain."

"OK, but don't blame me if you still don't understand, I just might not be able to put it into words."

"Try."

"Well," he began slowly, picking his way through his thoughts which were by now definitely fuzzy. "When you first married Harry, I liked him, but I didn't like how you changed – towards me and the twins. I know you tried, but somehow I felt left out. It wasn't so bad for the twins (maybe it was their age or something) but suddenly I wasn't important any more – nobody needed me. I thought Harry thought I was a nuisance. I thought he resented me being around; he wanted you all to himself. I was somewhere out in left field – nobody cared how I felt."

"That's not true."

"Maybe. But that's what I thought. "Till tonight," He stopped abruptly.

"And tonight he broke your nose and that made it all right?"

"For Christ-sake, Mum – you don't hit a person you don't care about!"

"Don't swear," Molly said automatically.

"He – I – oh, hell, I can't explain it any better than that. We had a long talk – "

"And a few drinks – "

" – and a few drinks, and we both feel – I feel – part of the family again."

"Oh good," said Molly, "that's why you're leaving, I suppose?"

"Mum!"

"It's all right. In my stupid feminine way I can see dimly what you're saying – and I'm glad."

"I think you'd better go to Harry now. He's pretty shaken up."

She looked at the young man on the bed, this son of hers who used to be her little boy, and marvelled that she had ever thought that this person who had sprung from her loins was not a free individual. I don't even know my own flesh that grew within me, how can I hope to know a man who had lived fifty years of his life before we met? If the circles of our consciousness can touch even ever so slightly and obliquely we are lucky. And we are lucky. We can work through this bad patch. Somehow.

She got up.

"Thank you, Rob. If you need anything in the night, call us."

Was Harry really shaken up? If so he was not showing it. He watched her warily with his good eye.

"I think," Molly said, "I've lost a son and gained a friend. Or lost a little boy and gained a son. Or something like that. I haven't worked it out yet." She gazed into the empty fireplace. "Have I lost a husband?" she asked in a low voice.

There was a pause while Harry seemed to consider this, standing very still and quiet beside her.

"No," he said at last, shortly, as though that was of little consequence.

Touch me! Her whole being screamed, put your arms around me, hold me, kiss me, tell me you love me; mental tears streamed down her cheeks, while in fact she remained as still and quiet as he, merely lowering her head slightly. Unless he was possessed of inner sight there was no way that Harry could guess the turmoil she was in. In fact, his train of thought was following a different tack – he had been expecting her to berate him for beating up her son and he was preparing to defend himself.

"Um," she said at last, surprised to find her voice was functioning normally, "before – before I went to talk to Rob you said something about... packing?"

"Hm-hmm," he grunted, "that was before I broke your son's

nose – or didn't you notice?" He was still expecting an angry tirade.

"I noticed. And he blackened your eye. I noticed that too. "But… packing?"

"Uh – huh."

"Dammit, don't grunt at me Harry. Talk. I need words."

"Very well." He pulled a clean folded handkerchief from his back pocket and held it out to her.

"What's this for?" Molly asked, taking it and noticing how careful they both were that their fingers did not touch.

"You'll probably need it by the time I've finished talking," Harry said grimly.

Molly looked at the handkerchief and knew that there was no way in the world that she was going to cry, no matter what he said, if only to prove she was not a 'weepy clinging vine' (those words had rankled hard). Not now that he was expecting it.

"When this heals," he touched his forehead, "I'll move out to the Bayshore –"

"Why wait?" Molly interrupted tersely.

" – and I'll live there during the rest of the shooting of this film" he continued, ignoring her interruption.

"And then?"

"I'll probably move back,"

"Oh. How nice of you. And this is all because I called you on your precious set this morning?"

"No. That brought it to a head. I've been feeling the strain for some time. Of course," he went on remotely, "I don't expect you to understand."

Oh God. Her stomach churned at the apparent coldness of the words.

"Try me," she managed to say.

"I'm an actor. When I'm working I, become involved in my part, in the whole movie; involved physically, mentally and emotionally. It's difficult to turn it off at the end of the day – you know that – I'm not easy to live with sometimes, and I'm sorry but there's nothing I can do about that. I can't come home to this kind of a hassle. I don't need it. It interferes with my work. This is a difficult script, the most complex character I've ever had to work on; I've got a bloody temperamental director and an inexperienced leading lady."

Unexpectedly Molly felt her gorge rising and began to calculate the distance to the bathroom door and how long it would take to get there without running.

"Before we married," Harry went on inexorably, "I always lived with the crew in a hotel. It helped my concentration. I can do it again."

"I'm sorry, I didn't realize," Molly said levelly, dry-eyed, handing him his handkerchief, "how inconvenient it was for you to have a wife and family. That was naive of me, wasn't it? But then Tom always said I was naive. Let me know when you want a divorce, I know the ropes you know, I might be able to help you." She swept past him grandly, head in the air.

"Now wait a minute, woman –" but she was already out of sight down the passage.

She made it to the bathroom just in time, flung up the toilet seat and retched violently on her knees in front of it.

Harry had followed her, furious, but when he heard the sounds coming from the other side of the bathroom door his anger dissipated quickly. He went in and sat on the edge of the bath and patted her heaving shoulders, and when she sat back on her heels, gasping, her eyes streaming, he wiped her face with a wet washcloth and handed her a glass of water.

"Sip," he said. "Rinse, don't swallow."

It was extraordinary, Molly had time to reflect before another bout of retching gripped her, she had never been so kindly tended when throwing up before, even in hospital, where the nurses had tactfully looked away, even at home as a child, when her mother had said 'some things are better done alone' and left the room, and here she was at her most vulnerable and Harry was being so matter-of-fact that she did not even feel embarrassed.

"Finished?" He wiped her face again and proffered fresh water.

"Yes."

"Deep breaths," he said; he flushed the toilet and closed the lid, handed her a towel. "Better?"

"Yes. Thank you, Harry. Much. That was my body

throwing up, not me. I'm OK" . She stood up without his assistance, feeling purged and somehow lighter and cleaner.

"What brought that on?" He followed her back to the living room. "I didn't say anything about divorce."

"I know. It was me, Harry. I've had a lousy day, remember; I had a dumb accident this afternoon, made a fool of myself by calling the studio, made my husband so angry he hung up on me – which I probably deserved – had to cope with a chauvinist pig of a driver, a bunch of suspicious policemen, and a snotty-nosed bitch of an insurance lady, all the time wondering what was going to happen when I got home. I had a bloody row with my husband and he stormed off and had another row with my son and they hit each other. Blood all over the place. What was I supposed to do? Who was I supposed to help? I was damned if I did and damned if I didn't, so I took off and dragged my other two kids to a rotten sexy horror movie that they assured me was labelled P.G. (and believe me if I'd been any kind of a Parent I'd have Guided them right out of there) which I can't remember a thing about, because I was too busy dreading to go home, and when I did come home, the living room looked like a casualty ward and my son and my husband were buddy-buddy in their cups. Then they both upped and told me thank you very much but we are leaving home. My poor stomach just rebelled."

"Next time cry," Harry said, not unsympathetically. "It's easier on the system."

"Does this mean" Molly asked, grinding the difficult words out one at a time, "does this mean – it's over? You're going to the Bayshore... do you want..."

Harry wondered how she could so misunderstand him, and it showed on his face. "No," he said shortly, knowing she wanted him to say, 'I love you' and deliberately not saying it. "It's the end of the honeymoon and the beginning of the marriage." It was a good line, he could not remember which show it was from, but it sounded right. Not sure how clean her mouth was, he leaned down and kissed Molly fastidiously on the forehead. "I had a lousy day, too," he added mildly.

Somewhat reassured by the kiss she said,

"I know – and it was all my fault."

"No, not at all. The row with Rob would have come, it's been brewing a long time. I didn't have to break his nose."

"Well," Molly flung out her arms, at a loss what to do next. "He probably deserved it. I guess I'd better see how the twins are," she said vaguely and started towards the kitchen thinking, no one really needs me around here; Rob's happily making plans to leave; Harry's making plans to leave; Ken and Sue get all the care they need from Mavis. She happened to glance back and saw that Harry had sunk down in his chair, both hands up to his head cradling his eye and cut eyebrow protectively, unaware that she was watching. For a moment he looked all that he was tired, and hurting, and lonely and – needing.

Molly went back and sat on the arm of his chair.

"Your poor face," she said gently, echoing Sue's reaction, and quoting from their second meeting at the Bayshore after he had been injured on the set, and realizing they were the first kind words she had said to him since the fight.

"Hmmm." He grunted with satisfaction and butted his head against her body below her heart. Molly put an arm around his shoulder and stroked his hair and he put an arm around her waist and pulled her closer, nuzzling her belly. She was just getting nicely sexually aroused when she realized by his steady breathing that reaction and alcohol had taken their toll and he was now fast asleep. This is how the marriage begins she thought wryly.

Hearing the silence, the twins came to the kitchen door and looked cautiously into the room.

"I think they've made up," said Sue.

"Boy," said Ken, "they sure don't behave like grown-ups, do they?"

A week later when Harry came back from the doctor's office, having had his stitches removed, he started to pack. It had not been an easy week for Molly. She had put on a front, being as normal as possible, pretending – hoping – that Harry would forget his declared intention of leaving to go and live in the Bayshore for the remainder of the shooting of the film, while at the same time, knowing in her bones that he would not.

Rob had had a difficult few days with his nose but he and

Harry had maintained the new warm relationship that the fight had engendered.

Harry acted normally, saying nothing of his intended departure on the assumption that having said it once there was no need to repeat it. It wasn't that he wanted to go – he had to. His work (however insignificant it might seem to his wife) took precedence over his marriage. It was as simple as that. So when he came home he started to pack.

Molly looked in at the door, trying to keep the bleakness she felt out of her face. She had long since realized that here was not your normal everyday marriage. The wife of a salesman expects him to leave home for weeks at a time, or a seaman or a truck driver, or a – a – helicopter logger (her mind grasped for unusual occupations), or even an actor doing an international tour, but an actor who was living ten minutes from the studio? It was hardly normal for him to go and live in a hotel, was it? Unless. Unless the marriage was a poor one? Could he have another woman and yet make love like he had to Molly just last night?

"Don't just stand there. Fill my toilet bag. And find me some more socks."

At the front door Harry put his arms around Molly and kissed her and her treacherous knees gave way and she sagged against him.

"O.K.," he said. "That's enough. I'll be back."

He threw his things into the Lincoln and then turned back.

"Don't call me," he said. "I'll call you." And he dropped one eyelid in an intimate wink that lifted her heart.

I did it to him, she thought. I took off and left him, I guess he's entitled to do it too? But I wish – then she had an idea!

Harry had been in his suite in the Bayshore barely an hour when a messenger delivered a small oblong parcel. Inside, in a nest of tissue paper, lay a Barbie-doll, a Barbie doll with the blonde haircut off short, and wearing blue jean bib-overalls and a T-shirt. There was no message; there did not have to be; the medium was the message. It was quite clearly "I'm your wife, please don't forget me, I love you." Harry smiled as he put it carefully away in the drawer of the bedside table next to the Gideon Bible.

Would he really come back? Sure, he had said 'I'll come back' but would he? Was it over? Had he felt like this when she had left – so lost and unsure? Would she ever know him?

The weeks of shooting stretched ahead interminably.

Chapter Seventeen

The End of the Affair

"A new star is born. Looks like young Wednesday Barnes, well-endowed leading lady in the new Harry Wentworth epic "Tiger's Eye" will make it to the top in short order."

"Richard," Molly said urgently, leaning across the table towards him, "I need your help. I don't know what to do about – Harry." (She had been going to say 'your father' but looking at the mature man in front of her, so close to her own age, it had suddenly seemed ridiculous.) "I'm afraid I'm losing him."

They were sitting at a tiny table at the back of the Beach House Tea Room in Stanley Park, where Molly had asked him to meet her. Outside in the sun waiting tennis players sprawled on the grass, while those playing on the many courts in front of them livened the air with the smack and plop and swing of balls being hit, and with shouted scores and whoops and exclamations of disgust – none of which Molly heard.

"Because he's going out with his current leading lady?"

"Going out with! He's moved out and living in the same hotel with. I never see him any more. He doesn't even call and the studio won't put me through to him. What do I do, Richard? Has he ever done this before?"

Richard shook his head in surprise.

"You mean you really don't know?"

"Don't know what? I was never a fan of his, remember?"

"Well, Dad's had an affair with every leading lady in every movie he's made since I can remember."

"When he was married to your mother?"

"No. I mean since she died. I used to read about him in the movie magazines and feel sick."

"I feel sick now. But not before she died?"

"I don't... think so. Maybe I just wouldn't have noticed at that age, and anyway we never had those magazines in the house then. I'm sorry, Molly. I'm really sorry you're going through this." Richard touched her hand and looked at her with real concern.

"But what do I do, Richard? Should I fight for him? Should I smile sweetly and graciously retire to the sidelines? Should I offer him a divorce – or start proceedings -?"

"No. My God, no. You really don't understand, do you? It's a thing some actors do – fall in love with their co-star, I mean. They say it helps their relationship on screen, or something – makes it more real. But when the movie's finished, so's the affair."

"Affair. I hate that word. Is that what happens with Harry, then? Does it always end when the filming finishes?"

"I guess so," Richard said, judiciously sipping his coffee. "He never stayed with any that I know of. Of course, I never really knew, only what I could glean from the magazines, and who knows how distorted they are? Maybe he didn't even have affairs."

"He is this time," Molly asserted grimly. "I've seen them working together and relaxing together. It's that girl with the silly name – Wednesday. She's an absolute stunner. Richard, I can't compete with a girl like that."

"You don't have to compete," Richard assured her. "You two are not even in the same class. My guess is that she's just part of the job to him – but you're his life."

"What a lovely corny line! Thanks, Richard, I wish I could believe that. But how can I be his 'life' when he never comes home to live it with me?"

"Maybe I should say 'his real life'. And Wednesday is part of his pretend life – on screen, in character."

"You make it sound so reasonable. Why am I so hurt and churned up inside?" She gave him a look of appeal and Richard dropped his eyes quickly so as not to meet her gaze and give away his own feeling.

"It's funny, isn't it?" he said. "I resented it terribly when I heard he was marrying you, and now I hate him for hurting you. I never thought I would accept anyone who took my mother's place."

"I didn't take your mother's place, Richard – at least, not for Harry. She's still got her place, and I've got mine – least I thought I had."

"I think you have too. Dad really loves you, Molly."

"He's got a helluva way of showing it."

They lapsed into silence, drank their coffee.

"So," Molly said finally, "I should do nothing, then. Just be patient. Is that what Dell – your mother – would have done?"

"I don't know." Richard looked out across the tennis courts. "I can't remember her that well. It's a long time since she died, and I was just a youngster."

"What was she like? Do you realize I've never even seen a picture of her? There aren't any in the house – anywhere?

Richard pulled out his wallet and went through it as he spoke.

"She was small and blonde with a pink and white complexion like a china doll: she had a beautiful figure and always dressed like a model. There," he put a small photograph on the table between them. "She was about thirty when that was taken."

Molly looked at the woman in the picture and felt – surprisingly – nothing.

"Well," she said wryly," we're not much alike, anyway."

Richard glanced up.

"More than you imagine, Molly. Mum wasn't interested in films either, though she had been a dancer before they married – and she was one-of-a-kind, like you."

"But I'm middle-aged and getting out of shape and awkward and a lot of the time I dress like a frump."

"But you're fun, Molly – and so was she. And if she were your age maybe she'd be getting plump by now.

"I don't think so." Molly laughed and handed him back the picture. "She wasn't the type. I am. Well, anyway, I love him. Even though he's treating me like this and looking moonstruck at that gorgeous young thing – which I hate him for doing – I love him. Does that make sense?"

"Yes."

"And you think if I'm good and patient he'll come back to me?"

"If he doesn't he's a fool," Richard said roughly.

"I'm not good at being patient and letting myself be trodden on. If I should rear up and take a poke at him will you be around to hold me back, or pick up the pieces?"

"Yes," said Richard, "You can count on it."

Had she not been so wrapped up in her own perspective of the problem Molly might have noticed the strangely fervent tone he used.

The long lonely days crept by, and in order to blunt her imagination Molly worked longer hours at the Day Care Centre, and when she came home threw herself into grandiose house cleaning projects, scorning the paid help who could have relieved her of these chores. Mavis watched sympathetically, having seen it all before, and the children became subdued and anxious in the face of their mother's obviously false acceptance of Harry's absence. They enjoyed Harry, and knew their mother did too, and not to have him coming back in the evening – even growling and pacing morosely and going over his lines – made the house a less exciting place to live.

Molly was swabbing the hall floor one afternoon when a car swept up to the door, sending up a shower of gravel, and her heart gave a funny lurch as she plunked the squeegee in the bucket and waited. Harry opened the door and her naked heart leapt to her face with joy – until Wednesday stepped in behind him and it zonked down to her stomach again.

They stared at her and she became very conscious of the old rolled-up jeans, the blouse knotted at the waist because the bottom two buttons were off, the worn down thongs on her feet and the cotton scarf covering her hair.

"Uh –" she said, groping for words. "Hallo, Mr. Wentworth. Your wife's out. I'm the new cleaning lady."

"Knock it off, Molly," Harry said briskly. "I thought we paid someone to scrub floors?"

"We did," she said lightly, "but since half my family left home I have time on my hands – I can save my poor hardworking husband some money." It was either talk like that or cry with frustration.

"Hmm." He grunted. "Just came back to pick up some evening clothes for the end-of-shooting party tonight. "He started down the corridor, turned back. "You know Wednesday, of course?"

Molly swallowed.

"Of course. Hallo Wednesday."

Wednesday was beautiful. She was poured into skintight designer jeans and a shiny satin blouse; her gorgeous copper-tinted hair framed her face in an artful tangle; her flawless complexion came out of a bottle and her fabulous eyelashes travelled in a little box when they were not stuck to her eyelids. She shifted from one stiletto heel to another.

"Hi, Mrs. Wentworth. May I come in?" She tip-tapped forward, looking around. "Sure like your house." She showed her teeth in a million-dollar dentist's smile, and took in the bucket and the mop and Molly with wide-eyed wonder. "Always do your own cleaning?" she asked in amazement.

Molly snatched the scarf off her head, that being the only improvement she could make in a hurry, and said darkly,

"Yes. He doesn't give me enough money to pay for a real cleaning lady. I even get down on my knees and scrub the oven." She shuddered at the memory.

Wednesday's eyes narrowed intelligently.

"You're joking me."

Of course she is," said Harry, coming down the corridor, his garment bag over one arm. He looked at Molly and actually saw her for the first time and shook his head in disapproval. "You're letting yourself go," he said sternly.

Didn't he know what he was doing to her, Molly wondered in despair. She looked him in the eye, holding his full attention.

"Harry," she said firmly, "Can I come to the party?" With

one foot she guided the bucket and mop to where she expected
Harry's next step would be.

"No. Cast and crew only. Wednesday and I are guests of
honour of course." He glanced down, stepped deliberately
over the bucket and led Wednesday out of the door.

"Urgh!" Molly sent the bucket flying down the hall with a
clatter and sat down suddenly, holding her foot.

A startled Wednesday peeped in the door and then turned
back and said in awe,

"Oh, Harry darling, she kicked the bucket."

Harry came in.

"I think I broke my toe."

He sloshed through the water and squatted down and took
her foot in one hand and wiggled the toe vigorously.

"It's O.K.," he said shortly, and stood up again. For a
moment – a split second – as he looked down at his soggy wife
sitting in the soapy water in her old clothes his gaze softened.
She was being so transparent he was, unwittingly, touched.

It was enough to give Molly hope, and when he had left,
she hobbled to the telephone.

"Richard," she said. "Can you please take me out to dinner
tonight?"

"Why tonight?"

"It's the end-of-shooting party at the Bayshore and I want
to be there. Harry's taking Wednesday and I'm not invited."

"Then how can you go?"

"Well, we can sit somewhere else in the dining-room, can't
we?"

"Is that wise?"

"Oh Richard, since when did I ever do anything wise?"

"Not often," he admitted.

"If you won't escort me I'll get Rob to."

"No, I'll do it, Molly. Rob's not old enough to handle you.
But I think you're asking to be hurt."

She called her hairdresser next, used her most imperious
voice, threw out Harry's name several times and persuaded
M. Roland – alias Bob Briggs – to abandon his present customer
to another operator and promise to do her hair immediately.

When she turned around, it was to find the twins quietly

mopping up the spilt water with clean bath towels.

"Thank you kids," she said humbly. "Aren't I silly? Why don't you have a good laugh?"

"You're not silly," said Ken.

"It's not funny, said Sue. "Nothing's funny anymore."

"Why don't you get Harry to come back?"

"I'm going to give it a damn good try. Believe me, I am."

Richard was not able to get a 'good' table at such short notice, but for Molly's purpose it was excellent. Set in a corner against a wall at the back of the room, it afforded a good view of the Cetapac tables without making her very noticeable.

Her hair was short and curly again. She wore a dress Harry had chosen for her, jewelry Harry had given her, and she smelled the way Harry liked her to smell. But she was sitting with Harry's son, and Harry was sitting with Wednesday Barnes. She arranged her chair so that three quarters of her back was towards the film group, but by glancing sideways she was able to take in all that happened there.

Harry and Wednesday were side-by-side directly facing her. Harry was listening to what the actress said, laughing in a charming way Molly was sure he had never laughed with her, looking down at her with tenderness, tolerance and admiration. He held the champagne glass up to her lips, he put his arm around her shoulders, he kissed her when a photographer held up his camera, and he stroked her forearm. Molly choked on her drink.

"I think I'm going to throw up. Let's go."

"No," said Richard sternly, "certainly not. It was your idea to do this, you're going to go-through-with-it."

"He'll kill me if he sees me. I'm wearing my heart on my sleeve – aren't I? – and he hates that."

"Then cover it up. You can carry this off. I'll help you."

"Dear Richard," she put her hand over his on the table and was surprised when he snatched his away.

"Don't do that!"

"Why not?"

"We don't want to start a scandal."

"Oh Richard!" she laughed. "I'm your step-mother!"

"It's a ridiculous situation and I've never felt about you that way, and you know it."

"I'm fond of you as a friend, a relative – but I love your father."

"And I love you, and that's why it hurts me when he hurts you, and that's why I'm helping you tonight."

They looked at each other, both a little shocked by what Richard had said, and then Molly spoke quietly.

"That was some speech, Richard."

"I'm sorry. It should have been left unsaid."

"If I hadn't been so stupidly self-centred, I would have realized ages ago. There were signs, I'm sure there were."

"I tried to hide them."

"And here I am asking you to help me win back your father's love. That's cruel."

"It's OK," Richard said. "If it works, it'll be OK. I'm just not sure how it's going to work."

"It's got to work," Molly said tersely. "I can't be a loving forgiving wife very much longer – I'm flying apart inside."

Their courses came and went, and the film people, who had arrived earlier than Molly and Richard, started to dance. Molly watched covertly as Harry danced with several women, and then more openly when he escorted Wednesday to the floor. But Wednesday could only disco and Harry looked nonplussed, and quickly relinquished her to a younger man and returned to his seat. Wednesday followed him back, took him by the hand, laughing, and dragged him back to the floor. She jigged and gyrated in front of him provocatively and laughed some more when Harry eventually responded with a few middle-aged twist steps.

Molly watched without smiling; she was feeling for Harry, who after a few minutes made a polite rueful gesture and returned to his table. She moved her chair to face him directly across the room. Harry sat back, lit a cigar and looked straight ahead and saw Molly. His hand hesitated for a fraction as he returned the lighter to the table, and his eyes met hers in a long hard look. Unconscious that she had even done it, Molly touched her hair, her necklace, her dress, crossed her legs, raised an eyebrow a tiny bit. I'm yours, come and get me.

"Harry's mouth hardened, he dropped his eyes then looked

away, apparently bored. Mortified, Molly turned her chair back to the table, gulped some wine, and stared at the cloth.

"It didn't work."

"Yes, it did," said Richard quietly. "He's coming over."

She felt rather than saw Harry's bulk beside her chair, saw his hand gesture towards the dance floor, got up, and preceded him to the edge of the floor. He put his arm around her and momentarily her legs turned to water at his touch (oh, no, not now, treacherous flesh!); he took her hand in an iron grip and held her up with a grunt; he drew her to him torso to torso, hip to hip, thigh to thigh, and she realized the band was playing a tango. They danced – not showily so that people would watch – quietly, harmoniously, with long smooth strides. Harry's cheek touched Molly's temple and a beautiful calm enveloped them for as long as the music played.

He guided her off the floor, cupping her elbow with a warm hand. Dear God, she thought, why am I trembling? The man's my husband. He pushed in her chair and as she reached for her glass he bent and said gruffly in her ear,

"Don't drink anymore wine, Molly." He left before she could respond.

She gulped down what was in the glass and held it out to Richard for a refill. Damn him! They had danced so well, why did he have to spoil it by being critical and masterful? She drank again, and turned her chair more resolutely away from the Cetapac table.

Richard, sympathetic, made no comment.

"What's he doing?" she asked presently.

"Talking to Wednesday."

And so Richard kept her informed as to what was happening across the room and for half-an-hour Molly drank, listened, asked questions, until she knew it was gone – the moment was past; nothing more would happen. The evening was over.

"Let's go," she said and started to stand up, only to sit down again quickly, gripping the arms of the chair. "Oh, no," she groaned. "It's happened again."

"The wine?"

"Everything's going round and round…"

"Just sit still and we'll have more coffee – lots of it." Richard signalled to the waiter.

"I wanted to leave before they did, but damn it, I can't go lurching out like this."

"Don't worry," Richard was smiling, "It'll pass. Anyway, I think they're moving out now."

Molly drank the coffee almost as quickly as she had the wine, cooling it with lots of cream.

"It's not working."

"Give it time. They're all out in the lobby. We'll have to wait until they disperse." Richard talked quietly, soothingly as the minutes dragged by; he had never seen Molly ashamed and he was strangely touched. Suddenly he stiffened and Molly saw his eyes (all three pairs) focus above and beyond her head.

"Dad's coming back," he said.

The two men, so alike, a generation apart, both loving her, stood on either side of Molly's chair.

"Bring your car to the door, Rich. I'll get her out there somehow."

The younger man nodded and left.

Harry helped her stand, linked his arm firmly in hers and gripped her wrist.

"Look up and ahead," he said, "and smile."

Molly beamed.

"Not like that."

She turned it down like a light.

"Better."

They moved slowly and regally into the lobby, making it look as though they were strolling casually. A flashbulb popped.

"I've been here before," said Molly.

"But this time," Harry said grimly, "you were pouring your own."

He helped her into the front seat of the car beside his son, apparently unaware of the incongruity of the situation.

"Thank you," she said. "All three of you." trying to sound bright and gay when in fact she felt humiliated. She had started out the evening strong and independent, and sure of herself, and now her chin was trembling and she had to grit her teeth hard to stop it. Then Harry leaned in and brushed her cheek with his lips.

"Goodnight, Molly."

"Goo'night – Mr. Wentworth."

"Take her straight home, Rich. Do not Pass Go; Do not Collect Two Hundred. That's a private joke."

Molly clamped one hand over her mouth and tried to will the tears to stay in her eyes – and failed. Harry pulled the silk handkerchief from his breast pocket and wiped her cheek and pushed the handkerchief into her hand. Then he shut the car door and turned away.

The twins heard the car in the driveway and scrambled to the window.

"Is it Harry?" Sue asked urgently.

"Nah. It's only Richard," said Ken flatly.

"Oh." Disconsolately they climbed back into their beds.

Molly felt wonderful the next morning. She slept late and woke to warm September sunshine flooding her room. No headache, no nausea from the wine, no guilt or shame or disappointment, just a buoyant hope, an illogical conviction that everything was all right filled her being. Call it a hunch, or intuition, she thought, or a just plain gut feeling, but I think things are working out.

She showered and dressed and joined Mavis in the kitchen.

"My, you look happy. How'd it go last night?"

"Very well. I got drunk and he helped me to the door."

Mavis raised an eyebrow.

"That's good?"

"That's good. Last week he would have ignored me."

"So now what'll you do?"

"Nothing. Something will happen – I know it will."

"Oh, the blind faith of the woman," said Mavis, putting toast and coffee on the table in front of Molly. "Your rotten husband dumps you for a two-bit floozy for six weeks and about breaks your heart, and then he helps you out of the room when you're drunk and suddenly everything's A.O.K."

"He's not a rotten husband – he's an actor."

"That's an excuse for his behaviour?"

"Not an excuse, a reason. He's on his way back – I know."

Molly giggled suddenly. "He couldn't keep up with Wednesday dancing last night – he's feeling his age. He's ready for good old middle-aged me."

"Drunk or sober?"

"Preferably sober, as he once said."

The telephone shrilled and Molly leapt up.

"That's him! Answer it, Mavis."

"How d'you know it's him?"

"How do I know how I know – I just know. Answer – please."

"Harry Wentworth residence, Mavis Topham speaking. Oh, my God -! I mean, good morning Mr. Wentworth. Molly? Yes, she – ah –" Molly signalled 'no' violently. "I'm not sure if she is in. Hold the line a minute." She covered the mouthpiece. "Are you in?"

"Tell him I'm out. Tell him I've gone for a walk," Molly hissed.

"Ah – I've found a note," Mavis extemporized. "Eh – she says – um – gone for a walk."

Harry's voice roared down the 'phone.

"When? Um – when?" She looked at Molly for help and she held up three fingers. "Oh – er – three hours –" Molly shook her head – "or rather, three minutes ago."

Again Harry's voice crackled down the receiver and Mavis held it away from her ear.

"Where? Do I know where?" She watched Molly mouthing an answer. "I... can't quite read it. Three?" Molly shook her head and tried again. "Oh, oh, yes – Third, that's it. Third what?" She was asking Molly, not Harry. "Third... Beach," she said triumphantly, reading Molly's lips."

"Put her on the 'phone, Mavis!" Harry shouted.

"I can't, she's gone." Mavis looked around. "She really has gone, Harry, that's the truth. I hear the car – oh –" She looked at the receiver – the line had gone dead.

Molly parked her car and ran down to the sand looking for Harry, hoping she had got there first. She had. The sand stretched golden and unsullied by footsteps, smooth from the ebbing tide, and beautifully empty of human occupation. The sun was bright, the waves broke in white showers, the sea was blue, and the breeze was pure and clean. Molly spread her arms and ran for the sheer joy of living.

"MOLLY!" A stentorian bellow from the Sea Wall. Harry stood there in his good sand-coloured three-piece suit, his feet apart, and his hands on his hips. "COME HERE!" he yelled.

Molly faced him, hands-on-hips, copying his stance.

"NO," she shouted back. "YOU COME HERE."

For a long few seconds he did not move, then deliberately he jumped down and started to walk towards her. She turned and ran. Without looking back she knew he was running too. She zigzagged through the soft dry sand and down to the firm damp sand and suddenly he was so close there was nowhere to go, but into the water. She plunged in up to her ankles, up to her knees, not yet feeling the cold of the autumn water.

"Molly, come out, you dumb nut."

She turned around panting and gasping and shook her head at Harry where he stood at the water's edge, his hands held out.

"No, Harry. You come to me."

"Very well," he said, and stripped off his jacket and threw it on the sand behind him and stepped into the water.

She waded further out, trying to jog in the water, missed her footing, was hit by a wave and fell with a shriek.

He reached her, grabbed her under the arms and dragged her up, dripping and spluttering, put his arms around her and held her tightly.

"Idiot, idiot, idiot…" he murmured, and cupped her face between his hands and kissed her, and then a bigger wave broke against his back and they both fell under the water. They struggled up together, hand-in-hand.

"My God," Harry said, "I'm freezing. We're too old for this."

They waded out of the water, gasping still with the cold and Harry picked up his jacket and they ran across the sand towards the Sea Wall. Panting, shivering, they almost collided with the mounted Policeman's horse.

"Morning," said the officer pleasantly, his face poker straight. "Enjoy your dip, Mr. Wentworth – Ma'am?"

"Hmm," said Harry. "A little brisk."

"Exactly," said Molly. "A little-ittle-ittle br-r-risk."

"I was on duty here when you two were married – quite a schmozzel wasn't it? Seen you often since – guess it's your favourite place? Well, I think you'd better dry off quickly before you catch cold." He touched his riding crop to his cap and urged his horse forward. He looked back and grinned. "I didn't see a thing," he said.

"Thank you, officer." Harry raised a hand.

The twins were home from school for their lunch and when they heard the two vehicles come into the driveway, they rushed to the window.

"It's them! It's them!" Sue cried. "Mum's wearing the picnic blanket and Harry's in Rob's old waders and oh – they're too small and he's walking all funny!"

Ken pushed her aside.

"They're carrying their clothes, and they're all wet!"

"Oh good," said Sue happily, settling back to her sandwich. "I think things are back to normal."

But they were not – not quite – and in fact never would be, for fate and Wednesday Barnes were preparing an even stiffer test for Harry and Molly.

Chapter Eighteen

Wednesday's Child

"Rugged Canadian actor Harry Wentworth, looking grim and refusing comment to reporters, arrived at the Courthouse this morning with his wife Molly smiling at his side. He is fighting the suit Wednesday Barnes is bringing against him."

Harry sat beside Molly on the front bench in the court room and presented his Mount Rushmore profile to the world – granite-like, imperious, expressionless, unmoved – only by the hand that uncharacteristically held hers on the seat between their thighs did he betray himself. That grip which he had taken when they sat down had not been to comfort or support her, Molly knew, but to draw strength from her presence; and for it she was suddenly grateful, for it meant that she was needed and useful (maybe, loved) and no matter what the outcome of the trial, no matter that she felt sick and desolate inside that there was a trial at all – there was a part of Harry that needed her, that no-one else was privy to, and for that part she could find love.

Molly was no actress, she could not do the Mount Rushmore imitation, she could not show the world coolness and detachment, and for that reason had argued forcibly that she should not come to the trial. Harry had insisted; it gave him credibility and dignity, he said, she must be seen to be on his side – at his side.

"I'll react," she had said.

"I know," he had answered grimly. "But come anyway."

Now she knew from the pressure of his hand he wanted her there for another reason, and it warmed her heart – the heart that had semi-frozen two weeks ago – and without thinking she turned her head and looked up at him with such tenderness that an artist in the court quickly sketched it for posterity.

The nightmare had actually started, Molly remembered, a week before the revelation was made; when Harry came in looking preoccupied and worried and hurried to the telephone before even greeting her. For days he had been aloof, removed from the family when he was home, but Molly had attributed it to problems at the Studio – often when filming he became superficially another person.

Again with hindsight Molly remembered Rob coming in from University, carrying a Movie magazine and looking concerned. The magazine was strange in itself as no one in the house read them – Harry refused to buy them, calling them dirt sheets, and worse. There had been an atmosphere of strain at the dinner table with Rob casting frequent hard glances at Harry; finally he had risen and said,

"Harry, can I talk to you, please? Downstairs."

Harry had shot him a look and evidently seen something in his face that caused him to get up unusually quickly.

"Of course."

They had gone down and Molly had heard their voices, quiet at first and then raised – both of them – in obvious anger. She gripped the arms of her chair, longing to go down and listen, but steeling herself to wait quietly. Eavesdropping is about as low as you can go, she thought.

Someone else in the house had no such qualms, for presently Sue came thoughtfully upstairs and across the room to Molly. She put her hand on Molly's stomach and said,

"Is there another baby in there, then?"

"No," Molly said sadly. "I'm afraid not. You know the doctor said I'd never have another one. Why d'you ask?"

"I heard Harry say to Rob 'well, how did you find out about this baby?' So I thought –"

"Oh now," said Molly quickly, relief flooding her soul. It was suddenly clear to her that Rob had got a girl in trouble and was asking Harry's advice, and though that was a problem, it was not an insurmountable one. "No, they're talking about someone else, not me I'm afraid."

Sue left and Molly cleared the table adjusting her thoughts to the idea of being a grandmother, or not being a grandmother if abortion should become the solution to Rob's problem – and wondering how she could accept that. At length she heard Harry coming back upstairs. He came into the living room, looking world-weary and sad and burdened. He put his hands on Molly's shoulders.

"I've got something to tell you," he said heavily.

She smiled to reassure him.

"I know."

"You do?"

"Yes. I guessed. It's Rob, isn't it? He's got a girl pregnant–"

"No. My God, no. I wish it was that simple." He reached one hand behind her head, put the fingers of the other hand across her lips. "Listen to me, Molly – don't say anything, just listen." Her insides turned to water, a ghastly premonition of disaster filled her and she stood mute. "Wednesday Barnes is having a baby. She's accusing me of being its father, and she's filing a paternity suit against me. It's not mine. I swear it. You have to believe me." Slowly he took his hands away from her head. "I'm sorry to have to tell you like this. I knew it was coming, but I hoped to keep it from you –"

"I'm sure you did." She blurted it out, wished it back immediately.

"– But Rob saw it in a Movie magazine – was shown it, I should say – and now we all have to deal with it."

Molly was heedless of the effort it must have taken for Harry to tell her this. All the jealousy, the hurt, the resentment and the fear she had felt during those long months when Harry had been filming with Wednesday came flooding back. It was so likely, it was so reasonable, it was so plausible; she had seen the way he put his arm around her when she forgot her lines; she had seen them rehearsing the love scene over and over again – of course there had been something between them then. And she had pretended to believe him, trust him. More fool her.

"Oh God, I feel betrayed."

"Believe me, Molly. Please."

"Believe you – why should I? Poor old middle-aged Molly could only give you a dead child, why shouldn't you try again with someone young and strong and beautiful, like her? Ah! – " She gasped as he slapped her across the cheek.

"Shut up!"

"Why do I hate you and love you at the same time? Why do you repel me and – and –"

"Molly, Molly…" he grabbed her, put his arms around her. "I'm sorry, I'm sorry…" He pushed the hair back from her face, kissed the cheek he had hit. "I told you at the time nothing had happened with Wednesday, and it was the truth. It's still the truth. You have to believe me."

"How can I?" Her voice was muffled against his shoulder.

"I don't know, love, but you're going to have to try, because I'm going to need you when the case comes up in court, because I'm going to fight it. Because it's not my child."

The weeks that followed were ones of almost intolerable strain – her heart wanted to believe him, but her intellect said 'no'. Somehow they went to parties and smiled, and even laughed. She took his arm and looked like his wife, and he cupped her elbow with his warm hand and looked like a faithful loving husband, but it was all sham and mockery. At home they were icily polite, remote strangers. The twins felt the tension and were quiet and good around the house, but Rob avoided Harry deliberately, bristling with hostility when they had to meet, and treated his mother with an unnatural consideration as though she had been bereaved.

A strange thing happened in bed one night. Lying apart from each other on their separate sides, each locked in a box of private misery, both afraid of the other's reaction if they touched, Molly felt she had never known such isolation and aloneness. She needed comfort and reassurance and there was no one in the world who could give it to her, for Harry was the one man who could comfort her, and Harry was the cause of her discomfort. Whom then could she turn to?

Opening her eyes, Molly saw the strong back turned to her and longed to tap its strength. She needed so much to touch. To touch something solid. To pull strength from someone strong. And Harry was the only one there. And the only one who knew what she was going through. But he was untouchable; he was the 'Enemy'.

She reached out a tentative hand and laid it gently on his back between his shoulder blades; he flinched and moved away and Molly withdrew her hand. Then Harry settled back in the bed and shifted a little closer to her, and once more, she touched his back. This time, instead of moving away, he leant into her hand and she felt his warmth and strength, and tension. And so they lay for minutes on end, in total awareness of each other's presence and need.

With a sigh – was he awake? – Harry shifted again so that his buttocks nudged into the curve of Molly's pelvis; her hand crept over his side and her arm curled around his chest. And so they lay again, silent, tentative, and aware. At last Harry's arm touched hers, his hand brushed then lightly covered hers. Now Molly sighed and butted her head against his shoulder blade, and warmed and comforted and no longer alone, she slept.

When they woke they were apart again and neither mentioned the happening in the night; both afraid (hoping?) the other had been asleep. Or awake...

The next night, an hour or so after turning out the light and mumbling a stiff and formal 'goodnight' to each other, their bodies touched again, accidentally, but on whose purpose? And their mutual emotional need overcame their intellectual disenchantment with each other. With eyes shut, reaching, groping, fearing rejection at each move, they caressed each other until at last Harry's arms encompassed Molly and they made careful, bittersweet love.

And so began a strange period in their lives when through the days they were stiff and guarded with each other – wounded and full of pride and caution and resentment, and obstinacy and pretense – and at night their bodies touched and comforted and made love, as though the darkness made them different people.

The night-people and the day-people did not verbally acknowledge each other's interdependence, but sometimes a glance, a small gesture; the lift of an eyebrow sparked a communication. How can we do this? Are you the person I knew last night? Where is my lover? Who is this daytime stranger?

Thus these communications and the nocturnal comings together made the difficult days before the trial more bearable. Without the nights, Molly thought, I don't think I would survive the days. She wondered if Harry felt the same, but the daytime Molly dare not ask the daytime Harry, and at night they never spoke.

Now they were sitting on the front bench in court beside their lawyer and Harry was holding Molly's hand and everyone, the public, the friends of both sides, the court officials, the reporters were watching them with eager gimlet eyes. Their slightest reaction would be noted, talked about, written about, exaggerated, twisted. They were on view, they were public property. They think we're not real people, Molly thought suddenly, who can be hurt and frightened. And that in itself was a frightening thought.

There was a rustle of excitement, a rising murmur of surprise as the doors flapped open and Wednesday Barnes swept in with her lawyer – Wednesday, all copper hair and high heels, expensive clothes and perfume, Wednesday 'The STAR' – and Wednesday followed by a nursemaid carrying a tiny baby well-wrapped in an acrylic shawl. It was High Drama, calculated and planned. She swept down the aisle and stopped in front of Harry and Molly, who had instinctively risen.

"Hallo Harry," she said in her husky little-girl voice.

He raised one ironic eyebrow in reply, meeting her eyes.

She pushed the nursemaid ahead of her.

"Meet your son," she said in clear crisp tones. "He's all yours – take him, why don't you?"

The nurse pulled the shawl back and the whole courtroom

behind them craned forward, holding their breath collectively. Harry glanced quickly at the baby and a flicker of expression crossed his Mount Rushmore features, like a volcanic tremor deep in a mountain's guts. Molly saw it and to divert attention from him, reached forward and took the baby from the nurse's arms and cradled him lovingly. The likeness was astonishing. She found she was looking down at Harry aged two weeks; Harry's eyebrows, Harry's nose, Harry's mouth, Harry's long face. To her he was a lovely baby.

"Wednesday," she said clearly, clearly enough for the whole courtroom to hear, "he's beautiful. How lucky you are to have a healthy living baby. What are you calling him?"

Wednesday had been making a moue of a scorn but the inquiry caught her off-stride and she answered quite naturally,

"Thomas Wentworth Barnes."

"Hallo, Thomas," Molly said and touched the soft cheek, triggering a brief toothless Harry-smile. Hallo Caroline, her mind said, goodbye Caroline. I want you, Thomas – the thought was like an explosion of light. She looked up quickly at Harry, who had been watching her closely and he saw the thought and shook his head in disbelief.

"Order in Court. All rise, please…"

"You never cease to surprise me", Harry murmured in Molly's ear as the Judge took his seat behind the Bench. "I love you." Mount Rushmore did not blink but he took her hand, free now that the nurse had taken the baby back, seemingly careless of whether anyone saw or not. Molly's stomach churned with a confusion of emotions.

They had barely seated themselves and the Judge was composing himself for an opening statement when the courtroom doors opened again, urgently and quick steps came down the aisle. Heads turned.

"Excuse me, Your Honour." Richard Worthington stood at the barrier. "I have something of importance to say concerning this case. May I approach the Bench, Sir?"

The Judge looked annoyed, glanced at the two Counsels, who nodded, and motioned him forward. Harry and Molly, in concert with everyone else in the court watched the young lawyer with astonishment and curiosity as he spoke quietly with the Judge. At last he turned.

"I have a statement to make to the court," he said firmly – a totally new Richard–personality whom neither Molly nor Harry had seen before. "I am claiming paternity of this child and offering total support to its mother."

"What?" Wednesday was up on her feet. "You can't do that!" she cried, but her voice was drowned in the general hubbub, and the Judge pounded with his gavel and called for 'Silence!' and added,

"Counsel, please control your client."

Her lawyer hauled Wednesday down into her seat.

"Continue. You have more to say, I believe."

"Yes, Your Honour. I think it's very obvious from the baby's facial features that I am the father, and I am prepared to take blood tests and answer any questions under Oath that Counsel may care to pose to prove my claim. In view of my claim, I respectfully suggest that Counsel for the Claimant, withdraw this suit from the Court.

The buzz of conversation broke out again as spectators and journalists alike, discussed the sensational development, but Harry and Molly exchanged not a word, riveting their attention on Richard. The Judge banged with his gavel again. "Court will recess while Counsels and I repair to Chambers, to discuss this counterclaim. Mr. Worthington will hold himself in readiness to attend our meeting."

"All rise!"

Richard, Harry and Molly stood in a tight threesome away from Wednesday and her friends, and Thomas Wentworth Barnes, his usefulness in attending Court having backfired on Wednesday was summarily dismissed in his nursemaid's care.

"You can't do this, Richard," Harry said.

"I'm the Dad, Dad. I have to. When I saw the baby outside just now, I knew I had no alternative."

"You'll ruin your career at the Bar."

"Possibly," he said evenly. "But what about your career on the screen?"

"Ah," Harry dismissed it – "it'll survive. When did you ever go out with Wednesday?"

"After you and Molly got together again – I figured she

needed some support. But she's no saint. I didn't think the baby was either yours or mine, until I saw it – and I don't think she did either. She doesn't want it, you know. She wants your money, lots of publicity and your head, if she can get it. I can prevent that by telling the truth – and marrying her."

"You love her?" Harry asked.

There was a slight pause while Richard – significantly – chose his words.

"I will give her all the love I have," he said carefully.

"Think she'll have you?" There was scepticism in Harry's voice.

Again Richard paused before answering.

"Yes. Not right away – but in time."

Molly had been listening, her eyes going from one to the other of the men in front of her, and now she spoke.

"Just a minute, you two. There's someone you're forgetting"

"Molly, it's –"

"Not me, Richard. Little Thomas, out there, whom everybody's busy rejecting. Harry doesn't want him, Wednesday doesn't want him, you don't really want him, and you're only prepared to acknowledge him to protect your father. Very noble. Well, I want him. A child has a right to be wanted, a right to a family, a mother, a father, love – we can give him all that, and to hell with your reputation, or your career."

"We can't do that, love."

"Why can't we? Why can't you go in there and tell the Judge that you're not contesting the suit any longer; you accept responsibility for the child and you're prepared to adopt him legally?"

The two men stared at her now.

"You want me," said Harry carefully, "to be noble and protect Richard?"

"No, I want you to be noble and give a child a home."

"And what about you?"

"What about me?"

"How will you survive the gossip, the pointing fingers – 'she took in her husband's bastard' – that sort of thing?"

"I'll manage."

"Now who's being noble?" said Richard.

"Don't get me wrong, gentlemen. I'm no do-goodie Pollyanna; I'm the one who stands to gain the most out of this. It's really a selfish suggestion. My arms have stayed empty after five pregnancies. I need a baby. Raising kids is what I do best. Or like doing best."

"Could you really do that?" Harry asked slowly, in wonder.

"Yes, I could. I love him already. He's so like you... and you..." She looked at Richard and a special message passed between them, a message Harry did not see.

"Get my Counsel out of Chambers and we'll talk about changing the Plea."

Molly took a deep breath. Her whole life was about to change – no, it had started to change from the moment Harry had told her about the paternity suit – and things were happening too fast.

In the car she was quiet until they turned off the Causeway into Stanley Park.

"Third Beach?"

"We have to talk before we get home." Harry parked facing the sea, sat staring through the windscreen. "I want to be sure that you really believe that's not my child."

"He has to be yours or Richard's, he's so like you both. It doesn't really matter."

"It does to me. I want to know that you trust me and believe me. Or our marriage isn't – good – anymore."

"Oh," Molly said in a small voice. "Just when I thought we were getting it together again."

"We are." He reached for her hand, knowing that she was thinking, as he was, of their nightly wordless understanding. "It's been a rotten two weeks for both of us. You may have thought I was hard to live with, but so were you." She smiled ruefully, her smile muscles out of practice. "I never went to bed with Wednesday, and that's not my child. Do you believe me?"

Molly looked down at her hands in her lap, his covering them. He was very convincing – but then he was a very good actor, wasn't he?

"I'll think about it."

They sat in silence, Harry leaning forward on the wheel,

his chin on his hands, waiting.

If I say yes, will I be lying? Is he lying? Is it better that we both lie than one lie and the other tells the truth? What's it all about? Trust? I trust him; I love him. I want him to trust me. So, of course, I must say I believe him. Even if I don't? Why not? But Molly, you're a rotten liar and he can always tell....

She turned, put a tentative hand on his thigh.

"I believe you, Harry."

He cupped her face in his hands, searched it.

"Look me in the eye and say it."

"I believe you Harry." She giggled suddenly. "Don't you believe me?"

He smiled. "I'll think about it," he mocked her.

"What bothers me," said Molly as they drove on, "is, I just can't imagine Richard in bed with Wednesday."

"Frankly," with a wry smile," neither can I. And speaking of bed..."

But before they could get to that, there had to be a family conference on the events of the day. This was a custom new to both Harry and Richard, and hitherto they had intended to enjoy it. This afternoon's conference promised to be a different proposition and they all approached it with hidden trepidation. They sat, all six of them, formally around the dining table, Harry and Molly at opposite ends.

"Your mother and I have a problem to share with you," Harry started.

"About the baby?" asked Sue.

"Yes. We –"

"On the T.V. News they said Richard said it was his."

"It is mine."

"Then why did – what's-her-name – say it was Harry's?"

"Because Harry has more money, of course," said Ken with his usual perception.

"Partly right."

"The problem is – your mother would like to adopt the baby."

Rob gave a snort and pushed his chair back angrily.

"You can't do that!"

"Why not?" Molly asked quietly.

"Because it's a – a – well, a bastard."

"He's a little boy who needs a home. Wednesday wants to go on being an actress, but I'd like to go on being a mother."

"It's not right!" Rob was still incensed. "You'd be a laughing stock, raising your – your – your son's -," he floundered. "It's ridiculous!"

"There's a way it wouldn't be ridiculous," Harry said carefully. "If I were to admit that he was mine –"

"My God! That makes it twice as bad!"

Molly sighed.

"That's silly," said Sue, with sweet reasonableness. "You can't pretend to be his father when you're really his grandpa. He'd be terribly mixed-up when he finds out."

"But why can't Richard just marry Wednesday?" Ken put in.

"She doesn't want to get married – yet. I asked her," Richard said. "Actually, neither do I until she wants to. First, she needs to be free to act anywhere in the world."

"But she had your baby!" Ken protested. Five curious pairs of eyes regarded Richard with sympathy rather than accusation.

"I know," he said shortly. "Any more suggestions?"

"It's so obvious," said Sue. "Richard takes the baby and gives him to Mum and Harry to look after 'till he and Wednesday gets married –"

"And I can't think of anyone I'd rather have to mother my child," said Richard warmly.

Molly dropped her eyes quickly, thinking, my God, that's a loaded statement if ever there was one, I wonder if Harry noticed? She said quietly,

"Thank you, Richard."

"Then he won't grow up thinking his father is his brother and his Granddad is his father," said Ken, logically following his twin's thought process.

There was a silence.

"A Solomon come to judgement," said Richard approvingly.

"Why don't we just hand over the government to children," said Harry. "They make everything so simple."

Molly smiled.

"What'll happen to you, Richard?"

"The Bar Association will probably discipline me. It'll blow over."

"That's settled then."

But of course, it was not as simple as that…

Rob, for one, remained antagonistic to the idea – and the child – believing in his heart that it was Harry's, and it was not until Thomas's arrival into the household brought with it the advent of the girl who was to become his wife that he relented his judgemental position.

Arrangements were made quickly since Wednesday had an offer to film in Europe and wanted to settle things before she left. Molly had to feel sorry for her; the girl appeared bewildered at the way the court case had backfired, and she found it difficult to look on Wednesday as a sexual rival for her husband's affections. She was even, at the last minute, surprised by her own depth of emotions in parting with the baby, to whom she had professed to be indifferent.

Molly, herself had moments of dire misgiving – which she only admitted to herself – wondering if this would, in fact, disrupt her marriage rather than cement it; wondering how Harry would accept the child….

THOMAS

To Molly's surprise and pleasure Harry accepted the baby immediately and without reserve. When he came home in the evening he would pluck him from the crib and walk around the house with him in the crook of his arm, or over his shoulder. He sat by the fireplace and studied his next day's lines with the baby on his lap, mumbling aloud, sometimes explaining the plot quite seriously as though the blue-eyed infant could actually understand him. He never used baby-talk and he never played with the child in the usual sense; he treated him as a small intelligent being. He taught him to make faces and to formulate sounds in imitation of him. He exercised his arms and legs and helped him coordinate his hands and eyes. He was a constant source of stimulation for the child, and little Thomas responded gratifying. Harry rarely kissed him and growled alarmingly when he cried, and when he roared he said "shut up" and called Molly or Mavis to attend to the routine physical needs such as changing and feeding and cleaning. One thing he left entirely to Molly was the swimming lessons; it gave him pleasure to watch them in the water together and he never interfered, even when he privately thought Molly was demanding too much of the little fellow.

Richard came over often to establish his rights as a father, but fell far short of Harry in his relationship to the child. Watching Harry one day as he exercised the little limbs he asked,

"Did you do this with me, Dad?"

"Of course," said Harry. "Why do you think you turned out to be such a bright young man?"

"You think Thomas will be a lawyer like me?"

"No," said Harry. "This lad's going to act – I guarantee it."

"Like his mother," said Richard.

"Yes. Like his mother," Harry said. That was all. They did not discuss Wednesday, by tactic unspoken agreement, and while she was absent filming, no comment was made about the fact that she never came to see her baby. It was accepted that was the way she was. If it saddened Richard, he never showed it.

As the weeks went by, Molly found that much as she enjoyed having a child to care for again, it was more time-consuming than she had anticipated. Mavis had her hands full, running the house, and while Ken and Sue loved having a baby to boss around, they were not reliable baby-sitters, and Rob, of course, remained judgementally aloof when he came over, doing his best to totally ignore a baby whose parentage he still looked upon as an insult to his mother. Molly acknowledged to herself – with a little guilt and regret – that she needed help, and without consulting Harry began to look around for a nursemaid.

The girl she found arrived just as Rob was leaving after one of his rare, short, visits, and they met in the hall. They shook hands and Molly was aware of a moment of stillness between them before Rob suddenly offered to carry the girl's suitcase to her room – which was in fact his old room.

When he came back to the front door, he said,

"I'll be back, Mum. Soon." And he glanced down the passage significantly.

Oh, Molly thought. Good.

That evening Harry came in and went as usual to the nursery to collect his grandson only to find the child being tucked up in his crib, protesting vehemently, by a strange young woman in a shapeless grey dress with a white Peter-Pan collar.

"Hi," said Harry briefly, pushed past her and leant over the crib and prepared to lift the child out.

"Oh no, sir," the young woman said quickly, her English accept crisp and precise. "Baby is just going to bed, you can't disturb him now."

"(A)," said Harry, pulling back the blankets and picking up his grandson, who was already making noises of recognition, "this is not Baby, this is Thomas; (b) he does not go to bed just when I get back from work; and (c) don't call me sir."

"I beg your pardon, Mr. Wentworth. I must ask you to put Baby Thomas down; this is a normal child's bedtime."

"Uh-huh? Well, this is not a normal house. Thomas sleeps when I'm at work and wakes when I come home. Otherwise how could we ever meet? Got that? Who are you, anyway?"

"My name is Pauline Tyndall. Mrs. Wentworth has engaged me as Nanny for Baby- Thomas." The girl was obviously afraid of Harry, who was coming across very strong and dominant, and had her hands clasped tightly in front of her, no doubt to hide the fact that they were shaking. She wore her dark hair pulled severely back from her face and screwed in to a bun at the back of her neck in an effort to make her appear older and more authoritarian; grey nylons and flat-heeled black shoes completed the drab dress. "You can call me Nanny or Nanny Tyndall."

"The hell I can," said Harry, tucking Thomas in the crook of his left arm. "In this house you'll be Pauline, or Nanny Pauline."

"But, sir – Mr. Wentworth – it's customary –"

"Yeah, maybe in England – but not here. While you're at it, you can dump that nineteenth century outfit and go and put on some real clothes." His eyes appraised her frankly, seeing the trim figure beneath the plain dress, making no bones about the fact that he was mentally undressing her.

Pauline's chin came up defiantly and she seemed on the point of saying something when Molly appeared in the door.

"Oh dear!" she said. "I meant to warn you two about each other."

At this moment Harry transferred the baby rapidly from one arm to the other and draped him over his forearm and Pauline stepped forward with a cry of dismay, hands outstretched to catch him.

" It's all right, Nanny," said Harry mockingly, with a wicked sideways look. "I won't drop Baby, I promise." Then seeing the genuine concern on the girl's face, he grinned and added, "I love the kid." He started to leave the room.

"What shall I do, Madam?"

"Not 'Madam'," Harry shouted back from the corridor. "My wife is not a Madam. She doesn't run a whorehouse."

"Just change into something less formal, Miss Tyndall," said Molly hastily, "and then come and join us in the living-room."

Pauline changed into a blouse and skirt, beige nylons and strap sandals with a two-inch heel. She was feeling lonely and disoriented as a new immigrant, with, as yet, no friends or family for support; the brief meeting with her employer's son Rob had been the only bright spot since she landed. She had hoped – expected – to get a position with a nice English family where she would feel secure in a familiar environment, and instead she had landed the only job on the Agency's books with this fierce actor whose name she remembered (too late) having seen splashed all over the front page of the News of the World as being involved in a paternity suit. Somehow she had assumed the child would be rejected and neglected and resented, not loved. Confused and shy, and somewhat bewildered by the Canadian informality she went out to the living room.

Mrs. Wentworth was sitting by the fireplace with the baby on her knee and Harry was leaning negligently against the mantelpiece looking down at them, but when he glanced up and saw Pauline he straightened at once and came towards her, hand outstretched.

"Good evening," he said suavely, affecting an English accent and emanating Charm and Sincerity, "my name is Harry Wentworth. You must be Pauline Tyndall. How nice to meet you. Do come in." She knew he was pulling her leg, but the warmth of the handshake he gave her was genuine, and when he put his arm around her shoulder and drew her towards the fireplace, she felt in a strangely prophetic way as though she was being welcomed into the family. "This is my wife Molly, and my grandson Thomas," he finished gravely.

Pauline giggled.

"We've already met," she said, dropping the pseudo-refined accent she had been adopting and letting the North Country flatness into her voice.

Molly was staring up at Harry.

"I didn't know you could talk like that," she said in amazement.

"There's a lot you don't know, ducks," he retorted, in Cockney this time. He turned to Pauline. "An' w'en we know yer be''er, luv, mybe you'll let yer 'air dahn fer us, eh!"

"Oh," said Pauline, putting her hand up to the bun which she hated. "Oh, yes, of course."

As the months went by, Pauline became very fond of her employers, and fonder still of Rob, but she was never quite to lose initial feeling of awe and fear of Harry. The twins summed it up one day:

"She likes Mum and us and Mavis; she loves Thomas; she's stuck on Rob and she doesn't understand Harry." That was Ken.

"Now we're a real TV family," said Sue comfortably, as though that was an accomplishment. "We've got a stepfather and a stepbrother and a maid and a Nanny—"

"And a Lincoln Continental," said Ken.

"— and a Nilligitimate baby. I bet we could write our own soap opera just about us."

Which explained why sometimes they caught each other's eye across the table during some crisis and dissolved in laughter.

But life after Thomas was not all jam for Molly. The restraint between her and Harry remained a real and bothersome thing. She sometimes wondered if it was destined to be a permanent part of the rest of their lives....

Chapter Nineteen

"Goo'bye, G'ampa."

"Wednesday Barnes, sexy international star who shot to fame after starring in "Tiger's Eye" with craggy Harry Wentworth two years ago, today married his son (and the father of her child) Richard Worthington, local lawyer.

Molly woke, and knew at the instant of waking that it was going to be a bad day, and a conscious moment later remembered why. This was the day Thomas went to Richard and Wednesday. Forever.

"Long face?" said Harry, looking at her reflection in the dressing-table mirror.

"He goes today," she said, knowing he knew whom she meant.

"Hmmph." He grunted and turned away. "High time. Two years is too damn long."

Damn you, she thought, you're as fond of him as I am – maybe fonder – why can't you be honest and admit that you're going to miss him? But you won't, of course; you'll grunt and shrug and turn away – anything but put your feelings into words.

They had slept in because Harry had been out on a night location shoot in the P.N.E. grounds until the small hours of the morning and Molly had waited up for him; today he was not due on the set until ten a.m. – an unusual luxury. The household was well into its routine by the time they had dressed – the twins had left for school long since, and Thomas was washed, dressed and breakfasted and sitting up in his high-chair in the kitchen listening intently while Mavis read the funnies to him.

"Morning kid," said Harry gruffly, tousling his hair as he passed on his way to pour himself coffee.

"Morning G'ampa."

"That's Grrampa," Harry corrected him automatically. "Read him the editorials, Mavis, the English is better."

"Oh, Harry, he won't understand them."

"Does he understand the funnies?"

"Yes."

"Then he'll understand the editorials. Won't you, Thomas?" The child laughed at the face Harry made at him and banged his high-chair tray. "See?" Harry took his coffee through to the dining room where Molly was toying with toast and marmalade. "Where's Pauline?" he asked.

"Packing."

"Cheer up," he said matter-of-factly. "Not as though he's leaving the country; they only live two miles away. Tell you what; I'll take you out to dinner tonight. OK?"

"OK" Molly said without enthusiasm.

Harry looked at his watch. "Gonna be late." He got up. "Pauline!" He started down the corridor. "Pauline!" he roared again.

She peeked out of her bedroom door for all the world like a nervous rabbit at the entrance to its warren, and when she saw that Harry was intent on coming in, she backed in, in front of him, trying to keep between him and the bed on which was spread all the intimate underwear she owned. But Harry was not interested in the underwear she owned, he was looking at Pauline.

After two years Pauline was still half-afraid of her employer, though she knew now that he was 90% bark and 10% bite. She had enjoyed living in the odd household with its strange mixture of people; the comings and goings; the chance to see well-known personalities relaxing; observing Harry's and Molly's dynamic relationship – as weirdly unsuited to each other though they seemed – and she respected Molly's ability to cope with it all. Especially she had come to respect Molly's acceptance of the child – in fact, her unreserved love for him. Of course, Thomas was a bright boy, made brighter by the constant stimulation he had had, - but there was that lingering question mark about his parentage.

Now Pauline stood in front of Harry and wondered if she would be as happy in Richard Worthington's home, working for the child's mother, the glamorous Wednesday Barnes.

"You're going," said Harry. "Want to thank you." He pulled a cheque out of his inside pocket and handed it to her. "Done a good job."

Pauline glanced at the cheque and almost dropped it when she saw it was for a thousand dollars.

"Oh, Mr. W...." (Mr. W. being the compromise they had agreed upon when she had flatly refused to call Harry by his first name and he had flatly refused to be called sir or Mr. Wentworth.) "... I can't accept this!"

"Course you can," Harry said gruffly. "Buy some new clothes. I don't want to see my future daughter-in-law in Wednesday's cast-offs."

"Oh, but – Rob and I – it'll be years before we can, you know, get married –"

"Save it then."

"Thank you." Pauline held out her hand, at a loss for further words.

Harry ignored the hand, took her shoulders and pulled her to him and kissed her soundly on both cheeks.

"Look after him," he said, and then left the room abruptly, shutting the door behind him. Pauline was astonished and touched; she had never felt too much warmth and emotion from Harry before.

Harry stomped down the passage and was ambushed by Thomas, just released from his high chair, who rushed at his legs and grappled them until he stopped walking.

"Thomas is going to Mama-Jo and Dad today," he said chattily.

"I know," Harry replied. "Good riddance. Now, get off my leg, kid, or I'll kick you against the wall."

Thomas was not deceived by Harry's fierce voice and only chortled and hung on the tighter saying,

"They got a new house, I got a new room, I got a new bed, Nana Pauly's going too. Will you come and see me?"

"Maybe," said Harry. "You're making me late for work." He bent down and pried the little fingers apart from behind his calf and when his face was only a few inches from Thomas's the child looked up at him and whispered,

"Don't want to go."

That was almost too much for Harry; he pushed the little boy away and started for the front door. Thomas sat down heavily and let out a wail, followed by a sweet little half-choked sob that was designed to break adult hearts.

"Shut up," Harry said sternly, turning. "You're faking, Thomas – you'll never win an Oscar that way."

"Thomas sad," the child said, pulling a long face.

Harry levelled his forefinger like a gun and said "Phhtt." And Thomas obediently flopped over backwards, rolled his eyes up and played dead.

"That's better," said Harry briskly, having a quick vision of Molly doing the same thing years ago, "goodbye, Thomas."

"Goo'bye, G'ampa."

"That's Grrrrampa. A good actor always sounds his R's, Thomas."

"Goo'bye, GrRRRRRRRAMPA!"

Harry shut the door quickly before the child could rush at him again.

Molly, watching from the kitchen, but unseen by either Harry or Thomas, guessed what the little exchange had cost her husband. He had forgotten to say goodbye to her for the first time in years. She watched through the kitchen window as Harry hurried to the car and then stopped with his hand on the door handle, looking back at the house thoughtfully. She moved out of his line of vision, not wanting him to think she was spying on him, feeling suddenly unbearably sad. The thin end of the wedge, she thought.

The kitchen door behind her opened quietly and Harry stepped in. He put his hand on Molly's bent neck, kissed her behind her ear.

"See you later, love," he murmured.

"You're going to live with Mum and Dad," Molly said brightly to Thomas as they sat on the floor in his room systematically packing his toys in cardboard cartons. At least Molly was systematically packing, Thomas was unsystematically unpacking. She said it to him yet again, no longer caring whether he understood or not, but simply because she was in the habit of telling him everything and more importantly because she had to say the words aloud in order to get used to the reality of what was about to happen.

Thomas had heard this now over and over for days and was bored with the information, so he answered with his hands, pulling the toys resolutely out of the boxes.

Oh dear, this is going to be harder than I anticipated.

Notwithstanding the initial barrier the child had raised between Harry and Molly, Thomas had lately become a bridge across which tentative love and at least an attempt at understanding passed. He had become part of their daily life; now he was leaving. What would fill the gap, and without him would the bridge collapse?

God, is it you making life difficult, or do I do it to myself?

Wednesday and Richard arrived on a wave of perfume and laughter and talk. Wednesday a mature woman now, a Star in her own right, no longer needing the freedom to move – husbandless and childless around the world making a name for herself. In fact, now needing a husband and child to give her image a warm boost – and to give her a feeling of deeper worth as a woman (or so she said). And Richard – Richard was a warmer person, than he had been, too; still a little amazed to find himself married to a glamorous star, and deeply fond of his son.

Wednesday sailed into the nursery and swooped down on Thomas and scooped him up and whirled him around in her arms, her eyes alight with love and joy. Like Harry, she emanated a vital charisma no matter how she dressed, and now in jeans and a T-shirt that would have made Molly meld into the woodwork, she positively sparkled, and the child shrieked with joy and clutched at her marvellous hair.

Molly felt a pang of jealousy and in turning away met Richard's steady gaze. He was observing both the women – and loving and understanding them both too – and the look on his face gave Molly the strength to pull herself together and say,

"Well, I'll leave you three to pack up here, and I'll go and help Pauline." Pauline did not need any help, but it was an excuse to get out of the room.

Wednesday found her later downstairs in the family room ostensibly sorting out children's books and records.

"Molly," she perched on the arm of the sofa. "Can I talk to you?"

"Of course." Molly went on sorting.

"Are we friends?" That got Molly's attention. "I want us to be friends."

She sat back on her heels and looked up at the actress.

"Yes, Wednesday, I think we are – we can be – friends."

"You're a marvellous person. I don't know anyone else who could have done what you did, taking in my son and raising him like your own for two years. Especially after I'd brought that dumb suit against Harry – and, well, that must have made things rough on your marriage – I don't know how you could forgive me." (Neither do I, thought Molly.) "I know you'll say you did it for Thomas's sake, and I know you did, but I want you to know what a lot it did for me too. I was young and stupid and naive then, and I needed to get a lot of stuff out of my system. If I'd had to marry and settle down, I'd have never grown up. So, thank you for that too, Molly. With the exception of my mother, I think you're the nicest person I ever met."

"Well –" Molly was amazed at the rush of words and their obvious sincerity. "What can I say, but – thank you? And do love Thomas, he's such a nice little boy. And Richard."

"I love them both most dearly. And you'll always, always be welcome at our house – you know that." She stooped and enveloped Molly in a fragrant bouncy hug, and willy-nilly, Molly found herself hugging her back.

This is ridiculous! Molly thought. It's unreal! This woman nearly wrecked my marriage, and in my heart of hearts I sometimes think she bore my husband's son (whom I raised while she gallivanted around the world making a name for herself, and whom she's now taking away from me) and I'm hugging her! As though I love her; as though we're bosom friends? Well, she's got the bosoms and I've got the friendship –

The thought was broken by Richard's appearance at the door with Thomas on his hip. By the look on his face, he also found the tableau that greeted his eyes incredible. Over Wednesday's shoulder Molly winked at him.

Thomas gave Molly a series of big wet kisses and patted her cheeks and pulled her hair and waved and laughed when Richard carried him out to the car, and she had to grit her teeth until her jaw ached to stop herself from crying. Pauline tactfully moved between Molly and the car and gave Molly a quick embarrassed hug and murmured in her ear,

"I'll look after him, I promise, Mrs. W.

The house rang with emptiness and silence. Molly and Mavis stood together in the kitchen. Not touching... but understanding. Molly said,

"I'm going for a walk around Stanley Park."

"For how long?"

"For as long as it takes."

Mavis nodded.

At first Molly walked blindly, not seeing, not thinking, her legs working automatically, her mind in hiatus – in retreat. Then gradually she began to think, aware that her cheeks were wet – but that just might have been her eyes watering in the wind, mightn't it? – and wonder. She loved Harry so much, and yet there seemed to have been a reserve between them ever since the paternity suit fiasco, as though they were both holding back afraid to fully trust the other with their true feelings. Thomas had been a godsend, a medium through whom they communicated and expressed themselves. Now that he was gone what would they do? They couldn't go back. Was there anything to go forward with?

She passed Third Beach and remembered how Harry had

swum out to share the nadir of her life with her, and how they had swum back together, and she marvelled that she had ever thought of drowning as a solution, even recognizing that it was triggered by the loss of her baby and the very normal onset of post-partum blues. Now she felt no suicidal impulse – a weary despair, perhaps, but only that.

She walked longer than she meant to, and it was getting dark when she finally got home, tired and cold, guiltily aware that people had probably been worrying about her. Harry leapt from his chair by the fireplace when he heard the door shut and was halfway across the room in two strides.

"I'm sorry," Molly said quickly, "I didn't mean…" She stopped, her mouth open in surprise. "Harry," she said. "What happened?"

He stood a few feet from her, almost embarrassed, a new Harry in brown slacks, an open-necked white shirt and a fawn coloured long-sleeved cashmere sweater.

"Well," he spread his arms. "Thought I'd try on a new image."

"I like it." Molly reached and touched the sweater, ran her hands down his arms feeling the softness of the wool. She leaned forward and laid her head on his chest experimentally and he leaned in to her so that her cheek pressed hard against him, and she murmured in satisfaction, rubbing her face against the softness, and at last, when he had almost given up waiting for her to do it, she wrapped her arms around his chest and held him.

"All right," he said gruffly after a moment, "don't make a meal of it." He pulled her arms apart and reached for a packet that lay on the hall table. "Take this, and get your toothbrush."

"What is it?"

"Present for you, fool."

"Why a toothbrush?"

"I booked a suite at the Bayshore. We'll have dinner and stay overnight. Open it."

Molly opened the box and pulled apart the tissue paper and lifted out the sheer red nightgown. She held it against herself and looked up at Harry, smiling her pleasure, all the sadness gone from her face. He's wooing me, she thought with delight. The darling, kind, perceptive man.

"I love you," she said, hearing herself say it quite unplanned."

"Hmmph." He grunted, pleased, meaning 'and I love you'. "Tomorrow," he said, "You'll go out and buy yourself a whole new wardrobe."

"But Harry, I don't need –"

"Yes, you do. Because we're going to Europe for three months. The opener for next season's "Stringer" is a two-hour special and we're shooting on location in five countries. You're coming too."

"But I never go on location with you, Harry."

"From now on, you will. Go and change for dinner, woman."

Molly paused on the way to the bedroom, looked at the new nightie in her hand, at the New Image Harry Wentworth in his cashmere sweater and asked,

"What's this all about, Harry?"

"New beginning."

"You mean – we're starting over?"

"No. You don't go back and start over, you make a new beginning from the place you've reached."

"And do we have to keep on making new beginnings?" Molly asked a little plaintively.

"Yeah. If we're to stay alive and vital. That's what life is all about, my love." He made his voice Deep and Portentous, for after all, he was an actor used to using his tools.

Ken and Sue, concealed in the stairwell, looked at each other. Sue's eyes were shining.

"Isn't he marvellous?" she breathed.

"Phoney," said Ken succinctly. "But Mum bought it."

"He meant it," said Sue. "They're going to make a New Beginning. Isn't it romantic?"

"Maybe," said Ken. "But if I know Mum," he added with prophetic certainty, "she'll mess it up somehow."

He was right, of course.

Chapter Twenty

Happy Birthday

"Trivia question: this day twenty-five years ago what famous Canadian actor's wife met an untimely death on the street in downtown Vancouver?"

Harry would be fifty-five in ten minutes. Dell would have been fifty-two. As usual for the four years since he had been married to Molly he had refused to acknowledge his birthday, and declined presents or a party without explanation.

He tried to imagine Dell at fifty-two. Would she have lost her dancer's figure and well-shaped legs? Would her blonde hair have faded and her well-defined features have blurred with age? Would her hands – Harry stopped himself because the pain was growing too much. After all the years, so much pain. He glanced guiltily at Molly asleep beside him, her face relaxed and soft, snoring gently. (Would Dell have snored?) He nudged Molly to stop the snoring, turned over and settled himself for sleep again.

The dream came. Again. It woke him, sweating, trembling and he lay still, shocked by the vividness of his inner pictures, and wondered if the cry he had made in the dream had been aloud. He waited, but Molly lay still and calm beside him.

The dream was always the same. He was walking West on Hastings and ahead of him at the intersection with Richards, he suddenly saw Dell, recognized her bright hair, her green raincoat, as she waited for the light to change. He waved but she did not see, so he started to hurry forward calling her name but his voice had no power, it was a whisper no matter how hard he tried to force the air past his vocal chords. She neither saw nor heard him, not expecting him to be there, happy within herself, intent on finding him a birthday present. The light changed and as she stepped off the curb a speeding car right-turning on the red caught her squarely and threw her up and to the side, a jumble of flying arms and legs, and she landed like a rag-doll on the hood of another car and rolled forward onto the street. And he knew – knew – knew – she was dead at that moment and a cry of dreadful anguish choked his throat. He tried to run forward, his feet slipping back and back the harder he ran. And the people crowded around and hid her from his sight and pushed him away, and he fought them, cursing, saying it's my wife, it's my wife, but they would not let him through, and always at that point he woke.

It had not been like that in real life for Harry had been filming at the Studio at the time and had seen nothing. But he knew how it happened because they told him – the police, the witnesses, the driver – and he had seen it at once in his mind's eye with his actor's imagination, and so he saw it over and over again, periodically, and the pain never got any less. He had not been there to shout a warning, to delay her the one second that would have saved her life – and he punished himself for that. If she had not been out to buy him a birthday present....

As long as he worked until he was so tired that he slept deeply, the dream stayed away. When he took time off, rested, relaxed, the dream came back. The dread of the dream drove him to work constantly. He knew this; no one else did. They thought he loved his work.

Harry's mouth was dry and he needed a drink and a smoke to soothe him so, with infinite care, he slipped from the bed, put on his robe and went to the bureau. He pulled out the top drawer and from under the pile of handkerchiefs he took out a small leather photo-frame and slipped it into his pocket. He did not need to look at it; he only needed to hold it, and know that Dell's likeness was there.

He went quietly to the living room, mixed himself a drink and lit a cigar, and then he opened the doors to the sundeck and stepped out into the mild summer night air and drew a deep breath.

Molly was awake. She had felt Harry's body shake, his pyjamas damp with sweat, had heard his teeth grind and the guttural sounds choked in his throat. For four years now, she had pretended to be asleep when he had the dream, had quietly put his soiled pyjamas in the wash the next day, said nothing. She had waited, knowing it was something very private, hoping he would confide in her without prompting. Her heart ached for him and his inability to share his horror with anyone else. There had to be an end to it some time; maybe tonight was as good a night as any.

This night followed another pattern – it was the night before the birthday he refused to celebrate. The dream came apparently haphazardly through the year, but always the night before his birthday.

With no particular plan in mind Molly got up, and pulling on her filmy summer negligée went through into the living room, moving silently in her bare feet on the warm floor. Harry was coming in from the deck, silhouetted against the moonlight, a glowing cigar in one hand, his glass in the other. Molly raised her arm and he saw her and started violently, and with a sharp exclamation dropped his glass. She knew that for one split second, he thought he had seen someone else. The glass landed with a small thud on the carpet and rolled in diminishing arcs.

"It's me," she said quickly. "It's me – Molly."

"Uh," he said. "Yeah — — well — — didn't mean to wake you." He bent to retrieve the glass. "Go back to bed, Molly."

"No."

"I'm all right. Go back to bed." His face was in the shadow, unreadable, hers fully exposed in the beam of moonlight coming in over Harry's shoulder. Carefully, she kept it smooth and unworried, feeling strongly that the next few seconds would be crucial.

"Since I'm awake I'll go and make some tea." She turned, apparently unconcerned, and went to the kitchen, praying that he would follow and at the same time dreading the difficult conversation that would inevitably ensue if he did. By the light from the control panel of the stove, she plugged in the kettle and got out the teapot. Harry came in, put his glass in the sink and sat down at the table, grateful for the dimness.

"Don't have to make it for me."

"I want a cup."

"OK".

She sat down.

"You had a bad dream." Statement... not question.

"Uh-huh."

"Again," she added.

He studied the mug she had set down in front of him, his private mug that no one else used.

"What d'you mean – again?"

"I've woken other times when you've had it."

"Sorry." He put up the shutters with the coldness in his voice, meaning subject closed, I don't want to talk about it.

"I think we should talk about it," Molly said, as though she had read his mind.

He studied the mug again.

"How many times?" he asked at last.

"Many. Over the years – ten – twelve. I don't know for sure."

"He expelled his breath in a small sigh.

"I'm sorry," he said again, more warmly. "I had no idea. What do I do?" It was painful for him to ask.

The kettle boiled and Molly made the tea and set the pot on the table before answering.

"You shudder and you thresh your legs. And you sweat and grind your teeth."

"Oh God. Do I say things?"

"No – not words. Mumble. Try to cry out, but don't, as though your throat closes."

"I didn't mean to bother you with this."

"No bother. I'm your wife. Isn't that what I'm here for – to listen if you want to talk?"

"Don't come the Mother-figure on me, Molly."

"I'm not. I just want to share your pain. Sometimes I feel so shut out. Don't shut me out, Harry."

He reached across the table but did not quite touch her.

"You've had enough pain of your own without having mine as well."

He sipped his tea, not tasting it. She had forgotten he did not like tea. His hand closed around the photo-frame in his pocket, and reluctantly, as though his hand was working at cross purposes with his mind, he drew it out; looked at it, surprised at what he had done. He laid it on the table.

"Know who this is?"

"Yes. It's Dell."

"How do you know that?"

"I've seen it before – many times. I put your handkerchiefs away in that drawer every week, Harry. Besides, your son Richard has one just like it. He showed it to me years ago."

Harry felt as though he had been caught naked in front of a mirror that was in fact two-way glass. She had no right to have been in the private places of his life. Molly felt him withdraw.

"You dream about her, don't you?" she said steadily. Having got this far she felt they had to carry on, even if it did mean her getting hurt, which she knew she would be if Harry rebuffed her. She had to put herself at that risk.

"I dream about her," he concurred heavily, after a lengthy pause.

"About..... how she died?"

"Yes." Tersely. "I don't like tea," he said, staring at the mug. "You know I don't like tea. She was killed on the crosswalk at Hastings and Richards." It came out suddenly as though he was afraid to hear the words himself.

"I'm sorry, darling. I never knew. People just said 'an accident'. I never asked what kind."

"You want to hear the gory details?" he asked harshly.

"If you want to tell me."

"I don't. But I will." And he told her, graphically, as he saw it in the dream, his voice expressive, dramatic, his timing and turn of phrase precise – these were the tools of his trade after all, when he had a story to tell he used them instinctively. The fact that he may have seemed to be acting it out detracted nothing from his sincerity for Molly, who knew him.

When he finished, Harry put his elbow on the table, and his hand up to his forehead, hiding his eyes. Molly gave him a moment of grace in which to compose himself.

"And this was twenty-five years ago?"

"Twenty-five," he said. "Yesterday."

"But it's over, Harry."

"It's never over."

"It is. It happened; it's finished, done. It wasn't your fault. Because she was out to buy you a present doesn't make it your fault, Harry. Has your subconscious been tormenting you with guilt all these years, just because –"

"Forget the amateur psychology, Molly," he cut in rudely "Just drop it."

"No. I think we should talk it out."

"I don't want to hurt you."

"I know that, I'm not a fool, Harry."

"When I said it's never over, I meant I still love her. God help me, Molly, I still love her."

It was like being kicked in the stomach. Help me, God, Molly prayed silently, give me words and give me courage and give me understanding. I don't want to lose this lovely man.

"Of course you love her," she forced herself to say gently. "I wouldn't expect you not to remember your love for her. But that was then, and this is now, and she's not here and I am. Dell is dead, Harry. She died twenty-five years ago, violently and unnecessarily, but she's dead. Let her go."

"I can't. If only –"

"Oh, Harry, forget the 'ifs', there's no profit in that line of thought. 'What if', 'if only', 'maybe if', - you don't know. It happened the way it happened. Don't try to live with the 'ifs', live with the facts, Harry, the reality."

"You don't know –"

"Yes, I do know," she interrupted quickly. "I know because I lost four babies before I met you, four of Tom's babies. So don't tell me I don't know."

"That's different."

"Damn right it's different. I could really blame myself. Those babies were people to me, Harry, little living people growing inside me, and my stupid body let them down, killed them. Rejected them, couldn't sustain them through a crisis. I had to let them go or I would have gone insane. As it was I nearly killed myself, so don't tell me I don't know." Angrily she scrubbed her cheeks with the backs of her hands and accepted Harry's handkerchief when he held it out to her. "Damn. I'm sorry. I didn't mean to cry."

"You never do." She was grateful for the sudden fondness in his voice. "And I suppose you're right, I should – let her go, as you call it. Damned if I know how to. How did you manage it, Love?"

Molly shrugged, blew her nose.

"It was difficult. I thought it out, and I guess I sort of said goodbye inside. Part of me loved each of those babies, but the whole of the rest of me that includes those parts had to go on living and loving in the present. So I manage to live with the memory, but not with the desperate yearning for time to turn back or things not to have happened. That way I can be fair to the twins."

"You're quite a woman." Harry stood up, characteristically abruptly. "Let's go back to bed."

Molly led the way and was surprised to feel not his arm around her, but his hand upon her shoulder, letting her lead him. Neither of them noticed that Harry had left the secret – but no longer secret – picture of Dell lying face up on the kitchen table.

Harry woke early and found himself in the crook of Molly's arm, his head on her shoulder, in an unusual reversal of roles, and smiling wryly he extricated himself without waking her. He lay and relived the strange interlude in the night, and reliving it, he found one piece missing. Dell's picture. He felt a moment of near panic. It was past eight, Molly's children would be having breakfast. Maybe – He got up quickly, put on his robe and slippers and went through to the kitchen.

There was a warm smell of toast and coffee and bacon, and the housekeeper, Mavis, and the twelve-year-old twins looked at him in surprise. When he was working, he was out of the house and gone for a seven-thirty call before they breakfasted; when he was between films, as now, he customarily slept in until they had left for school.

"Hi, Harry."

"Hi, kids."

"Good morning, Harry. Like some coffee?"

"Yeah. Thanks." He sat down glancing, apparently casually, at the clutter of cereal bowls and jam and juice glasses on the table.

"Looking for this?" Sue asked. The picture was set on it's stand neatly, facing her. Now she turned it to Harry.

"Er – yes, as a matter of fact."

"She's nice."

"Thank you. Know who she is?"

"Oh, yes. That's Dell. Your other wife."

"First wife," said Ken. "Not other wife, dummy."

Harry was taken aback at their knowledge.

"You've seen it before?" he asked sharply.

"Not that one," said Ken, collecting his books and stuffing toast in his mouth. "The one Richard has."

Once again Harry felt as though a rug had been pulled out from under him. He had thought Dell was his secret and here everyone seemed to know about her and take her picture for granted.

"I guess you really loved her," said Sue softly.

"Uh-huh."

"I'm sorry she died. You must have been very sad."

"I was," he said. "I was." He glanced at Mavis, who was standing transfixed at the stove, and cocked a rueful eyebrow.

He waited until the twins had left for school then he picked up the picture and went back to the bedroom, where he set it up on the bureau and looked at it for several minutes. Gently he put it away in the handkerchief drawer. He did not need it anymore, he realized. It was good not to have to keep it secret. He had not thought or spoken of Dell without pain for all these years. He hoped the years of the dreams were over.

Harry sat on the edge of the bed and looked down at Molly, not beautiful but not plain either, a little overweight, his wife, and was surprised by the warmth of the emotion that swept through him. I love her, he thought. I don't know why, but I really love her, just as I really loved Dell – and that's O.K.

Molly stirred.

"Happy Birthday," Harry said.

"Mmmm?" she opened her eyes. "Not my birthday," she murmured, half asleep.

"No," he said. "It's mine."

Chapter Twenty-One

Molly takes a Bath

"Cetapac Studios took Canadian actor Harry Wentworth and the entire cast and crew of "Stringer and his Men" on an European junket recently, shooting scenes for the up-and-coming series' season's opener in six or seven major cities. Surprise addition to the group was Wentworth's unpredictable wife Molly, who made headlines wherever she went."

The European tour to do on-the-spot location shots for the two hour opening episode of the new season of the "Stringer's Men" series was winding up in Britain. It had been successful not only in getting a lot of good film in the can but also in promoting the series to the European market – Harry and others in the cast had done many interviews, talk-shows and guest appearances. Nothing, however, had created quite so much continuous interest as Harry's wife's exploits.

For Molly the tour had been one disaster after another. In Paris she had spent two hours in a Rent-a-car, driving around and around the inside lane of a traffic circle unable to break out to an exit, until finally she had stopped and in the ensuing traffic snarl, had been rescued by a gallant French policeman. In Rome she had been lost for hours and had the entire City police alerted, suspecting a kidnapping. In Athens she had chased a bag-snatcher and succeeded in knocking him under a car, from whence he had been carted off to hospital with a broken leg. In Berlin, she almost created an international incident by wandering too close to the Wall, and while sight-seeing in Brussels, she had twisted an ankle and insisted on being pushed around in a wheelchair so as not to miss anything. Standing outside Buckingham Palace in London, she had snagged her blouse on the spur of a Horse Guardsman, leaving the wretched man to finish his duty with a large piece of gaily-patterned cotton hanging from his boot.

Harry was fed up with Molly, and as close to falling out of love with her, as he had ever been. Her antics jarred on him, and her apparent lack of concern about them frustrated him; the headlines embarrassed him, and if the truth were known, he was jealous of the attention the Press were giving her. To be honest, he wanted her out of the way, home in Canada. He wanted to concentrate on shooting the movie; he wanted to be the centre of attention. Bringing her to Europe had been a disastrous mistake – he would never do it again; if they got through this episode in their lives whole they would be lucky. He tried to ignore her; he tried to immerse himself in his part; he let Stringer take over his personality; he became a stranger to his wife.

Molly was fully aware of the effect her adventures were having on Harry, and wished he could understand that she did not initiate things, they just happened to her. In herself, and by herself, she tried to be as happy as she could – aware that there was more than the usual estrangement between Harry and her that always occurred when he was absorbed in filming. She wished they could have seen Europe together, as tourists, not with him doing a job and she tagging along for the ride. She, too, began to wonder if their marriage would survive what was turning out to be a monumental mistake.

Consequently, relations between them were very strained when they arrived at the final British location – Bath Spa, home of the ancient Roman Baths dating back to 50 A.D. Here Stringer and his Men were to do a chase sequence in and around the Baths themselves. The Baths were closed to the public for a day and the entire film crew and hanger's on were invited to a private tour and lecture.

Molly hovered on the outskirts of the crowd around the Tour Guide, her camera at the ready. The background of ancient Roman stonework twenty feet below the level of the modern city of Bath, was fantastic. Behind her the sun streamed down upon the warm green waters of the Great Bath, and under her feet were stones trodden and worn down by Roman feet nearly two thousand years before. Harry was standing near a column that supported a bust, and as Molly glanced at him, she noticed the striking resemblance between the bust and her currently grim-faced husband. She raised the camera – it was too good a shot to miss.

"Harry!" she called, to get him to look her way, and stepped back to get him balanced in the frame.

"Molly, don't –"

She stepped back again and fell into the Great Bath with a resounding splash, tossing the camera towards Harry as she fell. He caught it without thinking as he lunged to the edge.

She came up spluttering and splashing wildly, to see the film people lining the Bath and applauding.

"Good old Molly! Trust Molly! Who else – So what's new?"

A busy little man in a peaked cap pushed through to the front.

"There are signs everywhere," he said. "Don't touch the water, it may not be safe'. Please don't swallow any, madam."

Harry leaned over, holding out his hand.

"Come on," he said shortly. "Stop threshing around, it's only five feet deep. Get out."

She grasped his hand and he yanked her out unceremoniously and then stood back so that the water cascading from her would not wet him

"The water's fine," she said, trying to pass it off as a joke, wishing that Harry would catch her eye and smile. "Really warm. I can see why the Romans like to bathe here."

The little man was in front of her.

"There are signs, madam, warning that the stones are slippery. We take no responsibility –"

"I didn't slip, I stepped. It was my fault. It's all been my fault." She looked steadily at Harry.

"Someone call a cab," he said. "We'll go back to the hotel and continue the tour later."

Molly was beginning to feel foolish now; she was not hurt, not cold, not even shocked, but definitely feeling silly and in need of comfort. It arrived in the shape of a kind-faced woman, in a white uniform carrying a blanket.

"There you are, my dear," she said, draping the blanket around Molly's shoulders. "What a nasty shock. You're not the first, you know. It happens every so often. Now, you just follow me, and we'll go to the Ladies' Room and I'll get you a nice big towel and you can dry off a bit."

"Thank you," Molly said gratefully, pulling the blanket around her more firmly. "Harry – wait for me?"

"Of course." There was no warmth in his voice.

In a cubicle in the Ladies' Room, Molly stripped and rubbed herself down with the huge towel the woman handed in to her.

"Pass your things out, dearie, and I'll put them all in a plastic bag."

"But what will I wear?"

"I've got another towel here. Now just take your time, get properly dry. That man of yours can wait."

"He doesn't want to. He's fed up with me."

"Ah well, men are like that, aren't they? And him being a star and all, though I must say I don't like the films he makes, if you don't mind me saying so, Mrs. Wentworth?"

"I don't mind. Don't like them much myself, to be honest." Molly stuck her head over the door. "He's not a bit like the characters he plays, you know. Not really. He's just annoyed with me right now for doing dumb things. How did you know I was Harry Wentworth's wife?"

"Well, my dear," said the woman with a smile, "you have been on the telly quite a lot lately, you know. That time in Rome, and then that poor young man outside the Palace, and so on. Oh yes, I've seen you quite a bit. It must be an interesting life."

"The way I live it," Molly said grimly, "it sure is."

She wrapped the dry towel firmly around her, toga style – which seemed appropriate – and emerged.

"There now, my dear. Now here are your clothes. Just you get back to your hotel and have a little drink and a little rest and you'll be right as rain."

They came out onto the stairwell and found Harry waiting moodily, smoking a cigar.

"Here she is, Mr. Wentworth, none the worse for wear."

"Couldn't you have been quicker? Those damn television vultures are outside now."

"Now sir, it wouldn't have done her any good to go home in those wet things. Besides, the taxi-man probably wouldn't have let her get in, all wet like that. Now, you be nice to her, she's not feeling too good about it herself, you know."

Harry looked at the woman in surprise – he was not used to be being told off by washroom attendants. He pulled some money out of his wallet and put it into her hand.

"Thank you," he said, suddenly warmly. "Thank you for being so helpful." He turned on a powerful actor's smile. "These things happen, don't they?" He pressed her hand, gave her a knowing wink, both of which she would remember for months – years – to come. That Harry Wentworth's a really nice man, not a bit like on the telly, she would say.

They were let out of a side door, where a taxi waited on the street. Between them and the taxi were reporters with cameras, a portable television crew and a curious crowd.

"Don't say anything. No comment. Just keep your mouth shut," he grated in Molly's ear.

"Harry, don't be so miserable. They're only doing their job."

"Hey, Mrs. Wentworth, how was the water?"

"Fine!"

"Did you slip or were you pushed?"

"Neither, I stepped backwards."

"Your wife's been in a bit of trouble lately, Mr. Wentworth. Would you say she was in hot water today?" Cackles of laughter.

"When in ancient Rome," Molly said gaily, as Harry pushed her into the taxi, "Do as the ancient Romans did."

"My God," he said, sitting in the far corner. "This time you really did it."

"I'm a naughty girl," she said sarcastically. "Send me to bed with no juice and cookies."

"Of all times and places, to pull a stunt like this!"

"Just a minute!" she leant forward. "Driver, stop here, please."

"I'm sorry, my dear, I've got a double yellow line. Wait a tic till I can turn off." The taxi swung into an alley.

"Now," said Molly. "Let's get this straight. I fell in the Bath; I got soaked; I'm wrapped in a towel; my clothes are probably ruined. What have you got to gripe about?"

"What happens to you, happens to me."

"The hell it does. Did you sprain your ankle in Brussels, or drive around that bloody circle for two hours, or nearly get mugged? No, that was me, Molly. I felt the physical pain, the humiliation, the embarrassment – all you felt was annoyed that people should think you were married to an imbecile. Well, I'm sorry, but that's the way I am. Maybe it's because I'm in the change of life, or something. You used to say you loved me for being a bit wacky... I don't do these things on purpose – they just happen –"

"Be quiet, woman. We're behind schedule now. Let's get going."

"No," she reached across and unlatched his door. "No you get going. Go back to the Baths and do your tour – I don't need you to watch me get changed. I'll come back if I feel like it – or I won't if I don't." Her voice dropped. "It's not much fun to be around you when you don't like me."

"Very well." Harry got out some money and passed it forward to the taxi driver. "Take her back to the hotel." He gave Molly his best tight-lipped Mount Rushmore face, got out of the taxi, slammed the door and walked away.

The driver caught Molly's eye in the rear-view mirror.

"Never mind, my dear. We all have off days, don't we? The hotel it is then. We'll be there in a tic, and if I may make a suggestion, madam –"

"Of course."

"I could drop you off at the back entrance and get my friend who's a porter there, to show you up the service lift. That way you'd not have to go through the front hall, like, in your towel."

"You're a genius – thank you. Are all Bath people as kind as you, and the lady in charge of the washroom?"

"We do our best to make people feel welcome, madam. For me, it's a pleasure to meet you, my dear, and find out that show people aren't all stuck up and artificial, like some I could name."

"Oh, we're very human, I assure you. Did Harry give you enough money to cover waiting for me to change and taking me back to the Baths?"

The driver touched the pocket where he had put the ten-pound note.

"More than enough, my dear," he said.

Meanwhile, Harry strode, unseeing, still angry, through the crowded city streets towards the Roman Baths. If the pleasant West Country people recognized him, they politely pretended not to, and he was neither approached, nor stared at, nor accosted with fatuous remarks, as he may well have been in Vancouver or Toronto, or even Los Angeles. He was too immersed in his thoughts to appreciate fully the anonymity he was afforded; and his thoughts were at first a jumble of resentments, and recriminations, and guilt, and affection – a hodgepodge – of Me against her; My feelings over Her feelings; My importance, Her insignificance; My reputation, Her thoughtless disregard.

He turned in under the colonnade leading into the Abbey courtyard and found himself facing the great doors of Bath Abbey. As he mingled with the crowds, the pigeons flew up, but soon re-settled on the flagstones and strutted self-importantly looking for handouts. Harry stopped and joined the tourists in their camera-snapping contemplation of the impressive architecture. (Did tourists ever see anything with the naked eye, he wondered, or always neatly framed in a viewfinder?) Standing still, arms folded across his chest (holding his thoughts in), Harry, in his sand-coloured suit, with the brown silk-handkerchief in the top pocket, suddenly became conspicuous in his camera-less-ness, and in his relaxed immobility. Few people can stand as still and yet be as noticeable as a good actor.

Thoughtfully, he studied the front of the Abbey where on either side of the great doors, a ladder was carved in the stone reaching up to a God- or St. Peter-like figure, at the top; at intervals up the ladder little stone angels climbed from rung to rung, and between the aspiring angels less successful ones tumbled head-first down. How did it feel to be going down past the others coming up? Like a stone thrown in a pool that would spread ripples far into the future, the thought dropped into Harry's mind: 'I must make a film about this.'

He smiled to himself, somehow warmed by the humanness of the stone angels. At this moment Molly was undoubtedly feeling like an upside-down angel, and as he reviewed their conversation in the taxi, he finally heard what she had said, and thought about it. She was wet and uncomfortable and humiliated, why had he not been big enough and nice enough to put his arms around her and turn it into a joke? Why hadn't he defended her when the French and Italian police had complained about her Paris and Roman escapades? Why had he disassociated himself from her in Brussels, and London, preferring not to be seen with her? Was he ashamed of her forthrightness and naiveté, qualities he had once found endearing? Was he turning into another Tom Ash – God forbid – and finding her 'not good enough' for him? His face darkened in self-disgust.

A woman's voice intruded.

"Excuse me, but aren't you –"

"No!" He barked rudely in Stringer's voice. Then he looked at the woman, a nice enough middle class middle-aged lady – my God, a Molly Wentworth – and at the hurt and confusion on her face and regretted it. "Sorry," he said. "Yes, I am Harry Wentworth."

"That's all right, m'dear. You're probably worried about your poor wife. I saw you bring her out at the side door. Nasty slippery places them Baths – they'll have a bad accident one of these days, unless they put up some ropes or something. Is she all right?"

"Yes. Yes, thank you. She's fine."

"Such a nice lady. I saw her on the telly last night. My word, but she's had a few mishaps, hasn't she? Good thing she's got a sense of humour. I always say a sense of humour will get you through many a tight spot."

"You're right," Harry said, and he took the woman's hand and shook it warmly and in the deepest most vibrant tones in his lower register added, "I'll tell her you said that, she'll like it."

Damn, he thought, turning to go into the Baths, I've been too much Stringer and too little Harry. Work and life don't mix; I should never have brought her over here while I was filming. Molly, he commanded silently, get changed and come back here – any way, in shorts and a T-shirt if you like, but come back.

He had seen that to the outside world his wife was not a lame-brained imbecile, inept and accident prone, but a nice person to whom things happened, but who nevertheless managed to keep her chin up and smile – most of the time – despite her husband's lack of sympathy. He remembered his mother-in-law saying that Molly had been born with a label, warning that 'this model will attempt to self-destruct at regular intervals', and he smiled.

With the aid of the friendly porter Molly got up to the suite unnoticed by anyone. She changed quickly into a severe black suit, a high-necked blouse and flat-heeled shoes. She combed her damp hair straight back and twisted it into a bun on the nape of her neck; she put on large, very black dark glasses, gloves and a shoulder-bag and surveyed herself in the mirror. The effect was startlingly different. In fact, she felt she was unrecognizable until she walked out of the front door and her driver leapt out of his taxi without hesitation and held open the door for her.

"I thought you might not know me."

"Oh, I wouldn't, madam," he said earnestly. "Only that your shoes don't match."

"Oh hell." She looked down, and sure enough one was brown and one was blue – same style, but different colours. Interesting.

"Not to worry, my dear," the driver said, holding open the door as though he fully expected her not to go back in and change. "Nobody will notice, I'm sure."

Molly decided that it would not matter if they did and got into the car.

At the Baths she pulled in her chin, stuck out her bosom and sailed into the hall as imperiously as she could.

"I'm with Cetapac Films," she said crisply. "Where is the Film group, please? I'm to join them."

"Oh yes, madam. They finished the tour of the Baths, they're in the Grand Pump Room now having coffee. Straight through that door there."

Molly pushed open the door and stopped in awe. The Grand Pump Room was marvellous; she felt the parquet dance floor give under her feet, and was dazzled by the fantastic chandelier; the enormous windows twenty feet high took her breath away. To her left stood the fountain where the mineral waters flowed, waiting to be ingested as a panacea for a million ills; in front on a low stage sat three decrepit musicians, a pianist, a cellist and a violinist, playing gentle old-fashioned music. Between her and the stage the floor was carpeted and tables were set out for morning coffee; a pastry trolley stood between the tables presided over by a wizened waitress in a black uniform, with a little white collar. On the far right side of the room, several tables had been pushed together and the Cetapac people were clustered around in earnest, eager conversation, arms being waved, diagrams being drawn. Harry lounged at the end of the table, a thoughtful expression on his face, his hand caressing his chin.

At another large table sat the wives and husbands and friends, the hangers-on of the tour. Molly felt no more a part of them than she did of the actors and crew. In truth, for a moment, she felt rejected, unnoticed, unneeded, unwanted. Everyone was getting along very well without her; she might as well have stayed at the hotel. Whatever vague idea she had in mind, when putting on her disguise, eluded her now. She felt more foolish than when she had fallen into the Great Bath.

A waitress, just slightly more virile than the trolley lady, led her to an empty table and brought coffee and hot milk in silver pots, and Molly sat with her back to the Cetapac tables and sipped sadly.

Presently a coffee cup was placed on the table near hers, the chair beside her scraped back, and Harry sat down.

"Hi," he said laconically.

Speechless, Molly inclined her head in reply.

He sat back in the chair, his elbow on the arm, his hand up to his cheek and his head on one side, regarding her intently.

"Like the disguise," he said. "Had me fooled for at least five seconds, until I saw—"

"I know – odd shoes. The taxi-man told me," she said gloomily.

"No – really: you turned your back and I recognized your ass."

"Oh."

"Hey," he hooked a finger on her glasses and pulled them halfway down her nose, "are you really in there?" He saw her big sad eyes. "Oops!" He pushed the glasses up again. "Your soul is naked. I'm sorry, honey."

It was the first time he had ever called her honey and the moment was appropriately sweet. Molly felt physically embraced by his voice. She looked at him through the glasses, studying his face for actor's insincerity (it wasn't there) and wondering what was happening.

"And I do like you, idiot. Are you all right now?"

"If I'm forgiven."

"Nothing to forgive. You are you; that's why I married you. I've been a bastard lately." He stopped short of apologizing. "Stringer took over."

"Excuse me. Mr. Wentworth?" A little man in a shabby raincoat had stopped by the table.

"Yes, I'm Wentworth. What d'you want?"

"I wondered – I'm with the Bath Chronicle-News – if I could ask you a question or two?"

"I'm in conference," Harry said shortly "Can't you see?"

"Yes – but... er... I understand Mrs. Wentworth fell in the Great Bath... ?"

"Yes, she did."

Molly sat very still, her cup halfway between the table and her face.

"And is she all right? No injuries?"

"My companion can answer that better than I," Harry said with a wolfish grin, while Molly trod on his foot. "This is Mrs. Ash," he went on blandly. "She travels with the film company."

"Oh, really. What's your capacity with Cetapac Films, Mrs. Ash?"

"Uh-" said Molly, groping, "yes, well, I – as you might say – look after the – uh creature comforts of the actors."

His pen poised over his notebook the journalist asked,

"In what way, Mrs. Ash?"

"I make sure they're comfortable in their hotels – their beds – er – et cetera." The man wrote briskly.

"She's very good at her job," said Harry sincerely. "Especially with the beds. She always likes to see that I'm comfortable in bed." Molly choked and pressed her napkin to her lips. "Oh, and Mrs. Wentworth too, of course."

"And how is Mrs. Wentworth?"

Molly got her mouth under control.

"She's feeling a lot better." Harry's knee bumped hers under the table.

"I understand," he said gravely, "she's going to spend the afternoon in bed. Isn't that right, Mrs. Ash?" He looked at Molly.

"Oh yes," she said not knowing what had caused Harry's incredibly welcome change of mood but thanking God for it anyway. "Oh, definitely, Mr. Wentworth. If you say so. Honey." She pulled down her glasses and engaged his eyes directly, and was happy to find them warm and loving and speculative. "Thank you, Mr. Bath News, that's all the time we have for interview," she added without looking around, and a rather nonplussed journalist wandered away.

"What happened?" she asked Harry.

"I saw a falling angel," he replied enigmatically.

"Does that mean you've found our new beginning?"

"Definitely," he said.

"Then I like it."

But it would be several years before the full significance of Harry's falling angel would become apparent.

Chapter Twenty-Two

Don't Leave Me

"Rugged actor Harry Wentworth returned to Vancouver by air today from Hollywood, where he has been filming a Western. He was looking tired."

The handkerchiefs had bothered Molly from the very first. They were big squares of fine silk, white, coloured, spotted and patterned and Harry wore them in the breast pockets of his suits, a different one every day, chosen from the drawerful in his dresser. He wore them in extravagant puffs and points that soared and sometimes flopped across his chest. There were times when Molly hated them – oh, not the handkerchiefs themselves, they were things of beauty to see and feel – but the way he wore them. They were too... showy... exhibitionistic? for her; she hesitated to use the word 'tasteless' in her mind, but it hovered there unspoken by that inward voice.

One morning, as she had kissed him goodbye at the door, Molly's treacherous hand, obeying her instinct, had reached up and tucked in the silk display.

"Leave it," said Harry.

"It's too big, darling."

He pulled it up. "That's the way I wear it. Like my suits and my raincoat, it's part of me that way."

"But not so... big." She reached and tucked again.

"Molly!" There was a warning steely note in his voice. "Don't try to change me. I've worn my handkerchiefs like this for years, people know me by them. I like them. If you don't – too bad – you'll just have to get used to them. Have I tried to change you?"

"Yes. You had me cut and perm my hair."

"Well," he said reasonably, "it looked terrible the other way, didn't it? This..." he patted his breast pocket, "...is me."

So, Molly had learned to accept the colourful handkerchiefs, and over the years Harry had on several occasions taken one from his pocket and given it to her to stem her tears, and each time she had realized the significance of the act. It was a gesture with far more meaning than appeared, because by taking the handkerchief from his pocket – the handkerchief that was symbolic of his formed personality – he was giving her a part of himself; offering more than just comfort, offering a sacrifice, saying in effect 'comforting you is more important than maintaining my image, I can change when you really need me to.'

Each time Molly had kept the handkerchief and washed and ironed it and folded in a corner of her own drawer, until she had a small pile collected. When she went away on one of her periodic 'walkabouts' (when life at home crowded her, and she felt the need to withdraw for a while and think), or when Harry went on location, or simply when she felt depressed, she would take one from the pile and run it through her hands, bundle it, wipe her face, her eyes, rub it on her cheek and somehow feel closer to Harry. This was a little part of him that he had given her forever – for he never asked for one back, yet he must have known she had them. Whether he knew she felt about those handkerchiefs like this, Molly could not guess; she thought perhaps he did.

On this particular day, as she packed, her hand hovered over the pile of silken squares and almost – almost – she did not pick one out. As alienated as she felt from Harry as he struggled with his current role, yet at the last moment, she realised that she could not leave without this little symbol of his love and care. She chose a red Paisley patterned one and folded it small enough to go in her coat pocket where she could reach in and feel it for comfort at any given moment.

They were both missing Thomas, she knew, more than they would admit, and deep inside, almost hidden, she wondered – as she had wondered so many times – if he really was Harry's child and if this was why Harry had worked so hard in the past twelve months, with hardly a break between films and TV specials and guest appearances. Since the disastrous European tour they had zigzagged across the North American continent between Vancouver and Toronto, New York and Los Angeles, Chicago and Montreal, Miami and Hawaii, and Harry had doggedly insisted that Molly come everywhere with him, and as he now accepted her social gaffes more graciously so she made less of them.

But now Molly was tired, tired of travelling, tired of always being busy, tired of living in hotels and rented mansions, tired of brief visits with her children, tired of Harry always working. She wanted to stand on her sundeck in West Vancouver and take in the sweep of English Bay, the green lump of Stanley Park, the Lion's Gate Bridge busy with its toy cars, the towers of the University of B.C. rising ethereally through the mist across the water at West Point Grey. But she was stuck in the fog in L.A., a grass widow playing second fiddle to a horse.

Two months ago, just a bare three days after getting back from two weeks on location, in Anchorage, Alaska, Harry had breezed in looking pleased with himself.

"I'm going to make a Western," he said.

"A Western!" Molly pealed with laughter. "You!?"

"Why not?" he said huffily. "I've made Westerns before. Remember "Guns Alone"?"

"I know," said Molly. "But you're too old now, darling."

He gave her a withering look.

"It's about an old cowboy," he said. "It'll mean going to Hollywood again."

Molly hated Hollywood. She hated the opulent house, the studio rented for them; she hated the Tinsel Town social life; she hated the parties and the intrigue and the one-upmanship;

she hated the climate and the traffic and the armed policemen
and the freeways. The only things she liked were the beaches,
and the swimming pools. It got so that whenever they were
invited out, she took her swimsuit and, no matter what kind of
a party it was, she swam. She was Harry Wentworth's wife,
she was a nut, she could do it. While Harry mingled and
grunted at people and drank, he got used to seeing his wife
serenely ploughing up and down the hosts' pool. Sometimes
he envied her.

One day, Molly came to the side of the pool, after a brisk
twenty lengths and found herself looking up into a famous
face that even she recognized.

"Hi," he said. "I made a movie about a person like you
once. It was called The Swimmer. Remember?"

Molly wracked her brain.

"I'm sorry, I don't"

"Well, never mind. If it comes on the tube one night, watch
it; I think you'd appreciate it."

She got a videodisc of the film, watched it alone, and was
profoundly depressed by it.

Harry was looking older, and more tired, these days,
absorbed as he was in his Western, unapproachable and
uncommunicative as ever when he was filming; though capable
of turning on the charm in public, at home he was more difficult
to live with than ever before. Molly felt there was no point in
telling him she wanted to leave L.A., and go home, he'd just
shrug and turn away and say, "it's your decision." He was
busy; he didn't need her; she would just go. He had come to
accept her leavings – didn't like them, she knew, but accepted
them – just as she accepted his change of personality when he
was working. He never asked her not to go; he never asked
her to come back, took it for granted that she would.

She packed and called a cab.

Leaving seemed to be the only solution. To tell Harry – to
say goodbye – would be to break with tradition, yet this time
for some reason Molly had an instinct to go to the living-room
where he was sunk in a chair, absorbed in his script for
tomorrow's shooting, doing lines, and fling her arms around
his neck and kiss him. She disobeyed her instinct – steeled

herself to disobey it – and instead clenched her hand around the silk handkerchief in her pocket.

The cab arrived.

Harry was not as absorbed as Molly thought. He had felt in his bones for the past few days that she would be going soon. There was that withdrawal from him, a remoteness she unconsciously assumed (perhaps as a self-protection), a feeling that she was already spiritually moving away. He had never failed to notice the symptoms in his wife when they occurred, and always he had ignored them, made no comment, and then let her go. From the first traumatic time he had realized that this was something she had to do, that he should not stand in her way, that no arguments would dissuade her. Pleas might, but Harry was not a man to plead.

This time he almost wished he could. He felt so damnably tired. He needed her, if only to snarl at in the evenings – realizing at the same time, how unfair that was. The movie was going all right; but there was a heaviness about him that he could not shake. In the studio he functioned – at home he sagged.

He went to the window when the cab drew up, stood and watched, knowing that the moment had come – again. He hated being apart from Molly now, even when being with her was tiresome – a tiresome Molly to endure was better than no Molly at all.

For one blind moment he had an overwhelming desire to shout 'Don't go!' and run and physically restrain her, knowing that he could still melt her body with his touch – and knowing that was an unfair weapon to use. How many men of his age were lucky enough to have a wife whose knees buckled when he held her?

He smiled as he watched her go out to the cab, the small suitcase bumping her legs, no longer young, a little grey in her hair – but still his vital, original Molly, one-of-a-kind. He wanted her to look up and see him and, ambivalently, he wanted her to have the resolve not to, so that he would know she had no doubts about what she was doing. She did not look up, did not see his hand raised in a private gesture of farewell. Then he wished she had; wished she had smiled and waved.

There would be no note, he knew; there never was. She would go home to Vancouver, or to her mother, or perhaps to Richard or Rob, or a friend. When she was ready she would come back. It was a game. Harry could play it and enjoy the homecoming and appreciate that without the parting there would be no reunion – but today, now, he did not want to play the game. He wished he had told her. He wished he had told her a thousand things.

Two days later he collapsed on the set.

"Veteran Canadian tough-guy actor Harry Wentworth flew back to Vancouver today from Hollywood to be admitted to hospital with what was first diagnosed as a mild heart attack, and later amended by a hospital spokesman to "extreme exhaustion". He will remain in hospital for a few days, undergoing tests. Wentworth's wife Molly, son Richard, and stepchildren were not in Hollywood at the time of his collapse, and so far, have not arrived at his bedside. May we take this as a sign that his illness is not serious?"

Harry dropped the paper to the floor and lay back against the pillows. He reached and opened the drawer of the bedside locker and pulled out the little jean-clad Barbie doll. Where the hell are you, Molly? Dammit, don't you know I need you now? He was sensitive enough to know that she was probably feeling bad about being away when he collapsed, but surely that wouldn't keep her away? Surely she didn't think he was angry with her for leaving? With a deep – uncharacteristic – sigh he put the doll away. The tests had been variously tedious, tiring and unpleasant, and the verdict disturbing; he needed to rest, but could not.

A nurse bustled in with a wheelchair.

"I have to take you to see Doctor Hansen again, Mr. Wentworth."

"Can't he come here?"

"Apparently not. Will you get in the chair, please?"

"Do I have to? I'd rather walk."

"You have to – Doctor's orders. You'll need all your strength for the surgery tomorrow."

He felt too tired to object. He got in the wheelchair, pulled his dressing gown together over his knees and allowed the nurse to push him down the corridor without further comment. He was down— physically, mentally, and spiritually; and he was down about feeling down, it was such an unfamiliar sensation for him, and difficult to accept.

The nurse left him in a small office equipped starkly with desk, chairs and a screen, and Harry had an eerie feeling he was not alone. He looked around for a two-way mirror thinking perhaps it was an observation room, but there was none.

"What now, Hansen?" he asked when the Doctor came in. "I thought you'd done everything?"

"We have." The Doctor sat down looking rather awkward and embarrassed. "I have to ask you some questions of a personal nature."

"Well?"

"It's obvious, and rather surprising that your wife is not here."

"Obvious, yes, surprising, no. She's away. I told you."

"Have you contacted her?"

"No," he said shortly.

"Don't you think you should?"

"No."

"Well, will you let me? I don't want to operate without her being here."

"No."

"Why not? You're a sick man; she should know."

Harry sighed.

"Hansen, I don't know where she is. Oh, I could find out, I suppose, but I'd rather not. She'll come in her own time. She's like that."

The Doctor looked uncomfortable.

"I have to ask you," he said, as though it was a question in an oral exam, "are you sure you want her to come?"

"Dammit, of course I want her!" Harry exploded. "What d'you think I –"

"Ta-da!" The screen was pushed aside so violently it fell over with a crash and Molly stepped out and struck a pose, one hand in the air, one leg bent up. She glanced guiltily at the screen and back at Harry with a sickly smile.

"Oh God," he said in apparent disgust. "I should have known." He beat his hands together silently in ironic applause. "Nice entrance, love." He meant 'Thank God you're here.'

Molly knew that. She lowered her arm and leg.

"I messed it up." She meant "I came as soon as I could.'

"Of course." He watched the scarlet tide rise from her neck to her hairline. "What's the blush for?" he asked sharply. "I'm your husband. Remember?" That wasn't what he meant to say either.

"Blush!" she exclaimed with a gay forced laugh. "That's no blush— it's one of those middle-age hot flushes."

Neither of them noticed Doctor Hansen slip out of the room.

"It's a blush," Harry said quietly, "and I love you for it." He held out his hands. "Come here, woman."

Molly wobbled across the room and as soon as she took his hands dropped to her knees beside the wheelchair.

"No! Stand up, Molly."

"I can't," she said hopelessly, "my knees just gave way." She was surprised by the lightness of his grip; her heart was torn by the lines of weariness and strain around his eyes and mouth, the slump of his usually firm shoulders. "Poor Doctor Hansen, I shouldn't have made him do that, should I? I should have come quietly to your bedside with a brave smile and a bunch of flowers."

He stroked her hair.

"I didn't expect you that way."

She laid her head on his knees.

"Better still, I should never have left. I should have known – seen – something was deeply wrong."

"You're here now."

"I came as fast as I could. It was on the radio, you know a few hours after – I rushed to the Airport, but by the time I got to L.A. you'd left for here – I could have screamed –"

"Sorry. I just wanted to get home."

"Harry," she raised her head and looked him directly in the eyes. "What's wrong with you?"

"I have cancer. In one lung. Not like Steve's – like Duke's. Operable. Then there'll be therapy. I'll survive." His voice was gruff, abrupt; he was trying to make it sound matter-of-fact, afraid of Molly's reaction (a little afraid of his own).

She took it calmly, looking at him steadily, her face taking on strength and determination as he watched.

"We'll beat it," she said. She raised his hand to her lips and kissed the knuckles, then turned it over and kissed the palm and pressed it hard across her mouth for a moment. "Are you afraid, darling?" she asked softly.

"Not of pain, not of death. Of being helpless, an invalid, a burden to you, yes." He gripped her hand hard, the sweat standing in drops on his temples, and looked away. He was incredibly glad she was there.

Molly dug in her pocket and pulled out the red paisley patterned handkerchief. "Here," she said.

He took it and wiped his temples and his forehead and his eyes.

"Where did that come from?"

"You gave it to me once, remember? When I was crying? I've kept it in my drawer; with the others you've given me over the years. When you're away – or when I leave you – ("'God forgive me for that', she added silently) – I always carry one with me, to feel close to you."

"Sentimental fool," he growled, remembering the Barbie doll in his own drawer.

Molly made a face, and Harry sighed a great sigh of relief. He shaped the handkerchief and put it into the top pocket of his dressing gown, pulled it up in a big puff, glanced at Molly and then tucked it neatly down so that a bare half-inch protruded.

"Good?"

"Good."

He pulled himself up in the wheelchair and squared his shoulders.

"Now, take me back to my room. We have things to talk about –"

"__ and do!"

" – and do before the operation tomorrow."

Molly pulled a chair up beside the bed and for a while they simply held hands and said nothing, organizing their thoughts.

"Time," she said. "Time is important now. I won't leave

you."

"Tonight?"

"Tonight – or tomorrow – or ever again. I mean, I'll never take off again.

"You know I understand about that."

"I don't know whether you understand, but I do know you've been more tolerant and kind about it than I deserve."

"I've owed you that, Molly, ever since the baby died."

She shook her head. "What d'you mean? You owe me nothing."

"You're a very strong woman, my love, whether you know it or not. When Caroline died you supported us all, and I did nothing to help. All I did was insult you –"

"I forgave you years ago."

"I know, but I've never had the guts to apologize or ask your forgiveness before. I do now." He leant forward and kissed her gently.

"You might die," Molly said. "Tomorrow, during the operation."

"Or next month, or next year." They regarded each other with terrible seriousness.

"So time is terribly important. And so is now, this moment." She got up suddenly and went and closed the door and finding it had no lock on it, she dragged over a chair and propped it up under the handle, to jam it shut. She stood in the middle of the room and started to hum, with bumps and grinds she took off every stitch of her clothing, throwing the pieces aside around the room, until she stood completely naked except for her knee-high leather boots.

Harry appreciated every moment, his heart warming with love for this gloriously unpredictable woman who was his wife; her figure still good, a little thicker round the waist and hips than when they married, her breasts still firm and round and unsagging, her skin smooth, except for the few stretch-marks on her belly.

"Not bad, for a grandmother," he said with a grin. "Get those boots off and come in here before you catch pneumonia." He held open the bed covers.

They made love with infinite bittersweet tenderness – Harry

slow to come, a little weak, having to cough a few times – Molly gentle, undemanding, comforting, keenly aware that each shared sensation might be being experienced for the last time.

Then they lay entwined in each other's arms, their faces wet with each other's silent tears, holding each other with newly rediscovered urgency.

Harry thought 'I never had this chance with Dell, she died so suddenly – I wish I had, maybe I could have let her go sooner'. And for once he thought of her while holding Molly without feeling guilty, and that was a sweet release for him.

The door handle rattled suddenly and the chair slid from under it and crashed to the floor, and Doctor Hansen came in. Harry pushed Molly's head down under the blankets and held it there.

The Doctor, without seeming to, took in the fallen chair, the scattered clothes and the lumpy bed.

"I think your wife is suffocating," he said. "I'll come back later."

For three days Molly ate and slept in a chair beside Harry, one hand always on the bed, either over or under his, never losing contact. Sometimes his eyes opened, sometimes his hand moved, sometimes he sighed and groaned. He knew she was there but was incapable of further communication.

Molly regretted bitterly the days apart from him and resolved there would be no more of her initiating.

Unexpectedly Harry's eyes opened and fastened on Molly in evident surprise.

"They let you stay," he murmured, his voice a whisper.

"Of course," she said. "They knew they'd have had to drag me out kicking and screaming. No one had the courage."

He smiled, well satisfied, a mental image of Molly defying the nursing staff to move her from his side coming easily to mind. He drifted into sleep.

"You look awful," he said, when he woke again. Her face was creased with sleeplessness and grubby, her hair untidy.

"Thanks a lot," she said. She stood up, letting go her grasp on his hand and stretched mightily.

"Don't leave me."

"I'm not – ever again, Harry. But once in a while I may

have to go and pee."

If he could have laughed he would have. Instead he slept again.

"I'm alive," he said, and his eyes were clearer this time and his voice stronger.

"Are you?" Molly slipped her hand under the bedclothes and down between his thighs. She encountered the catheter and almost withdraw, but Harry grunted in satisfaction, his eyes on her face.

"Ignore it," he said.

She did.

Doctor Hansen backed quietly out of the door, closing it behind him.

"Your father's doing very well," he said blandly to Richard. "He's having therapy. I shouldn't go in for a while if I were you."

He went jauntily down the corridor, inexplicably heartened by his famous patient's behaviour. Notwithstanding his own skills, he was convinced that it was Molly Wentworth who had contributed most to her husband's recovery in those first few dicey days following the operation. She simply would not let him die. A remarkable woman, he thought, married to a remarkable man. There was no doubt in his mind, but that Harry Wentworth would be back making films in less than a year.

Chapter Twenty-Three

Frankenstein's Monster

"*Filming of Drug Squad – being shot in Cetapac Studios and on location at Lion's Gate Hospital – will be delayed for a few days following an accident on the set said to have involved veteran star Harry Wentworth, fully recovered now from his bout with cancer last year.*"

It was not so much the lateness that Molly minded – she was used to that when he was filming – it was that tonight there had been no message warning her, from him, or Sam or anyone. To prevent herself from becoming overanxious she made a conscious decision to become angry instead. She told Mavis to hold dinner. (Mavis had the ability to delay a meal for an hour and a half and then reproduce it just as fresh and tasty as though it had that minute finished cooking, which Molly considered a major talent in the light of her own delayed meals which invariably arrived at the table as tough brown blobs.) She had told the twins to do their homework now and postponed their TV watching till after dinner. Finally, she sat down in Harry's chair, the one with its back to the door (and that was a conscious symbolic act too), and stared blindly at a book she did not want to read. Had she remembered she had some knitting on the go, she would have knitted furiously – in several senses of the word.

It was impossible to deny the enormous wave of relief that flooded over her at the familiar sound of the Lincoln in the driveway, but she remained resolutely in the chair. Damned if she was going to run to the door all big-eyed and thank-God-ing. Besides, he would not appreciate it.

"Molly?" He shut the door carefully, and his voice was careful too.

"Here." She raised a casual hand and flapped it above the top of the chair.

"Don't move," he said sharply. "Don't turn around."

She sat still, taken by surprise by the lack of apology in his tone, and by something else that she could not quite identify. His footsteps crossed behind the chair. Without warning, his hands clamped down over her eyes. She started…

"What's this about?"

"You'll see. In good time." Again there was that unusual quality to his voice, and Molly became aware of a strange odour that she could not readily pin down.

"I'm late."

"I noticed," she said dryly. And suddenly, she realized that he was going to explain and apologize and give her a present, and that was why he had covered her eyes – so that it would be a surprise – and her heart lightened and her anger evaporated. She loved Harry's unexpected presents.

"There was… an accident," he said.

"Oh God." A yawning pit opened in her stomach and her mental vision of a present crumpled and melted like burning plastic. She put her hands over his, not so much to tear them away from her eyes, as to actively touch rather than passively be touched.

"I'm all right," he said quickly, correctly interpreting her movement.

"But –?"

"But I have a few stitches in my face."

A few. Molly knew at once that was an understatement, and the yawning pit yawned a little wider. She recognized the smell then, hospitals, and antiseptic.

"Don't look until I tell you to, and when you do for God's sake, don't come the Earth-Mother on me; don't swoon and sob and hold me to your bosom – what there is of it."

Does he really think I would? No, he's talking to cover his anxiety, surely?

"Don't make a fuss, Molly. Please." There – the unexpected 'please', it still took her by surprise.

He took his hands from her head and she heard him move away but kept her eyes shut until he said,

"OK".

He was standing in his favourite pose in front of the fireplace, one elbow on the mantelpiece, his hand negligently dangling, and the other hand in his trouser pocket. His back was to the light so that his face was in shadow. But not enough shadow to hide the mass of sutures that zigzagged across it. There was a ragged five inch cut from the temple to temple on his forehead, and another from the right side of his nose near the eye across the bridge of the nose and down to the flare of the left nostril; another along the line of the right side of his jaw and one vertically under his chin; his right earlobe appeared to have been reattached and there was a two-inch long gash from his upper lip to the right side of his nose. Add to all that the colouration from disinfectant, dribbles of dried blood and the bruising and puffiness that was beginning to come out, and Harry was a fearsome sight.

Of course Molly wanted to rush to him and enfold him in her arms and murmur, 'Oh Darling, how awful. Does it hurt much? It looks so uncomfortable… what can I do? Never mind, never mind.' But, she did not, since he had explicitly told her not to. She turned in the chair instead.

"Well!" she said, leaping to her feet. "You've got a nerve I must say! Two hours late and not a word, not a message from anyone. What was I supposed to think? I was worried sick!" She started to stride up and down in front of him waving her arms. "And then you have the gall to come in, without any warning, looking like Frankenstein's monster and say 'Don't look at me, there's been an accident – but don't look at me, I'm all right, but I have a few stitches in my face–"

"Molly!"

"A few! You look like a voodoo doll that's been slashed up and cobbled together again. And I'm not to get upset?! What the hell happened?"

"There was a fight scene. A few things went wrong."

"Wrong! I'll say they went wrong. They just cut their star to ribbons."

"I thought you didn't care about my being a star?"

"I don't! But I care about you being my husband. And I didn't bargain on my husband being held together with catgut and clamps. After all, this is not the first time this has happened."

"And it won't be the last," he snapped. "It goes with the job. That's the kind a' guy I am and the kind a' part I play. Men. So the stair rail broke where it wasn't supposed to break and the chair that was supposed to break didn't, and a mirror got smashed, what the hell!, it was a good fight and we got it in the can."

"Real blood and all! I'm sure the director was ecstatic," Molly cried sarcastically.

"Yes, he was."

"Too bad the 'STAR' has to be out of commission for a few weeks while he heals up. Whatever happened to stand-ins and stuntmen? I thought 'STARS' had other people to do the dangerous stuff for them? – or aren't you a big enough 'STAR'? –"

"Shut up and stand still!" Harry grabbed her arm and made her stop in front of him; she tried to break his grip and turn away, but he jerked her back.

"You're hurting me, Harry."

"I don't care. Stop waving your arms and listen. I'm Harry Wentworth, and Harry Wentworth has always done his own fights and his own action shots. When people see me up there on that screen, they know it's me, not some double in my clothes. That's what I've built my reputation on; that's what my fans expect."

"When Harry Wentworth bleeds that's real blood, boys and girls, not the wizardry of the make-up man. Oh, grow up, Harry. You're past fifty. Let somebody else do that stuff for you."

"No," he said stubbornly. "Won't you ever understand? What's the matter with you Molly?"

"The matter!" Molly cried. "What – is – the – matter? I'll tell you what the matter is, Harry bloody Wentworth. I'm upset, distraught, beside myself. My husband is hurt and he doesn't bother to call me; he spends two hours or so at the hospital getting his face sewn back together, like a patchwork-quilt – while the dinner congeals in the oven and the family wonders where the hell he is – and when he comes in, he says 'don't faint, don't cry, don't fuss' – Dear God! What does that leave me to do except get blazing mad!" Her voice broke on the last word and she clamped her free hand over her mouth, and though she did not mean there to be, there were tears in the eyes that she raised to Harry.

He saw, and understood. He let go of her arm and rubbed it gently, where he had gripped so hard and then let his hand drop to his side. They looked at each other in silence, and Harry remembered the tirade he had levelled at Molly when he had gone to visit her at the hospital after her car accident, and realized he knew what she was going through.

"Yeah," he said quietly. "Well." He tried to cock his eyebrow, but the stitches in his forehead pulled too much; when he tried to smile, the cut on his upper lip hurt too much, and it came out lopsided.

"Oh Harry," Molly said warmly, and her voice was steady again. "You shouldn't talk so much, you're bleeding all over the place. Give me your handkerchief." When he had given it to her she said, "Bend forward," and gently she blotted the trickles of blood from his forehead, his nose and his chin, and had a quick memory of the time at the Bayshore when she had tried to do the same thing and with an exclamation of annoyance, he had impatiently pushed her hand away. Now he stood quietly with his eyes shut and submitted to her ministrations. When it was done and while his eyes were still shut, she selected an unblemished patch of skin on his left cheek and kissed him lightly.

With a sigh Harry crossed his hands behind her waist and gathered her to him, and as they stood there together, Molly felt the fine tremor that shook his body and was comforted to know that he was human.

"You remind me," she said against his shoulder," of the little boy who comes home from school two hours late, with a black eye, and a split lip, and he doesn't know whether his mother is going to burst into tears or wallop him. And it reminds me of the mother because whichever she does, it's because she loves him."

"Um-hmm."

"I'd better tell Mavis to put dinner on, and call the twins." She moved across the room.

"Molly " he said. "Warn then."

She nodded, aware for the first time that even tough-guy Harry Wentworth could feel embarrassment, and loving him the more for his vulnerability. We live and learn – constantly – she thought.

Mavis had seen Harry come in and been appalled and was ready to sympathize, but agreed reluctantly to act as though nothing was wrong. The twins were easier. They too had seen Harry when he came in, and in fact, had heard most of the conversation between him and Molly. When she said,

"Darlings, don't say anything about Harry's face," they said,

"Of course not."

"You see, he's feeling –"

"We know," said Ken.

"You don't have to tell us," said Sue.

She believed them; there had always been something incredibly perceptive about the twins.

They sat down to dinner and strangely Mavis seemed to have set all the places in a cluster down Harry's end of the table.

They talked and ate and passed the food, laughing and chatting as though it was any other evening, and the man of the house was not scarred and bruised as though a sheet of glass had fallen in on him, (which in fact it had), and no-one looked askance at his face, or mentioned it or made unctuous kind remarks about it. But love poured out towards him, and Harry felt it.

He sat as in a pool of warmth, basking. The local anaesthesia was wearing off and his stitches were hurting; with every attempted mouthful he became more aware of how sore his whole face was – his head, his nose, his jaw, his chin, his lip. He sipped, carefully, the rye-on-the-rocks that Molly had made for him (not unaware that it was least a double, if not a triple – good girl, she knew what he needed) and was grateful for the gradual numbing effect it was having on his body – and soul.

He was removed from the conversation, and yet part of it – included but not involved. He was suspended in time, as it were, and knew that shock was beginning its onset; he noted as his fork rattled against his teeth that he was beginning to shake, and regarded his body with disgust for its weakness. However, he wanted to do nothing more than sit there and let life flow around him. It was very comforting.

He remembered previous times when he had been injured accidentally on the set; how, usually, after repairs had been done, he had been taken out by a group of his buddies who had solicitously filled him with liquor and when he passed out, equally solicitously heaved him into bed, pulled off his boots and left him there to wake up alone, and hurting and hung over, but with a bottle close by to nip the pain in the bud. He had believed they were good friends who had stood him in good stead, and in their time and in their way they had been.

He thought, while he was being stitched up, nostalgically of those good old days; he had dreaded the thought of going home to a wife and children. He had feared their reaction far more than he had worried about the cuts and bruises. But somehow, now, he felt cheated.

"Dammit!" he said suddenly. "Has no one noticed anything about me?"

Four bland inquiring faces turned to him.

"I look like Frankenstein's monster, as your mother said. I have ninety-seven stitches in my face."

"Ninety-six," said Ken matter-of-factly. "I just counted."

"You look like Harry to me," said Sue. "Harry with a few cuts. We still love you." It was too glib and sweet by far.

"Now tell me how you really feel."

Sue's face crumpled and her eyes filled with real tears.

"It's awful!" she cried. "Oh, Harry, it's awful!" She flung herself at him and buried her face on his chest.

Harry put his arm around her shoulders, satisfied. He decided this was better than getting drunk and being put to bed by his buddies. Now, he felt more like a suffering hero, especially when he saw the admiration in Ken's eyes. He patted Sue and looked to Mavis for her honest reaction and was not disappointed. Her face suffused with sympathy, she shook a wondering head.

"I don't know how they could have let you out of the hospital, looking like that,"

"They didn't – I walked out. Felt OK. Wanted to come home." That was not true; it was rather that he had not wanted to stay in hospital than that he wanted to come home.

"But... no bandages?"

"Heal better this way. Besides, then I'd have looked like The Curse of the Mummy."

Ken found that funny and laughed and Sue began to calm down. Harry looked at Molly but she remained aloof, keeping up the pretense of being unperturbed, watching the others with a small cool smile. Unable to interpret it, his mind slowed by the alcohol, he decided to put her on a back-burner and concentrate on enjoying the sympathy of Mavis and the children.

Presently, when they had finished dinner and got up to move to the living room, Harry found his shoulder and hip stiffened painfully. He tried to walk casually, strolling, tried to mask his efforts, not to favour his right leg, but catching Molly's sharp look knew that she was not deceived.

The twins exclaimed in awe, but Molly's reaction was sharper.

"You could have broken your hip, or lost an eye or severed an artery and bled to death," she said bleakly.

"Then I'd have been the wife of a blind cripple, or a widow."

"Oh Mum!" the twins protested. "It was only a movie!"

"Those stitches are for real," Molly pointed out. "Now I think it's time you went to bed."

When the children had gone and Mavis had retired to the kitchen to feed the dishwasher, Harry stretched out on the sofa, pulling a cushion under his head, and looked across the hearth at Molly. She had found her wool and sat knitting briskly.

"Still mad at me?"

"Oh," she shrugged. "No – Yes, I guess so." She counted stitches.

"Don't be." He used his sexy voice.

"What?"

"Mad." He stretched out a hand. "Come here." He managed to capitalize both words with his voice, richly velvet.

She shook her head.

"Can't trust myself."

"Meaning?"

"I might turn into the Earth-Mother and suddenly give in to a desire to cradle you against my bosom, 'what there is of it' " she added.

"Didn't mean that. Put down that bloody knitting, woman."

She put it down and with a sigh got up and walked across the rug to stand beside the sofa looking at him.

"Will there be scars?"

"Hansen says probably not. If there are, a plastic surgeon can tidy them up."

"Good thing I didn't marry you for your pretty face."

Harry pushed a cushion onto the floor and Molly knelt down on it, so that their heads were on a level.

"What did you marry me for?"

"The truth?"

"The truth."

"You won't like it."

He raised an eyebrow painfully.

"Try me."

"Your gentleness and vulnerability."

"Huh!" he grunted. "Don't tell my fans."

"I won't. It's my secret," Molly said.

"And I thought it was my masculinity and charm."

"Those too," Molly said softly, and smiled at last.

"Want to know what I married you for?"

"I'm afraid to ask," she said.

"Your strength and integrity," said Harry seriously.

"Oh," she responded in a small wondering voice.

"Of course some people might call it bloody stubbornness, but," Harry raised a hand and touched her cheek, "to me it's strength. You know you're strong, don't you?"

"Yes." She signed, holding her hand over his against her cheek," to me it's strength. You know you're strong, don't you?"

"And I'll admit my vulnerability. But only to you."

They sat quietly, contemplating the paradoxes of the qualities they saw in each other, vulnerability and gentleness in the man, strength and integrity in the woman. Opposites of the sexual stereotypes – complementary to each other. A bonding had taken place during that conversation that was to carry them through their remaining years together.

Molly stood up.

"You should go to bed, Harry."

He slipped his hand up her thigh under her skirt.

"Good idea," he said.

But the idea he was referring to was one he had just had, and had nothing to do with sex or sleep. It had to do with Molly gaining an insight into his world— something that was long overdue, he recognized at last. It was an idea that he remembered considering briefly years ago and discarding as unworkable at that time. Perhaps now, with the closeness and understanding they had reached during his illness and convalescence, it would work?

As he floated in the comfortable limbo between waking and sleep, feeling Molly's hand gently stroke his head, Harry determined that as soon as he was healed he would set the wheels in motion. He knew exactly what he wanted to do with her.

Chapter Twenty-Four

'Trust me.'

"Gala Opening. The World Premiere of Drug Squad attracted big crowds to the Stanley last night. Rumours that star Harry Wentworth had been badly scarred in an accident while shooting the film proved to be unfounded. He looked fit and strong and completely recovered from his bout with cancer."

Harry came back from the doctor's office two weeks later, in a very good mood, having had the last of the stitches removed.

"Well?" he said, presenting himself to Molly.

"Well," she responded, examining him critically, well aware that he was a great deal more sensitive about his appearance than he pretended. (It had been a shock to him to find that people were actually nauseated by the sight of his battered face, and Pauline had almost fainted on seeing him.) "It's a lot better than it was, isn't it?" She saw his disappointment. "Harry," she said, "since we've been married, I've lived with you with long hair, and short hair, and even a shaven pate; you've had a bushy moustache and a Doug Fairbanks and a long beard, and stubble – oh, lots of stubble. But I've always known that eventually you'd go back to being the Harry I married. This is different, because you won't go back to being the same Harry, ever. You'll always have scars, and I have to adjust to the scars being a permanent part of you."

"So do I," he said soberly.

"I know." She put her arms around his neck. "Don't worry, I'll love you with your new scarred face."

He wanted to thank her for not pretending that it made any difference – her honesty always warmed him – but he could not find the right words, so he kissed her instead.

"Ugh!" she said. "Speaking of stubble –"

"O.K., I'll shave now. Tomorrow it's back to work, and you're coming with me."

"I'm what?"

"Coming with me. I've got you in as an extra."

"Harry, I can't act." Molly was appalled.

"You don't have to."

"And I'm too old."

"You'll be a middle-aged nurse and you'll walk down a corridor. That's all."

"But – why?"

"Remember when I was making a film with Wednesday and you visited the set? You said you wanted to see what went on –?"

"But that was years ago –"

"It took a while to set up," he said blandly.

"You really want me to come?" Molly was incredulous.

"Yes, I want you to understand what makes me tick. What happens between actors."

"Are you in the scene I'll be in?"

"Yes."

"But – your face?"

"Won't show."

"Oh."

On the way to the Studio in the car the next morning, Harry seemed to be withdrawn and moody, and Molly was curious.

"Having second thoughts?" she asked brightly.

"Maybe," he said shortly. "By the way," he added, "We don't know each other. You're registered with casting as Maureen Bragg." He pulled over to the curb and stopped, though they were still two blocks from the Cetapac lot. "In this bag," he passed her a plastic shopping bag, "you'll find a wig. Put it on. This is your pass to get in at the gate. Jack'll tell you where to report to." He adjusted the wig. "That's good. Off you go."

Speechless for a moment, Molly finally found her voice.

"You mean I walk in from here?" she asked faintly.

"Right. Wait a minute." He leaned over and kissed her. "Good luck. Keep your eyes open and enjoy yourself."

Molly, however, was still too mystified by Harry's sudden decision to invite her in to his hitherto sacrosanct domain to enjoy herself. As she checked in, she was issued a nurse's uniform and set over to Make-up. Here she found herself sitting beside a peasant-faced woman of much her own age, who looked her over and said,

"My name's Jane McQuarrie. You look as though you've never done this before."

"I haven't," Molly said, turning with relief. "Maureen Bragg," she introduced herself, feeling strange at using her maiden name. "My husband got me into this."

"Um-hm. Mine too. 'Get out and bring in some money' he said. The kids are all in school, go 'do something useful.' So here I am. I was a showgirl before I married. This is the only business I can hack. You want I should show you the ropes?"

"Please."

"Maureen Bragg?" said another girl. "You're the one that's doing a scene with Harry Wentworth, then?"

"Am I?"

"You mean you don't know?"

"Well," Molly temporized hastily, "casting just said he'd be in it."

"In it!" the girl snorted. "I take it you haven't read the script? No? Well, neither have I, but I heard what happens. I won't spoil it by telling you."

"Hey," said Molly, "that's not fair –!"

"Don't worry, dear," said Jane comfortingly. "Our Harry's a pro. He's no Laurence Olivier but he is a pro. He'll help you – and you don't need to be afraid of him. I've been in two pictures with him before. He's a gentleman; real nice to everyone on the set, including extras and crew."

"Oh?" Molly feigned surprise, curious to hear what these women knew about her husband that she did not. "I thought he was real rough and tough – you know – macho – chauvinistic?"

"Nah. That's just the parts he plays. He's a softie underneath, a real pussy-cat," Jane said. "Isn't that right Brenda?"

"Specially since he married," the other girl chimed in. "He's a lot nicer now."

Molly wondered if this was what Harry intended her to hear.

"Look, you've got nothing to worry about, Maureen." It was Jane again. "You can trust Harry Wentworth. Whatever you have to do, he'll help you. That's what I mean when I say he's a pro. It's that Lucy Finn you have to watch out for – she's a bitch. Stuck up little tart, if you ask me. She's playing the lady doctor – steer clear of her if you can."

"Thanks. Thanks for the advice, girls." Notwithstanding they were all in their forties and thirties, Molly felt that the term 'girls' was appropriate. And in a strange and enjoyable way she now felt like 'one of the girls'.

With a crowd of other extras variously dressed as doctors, nurses, orderlies and patients, Molly was bussed up to Lion's Gate Hospital, in an empty wing of which the scenes were to be shot. She had no idea what the movie was about, but the others told her it was to do with drug trafficking, and Harry Wentworth was an undercover policeman masquerading as a crook.

During the morning Molly walked back and forth in front of a Nursing Station, sometimes pushing 'patients' in wheelchairs, sometimes carrying charts or pulling a drug cart, and always bewildered. There was no sign of Harry, but other leading actors – including the notorious Lucy Finn – came and went across or through the set speaking lines which, when one had no knowledge of the plot, made very little sense. There was a lot of standing around waiting, while lights and cameras were positioned and the leads rehearsed their moves and lines, and while this was boring, Molly did catch a feeling of excitement, of being part of a larger mosaic, of being a cog which helped the main wheels go round. There was a friendliness amongst the extras that was warming, and when they heard it was Molly's first experience, they went out of their way to help her to understand what the director was telling them to do.

After a bag lunch, supplied by the Studio, Molly was taken to one side by an Assistant to the Director, Terry Young.

"Miss Bragg? Maureen?"

"Yes."

"We'll just go over your scene with Harry. First, we'll walk through it with his stand-in. Over here, Bert. This is Bert Melrose."

"Hi, baby." She had never seen the man before, never even heard his name, but his size and shape and short white hair were Harry's. "Your big moment, eh?"

"I guess," Molly said guardedly, suddenly a little apprehensive.

They told her to walk busily down the corridor, keeping close to the wall, intent on the imaginary place she had to go to. Where her corridor met another, at right angles, she was to go straight across, not glancing to her left, where Bert Melrose was hiding flat against the wall. As she passed, he reached out and took hold of her, one arm loosely around her neck and one around her waist, and pulled her backwards in slow motion – step-step-step. At a closet door he stopped, let go her waist, faked a karate chop to her neck, and the Director said,

"Fall! Collapse, woman, you're out cold."

Molly sagged obediently and Bert Melrose opened the closet door and lifted her inside.

"Good. Good. Let's walk through that again, a couple of times."

And while they walked through it – literally – the cameras and lights were positioned, and Molly had time to reflect. She looked around for Harry and finally spotted him behind the camera talking to the Director, his back to her. He was wearing a black leather jacket, black pants and sneakers. She wished very much he would turn around and catch her eye, wave, drop an intimate eyelid or in some other way make a contact that would reassure her. It bothered her that she was feeling nervous. She had no lines to remember; all she had to do was walk, be pulled backwards, and pushed into a closet. Surely any fool could do that? Any fool but me, she thought gloomily. I'll botch it for sure. Is that what Harry wants – to show me how expert he is, to prove his job is challenging, that it's not something any fool can do?

She was called to her position, and looking for Harry found he had vanished, so presumed he was already flattened against the wall out of her sight.

"This is just a walk-through," the Director said. "Ready? Lights. Action."

Molly walked briskly along the corridor trying not to be conscious of the camera tracking backwards ahead of her, trying hard to look like a nurse on her way to somewhere important, and succeeding so well that what happened next took her completely by surprise.

It was like an explosion. She was yanked backwards off her feet, a heavy gloved hand clamped over her mouth, and a vice-like arm squeezing the breath from her chest. Totally panicked, she scrabbled wildly with her feet, made frantic noises under the hand and desperately scratched and clawed at the arms that held her. Nearly out of breath, she rolled her eyes up and back, and was shocked by the black-masked face looking down at her, the eyes through the holes in the ski toque cold and hard, the mouth visible only as a tight slit. Oh God, I'm going to wet my pants, she thought.

"Cut!"

Harry released her immediately and set her on her feet, where she stood gulping in air and rubbing her mouth.

"All right, Miss. Bragg?" he asked mildly.

She wanted to shout 'No, you bastard! How dare you set me up like this? I'll never forgive you, never,' but the Director's voice overrode her thoughts.

"That was pretty good, Harry. Miss. Bragg, I liked what you were doing with your hands, and the rolling of the eyes was excellent." Sheer terror, she wanted to retort. "But your legs were terrible. Don't let them kick out like that. Back pedal as he pulls you. Let's go through it again.

'No, no way,', Molly wanted to say, not again, but Harry's

hand between her shoulders propelled her back to her starting point. The make-up girl repaired her smudged lipstick, and willy-nilly, she was off again down the corridor. She cringed involuntarily as she passed the opening.

"Cut! You anticipated, Miss. Bragg. Do it again."

This time she managed not to cringe and once again was jerked off her feet and dragged backwards, suffocating, off balance, her ribs cracking in Harry's grip; once again she looked up in disbelief at his steely hard eyes, his cruel mouth. She thought, he's doing this on purpose; he wants to frighten me and hurt me – but why? Why? One arm released her, his hand came up and chopped down at the back of her neck; he pulled the blow and barely touched her, but when she remained upright, he pushed her forward and bundled her, a tangle of flopping arms and legs into the closet and shut the door.

"That was terrible," he said, opening the door. "Sorry, Terry, let's try it again. Remember to collapse when I hit you, Miss. Bragg," and once more he propelled her back down the corridor. She was incensed; she dared not look at him in case he saw her fury.

Again they did it – the cameras turning now – and again and again, until Molly felt bruised, battered and dishevelled (notwithstanding the make-up girl's repairs to her face and hair and the smoothing down of the nurse's uniform) – the dishevelment was internal.

"Let's get it right this time, people," the Director said wearily. "Harry use your right hand to open the door, left arm to hold her up. And don't forget to glance up and down the corridor as you do it. Let's go. Lights. Camera. Action!"

Molly was angry. This time it seemed to her that Harry grabbed her more roughly than ever and in retaliation she kicked back and caught his shin with her heel.

"Hell!" He let her go and hopped away, cursing and rubbing his leg.

"I think," said Terry, the Director, judiciously, "we're all getting too realistic here. You only pretend to fight him off, Miss. Bragg."

"I can't do it," Molly said desperately. "I'm sorry. Get someone else. Get Jane McQuarrie, she's had more experience."

"Casting sent me you, Miss Bragg, and you'll do it."

"I can't. Please, I really can't –"

"Let me talk to her." Harry had come back to them. "Come along, Miss. Bragg." He took Molly's arm and led her down the corridor. When they were out of earshot he turned and faced her. "Now," he said calmly. "What's the matter, Molly?"

She looked up at him – a sinister figure in black masked face, impersonal, unknown, menacing – what was he trying to do to her?

"I'm afraid," she said shortly.

"Of me?" Harry was incredulous.

"Take that damn thing off your head."

"No." His voice was very level now and he shook his head. "No. This is Rex Mallory, wearing this ski-mask, but inside Rex Mallory is me, Harry. I'm still Harry no matter how much I look like Rex; I'm still Harry when I act like Rex. Actors have to trust each other, Molly – especially in situations like this. Trust me. I'm not trying to hurt you. Don't be afraid, just act afraid. Don't fight me, pretend to. Relax. Molly?" He put his hands on her shoulders. "Do you hear me? When I look at you like that I'm not seeing you, Rex is seeing a nurse who's getting in his way, and he has to get rid of her –"

"But I can't see you," Molly said miserably, searching the face above her.

"I'm here," he said, pouring warmth into his voice. "Trust me. And let me trust you – that means no kicking. Eh?"

Molly dropped her eyes. She felt about fourteen, not forty-four.

"Sorry," she said.

"That's O.K. Sometimes we react instinctively in character – then there's no hard feelings, nothing personal – it's one character against another, not you and me fighting. You understand?"

"I think so." Slowly.

"Even when people get hurt. No fear. No hard feelings. Trust. OK?"

"OK," she said, having made up her mind. "Let's do it again."

"Good girl." He squeezed her shoulders, put an arm

around her and walked her back down the corridor. "We'll get it right this time, Terry," he said. "Maureen and I understand each other now."

It was strange to hear Harry call her by her given name; even for the wedding ceremony he had used her pet name Molly. As she went back to her starting place, she noticed Jane McQuarrie in the background behind the camera and caught her eye, and Jane gave her a grin and a thumbs up sign.

It went perfectly this time. Though Harry was as necessarily rough as ever, Molly got her timing right for once and the weight of his hands on her seemed less, and the backwards drag less awkward. She rolled her eyes up and back as rehearsed, saw Harry's hand come down in the karate chop and then – nothing. Total blackness.

Eons later Molly became vaguely aware of voices, tiny-tiny voices a long, long way away. It seemed as though she was at the bottom of an incredibly deep well, or looking through the wrong end of a telescope. Life was dimly perceived in the far distance. It hardly seemed worth it to struggle up; she relapsed into the comfortable darkness, only to have it shattered into fragments as her body was roughly shaken.

"Wake up!" someone was saying loudly, close to her face. She knew it was probably loud, but it did not sound loud.

"Here. I'll do that." Harry's voice. She recognized it. "Wake up!" he said sharply, and delivered a slap to the side of her face. She grunted involuntarily, and he slapped her lightly again and her eyes flew open momentarily with shock.

Bastard, bastard. She remembered then, he had hit her, had knocked her out. She shut her eyes tight, let her body slump, but Harry's arm was around her raising her head and shoulders.

"She's all right," he was saying. "She's coming round now. Gimme some water. Not the cup – the jug." He threw the jug full of cold water in her face and she could no longer pretend to be unconscious, and reared forward, spluttering and gasping with fury.

She was on a hospital bed, a ring of anxious faces surrounding her, the warmth she felt was due to Harry's black jacket wrapped around her shoulders. He was holding her with both arms now and she noted irrelevantly how taut and lean his body was in the black T-shirt; also that he still wore the ski mask. When he saw her eyes on his face, he reached up to the crown of his head and ripped the mask off in one quick motion, and Molly heard distinctly the gasps as members of the cast and crew saw his scarred face. But she did not see the scars, she saw only his look of such concern that the angry words rising to her lips subsided unsaid.

Jane McQuarrie, too, saw Harry's look and drew her own conclusions.

"Lie still," Harry was saying. "You hit your head as you fell. There's a doctor coming." Since Molly had now discovered a throbbing pain in her right temple as well as a deep ache in the left side of her neck, she was content, for the moment, to lie comfortably in the crook of Harry's arm.

While the young doctor summoned from the main hospital examined her for signs of concussion, she listened to snatches of conversation going on around her.

"It's all in the can then?"

"Can't improve on that."

"Good day's shooting."

"Let's wrap it up for today."

"Same time tomorrow, people."

The crowd had thinned to two or three by the time the doctor was satisfied she had no serious symptoms, and had supplied her with the classic advice to take two aspirins and rest. He and Harry helped her to her feet, where she swayed at first on rubbery legs. Then Jane came forward carrying her coat.

"They're holding the bus for us in the parking lot," she said.

"I'll take her home," Harry said shortly.

"My stuff's at the Studio."

"OK." He slipped his jacket off Molly's shoulders and took the coat Jane offered and wrapped it around her instead. "Look after her," he said to Jane. "And I'll take you home from the Studio – Miss. Bragg." It was not an offer or a question, it was a statement.

"Thank you," Molly said quietly.

Walking slowly down to the bus, Jane's arm giving her

support, Molly asked what – exactly – what happened.

"Well, Harry chopped you, but you must have moved or something and he really hit you, and as you fell, you clonked your head on the door handle of the closet. Good old Harry, being a trooper, never missed a beat. He picked you up, stuffed you in the closet, shut the door and did his exit down the corridor. Then he came charging back and dragged you out, and that was the first time anyone realized that you really were out cold. I guess he knew it from the moment you fell."

"Yet he finished the scene anyway?"

"Told you he was a pro. Anyway, it was a take. Director was ever so pleased. You should be so lucky, you don't have to do it all over again tomorrow."

"I won't be here tomorrow," Molly said.

"Not cut out for show-biz, dear?"

"Definitely not."

"Geez!" said another girl on the bus. "I'd give my eye-teeth to do a scene like that with Harry Wentworth. What'd he say to you when he took you aside?"

"Oh, stuff like this is the character being nasty, not me; don't be afraid of me."

"Were you?"

"Yes," Molly said shortly. "Then he said trust me, and I did and look what happened."

"I'd say it would be worth being knocked out to wake up with Harry Wentworth's arms around me," the girl sighed. Molly was surprised she had not realized Harry's sex appeal spanned so many years.

"He slapped me and threw water at me," she pointed out. "And that was after he bruised my mouth and cracked my ribs about twenty times."

"Well, whatever," said Jane. "He's trying to be nice and make it up to now, you know. Accept it. Go along with it. You're a lucky devil. He'll maybe get you a speaking part in his next movie."

"Yeah, he's like that," someone else agreed. "Remembers names and faces, and that."

"He's taking her home," said Jane as they left the bus and went in to get changed.

"Better not let his wife see you in the car," Brenda said darkly.

"Oh. Why not?" Molly asked faintly, dreading the answer.

"Story goes she came down on the set a few years ago when he was making a film with Joanie Barnes. Happened to come in on a love scene and fairly took the place apart, lights knocked down and everything. Quite a scene."

"Oh God," said Molly hollowly, appalled by the corruption of the truth. "And what did he do?" This she had to hear.

"Threw her out. She was in her bare feet too – must have chucked her shoes at him or something. Anyway, Barnes had hysterics and Harry took his wife on a torrid weekend somewhere, and after that everything was O.K."

"Oh good," said Molly with sarcastic emphasis, and Jane gave her a curious, speculative look.

"Maureen Bragg?" A man stuck his head in at the door. "There's a bloody great Lincoln waiting outside to take you home. The beat-up old actor at the wheel told me to tell you to hurry up."

Beat-up old actor – Harry wouldn't like that, Molly reflected as she and Jane left the building, though there had been a note of fondness in the man's voice.

Once Molly was settled in the car, Harry took Jane's hand and shook it warmly.

"Thank you, Jane," he said, and gave her a look so full of personal warmth, that even hard-boiled Jane McQuarrie felt a blush rising to her cheeks. He had taken the trouble to find out her name. That was the kind man he was!

Molly was not at all sure what kind of a man he was as they drove swiftly away from the Studio – and not in the direction of home. She forebore to ask him where they were going. His stern profile discouraged conversation. Besides, all at once, she felt too tired to say anything. He drove down to Ambleside Park and stopped in the parking lot at the very end of the road, facing the sea. He folded his arms over the wheel and gazed across the water to the green lump of Stanley Park, where tiny joggers slogged around the seven-mile Sea Wall under the tree-clad cliffs.

"Say something," he commanded, with a brief sideways

look at his wife.

So he wanted her to castigate him, did he? Well, she was ready to oblige.

"Why?" Molly said, straight to the point. "In God's name, why? Why get me down there to manhandle me, and drag me around, and hit me? Why me? What kind of a sadist are you? What were you trying to prove? Were you trying to humiliate me, make me feel useless and inept and clumsy? You certainly succeeded."

"I don't know why," he said harshly. "I only know when I read the scene I wanted to do it with you."

"Am I supposed to be flattered?"

"I just couldn't see knocking another woman around like that. I've never hit a woman in my life."

"And the only one you felt right about hitting, was your wife. Thanks." Molly sounded sarcastic and bitter. "You don't understand –"

"Well, neither do I," Harry admitted wearily. "But that's the way I felt. I thought if we did the scene together, you'd learn a bit about the mutual trust and understanding that actors have to have."

"I trusted you and you belted me," she pointed out.

"I know. I don't know what went wrong." He stopped abruptly at the point where it would have been natural to say 'I'm sorry'. Apologizing did not come easy to Harry, Molly knew that, and she waited pointedly for him to go on. When he did not, she said levelly,

"Maybe you wanted to knock me out."

"I did not! You stupid fool woman, Molly, can't you understand? – I thought I'd killed you!" He banged his forehead on his hands clasped on the steering wheel, his voice loud and rough with an emotion Molly had never heard before. She was shocked into stillness. "For one goddamned awful moment I thought I had killed you," he repeated very quietly.

"But you –" she was going to say 'finished the scene anyway' but bit the words back, seeing that he was genuinely upset.

"I know," Harry said grimly, reading her thought. "I went right on with the scene to the end before finding out. That's what I don't understand." Without warning he got out of the car, slammed the door, and walked off across the beach towards the sea, his fists rammed hard in his pants' pockets.

Molly was disturbed; she had never seen Harry unsure of himself, question his own actions. She looked at his rigid back, watched him flex his shoulders, and realized that in a strange way this new vulnerability made him more lovable. What he had said did not make sense – he'd never hit a woman and the only one he could feel right about roughing up and hitting was his wife, and in some complex way that was supposed to be a compliment? He was afraid he'd killed her when she collapsed from his blow to the neck, yet he went right on acting the scene before going back to find out? How genuine was his feeling for her? Was the film actually more important than life? Or was he just dramatizing his feeling, and in his heart he had known she wasn't really dead?

Her head throbbing, Molly plodded across the shingle to his side.

"My head hurts," she said. "Let's go home and be miserable together. And if you want me to say I forgive you, I do, Harry."

"Thanks. But I need to forgive myself more." He looked down at her and she saw that the whipping wind had brought tears to the corners of his eyes. Or was it the wind? He reached out and gently touched the lump on her forehead before taking her arm and turning back to the car.

In the car, he shut himself behind a wall of guilt and self-doubt and condemnation and drove in silence. Molly yawned and slid across the seat and leant against his unyielding shoulder.

"Hey," said Harry softly, after a little while, pouring Tenderness and Warmth and Sincerity into his voice. "Hey! I love you."

When she did not respond he glanced down and saw that she was asleep, and he smiled wryly at his wasted histrionics. Well, at least she seemed to trust him, he reflected. And after all, that had been the object of the exercise. Hadn't it?

The payoff was to come some nine months later when the film was released for a sneak preview.

Drug Squad had a Gala Canadian Premiere at the Tinseltown Theatre on Pender, and for once Molly had a real incentive to attend. Harry's face had healed well, but she was amused when he touched up some of the worst looking places with some special make-up. She was so used to the scars and stitch marks herself and had come to accept them as part of Harry, that she overlooked the fact that many of his fans did not realize that he had been injured and might be unpleasantly shocked at his appearance.

Harry, resplendent and commanding in tuxedo and black tie, was the centre of attention in the lobby and Molly, and Ken and Sue – who were accompanying them for the first time – faded discreetly into the background while he was introduced to the Mayor of Vancouver and some prominent film and theatre people. And thus it was that as Molly stood to one side with the twins, idly scanning the crowds, surging behind the red velvet ropes she spotted Jane McQuarrie, and their eyes met, with immediate recognition. Jane smiled and raised a quick hand in a small secret greeting, and before she could think it out Molly had grinned back.

Oh damn, she thought, turning away, now I've given myself away, Jane knows who I really am, and the story'll be in all the papers tomorrow and Harry'll be furious. (It was O.K. for him to be in the papers, but not for his family. Harry believed in keeping his private life private.) The twins looked at Jane with interest; she was dressed like a middle-aged hippy and had children of their own age with her.

The film was what Molly perceived as a run-of-the-mill Harry Wentworth vehicle – lots of sinister characters plotting and counter-plotting and straight cops and one crooked cop chasing them, and Harry chasing the crooked cop. She was really only interested in the hospital scene and was taken by surprise when the fight scene erupted and found herself gasping with the rest of the audience when Harry fell through the bannisters; and then again when the chair was smashed over his head and only partially broke, and she actually joined in the universal exclamation of shock when the plate glass mirror crashed down on Harry; and when he emerged from the wreckage, face streaming with blood, she too, gave a groan of horror and revulsion, and was surprised when his hand found hers and gripped it hard. The scene carried straight on with no signs of a break and Harry delivered his lines and completed the action apparently oblivious of the wreckage of a face from which he spoke. Here was the man, Molly perceived, who, being a 'real pro', finished a scene first and then attended to the wounds (as he had with her).

"Great make-up job," she whispered sarcastically, and Harry trod on her foot and let go her hand.

The hospital scene arrived and Molly was hard put to recognize herself in the middle-aged curly-brown-haired nurse walking back and forth in front of the Nursing Station. She was made well aware that the twins had spotted her by the stifled giggles coming from her left, and she thought grimly, you wait, kids, and see what happens next; for she had not told them this part.

But, it never happened. Harry's sinister black-clad masked figure skulked and flitted through the hospital corridors and stairwells (bringing to Molly's mind the disloyal thought that if Rex Mallory had really wanted to infiltrate the hospital, he'd have been a lot less conspicuous if he'd worn a white coat with a stethoscope in one pocket) and never once did he leap out and overpower a curly-haired middle-aged nurse, knock her out and stuff her in a closet.

"What happened to my bit?" she hissed urgently to Harry.

"Guess you ended up on the cutting-room floor, love," he murmured back, amusement in his voice, putting a sympathetic arm around her shoulders.

"That's not fair! You mean I went through all that for nothing?"

"Oh, well," he responded mockingly, "That's show-biz, dahling."

You knew, she thought, you knew my bit had been cut and you never even told me. Maybe it was all a setup and it was never going to be in anyway and you fixed the whole thing just to do that to me? She looked at Harry's intent profile. No, I won't believe you're that devious. Or are you?

The movie received an ovation at the end –

incomprehensibly to Molly – and Harry was sufficiently flattered by it to stand in the lobby afterwards showing his teeth in his familiar tough-guy grin autographing programs – while Ken and Sue collected the other actors' autographs. When Jane McQuarrie approached with her two children, Harry looked quickly from her to Molly, unaware that the two women had already recognised each other, and said,

"Jane. I don't think you've met my wife, Molly, have you? Jane McQuarrie. She had a bit part in the film."

"No," said Jane, looking up with an exaggerated bland frankness. "Nice to meet you, Mrs. Wentworth." They shook hands solemnly.

"So," said Molly brightly, playing the game, "you were in the film, too?"

"Sure was. Would you sign my kids' programs, Mr. Wentworth?"

"My pleasure," Harry murmured, taking them. "They're casting my new picture next month. Why don't you see your agent – you might get a small part."

"Gosh, thanks, Harry."

"I suppose," said Molly apparently seriously, "some of the movie was cut?"

"Oh yes," Jane responded. "One of the best parts, as I remember."

"Would that be the scene where Rex Mallory beats up a middle-aged curly-haired nurse and knocks her out and stuffs her in a cupboard?"

"Why, yes, Mrs. Wentworth, that's the one I was thinking about. How did you guess?" And suddenly the two women were hooting with laughter and Harry was looking disconcerted.

For the first time he saw a movie of his, through Molly's eyes and was vastly dissatisfied. Drug Squad was nine months in the past, Fallen Man was still in the planning stages, but already he knew it was going to be very different. How different, he had no intention of telling Molly. He remembered how he had felt standing in front of Bath Abbey looking up at the falling angels carved on either side of the great door, and his gut feeling told him the whole concept was good.

"I thought Mum looked a fright," said Sue sympathetically, breaking his train of thought.

"She looked weird," said Ken.

"Ah. Like the movie?" Harry asked quickly.

"Bam! Pow! Splat!," said Ken drily. "I liked the fight. No wonder your face got busted up."

"Can I be in your next movie?" Sue asked.

"No. Never act with dogs or children."

"I'm not a child, I'm Susan Ash."

Harry looked at her thoughtfully.

"So you are," he said, seeing the woman within the girl. "So you are."

"Are you going to be in any more of Harry's movies, Mum?" Ken asked.

"No," said Molly. "Definitely not."

"Good," the boy said, "one actor in the family is enough."

Sue drew a quick breath to protest but Harry dropped her a wink and she subsided. The link between her and Harry was strong, forged on the implicit knowledge that she would act one day. This unspoken secret bonded them; but for Sue it was deeper than just a shared professional ambition – she loved Harry.

Later that night, in bed, Harry said casually,

"I'm going to England again next month, for a new movie. Want to come?"

Attuned to the subtleties of his voice, Molly knew at once, he did not want her to, and after a brief struggle with the stubborn side of her nature, she managed to say with false sincerity,

"Oh, what a shame! I'm committed up to my ears with things. I'm sorry, Harry, I really don't think I should."

"Hmmph." He grunted, satisfied and not deceived. A good wife, he thought, is more precious than rubies. You won't regret it, love, when you see what I can do when I really try. I hope.

He kissed her and they settled down to sleep. Like a flicker of lightning far below the distant horizon, the pain flared briefly and was gone.

Chapter Twenty-Five

The Oscar

"Seen at Vancouver International Airport last night, popular craggy actor Harry Wentworth and his smiling wife Molly. Harry is a nominee for Best Actor this year."

The call from Richard came as a complete surprise.

"Will you have lunch with me, Molly?"

"Today?"

"Today."

"Why?"

"I want to talk to you."

"That's nice. What about?"

"Not over the 'phone."

"Now I've got a sinking feeling in my stomach. Is it nice or nasty?"

"It's about Harry. I've booked a table at the Ferguson Point Teahouse for one o'clock. Can you be there?"

"Of course. I'm consumed with curiosity."

About Harry. What could Richard want to discuss about his father with Molly? Was he sick again? No, please God, not that. But Richard wouldn't keep her in suspense about a thing like that. Would he?

Normally a window table at the Teahouse would have afforded a fabulous view of English Bay and all the freighters at anchor waiting to get in or out of the Harbour, sail boats of all shapes and sizes, fishing boats, runabouts, dinghies, wind surfers, the sun on the sparkling sea, Atkinson Point Light blinking away at the right, the University buildings to the left. Today there was nothing but a blanket of white fog; beyond the green lawn on top of the bluff was nothing, a nothing that billowed occasionally in thicker or lighter rolls but never allowed so much as a glimpse of the sea. It gave one a sense of isolation, suspension, privacy – maybe that was why Richard had chosen the place on such a poor day?

They sat across from each other and drank sherry.

Richard, approaching forty, had reached that plateau, Molly decided, when his age would be un-guessable for fifteen years. His hair was longer now, perhaps in an attempt to abnegate his still astonishing likeness to his famous father, perhaps simply to be in style with the current trend. He looked like what he was, a reasonably prosperous young lawyer with a wife and children, a house in the suburbs and a condo in Hawaii.

Since he seemed to be in no hurry to broach the subject of Harry, Molly did a little social back-scratching.

"How's Wednesday?"

"As beautiful and predictable and immature as ever." Richard gave her a look that said not as admirable as you, and Molly shifted her gaze quickly to the fog.

"Don't do that, Richard," she murmured.

"I'm the envy of my colleagues. Fancy, stuffy, conventional, old Richard Worthington married to a gorgeous movie-star – how did he do it?"

"I've often wondered – how did you do it, Richard?"

"Just stood around and looked like my father," he said bitterly.

"Don't sound like that. Wednesday loves you, doesn't she?"

"In her way."

"And you –"

"In my way. You know about that. I'm a lucky man and I

know it, and I'm not complaining, Molly. These last few years living close to Dad have been a revelation to me – I just wish I'd got to know him sooner."

"And Thomas?"

"Growing like a weed, and talking like a child twice his age. That's Dad's influence."

"Harry?" Molly tried not to sound anxious.

"Ah, yes – Harry. Dad. How is he?"

"Why, fine – totally clear at his last checkup."

"Excited about anything?"

"No-o-o I don't think – no, wait, I know what you mean. The Oscar nomination?"

Richard leaned across the table and spoke urgently.

"Molly, do you honestly not realize that this is the biggest thing that's happened to him in his whole life? Nearly forty years he's been acting and this is the first recognition he's ever had from the profession. Don't you know how excited he is?"

Molly looked astonished.

"He is? He never said anything like that to me."

"No, because you've never shown any interest in his career. You love him – and that's fine – but you've always made it quite clear that you don't think much of him as an actor."

"Oh dear," said Molly. "What are you telling me, Richard?"

"That I think it's time you took another look at Harry Wentworth the film star. He's been growing a lot lately."

"How come you're suddenly an expert?"

"I'm not. Wednesday keeps me up to date. He's been talking to her, you know – about the Oscar nomination – that's how I know he's excited. I guess she's the only one in the family who really understands. Except Sue."

Molly made a wry face.

"We four do have a strange relationship, don't we? Here's Harry confiding in his daughter-in-law, and his son telling me I've been remiss as a wife. And we all love each other, this way, and that way, and that way..." she said, drawing lines diagonally and horizontally and perpendicularly in the air.

Richard caught her waving hands and held them down on the table.

"Don't you know," he said earnestly, "how Harry longs for

you to admire his work on the screen? You're his wife, Molly and you've never once said 'that was a good movie' or 'you gave a great performance'. Of all people in the world a man needs his wife's approval more than anyone else. I know. I need Wednesday's and she couldn't care less about the Law."

"Oh, Richard! Are you sure about Harry. He's never said anything to me."

"Molly, I've seen his face when he's mentioned a new part and you've turned away and talked about something else. You know how his face turns to stone?"

"I know, I know. God, Richard, I feel terrible." Her voice was low. "Are you sure?"

He nodded.

"Wednesday told me, and I believe her. She knows Harry as an actor, as a fellow professional. And I know Wednesday. And, Molly, I know that my opinion means more to Wednesday than all the fawning critics or flattering directors; she wants me to approve because I honestly do know her better than anyone else. And I think you know Dad in the same way."

"How can you say that!" Molly cried. "When I didn't even know this about him? Have I really been so blind and selfish and callous and – and – unfeeling – all these years? What can I do? I can't suddenly fake an interest I don't feel – Harry can read me like a book, he'd know I wasn't sincere."

"He might appreciate you just making the effort. No, that wasn't what I was getting at." Richard paused and took a breath. "I take it you haven't seen "The Fallen Man"? I thought not. Neither had I until last night when Wednesday made me go. Molly, you have to see the movie. Harry is – I can't describe what I felt about his performance. Would you believe I felt like a kid whose father just hit a winning home run? I wanted to stand up in the cinema and shout 'Hey, everybody! That's my Dad!' " He stopped suddenly, looking embarrassed, and busied himself with his lunch.

Molly ate, too, thoughtfully, glancing occasionally out at the fog. Why did I ever assume that he didn't take his work anymore seriously than I did? Was I so busy being clever about his films that I never noticed I was hurting him? How could I have done that? How could he have taken it all these years?

"Look, Molly, it's not the end of the world," Richard said gently, seeing the sadness and guilt on her face. "Remember that first time we met and you told me that Dad hadn't deserted me after Mum died, and had tried to keep in touch, but my grandparents had kept us apart? Remember how hard it was for me to accept that? But, I did in the end, and Dad and I have built a good relationship since then – and don't forget, it's not one-sided. You and Harry already have a terrific thing going together."

"But how can I expect him to forgive me?"

"You've forgiven him bigger things. I know. I know what happened when the baby died. I know how desperately he hurt you, and how marvellous you were about it."

"We don't talk about that."

"No. But you both know it happened – it's part of your life together. Make the Oscar a part too. He may not win – in fact, he probably won't – but Molly it's such a triumph for him even to be nominated. Why don't you share that joy with him?"

"Where's the film showing?" Molly asked, making an impulsive decision. "I'll go this afternoon. Then I'll see what I can do, Richard. Is that good enough?"

He smiled one of his rare warm smiles, and Molly realized suddenly that he was not a happy man.

'I just want to see the two people I love, happy together', he thought. But, he did not say it because it sounded too corny.

Watching Harry in The Fallen Man was a strange experience for Molly. He was her husband and yet, he was not, he was a man called Morgan Steele; she knew every line of his face and yet this was another man's face.

She saw torture in his eyes and fear in his mouth and guilt on his brow that she had never seen, had never known he was capable of showing. His voice was different, accented, a new rhythm to his speech she had never heard before. His body – so familiar – was new, it moved a different way, it reflected moods and feelings that were foreign to her.

Though she knew the man on the screen so well – had made love with him three nights ago, wiped gravy off his chin, folded his clean underwear – she did not know him at all because he was not Harry Wentworth, he was Morgan Steele, adventurer, soldier of fortune, whose past had come to haunt and challenge him and lay him low. Molly became involved with Morgan Steele, she agonized with him, feared with him, loved with him the girl – the only person in his world who could comfort him – and felt no jealousy when he caressed and kissed her because Morgan Steele was not her husband. Finally, when he turned and walked slowly, wearily, up the street and stopped and looked up at the Abbey wall, at the carved stone angels climbing the ladder to heaven, and the camera lingered on the upside-down angel, that was falling from grace, and on Morgan Steele's face, and then back to a climbing angel on a lower rung, and she understood that the Fallen Man believed he had another chance, the tears rolled down her cheeks.

She sat unmoving, and so did most of the people in the theatre, so powerful and moving an experience had it been. She understood now Richard's reaction of wanting to jump up and claim his relationship, and yet she felt ashamed because though she longed to say 'that's my husband', she would also have to add 'and I never knew he could act like that.' So she sat with her hands in her lap and her eyes down.

Harry, Harry, where have I been? Why didn't someone tell me you could act like this? How did I not know that you were making different films? Did people tell me and I never heard? She hurried home, eager to shower praise on him, apologize and ask forgiveness.

Yet, when Molly entered the house and saw Harry sitting in his chair to the right of the fireplace, she was suddenly stricken with shyness and awe. For the very first time, she realized that she was privileged to be married to someone famous, a celebrity, a vastly talented man – a stranger full of depths and sensibilities she had never even guessed at, and it made her absurdly afraid.

Afraid of my husband, Harry Wentworth? That's ridiculous.

"Hi," he said, glancing up from the paper. "You're late."

"I know, I went to the movies," she said in a breathy rush.

"Hmm." He went back to the paper.

"I went to see The Fallen Man." She waited, swallowing. Harry turned a page.

"So?" he said without looking up, apparently disinterested. Was he so used to her sneering at his pictures that he had to pretend he didn't care what she thought? Molly flagellated herself mentally.

"Harry," she stood like a little girl, twisting her hands together. "Harry, it was marvellous. You were terrific."

"Mmm-hmm." He turned a page, still not looking up.

"Harry!" she swiped at the paper, knocking it out of his hands. "I'm trying to tell you something!"

"Really?" Now he looked up, maddeningly mild and unimpressed. "What?"

"You're a great actor."

"Had a good director, good cameraman, good lighting, that's all."

"That's not all! –"

"Good script –"

"If they don't give you an Oscar I will –"

"Good editing, good cutting –"

"Dammit, how can I convince you I think you were wonderful?"

He cocked his head judiciously, one eyebrow up, a smile twitching his lips.

"You could kiss my feet –Hey!" For Molly was on her knees at once, pulling at his shoelaces. "Don't do that!" He laughed and stood, his hands under her arms pulling her up with him. "You wash my socks, you know, I've feet of clay. I've always loved you for not treating me like a star – don't start now."

"I should at least have given you credit for being good at your job."

"You kept me humble."

"Now I'm humble." Molly crossed her wrists at the back of his neck and searched his eyes. "How can I make it up?"

"You don't have to. You gave me back the feeling of being a real person by loving me not because I was famous – in fact, in spite of it – but because I was me, Harry. I needed that, Molly. I had been an actor so long I was beginning to forget I was a real person, too. Then you came along. So – you didn't respect my craft or my talent, but you gave me a reason for living that I hadn't had for a long time."

Since Dell died. The phrase hung between them unspoken. Molly was surprised to find that the twinge of jealousy was not there.

"So," she said carefully, not looking at him now, "you're saying it doesn't matter to you that I think, now, you're a fine actor?"

"Don't let it make a difference to the way you see me."

"A difference? It has to, Harry. Seeing The Fallen Man has shown me a whole new dimension in you that I think is marvellous. I thought you'd be pleased…"

"Pleased!" he said, and at last he let the joy and pleasure show on his face. "Oh my God, darling – pleased!" and he put his arms around her in a rough and clumsy hug, that did more to express his real feelings than any words could have. He buried his face in her hair and held her tightly and she felt his heart beating and his body quivering, and at last she knew that he was accepting her praise, and acknowledging that he had waited a long time for it, and it was worth it!

Now, Molly was not shy of him anymore. Despite her discovery of his enormous talent, he was Harry her husband – the one with the moods and imperfections and inconsistencies, the one who loved her because she loved him. He was Harry Wentworth the Star she could admire, and he was at the same time, Harry-my-husband whom she could love unreservedly and without awe or shyness. It seemed to her that in that moment their relationship became more complete than ever before.

"When do we leave for Hollywood for the Oscars?"

"I hadn't planned on going."

"I know. But that was before –""

"Do you want to go?"

"I wouldn't miss it for the world! Don't you want to win?"

"With you in my corner now," Harry said seriously, "I've won even if I don't win."

"Of course you'll win. And in view of the elegance of the occasion, I think Ken had better buy Barbie a new dress."

"You're on."

In the end Molly, waited until they got to Los Angeles and

then took the money and went shopping for the dress by herself. She wanted it to be a complete surprise for Harry. For once, she determined, she would look like a movie star's wife; for once she would be glamorous and glittery and impractical and frothy and superficial – and never mind, the fact that she was prostituting her personal integrity to do it, that in fact, doing it for Harry was denying her liberation from the bonds of husband-pleasing female. He deserved it. It would be worth it!

She bought the dress on the day of the Oscars and had it delivered to their suite while Harry was out. She laid it on the bed and had second thoughts. It was a deep mauve (the 'in' colour), the material shot through with metallic thread, and spangles and sequins blazing in patches, and had an uneven hemline dipping to the ankles at the back, mid-calf at the front; the skirt was a series of overlapping panels that flowed freely with the slightest movement; the halter top with a choker neck left her shoulders and back bare. There was a filmy stole to match, also sparkling, and shoes with high heels and ankle straps. It would look fabulous on anyone in their twenties – or thirties – but, forties? She had a twinge of doubt.

In the afternoon she summoned Perc – who had travelled with them for this specific purpose – and retired behind closed doors to get ready. Harry changed in the other bedroom and waited – and waited – and waited.

"The limo is turning into a pumpkin," he shouted through the door at last.

Molly was standing in front of the mirror adjusting to her new image.

"Perc, you've outdone yourself."

He beamed.

The dress, not originally intended for a more mature figure, had been let out and fitted Molly like a glove. It shimmered as she moved. Perc had made her up in brilliant tones, highlighting her cheekbones and chin and skilfully diminishing her nose; the eye-shadow picked up the colour of the dress, and sparkled in harmony with it; her lips were full and glossy; eyebrows gracefully arched, eyelashes (false), lustrous and full, touching her cheeks when she blinked. Her hair, blonde rinsed to lighten it, was piled in immaculate waves, and curls and sprayed into basket-like immobility. She looked at least fifteen years younger. She did not look much like Molly Wentworth, but she did look like the wife of a Star. She hated and despised her image on sight.

"Open the door, Perc."

She swept out, moving in quite a different way in the unusually high heels, and struck a pose.

"I'm ready, dahling," she drawled.

Harry had expected to be surprised, but not jolted like this. He kept his face impassive, absorbing the shock. The creature provocatively posed in front of him, hands on hips, one eyebrow cocked invitingly, was certainly striking and gasp-worthy and stellar and highly appropriately attired for a tinsel-town gala event – the trouble was he couldn't see his wife Molly anywhere inside her. His instinct was to say, 'you look silly, take it off, wash your face, and try again', but a slight hesitancy in the way Molly's hands dropped from her hips and her fingers quickly clenched and unclenched, telegraphed her anxiety and he looked down, grinding out his cigar in an ashtray.

She's done this for me, she thinks it's what I want. My God, how can I ever have given her that impression? If I tell her to change she'll be shattered, her evening spoilt. I may know who she is under all that, but nobody else will. I wanted people to see Molly my wife, not this strange gaudy person; but, if that's the way she wants it, that's the way it'll be.

He crushed his disappointment and looked up with a big Sincere Smile.

"You took me by surprise, love. You look stunning. Let's go." He took her elbow, as usual, and guided her to the door.

Oh God, Molly thought, looking at his face from the new angle her high heels gave her, he hates it, but he's too nice to say so. He's prepared to take me like this, rather than hurt me, and I was only prepared to go like this because that was what I thought he wanted. Someone's got to start being honest – and quickly.

"Wait," she said, at the door. "I've forgotten something. Can you wait? Please?"

"Of course." Harry spread his hands. "As long as you like."

She shut the bedroom door behind her.

"Help me, Perc. Unzip me, quick. I have to change."

"My dear! He didn't like it?"

"No, he didn't say so, but I could tell." The dress fell in a heap on the floor and she stepped out of it. In two minutes she had found and put on a cream jersey blouse with full bishop's sleeves and a crossover neckline, and the black evening skirt that she liked to dance in. Without being asked Perc creamed her face and swiftly wiped off the excessive eye shadow, lipstick and blusher. With quick expert strokes he redid her make-up to match the feeling of the new outfit.

"Not diamonds," he said, stripping off her earrings. "The gold hoops."

"And the three-strand gold necklace," Molly said.

She looked at her new image in the mirror.

"Better?"

"Different," said Perc tactfully. "You were good before, dear. You're good now."

"Now I'm me." Molly bent to pull on gold strap sandals, and noticed Perc reverently on one knee picking up the purple spangled dress.

"You want, Perc, you can have it," she said gently.

He turned an aggrieved face to her.

"I'm not a transvestite, Molly," he said huffily.

"No, no, I didn't mean for you. I thought perhaps, if you had a friend… " she nearly said 'of either sex' but stopped in time.

"Yes," his face softened. "Thank you, Molly, I have."

She went out quickly and straight to Harry's side without posing, as before.

"I'm sorry, Harry," she said, "I had to change. I just didn't feel right. Do you mind terribly?"

He kept his face straight, neither fake disappointment nor relief showed.

"If you feel more comfortable like that, love," he said gravely, "then that's all right with me."

She looked at him.

Bloody liar, why can't you say you hated it?

But he would not, she knew; he did not have to anyway.

Unexpectedly Harry reached out and pushed his hands up into her hair at either temple and shook and loosened the hair-sprayed curls and waves out of their immaculate order, pulled a tendril down on each side in front of her ear.

"Good," he said, and took her elbow again, giving it an extra warm squeeze of appreciation.

This wordless communication is all very well, Molly thought, but wouldn't it be nice just once to say what we really feel? And let the chips fall where they may. Internally she sighed and shrugged, knowing that it would never happen with Harry, knowing that she would continue to take the initiative, as she just had, and accepting that through the years there had indeed been many times when Harry had done just that, on occasions when she had not been prepared to be honest.

For almost the first time in their married life, Molly became aware that Harry was very nervous. No, it did not show much on the outside, he did not shake or stammer or wave his hands about (as she would have done), but it manifested itself in a glacial repose, an exaggerated at-ease-ness; he wore his Mount Rushmore face as he had in court during Wednesday's paternity suit, and she could feel the tension in him, see small differences in his behaviour – a blood vessel in his cheek pulsing, his jaw taut, a slight difference in his voice – the pace of his speech – things only a person who lived with him would notice. To the world he was Harry Wentworth, tough-guy actor, somewhat scornful of the Hollywood scene, totally in control of himself and his world, and somewhat amused, in a cynical way, by the gaudy trappings of the whole affair. He had one arm protectively around the waist of the calm blonde woman who accompanied him – the wife so few people in the film world had met – her simple evening clothes and make-up an island of taste in a sea of theatricality; the occasional glances of such open affection that she gave her husband positively embarrassing to the company of people around her who customarily hid their deepest feelings and overpowered each other with their superficial ones.

Since Harry was a Best Actor Nominee, the TV cameras constantly picked him out of the crowd, and Molly found herself beaming automatically whenever Harry nudged or squeezed her. He spoke to so many people in the theatre lobby as they stood with Richard and Wednesday, that she hardly had time to pick out and gawk at the famous faces. Harry's friends in the industry tended to be people she had never heard of, bit players, stuntmen, camera crewmen, this was the first time she had seen him mix with stars. Everybody came over to wish him luck, including a succession of good-looking younger women stars who all seemed to find Harry quite as sexually attractive as she did, judging by the way they touched him as they spoke and lingered over their good luck kisses – many of which were on the mouth. Molly stood at his side appraising the girls with older eyes. Most of them could be my daughters, she thought, and they're lovely. How can I be so lucky that he's mine – in so far as anyone can belong to anyone else? She glanced at Wednesday and surprised a look of naked jealousy on her face, and was able to feel compassion for the girl who had married the son of the man she loved. Then she saw that Richard had noticed too, and his face had momentarily clouded with sadness, and she caught his eye and smiled her fondness and understanding to him, and was gratified by the wry and adult smile he gave her in return. Richard at least knew who he was and where he was, and how to cope. Watching Harry with the younger women, Molly hoped that she was equally as adult. He smiled his actor's smile, and glanced from face to face with expressive actor's eyes, and spoke with his vibrant actor's voice, but when he took Molly's arm to escort her to their seats, it was not for the cameras, his touch was the touch of a husband, and the grunt of relief that that part of the evening was over, was for her ears alone.

They filed into their seats, Wednesday, Richard, Molly and Harry on the aisle, in that order, so that if (when?) Harry was called to receive his Oscar, he would not have to climb over anyone's knees.

For almost three hours the presentations continued and they sat and smiled and clapped and enjoyed other people's triumphs, and silently empathized with other people's disappointments – their set smiles and gracious concessions of defeat, the acknowledgment of another's superior talent, at least as far as the Academy was concerned. As they came into the final stretch, Molly would have liked to hold Harry's hand, but he had arranged himself in an elaborately relaxed position leaning on the aisle-side-arm of his seat, his elbow on the armrest, his hand in a fist under his chin, one finger along his cheek; his legs were elegantly crossed, and he looked the picture of interested, amused, unconcern. He was seething inside. This was probably his last chance for a genuine Oscar, nominated, and won on the merit of a specific performance – after this, his only chance would be for a special award for services to the film industry. He desperately wanted the Oscar. And he despised himself for wanting it so badly. He had no speech prepared, and trusted that he would be able to accept it, - if he won it – without a lot of emotional gibberish, with a dignity and reserve that would please the three people to his right, who singly and collectively, meant more to him than fame or popularity or money.

He sensed Molly's leaning towards him, wanting to share these moments of tense expectation, but to hold himself together in the image that he wanted to project to the TV audience that was undoubtedly getting close-ups of him every few minutes, he felt impelled to remain aloof, to pull himself away from her. These were moments and emotions that he could not share. Like a woman in labour, he felt himself removed from the world around him, totally self-absorbed. Molly would have to make out as best she could, whether she understood or not.

Molly was hurt; there was no denying the ache of rejection she felt. I love him, and I cannot help him, because he doesn't need – or want – my support – and I don't know why. As well as I think I know him, I guess he has secret places, just like I do, where he doesn't want me to be. And if I expect the privilege of privacy, then I guess he's entitled to it too. The realization that they shared a need brought her closer to him again and the pain receded, and unconsciously she released a sigh. Richard moved his legs against hers in a rare physical demonstration of his feeling for her. And she thought, wryly, the wrong man, but the right time, and she looked at the stage and smiled for the benefit of the cameras that might be on Harry and include her in their picture.

Clips of the films for the nominees for Best Actor were shown, including the now famous shot of Harry looking at the falling angel, and enthusiastic applause greeted each one.

Molly felt sick.

Harry, with his great pretense of calm, seemed to her terribly vulnerable, and she hoped fervently that if he lost, he would not withdraw even further from her. Harry Wentworth vulnerable? Harry Wentworth capable of being hurt? Harry Wentworth actually caring, whether he won an Oscar or not? You've gotta be kidding! Oh no, I'm not, said Molly silently to herself, he cares and he can be hurt and that's why I love him, because he'll let me know that – and not many other people in the world do.

The Fondas, brother and sister, were doing the presenting, and now Jane reached for the envelope, slit it... opened it –

"The winner is – Harry Wentworth for Fallen Man!" A roar of applause.

In one movement Harry uncrossed his legs and stood up, and Molly raised her arms and her face full of love and joy, for him to kiss, but he was already in the aisle, striding towards the stage without once looking at her. She sank back mortified and angry, both, hoping that no camera had recorded her little moment of humiliation.

("Bastard!" said Rob, leaping from his chair in front of the TV. "Selfish egocentric bastard! Did you see that?" But Sue was too busy mopping up tears of joy to answer and Ken had returned to his book.)

Richard's hand found Molly's and held it in her lap.

Harry was at the podium now, shaking hands with Peter and kissing Jane Fonda, hefting his Oscar delightedly. He moved to the microphone and the theatre fell silent, and waited as he considered the statue thoughtfully, before setting it on the lectern in front of him. Just when the tension was almost unbearable, he looked up and spoke quietly.

"I never expected to win an Oscar. And when I was nominated, I never expected winning it would mean anything to me. But it does. This is probably the most... serious... moment of my life, believe it or not."

Molly relaxed. Bless him, he was being himself, for once in his public life he was being sincere and natural – the man she knew.

"I have to thank the producer, the director, and particularly the writer of Fallen Man of course, but more particularly, still I have to thank my wife for my being here tonight." Molly felt a silly grin spread across her face. "Without Dell's support in the early years –" Molly's smile froze "—I would have quit the business. Dell believed in me." Dell. Damn his eyes. I can't believe this is happening. Molly wrenched her hand from Richard's tightening grip, and would have stood then, but for his other hand on her arm.

"Molly, don't!" he whispered urgently.

"Dell saw a potential in me that maybe no-one else did. She convinced me I could act."

No, dammit, I will not sit and listen to this! I have to get out of here. Molly stood up, freeing herself from Richard's restraining hand, and stepping into the aisle, turned her back on the stage and started towards the exit a mile and a half away up sixteen million shallow steps, not hearing the murmur of consternation around her.

"Otherwise I would probably still be selling encyclopedias."

Molly lifted her skirt and moved slowly, walking through heavy mud, and when the aisle was inexplicably bathed in light, she lifted her head and wiped all expression from her face – or so she thought. The spotlight moved with her.

"Molly."

It was as though Harry was standing at her shoulder; he must have leant forward, and spoken directly into the microphone, his voice was so warm and intimate. "Don't go. Please." She stopped. "Hear me out." The whole theatre turned now to watch and listen in hushed expectancy to the real-life drama being acted out before them, and before millions of movie fans watching TV around the world.

Oh, damn, damn, now I've really messed it up. Molly took a deep breath and turned around to face the stage – and Harry. He was looking directly at her, and it was all right.

"Dell, gave me the confidence to act," he went on. "But most of you know that Dell died thirty years ago." (Thirty years, is it really that long and the memory as clear as ever? And have I really – at last – accepted the fact she's dead and let her go?) A corporate sigh rose like a vocal mist in the theatre. "And it's Molly, my present wife, who turned me into an actor, good enough to win this," he touched the Oscar. "Molly, come up here. Please. I want you to share this moment because this Oscar is half yours."

Someone took Molly's arm and led her quickly down the aisle and up onto the stage, while Harry continued talking.

"For years I acted from the outside in. Then I met Molly and from her and her young family, I learned what it was like to be a real person. Molly," he put his arm around her and gathered her to his side, not quite sure what she might do or say, "you gave me the warmth and depth and compassion, that I needed for Morgan Steele. The Oscar's yours as much as mine!"

He looked at her face, and quickly put his hand over the microphone. Through teeth bared in his favourite tough-guy grin he said,

"Don't say anything – smile."

Through a huge and beaming smile Molly said,

"I could kill you –!" and that was as far as she got because he then smothered her mouth with a kiss, not a peck, but a real 'knees-to-water' bedroom kiss. And the crowd loved it, and whistled and applauded and the TV director knew it was worth every minute they were running overtime and ceased making frantic hand signals and just let the cameras run.

He doesn't know, Molly thought incredulously, he really doesn't know what he did to me just then. Accept it. That's the way he is. Love him with his faults and blind spots. I have to tell him – no, you don't. It really doesn't matter – let it go, let it go.

The band struck up the Fallen Man theme, which happened to be a waltz and before she knew it, Harry had his arm around Molly's waist and between them, with their other hands, they held the Oscar, and he was dancing her across the huge floodlit stage, their bodies dipping and gliding and flowing in the old perfect, pre-operation harmony. As her skirt swirled gracefully around her, Harry said,

"I'm glad you changed.   The other thing made you look like a high class hooker from Georgia and Howe."

"Well, thanks for the high class, anyway."   Her anger dissipated, she looked up at him coquettishly.   "Will you be my trick tonight?"

"What do you charge, lady?"

"I'm into small gold statues right now."

"Done."   He spun her into the wings and they stood and listened to the applause until someone pushed them out to take a final bow.

After that, Best Actress and Best Picture Awards could only be an anticlimax.   Even Sue stopped watching; she was too busy calling Harry person-to-person at the theatre.   Amazingly, she got through to him and, dragged from the exuberant crowd backstage to the telephone Harry answered curtly.

"Yes?"

"Harry, it's me, Sue.   You were wonderful.   I'm so glad.   I'm so happy I've been crying for the last ten minutes.   And I'm so proud – and glad – and—"

Rob's voice cut in from the extension.

"Harry? I thought that was a rotten thing you did to Mum."

"Rotten?"

"Rob, you beast, get off the line!"

"What thing?" Harry asked, puzzled.

"You know damn well."

"This is my call, Rob," Sue shouted.

Harry handed the squeaking receiver to the stage manager.

"When they stop yelling at each other," he said, "hang up".

Richard shoved his way through the melee to Harry's side and gripped his hand.

"Congratulations, Dad.   And thanks – for the nice words about Mum.   I was afraid at first Molly was upset –"

"Upset?" Harry looked astonished.   He put his hand on the nape of Molly's neck.   "You weren't upset, were you Molly?"

She met the steady gaze of his steely-blues that frightened so many people but not her, and answered,

"No, of course not."

"She understands me, Rich."

"I do?" She caught herself in the rising inflection and

changed it with a wry smile to an affirmative, "I do."

His fingers gently squeezed her neck in appreciation. He understands that I don't understand him sometimes, she thought. Damn, but relationships are complicated. I understand that he doesn't understand me – and he understands that – no, I'm going in circles. We both understand that there are things we don't understand about each other –

Someone put a glass of champagne in Molly's hand.

"My wife doesn't drink," said Harry.

"We have an understanding," said Molly, taking a bubbly gulp.

"She only drinks when I'm there to hold her up," Harry finished for her.

And she looked up and saw the twinge of pain across his face.

Chapter Twenty-Six

The Interview

"Molly Wentworth reveals all in a stunningly frank interview about her twelve-year marriage to Canadian star Harry Wentworth."

"Molly Ash Wentworth – A Rather Special Lady."
By Beryl Lonsdale

This morning I went to interview Molly Wentworth, wife of the veteran and much-respected Canadian actor, Harry Wentworth, who won the Best Actor Oscar, last year for his role in Fallen Man. We sat in the living-room of their house in the British Properties in West Vancouver – It's a modest house by celebrity standards, and looks well lived-in, as you might expect in a family where there are two teenagers still at home, and a grandson of six who is a constant visitor. Molly, who does much of her own cooking, served me with coffee and brownies. Below is a direct transcription of the interview I taped.

Beryl: These brownies are delicious. Do you have a recipe?
Molly: I suppose I did once. Now I just throw things

together and most of the time they come out right. Did you come here to discuss my housekeeping prowess? You might notice the plates don't match the cups and saucers.

Beryl: Would you call that typical of yourself?

Molly: Fairly typical. Does it bother you? I can get the right ones in a moment.

Beryl: No – no, please don't. I really came to discuss your marriage to Harry Wentworth.

Molly: I thought you came to interview me.

Beryl: Well, yes, but you are married to Harry. That has to have a bearing.

Molly: Oh really? I was me long before I married Harry.

Beryl: Our readers would like to know what it's like to be the wife of a star.

Molly: I don't know.

Beryl: Oh, come now –

Molly: Harry is Harry; whether he's a star or not, has nothing to do with our marriage.

Beryl: I can hardly believe that. It must be an exciting life, meeting other celebrities, parties –

Molly: Oh, - parties. It's an exciting life with Harry all right, but not because of the parties. I'm not very good at parties anyway. I tend to gravitate to a corner and watch. Show business people are like any other professionals, when they get in a group they talk shop. If their shop isn't your shop, then it can be quite boring.

Beryl: You're noted for your conservative style of dressing. Is this a reflection of Harry Wentworth's taste?

Molly: If you mean did he make me over, the answer is no. He tried once or twice, mind you, but it didn't work.

Beryl: But don't you dress to please him?

Molly: No. I undress to please him.

Beryl: Er – yes. What first attracted you to Harry Wentworth?

Molly: Nothing. I thought he was an arrogant, conceited, domineering bore.

Beryl: But you were a fan of his?

Molly: Good heavens, no! I thought his movies were cra... – dreadful – violent – crude, unsubtle.

Beryl: But you won a contest about his movies.

Molly: I didn't – my son did, but he put my name on the form.

Beryl: And so it was you who got to have dinner with Harry at the Bayshore.

Molly: Which I resented strongly. I'd rather have had the fifty dollars second prize. I needed the money.

Beryl: Why did you resent the dinner?

Molly: I found it belittling and demeaning – to both of us. It was a promotional gimmick. We weren't people. I wasn't Molly Ash, he wasn't Harry Wentworth. We were symbols, ciphers, pawns of the P.R. people. The Winner – God save us, that was me – and the Prize – Harry, and the object was to glorify Cetapac Films.

Beryl: You didn't enjoy the dinner, then?

Molly: Not at first. Not until we danced together and that was briefly beautiful, our steps fit together so well, it was like a revelation.

Beryl: But you still found him arrogant, conceited –?

Molly: No. Not then. I found him gentle and considerate.

Beryl: That must have been a surprise.

Molly: It was. I'm probably ruining his image by saying this – he's supposed to be such a tough-guy – but really he's a very sensitive man.

Beryl: So you never have any arguments?

Molly: Heavens, yes. Slam-bang drag-em-out rows. We're not very much alike, you know. We have different philosophies.

Beryl: So how do you cope with that?

Molly: Our marriage is founded on the two C's. Conflict and Compromise.

Beryl: I can understand the compromise – but is conflict really necessary in a good marriage, would you say?

Molly: I guess it is in ours. Without it life would be a lot duller. And we learn and grow through it.

Beryl: That's interesting. Do you still feel after – what? – 12 years of marriage that you're learning and growing?

Molly: Yes.

Beryl: What about the problems of being an actor's wife? Particularly when your husband acts in the kind of films that don't appeal to you?

Molly: The personality change, you mean, when he gets into a role? Yes, I've had to deal with that, and come to accept it.

Beryl: Does it bother you to see him making love to an actress on the screen?

Molly: No.

Beryl: No jealousy?

Molly: No. Not now. You see, Beryl, I know that man up there – thirteen feet tall – kissing that woman is not Harry-my-husband, he's Dick or Joe or Phil, or whatever the character's name is. Harry-my-husband is another man who lives with me and makes love to me and sometimes shouts at me. I don't identify Harry-on-the-screen with Harry-at-home.

Beryl: I'm sure you're very lucky to be able to do that.

Molly: I couldn't always. I had to work on it.

Beryl: Isn't it true that he had an affair with Wednesday Barnes some years ago?

Molly: An affair? You'll have to ask him about that.

Beryl: How did you cope with that situation? I remember reading he went to live in the same hotel as her.

Molly: You're very nosy. Wednesday became a friend of the family, and married Harry's son Richard – you must know that? We're a very happy family group.

Beryl: But you raised their son for the first two years of his life –

Molly: Yes. If you remember, Harry and I lost our own baby at birth. My arms were still feeling very empty when it became evident that Wednesday's career was going to take her away from little Thomas for long periods at a time. I volunteered to look after him, and it worked out very well. Harry adores him.

Beryl: He likes being a grandfather?

Molly: He enjoys the relationship he has with the boy – I don't think he puts a label on it. They're not Grandpa and Grandson so much as just two people of different ages who like each other.

Beryl: There are a lot of second marriages now, with stepchildren involved. Did you and Harry encounter any problems with your respective families? And if so, how did you deal with them?

Molly: Conflict and Compromise. We were lucky – the twins liked Harry, and I liked Richard. And vice versa.

Beryl: Your stepson is very close to your own age. Did that make for problems?

Molly: No. We have a – good relationship.

Beryl: How would you describe it?

Molly: Warm. And friendly.

Beryl: And your eldest son? The lawyer?

Molly: We had to learn to let each other live our own lives. There were a few rows. But doors were never permanently shut. That's important, you know. Doors give you privacy – but they also give you access.

Beryl: Harry Wentworth is a very strong personality – yet you never seem to be overshadowed. How do you manage that?

Molly: I don't think husbands and wives should subjugate themselves to each other. They were individuals before they met, they should remain individuals – but in partnership. I needed to remain being me. However, I had to fight for my right to do that. Harry was quite a chauvinist at first, and yes, he did try to make me over. Things were a lot better when he gave up. And when I gave up expecting him to be another kind of Harry than he was.

Beryl: You accepted each other, then, just as you were.

Molly: Yes, but with the understanding that we were both able and free to grow and change.

Beryl: Supposing one grew and changed more than the other?

Molly: Then the other had to adapt. Compromise.

Beryl: Mrs. Wentworth, how would you describe your love for your husband?

Molly: Passionate. My knees buckle when he touches me.

Beryl: How do you manage to retain that – that excitement after twelve years? So many marriages seem to go stale by then.

Molly: We keep surprising each other. I'll never know Harry; he'll never know me.

Beryl: I think you're special people if you can do that.

Would you like to tell me about your first marriage?

Molly: No. For Tom's sake, no. He wouldn't like it, and I respect that. I can't deny the experience must have shaped me to what I am now.

Beryl: If you'd rather not talk about it, I understand, but losing your baby must have been a terrible blow for you and Harry?

Molly: It was. Harry got drunk and I got suicidal, but we survived. We let her go, and we survived. That's all I can say.

Beryl: Is it true you have a drinking problem?

Molly: Wine goes to my head, if that's what you mean. Harry has the problem accepting it, not me. We have an understanding about that now. I don't drink more than I can take unless he's there to hold me up.

Beryl: I understand you're still working – ?

Molly: Yes, I'm involved in the Day Care Centre, at the administrative level. Single parents are my hobbyhorse. But that's another subject.

Beryl: Yes. You must have been very proud and happy when Harry won the Oscar?

Molly: Oh, I was. I thought Fallen Man was marvellous.

Beryl: Where is it? The Oscar? I don't see it anywhere.

Molly: Oh – gosh – I don't know. Maybe Sue has it in her room. She's going to be an actress, you know. And Thomas will act, too, I think.

Beryl: Harry paid you quite a tribute when he received the Oscar. Those of us who were watching were very moved by it.

Molly: Were you?

Beryl: I don't think I've ever seen that happen at the Academy Awards. I liked the way he kissed you. Was it all planned?

Molly: Yes.

Beryl: Is that one of the things you and Harry do together?

Molly: No. Sometimes. When it's important. Actually, we don't have a lot in common, you know. Our tastes are very different. It's just that we love each other. And I don't know why he loves me, any more than I can tell you coherently why I love him. I could say he's strong and gentle and kind and vulnerable and sad, and original and alive and different and perceptive and stubborn and talented, and it'd all be true. But sometimes he's weak and rough and cruel and infallible and happy-go-lucky and stuffy and insensitive and conventional and malleable and a rotten actor and that would be true too. And I love him for those things as well. Isn't that dumb?

Beryl: No, I don't think it's dumb, and neither do you, Molly. But really who is Molly Wentworth? We've all seen the calm, mature blonde woman at Harry Wentworth's side at First Nights and Fund Raising Dinners and heard her cryptic responses to the Press, but nobody really knows who she is. Can you tell us?

Molly: I'm Harry's wife and my children's mother and my mother's daughter. I'm the lady who runs the Day Care Centre and Harry's wife. I'm Perc's friend and Richard's stepmother and Pauline's mother-in-law and Harry's wife. I'm a dancer and a swimmer and a dreamer and a degree-holding women's libber; a cook, a first-aid-attendant, a nurse, an organizer, a dishwasher and a floor-scrubber. And Harry's wife. I'm none of those things by itself and all of them together. Take away one of them, and I wouldn't be the me I am.

Beryl: How do you see yourself?

Molly: Like a stone with a hundred faces. The faces are all different shapes and colours but the whole stone is me.

Beryl: That's very poetic.

Molly: I majored in English. Years ago.

Beryl: People wonder why of all the glamorous women he could have had Harry chose to marry you? You must know that?

Molly: Yes.

Beryl: Do you have an answer?

Molly: No. Except that he gets the male equivalent of my buckling knees when he touches me. I guess you'd call that chemistry. Logically and reasonable we're hopelessly mismatched.

Beryl: I know he's proud of you.

Molly: Oh, really? He may not be after this is published. I may end up in hospital.

Beryl: Of course you're joking.

Molly: Of course.

Beryl: One last question. Is being a celebrity's wife what you expected?

Molly: I didn't expect anything. I didn't marry a celebrity. I married a guy called Harry. Whether he was a celebrity or a garbage man had no bearing on my expectations. I thought I told you that? Marriage is a very personal private thing. Harry is Harry and Molly is Molly – and that's how we relate.

Beryl: I think, - and I'm sure our readers will agree with me – that you're very lucky.

Molly: Lucky – hell! What we've got, we worked for. And you can quote me on that!

Harry put down the magazine thoughtfully and grunted. He got up and moved out onto the deck to look at the familiar – spectacular – view, and winced. The pain was back. He leant on the rail, smiling to himself.

Sue found him there.

"Harry!" she cried dramatically. "Poor Harry! I read it. Oh, how could mother say those things about you!" She turned on him huge eyes brimming with sympathy. In fact they overflowed and three or four perfectly formed tears slid artistically down her cheeks, and Harry noticed with an inward grin that she leaned forward a little so that they fell directly to the floor and did not drop onto her bosom and spot her shirt. The girl was a natural actress, she could laugh or cry at the drop of a hat.

"What things?" he asked.

"About being weak and having rows and– oh–so much --"

"Thought it was pretty good myself."

"Oh, Harry, you're so loyal – and brave!" She opened her arms and flung herself at him and Harry prepared to hug her in response (she was the only person other than Molly that he had ever felt natural hugging), but found instead that she was kissing him on the mouth. Not a daughter's kiss, certainly, nor a little girl's kiss, but a tremulous, passionate, love-hungry, newly-awakened young woman's kiss. To his consternation, he found himself suddenly aware of her perfume, her full breasts pressed against him, her abdomen, her thighs, and unwittingly his body began to respond.

Quickly he took her by the shoulders and pushed her away, drawing his mouth off hers with an audible smack that made a small independent part of his mind grin.

"No, Sue," he said roughly.

"I love you, Harry," Sue whispered. "I always have."

He grunted; turned away; leaned on the rail again, trying to be casual, kicking himself mentally. I saw it – for years I've seen it, but I didn't take it seriously. Damn.

"I think," he said, "you should go to the National Theatre School in Montreal. As soon as possible. For both our sakes." He added that as a face-saver.

Sue gasped with joy, and then quickly remembered to be shattered and commanded another rush of tears to her eyes.

"I can't," she said tragically "Harry, let me go to the Playhouse School here in Vancouver. I can't live without you!"

"You can. You'll learn," he said, firmly but kindly.

And so will you, Molly. You'll have to. Not yet – but soon. I feel it: I know it.

Chapter Twenty-Seven

The End

The vigil had gone on for a week, a long week, since the day Harry had said,

"Tell them to take the tubes out; unhook me. Give me the 'cocktail' and let me die my way. Can you do that?"

"Yes."

"Make them understand."

"Don't worry."

"Is that too hard on you?"

"No, you know it isn't. Is there anything else, Harry, anything special I can do?"

"You're doing it already. Just being there when I open my eyes. It's a lot to ask. Staying here twenty-four hours a day –"

"There's nothing else I want to do."

"How long can you take it?"

"As long as it takes." And she was conscious of quoting the very words he had said as he had swum beside her that day in English Bay when she had been bent on suicide. He knew it too, and there was no need for them to vocalize the thought.

"If you cry," he said, "use this." He pulled the red silk paisley patterned handkerchief from under his pillow.

"I won't cry," she said. "I only cry for little things,

remember? Big things I can take. But I'll need this anyway."
She rubbed the silk across her cheek, across his and then put it
in her pocket.

He said, "Molly stand up where I can see you. Or turn my
head."

She did both. She stood by the bed and leaned over and
gently turned his head on the single pillow, very gently because
the lightest touch now gave him pain, he could hardly even
stand a sheet on his body. His eyes were open wider, brighter,
less clouded with drugs than they had been for days.

"Oh hell," he said.

"What's the matter?"

"I'm dying." He sounded surprised and annoyed. "Come
here." Amazingly he opened his arms and when Molly homed
into them, he pulled her down on top of him and hugged her,
and the hands that for two days had been too weak to lift a
spoon, gripped her body hard, and his lips were on her cheek,
and his breath was warm on her neck.

And so they lay until his embrace slackened and his arms
were merely heavy on her back and there was no more warmth
on her neck, and Molly knew he was dead. Gradually she eased
herself out of his arms; arranged him neatly in the bed; pulled
the sheet and coverlet up to his neck. By the door she raised
one hand.

" 'Bye, Harry," she said softly.

Richard saw her face and knew at once. She nodded to the
door.

"Go in," she said. "Say your farewells."

"Wait for me. I'll drive you home."

"No." She shook her head. Calm, remote, not needing
him, having Harry. "I'm all right, Richard."

"Don't go out the front way – the reporters are there."

She smiled at his lack of understanding, and punched the
button for the elevator down to the main lobby. The reporters
surrounded her immediately.

"Molly – Mrs. Wentworth – how is he? How's Harry?"

"He's fine," she said, her head up, looking from one familiar
face to another. "He's dead."

There was a murmur of consternation.

"How did he die, Molly?"

"You said he's fine –"

"What was the cause of death?"

She took a deep breath and looked at them again, one by one, and they were silenced. Wendy Hill shoved her microphone in her shoulder bag and put her hand on Molly's arm.

"I'm so sorry," she said.

Molly moved forward and the reporters made a box around her, protecting her from the curious stares of the people thronging the busy lobby, and their sympathy embraced her and carried her down the steps and out to the car park. Here the cameras turned and clicked discreetly, but no microphones were used.

She paused by the door of the car, remembering her handbag upstairs in Harry's room.

"I left my keys," she said. "Can someone give me a ride home?"

At home Molly changed and slipped into the pool and swam.

Molly shepherded the family out of the house and into the two large funeral cars, but when the driver held the door open for her, she shook her head and stepped back.

"No," she said. "You go on ahead. I'll come in my own car."

There was a moment of impasse; everybody seemed to be about to say something, but nobody actually spoke. There are some advantages to having a reputation for being an oddball, Molly thought. Young Thomas started to climb out of the car, but Molly held up her hand and shook her head again.

"No, Thomas." Obediently the boy sat down.

When the cars had pulled out of the driveway, she went back into the empty house – even Mavis had gone – and up in her room she changed from the correct conservative suit into slacks and a blouse and Harry's (and her) favourite jacket – the midnight blue crushed velvet one that he had given her to come home from the hospital, on the day he had proposed; it was

faded and scuffed, but still wearable and very dear. She fluffed
up her hair and then brushed it down into a pageboy, folded a
scarf into a bandeau and tied it in place; she put on dark glasses,
and looked at herself in the mirror. Never having been
conspicuously recognizable the barest efforts at disguise were
enough to ensure her anonymity.

She studied her face critically. There were no signs that
she was shattered, grief-stricken, bereaved. To herself, she
looked like herself; inside she was different, she knew, but
outwardly the same. She was satisfied. Some things are meant
to remain private. She put the small cardboard carton in her
shoulder bag and left the house.

Police were directing traffic on Burrard and Georgia in front
of the Cathedral, and as she inched slowly past she recognized
many stars from both Western and Eastern Canada, from Britain
and the States, standing in the sun chatting as they waited to
be ushered in and seated in the Cathedral. Mingling with the
stars were hundreds of ordinary people too, fans, audience,
celebrity watchers. Molly parked a few blocks away and
wandered back and joined the crowd in the courtyard, standing
under the loudspeakers that would broadcast the service to
the many who could not get in.

She stood beside a small pixie-like man with white hair in
tufts leaping out from under an old toque.

"Harry wouldn't have given two hoots for this lark," he
said conversationally to Molly, nodding at the reverent
upturned faces and the traffic snarled to a halt for two blocks
in all four directions.

"No," said Molly with conviction, "He sure wouldn't. Did
you know him?"

"Know him. Ma'am, I was an extra in six-seven movies he
made here in town."

"Mmm. So was I," said Molly warmly. "An extra. Seven
Souls."

"You were? Seven Souls, eh? No, I wasn't in that one. He
was a grand guy, was Harry Wentworth. No side to him. Once
when we were packing up for the day, he came up to me and
'Paddy,' he said (he always took the trouble to remember
people's names) 'Paddy' – and he looked at me real fierce and

angry, so I began to wonder what I'd done wrong, 'Paddy', he said, 'do me a favour and buy yourself some new shoes', and he stuck a fifty in my hand and gave me a wink and walked away real quick. He was like that."

"Yes, he was." Molly smoothed the well-worn jacket fondly.

"There was times," Paddy went on, leaning in to Molly as the crowd pushed them closer together, "times when he looked so damn tough and mean you'd think he's cheating his own mother, face-like a damn granite block – but you just look in the back of his eyes there, and you could see he was soft as butter inside."

For the first time Molly felt tears prick her eyes and she pushed up her sunglasses and wiped her cheeks with her fingers. The little man beside her looked up at her intently and then, as the organ pealed forth drowning the traffic noises, he looked to the front again and reached out and took Molly's hand in his, knotted and calloused as it was.

"I'm thinkin'," he said out of the corner of his mouth, "that you should be inside, Ma'am. Like in the front pew."

She squeezed his hand in answer. I was never any good at disguises, she thought.

"No," she said. "I belong here. He'd expect me to be here."

The service proceeded, but when the eulogies started, Molly gently disengaged her hand and eased her way out of the crowd. She drove to Third Beach, parked, and walked down on the sand. It was half-tide and the rocks were bare and dry on the top, so she walked out as far as she could and sat down, her knees up to her chin.

Hallo Harry.

They told me I should go to the service; they told me it would help me realize once and for all that you really were dead. How stupid can they get? Don't they know I realised you were dead from the first night I climbed into bed by myself and your side was empty; I knew when I looked in the closet at all the suits you're never going to wear again; I knew when I put away your special coffee mug that no one else ever used. I know you're dead better than they do. But what's dead? I remember you – I feel you – I feel you here – as no one else can.

Have you met Caroline yet, wherever you are – if there is a

wherever? (Does it matter?) Thank you, God, for giving us the years we did have together. Dying took you by surprise, didn't it? Did you think you were immortal? Paddy said you were a grand guy – could anyone ask for a better epitaph? I'm glad I shared you with the world for a while. And if I really did help you win that Oscar like you said, then I'm glad because I know that meant so much to you, and in a vicarious way, through you, I have contributed to the world too.

Have you met Dell? If she loved you and you loved her, I guess, she and I have a lot in common. I never thought of it like that before.

Harry, how am I going to live through twenty-five more years without you?

A picture of young Thomas came to her mind's eye.

Yes, Thomas will be a help. (And so will Richard.)

She opened her shoulder bag and took out the cardboard carton and opened that, and unloaded the container of ashes and shook some out into her hand. She held her hand out over the rocks and the sea and let the ashes sift down through her fingers.

They didn't leave much of you, Harry, but now a part of you will always be here on this beach, in the sea, in the sand, among the seaweed. So when I come down here, I'll always be able to find you. Now I suppose I must go back to the others.

Goodbye, Harry.

Molly stood up and stretched. "Damn," she said. The tide had come in and surrounded her rock. On the Sea Wall people were walking more slowly as they passed abreast of her, looking at her curiously, their heads turning guiltily forward again when they saw that she had seen them.

"Oh, well," she said. She took off her shoes and stripped off her knee-highs and rolled up her pant legs. I know, Harry, I know, she said inwardly, I can see your eyebrow going up and your teeth shining in a grin and hear you saying "Mm-hmm" as though you expected no less of me.

She stepped off the rock and immediately discovered she had misjudged the depth of the water, and in grabbing her pant legs to pull them up higher, she dropped her shoes.

She laughed. Laughed as she would have done, had Harry

been there to share the joke with her. Laughed on the day of her husband's funeral. Because she loved him.

She stood up in the water and looking to the beach, saw the tight little group coming down the steps from the car park; Rob and Pauline, who never quite got over being afraid of Harry; Ken and his girlfriend, both suitably solemn; Richard – bringing with him his strange warm relationship to Molly – and Wednesday, Wednesday who looked stunning in black and knew it, and had planned to impress the media, with an improvised grief and had been astonished to find it real, and painful, she clung to Richard's arm, pale and discomposed, she who owed her career to Harry, and her marriage in a way, and... maybe... her son? To one side stood Sue, alone, rejecting her boyfriend's arm, alone in her grief, loaded with tears; she had loved Harry – Molly knew this – not as a stepdaughter, but always, from the age of eight, with a passionate sexual love. Like me, Molly thought, she felt as captured by his charm as I was for thirteen years.

Pushing through to the front came young Thomas, resplendent in his three-piece suit, as casual and comfortable in it as a man – like Harry. Harry's son? Grandson? Did it matter? A part of Harry anyway. The boy detached himself from the group and ran across the sand to Molly.

"Hallo, Gramma," he said. "You got your pants wet."

"I know, Thomas. I also dropped my shoes in the water."

"That doesn't matter, Gramma."

"Not a bit," she agreed.

"They all thought you'd run away, but I told them you'd be here. Grandpa Harry said this was your special place. I told them you'd be here with him. You were, weren't you?"

"I was."

"He was with me all morning. That's all right, isn't it, Gramma?"

"Of course it's all right. He can be with you and with me at the same time."

"Even if we're in different places?"

"Even then."

"I hope it's nice for him, being dead." Suddenly he felt like crying, but people had been saying to him all day 'Don't cry,

Thomas, be a man; keep your chin up; be brave; be a good soldier and when he felt his chin trembling he looked up at Molly guiltily.

"It is all right to cry, Thomas," she said gently, and somehow once she had said that he did not need to cry any more and the single tear in each eye spilled down his cheeks and no more came.

Molly searched in her shoulder bag and found Harry's red paisley-patterned silk handkerchief and handed it to the boy.

He wiped his cheeks.

"That's Grandpa's hanky."

"Yes, you can keep it if you like." She had seen the admiration for it in his eyes.

"Oh, thank you." He crunched it up and was going to put it in his pants pocket when he thought better of it and opening the tiny split of the breast pocket of his suit he started to stuff it in. It made a bulge on his chest which he patted with satisfaction, then he pulled up a tongue of silk to show above the pocket and looked up at Molly for approval.

"A little bit more, I think," she said judiciously, and he pulled up some more so that a brave splash of colour soared from the pocket.

Oh God – another Harry.

Then the boy slipped his hand inside Molly's elbow – Harry again – and led her up the beach to the Sea Wall. The family formed a phalanx around her and they all walked up the steps to the car-park through the crowd – the unaware strollers, the curious, the stargazers, the reporters who had followed the family from the cathedral and Molly, despite her wet pants and bare sandy feet, displayed the unconscious dignity that she had always had and looked around and smiled kindly on the world.

The End

"*Molly Wentworth was conspicuous by her absence at her husband Harry's Memorial Service at Christ Church Cathedral yesterday. Harry Wentworth, veteran Canadian actor of international stature, will be missed by millions. He died of cancer at the age of sixty-three, leaving to mourn his passing, besides his wife, a son Richard Worthington, daughter-in-law Wednesday Barnes, and grandson Thomas; three stepchildren, Rob Ash, Ken Ash and Susan Ash (the Stratford star). No explanation was given for Molly's absence but the entire family disappeared for a time following the service and when they returned for the reception, Mrs. Wentworth was with them. Dressed very casually and looking surprisingly relaxed she had a handshake and a word of comfort for everyone there.*"

EPILOGUE

She's in her sixties now, and she still swims from Third Beach. Everyone down there knows her – the lifeguards, the mounted Park policemen, the people in the concession, the park staff and the regulars on the beach.

Sometimes I go and I stand on the platform where she and Harry were married and I watch her. When the tide is low, she'll go out and sit on the rocks with her chin on her knees and her arms wrapped around her legs, and from the back she looks the most desolate, lonely lady in the world; then the sea comes in and surrounds her rock, and all of the sudden she'll jump off into thigh-deep water and stride back up to the beach and I swear to you she's smiling like the happiest person in the world, and there's a warmth and sincerity emanating from her that attracts all the kids and dogs in the area.

And now, I've written all this, I have to tell you, I don't care whether she's my stepmother, or my step-grand-mother. It doesn't bother me anymore whether I am Richard Worthington's son or Harry Wentworth's; and I don't believe it matters to Dear Joan either, or if even she really knows. Because I know now that the most important thing is to accept the ME that I am and make the most of it.

That's what Harry and Molly did.

--- *Tom Worth*